Gaming with Attitudes

A Novel from Berlin

With her ex-husband bankrupt and her drug designer Father
making forays into the world of online gaming,
Caro(-lina) contacts Berlin investigator Dani(-ela)
to work out what the hell is going on, though when
Maria from Miami comes to town, it really isn't
clear who is going to prevail.......

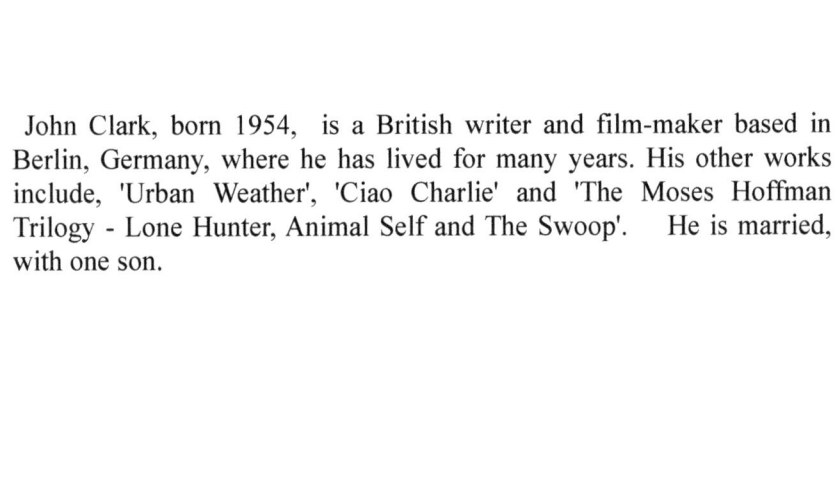

John Clark, born 1954, is a British writer and film-maker based in Berlin, Germany, where he has lived for many years. His other works include, 'Urban Weather', 'Ciao Charlie' and 'The Moses Hoffman Trilogy - Lone Hunter, Animal Self and The Swoop'. He is married, with one son.

GAMING WITH ATTITUDES

by

JOHN CLARK

A Novel from Berlin.

'Gaming with Attitudes'
by John Clark

First published 2018

'Gaming with Attitudes' is a work of fiction and any resemblance to events and characters either living or dead, outside those clearly in the public domain are entirely coincidental.

Bibliografische Information der Deutschen Nationalbibliothek: Die Deutsche Nationalbibliothek verzeichnet diese Publikation in der Deutschen Nationalbibliografie; detaillierte bibliografische Daten sind im Internet über dnb.dnb.de abrufbar.

Herstellung und Verlag: BoD – Books on Demand, Norderstedt
This edition published and distributed by BoD, Norderstedt, Germany.

ISBN: 9783746066257

GAMING WITH ATTITUDES

A Novel from Berlin

Chapter 1

Later, with all the lucid clarity of blue sky hindsight, among the puzzled few who could be bothered, people would ask why no-one with half a sense of responsibility had recognised what was going on before the situation went so wildly out of control in such a distressing, confusing and destructive fashion.

Why had none of the women recognised why they had been thrown together in such seemingly improbable circumstances?

Hindsight is treacherous, a remarkably confusing tool, with that uncomfortable tendency to make everything seem so glaringly obvious, but foresight is a rarer gift that no-one in this situation seems to have possessed.

But begin at the beginning, whenever that might have been, when nothing was as clear as would eventually seem to have been the case, which as Wittgenstein had ventured about the world was everything that was the case, and the whole situation was most obscure at best and blindingly opaque by any other measure.

More surprisingly, apart from a minor ripple of posts from young online gamers complaining about the crude way Berlin handles innovation and the hopelessly inadequate airports, the media didn't seem to notice that anything very unusual had happened at all.

Maybe it hadn't.

Maybe all this stuff was normal.

By now, it almost certainly is, assuming the implausible becomes normality.

For a whole host of reasons, that there is no particular reason to go into, in the beginning was indeed Berlin and the first to become involved was Caro.

Caro had been entangled in the situation for years before anything had surfaced. Some might say it had started when she was a kid, thanks to her irrepressible and determined Dad, the inimitable Bernhardt Hilberg, but no-one would deny that her husband Klaus had been the principle antagonist once she had grown up and they'd lived together, settling first in Schöneberg, until they'd found this five roomed apartment in Charlottenburg and finally got married.

She is tall, makes a slim silhouette watching from her balcony window on the second floor of the old Berlin apartment house as first there are ten, then twenty, then fifty or more noisy birds, all wheeling and cawing, swooping and swirling and diving against the background of a dull grey sky.

Caro had been wondering whether the window frames need painting, when she was distracted by the noise of the crows clashing with unsuccessful sounds of Chopin. Someone across the street is playing nocturnes very slowly on an old piano that has a twang.

Then a car drives past followed by a white van.

From another direction there's a radio tuned to Rundfunk Berlin Brandenburg, RBB, with the news. American fresh-water crabs are colonising the Tiergarten, says the reporter, and are click clacking their ways along the footpaths scaring the walkers and bemusing the dogs, before being captured by chefs from local Chinese restaurants, who intend them for the pot.

Maybe the car was an Audi, maybe not.

The van was anonymous.

Could have been a Toyota, as so many are.

The piano player has stopped, mercifully defeated.

Why does Caro keep getting messages saying she can share her contacts with this insurance salesman somebody someone. She doesn't share her contacts with anyone. The social networks have no way of knowing that she has sworn never to speak to that lying bastard again and no she does not want to be his friend, or a friend of his friends. They're creeps of the first order, every single one of them. She shudders, mildly repulsed.

Sometimes Caro, sometimes Lina, Carolina used to think of herself as an anthropologist, of sorts, but she isn't too certain any more. No-one had ever given her an office with her name and 'anthropologist' written on the door, but her study does have bookshelves that are full and a couple of filing cabinets stuffed with papers from old projects. There are degree certificates somewhere.

Apart from the books, the only colour in her study comes from the blue and red carpet, which is a modern copy of a jugendstyl design from 1900. Caro decides she'll repaint the white walls a relaxing apple green, then she notices the bunch of grey and black crows are making an even bigger fuss as they circle the apartment house across the road and supposes this is what crows do, though she hasn't seen anything like it before.

She's no kind of ornithologist, that's for sure. Sparrow, robin, blackbird, crow, seagull, buzzard, eagle, pretty polly, pieces of eight, parrot, penguin, peacock, roc and phoenix, that's about it, apart from chicken and duck, which she relates to from a culinary standpoint, like the slow roast goose at Christmas.

Having tried a search for information about crows, she starts to see adverts for corvine products when she's online and it's still only nine o'clock in the morning. Some-one has a company called Crow Investments in South Bend Indiana, some-one else is producing Crow Feather Gin in New Zealand and there's a new restaurant in Copenhagen threatening the world with crow pie. Somewhere people are being billed for this garbage to be sent to her laptop as targetted advertising. With a 'e', there are famous cricketers and an actor. A Museum in Manchester has included some sacred crow feathers in an exhibition, which Caro actually thinks might interest her.

She had never done the South Sea Island raw, cooked shaman stuff usually required of anthropologists, nor had she lived in Papua New Guinea, or the Amazonian rainforests, but she's networked and charmed her way into the circle of people who think of themselves as someone or something in the Berlin business community, people who in her eyes are a genuinely primitive society, backward, under-developed and in a self-serving sense banal as well as greedy, a community of insiders, outsiders and backsliders.

Men do like to believe what women tell them, so Caro is quite successful in her latest role as an anthropo-business advisor, a job title she claims to have invented for her own purposes.

Before turning to entrepreneurial advice as a way of making a living, Caro had managed a couple of businesses. For a while she'd bought and sold apartments with her former husband Klaus then she decided it was bad for their relationship, so she'd jumped ship and went on to advise other people about Berlin property.

The divorce had been due to happen anyway. It didn't take hindsight to recognise that it was inevitable. People had been expecting them to split up long before.

She and Klaus had been together for 23 years, half of the time married. She still lives in the apartment they shared, which is full of stuff they'd bought together. Should she have been more ruthless and thrown things away, even though she'd chosen it? The place is her home, despite his money having paid for most of it.

Is it obligatory to live a spartan existence after a divorce?

Hell no.

Neither of them had ever subscribed to anything like that.

Among her newer clients, her favourites are the developers at 'Network Check', who'd given her a pile of shares for helping them build some of her ideas into their artificial intelligence system, though she knows nothing at all about programming, or computing. Mainly, it just seemed like marketing, identifying new groups of customers and consumers, but they told her she'd helped them with their analog. Tropes, koans, agents of this and subjects of that, or the other. Terminology from ritual, or poetics degrades into algorithmic jargon; it can go either way, or both at the same time, depending on the breaks.

The young developers do the rhetoric without the analysis and catch on fast, adapting terminology as business patter, like market stall barrowboys crying their wares with phrases from theoretical physics. In their mouths, the subtlety of a Buddhist koan became high sounding synonyms for platitude and cliché. Anything you can express statistically is potentially sucked in.

The killer concept she devised for them became known as promantics, a marketing strategy to identify the key motifs and themes for promotional work that plays on personalised romantic associations. You can admit to going weak at the knees without being flagged up as a potential patient in orthopaedics. Going a stage further than place marketing to concentrate on the fantasies of group psychology in time and place, according to the advertising crap, promantics promises individual euphoria and the rapture of deeply personalised sentimental passions.

It reminds her of her Dad and his dope.

He does euphoria on demand.

She won't complain about their generosity. That would seem churlish, ungrateful. Don't bite the hand that feeds you, her Dad had always insisted. The little heap of shares are now worth over half a million and look set to carry on rising.

Then Frau Hedwig Trautmann calls and asks for an appointment. Caro confirms she is fully booked for the foreseeable future and unfortunately has no time to spare.

"Fuck my knee," says the woman, "Fick mich am knee".

She'll phone again tomorrow at nine fifteen, as she does every day.

Caro is tidying the clutter of papers on her desk when she realises that more and more birds are joining the crowd and soon there are at least a hundred, flapping, circling and stalking the rooftop opposite, loud and aggressive, aggrieved by something she cannot ascertain.

There's something amiss, but what?

Then she sees the predator take flight, the floppy corpse of a dead crow in its talons. The mass of crows harry and mob the buzzard until it drops the cadavre, which falls with a dull thud and a splash of fresh blood onto the pavement.

They caw a rallying cry of protest.

Then they chase.

The buzzard makes its escape and flies off into the distance.

Predator and prey were clear enough to recognise, but what were the flock of crows up to? Which of them were making the decisions, pushing and cajoling, leading them on as a group?

Someone has tethered three brightly coloured kites to fly over the roof, but that hadn't bothered the crows, so Caro paid no more attention to them than she does to the jingle jangle ring tones on other people's mobile phones.

Caro found it impossible to tell how individual behaviour steered the collective.

Which were leading and which were following?

Which of them were setting the pace, those leading the pack to flap and bluster at the buzzard, or those that stood cawing and bowing their aggression from the ridge of the pantiled roof?

A bird the size of a crow is normally considered to be too large to fall prey to a buzzard. Whether wildlife, or people, it doesn't seem to matter, there are hunters who seek out prey that are simply a size too big for them. Berlin is prone to this kind of thing, 'typische Berlin', the throwaway response. Some folk are too big to hunt, then one day, *hoppla!*, they're prey, which is what happened to Caro's ex-husband, 'dear old Klaus'. Despite the ruthless side of business, he was kind, considerate and gentle, but it hadn't helped at all when the wolves were at the door.

She's due to pick Klaus up from the airport at Tegel, but first she needs coffee, then she'll change.
She'll wear greys and black, like the crows.
A bright red smudge of lipstick is intended as a 'don't mess me about' warning that she's feeling fierce and singularly determined, deeply angry with the man and the games he's played and lost.
A sorry tale that left her sad.

As she leaves her apartment, Caro overhears the voice of an old man. "What we're facing now is like the situation in 1932." He was talking to someone she recognised, Frank something-somebody, a lawyer who has his office around the corner.
The old man is talking about the forthcoming elections. Maybe he's right, Caro allowed. He's upset. Klaus would have agreed with him. She knows that.
The lawyer does his best to mollify his concerns. "We aren't Nazi's, you know, not in the AfD, we are sincere about the Alternatives für Deutschland."
They must have been walking towards one another as they met, now they're uneasy, facing one another on the pavement, then moving aside as Caro leaves the house. She hopes they aren't going to start fighting.
"Frank, just because you're sincere, it doesn't mean you're not a fascist bastard. I've known you since you were a kid. You worry me. It wouldn't matter what you belong to, you're trouble. Your father was the same and his father was a fucking disgrace who was lucky

to die when he did, before they invented war crimes trials."

"Fuck you too, Sacha," said the Frank to the old man and stalked away with a mutter on his lips, "Scheiss kommunist."

Caro turned to look at the old man.

"The grandfather was a grade one Nazi, that one, and so is he, even if he won't admit it to himself," said the old man emphatically, looking Caro direct in the eye.

"What happened to the grandfather?"

"A bomb got him, served him right." The old man laughs, then justifies himself. "He taught round ups and deportations at the Gestapo training centre on the Schloßstrasse, you know, where the Berggruen Museum is now. He'd been giving lessons, officer training, how to be a war criminal, HA! A piece of shit, well paid too, highly praised and generously rewarded. The man was a popular psychopath, as genial a war criminal as he was cruel. They lived on the Kaiserdamm, not far from Hermann Goering's old place, where the filling station is now, the up the road from Alfred Döblin's house. His wife's custom was sought after among the local shopkeepers. You can imagine why. They had extra ration coupons too, which could have been another explanation for their eagerness. She was polite, if arrogant, so I'm told, a quietly spoken woman and a grade A anti-semite. Autumn 1944, when they got him in that air raid. On his way home from giving evening classes to officers on leave. He'd been in France, of course, in Lyons with Klaus Barbie and in Poland, 'not so far from Cracow'. It was a good thing they got him when they did in my opinion. I went to school with the younger son, Rudolf, 'Dolph', like Adolf. He was a sadistic bastard too. It's what they call continuity."

"I have to get moving, or I'll be late," said Caro as she started to walk to the car and shrug off the attention of this nearly blind old seer.

"Na ja, just you remember what I told you."

"I will, I promise." She wants to get to the car.

"Just one more thing." "What's that?"

"Remember, it is incredibly easy to kill people, and that means it's also incredibly easy to get killed, if that's what someone has decided. If I can find out who you are, then so can anyone else who wants to look."

He makes it sound like a warning, not too far removed from a threat.

Had he meant it that way? Perhaps not. She turns away from the old man and whispers a hurried goodbye.

"I have to go."

"You be careful, we have troubles to spare around here. Maybe I'll see you in the 'Esel' tonight for a shit of gold and a beer. Auf wedersehen."

He's unnerved her.

She's never seen him in the 'Gold-Esel', the 'Golden Ass' before, but she doesn't drink there often and she certainly won't be there that evening. Prophesying doom and disaster is a kind of hobby among Berliners, but some days it touches a nerve and this is one of them.

She's frustrated to have been delayed starting out for the airport, but there isn't a lot of traffic, so once she's picked up some flowers, she's there in less than fifteen minutes and parks the car within the inner ring of the polygonal Tegel terminal.

Everything is quiet.

She wants to get things over with.

Her errand really is a thankless task.

At least the Terminals are convenient.

A crowd of youngsters arriving Berlin for a games convention are clustered near the arrivals board, but apart from them, there aren't any crowds or queues at all.

The Tegel Airport has a wonderfully efficient design from the traveller's point of view. It's due to be closed. There are not enough shops there to sate the modern airport business model of security checks and futile delay, entrapping passengers as paying captives in shopping malls filled with over priced junk.

Besides the question of resurgent right wing local politicians, Caro has other preoccupations, mainly connected to Klaus.

The gambit that made Klaus rich was simple. Find some pleasant slightly run down apartment building, buy it up via a friendly Danish investment fund then lean on the sitting tenants until they finally realise that resistance is futile and chose to accept the compensation on offer and move out. The moment he had control, he sold on. Klaus was an everyday property shark. Lots of them about.

His argument was that there's far too much money in the world and a lot of it needs throwing away, which is what investors and the funds are up to in Berlin. Keynes made a similar point about the benefit of digging unneeded holes to ensure money stayed in circulation. It costs too much to leave cash in the bank. Investors are desperately trying to dispose of money with no-where else to go, injecting the city with the virulent disease of low cost finance and burgeoning housing costs under the dubious name of gentrification. Anything goes, so long as it's not yet illegal and there's the paperwork to go with it, so Klaus had volunteered to help.

They threw. He pocketed. The investment managers anticipate huge profits and swiftly sell everything on. It was beautiful. It was even legal. The tax people seemed happy.

Politicians flocked to sing his praises. Here at last was the new dynamic Berlin they'd been romanticising about for years.

You have to laugh.

Klaus' fetish was finance and he played by the first law of bubbles, get in early, pump like hell, then get out fast and look on, incredibly relaxed as other people twitch with panic when they recognise they've been well and truly fucked over.

He didn't even need to use his own money.

His investors stood in line. And the Next!!!

Everyone Klaus met had been a potential target for his ploys, rich, poor, frail, or smug, it mattered not one jot. Eventually even the know-all foreign investors would look around, puzzled and wonder where their money had gone.

But business is business, so who cares? It's a game, or rather it isn't, but it is open to being gamed according to the jargon that no-one really believes about their over simplified versions of events in the business world. The economists will tell you how their outcomes come replete with self-fulfilling calculations that look good whichever way you choose.

When his house of cards collapsed Caro felt as embarrassed on Klaus' behalf as she did over her own tangential role in his affairs and the need for as much creditor evasion as humanly possible in a city of only three million people.

Spartan lifestyle, humble pie, stay away from the crowds, a tedious, but symbolic necessity.

After ten good years, they'd finally caught Klaus twiddling the numbers to flatter his personal bank balance and that was endgame, not even the chance of a final spin of the market roulette wheel. It had been too late for a rescue from the moment the accountant uttered the word 'insolvent'. With hindsight his downfall was seen to be inevitable.

Maybe Klaus resembled the city more closely than anyone but he himself had recognised. He was totally discredited, a laughing stock. His opinions counted for less than little.

Forty three years old and he'd never even got round to owning a football club, or building a folly. Yet he had creditors on every continent except Antarctica.

The judge had said that Klaus was morally and ethically bankrupt.

Secretly, he agreed.

The bankers had simply said he was bankrupt, 'pleite' was their word, insolvent, broke.

So were they, he'd told himself bitterly, "The bastards".

The investors let it be known he was toast. Fair weather friends, he'd shrugged. They'd been happy enough to bank the profits of his earlier successes.

To Caro's profound discomfort, 'Dear old Klaus' became a source of entertainment, the subject of gossip on every Charlottenburg street and a variety of shady corners, some of them very shady indeed.

Whatever else he may have been, Klaus was neither Keyser, nor Söze, not a Moriaty, or even a Harry Lime. He would never have hurt anyone physically. He had never been malicious, on that much, everyone agreed. Klaus wanted to be nice to everyone and, like him, help themselves towards a happier future.

The insolvency process seemed so unfair. Even the insolvency people had told Caro that much. Everyone liked Klaus. Eventually, he'd taken himself off to Greece, leaving Caro angry and alone to face the people who ignored the fact that they were divorced and assumed she'd shared in the spoils. He sold the Merc in Austria and bought a modest house on a Peloponnesian mountain side with the last of his resources. Caro was still angry and alone, without it looking as though things were about to change.

Klaus planted lettuce, carrots and cannabis, drank Becks from the bottle and supermarket wine, charmed the English lady tourists, then got caught out a second time in a wave of collapsing property values as another round of the financial crisis refused to go away.

Then a Balkan Bank had yanked on his last paltry line of credit till it snapped.

And now he was dead.

Falling from the Parthenon into the Theatre of Dionysis was a spectacular, technically demanding farewell, involving an improvised paraglider to fly over the ancient stone stage, but Klaus had managed it with panache, floating gentle over the arcs of seating to slip out of the safety harness and land in a heap of splashing blood and crunching bone to the applause of a group of bekilted Scottish tourists who assumed the deed was a gag put on for their benefit.

The body had been rushed away to the morgue as fast as possible. The city authorities don't like corpses littering major tourist attractions. He was identified by the wad of 23 credit cards in his wallet and a yellow jacketed copy of Sophocles' 'Theban Plays' in a dual language Ancient Greek and German edition, which was found in his pocket. His name had been scrawled on the back cover almost thirty years earlier. Klaus had signed that as a gangly fifteen year old condemned to classics.

Thus for everyone who knew him, the death of Klaus was forever linked to the birth of tragedy.

When she heard the news, Caro was left speechless and quite frankly, to begin with she didn't believe a word. Then, report by report, on radio, on the net, on tv, then in the press, she realised it must be true and prepared herself to begin from the beginning once again.

She had been flown out to identify the body and now she's come to the airport for the ashes. By this time, Caro is not in the best of moods, what with crows, cantankerous old men and neo-Nazi's in denial. At least it has arrived as the undertaker had promised and she takes possession of the gritty grey dust. He'd been a part of her life for such a long time, it's difficult to believe these ashes are all that is left. They just don't feel authentic. They aren't at all like Klaus. They're more like that organic fertiliser you use for roses. Maybe she should talk to one of the local potters about having them ground up to make bone china. There should be sufficient for a paperweight, or two to remember him by.

He'd done the deed and succeeded, which is why there is a modest crowd of fourteen or fifteen, maybe twenty people gathered around the small square of a modern open grave in the old cemetery in Schöneberg, where the Brothers Grimm, a broad spectrum of Berlin's bigwigs and a tragic list of Aids victims are buried in the shade of four hundred trees. The mourners wear black, or grey and so do the birds. Were these those same crows who'd chased the predator and is there a buzzard among them who'd held Klaus in his claws, or are they just a flock of scruffy city pigeons fluttering about and pecking in the Brandenburg sand?

The mourners mumble among themselves. The birds twitter and caw. The S-bahn rattles past. The rain has stopped.

There's a gentle breeze and a nightingale sings in the sunshine.

Caro had driven with the remains direct from the airport and had a rush to get the paperwork finished in time for the burial. The Greek death certificate had to be translated and a fistful of forms needed to be filled out before she was allowed to take possession of the 'human remains'. Talk about 'last minute'. The man really looked like being late for his own funeral, but now he's there and his ashes will vibrate and gradually settle to the reassuring rumble of cream and red S-bahn trains passing on their way between Wannsee and Oranienburg, but it doesn't matter, does it?

Ashes are ashes, dust is dust, what's over is over and Klaus is certainly that, laid to rest in a green and gold Grecian urn.

Some of the mourners are friends and former colleagues, three are actors and among the others are folk who wished they'd gotten their revenge in first. Caro has shaken hands, avoided smiling, embraced women she never liked and pecked kisses with menfolk she detests. She is as stricken as anyone can be without actually weeping and wailing, bemoaning her fate.

There had been a couple of reports on local radio that morning about 'the Icarus of Berlin finance', and the 'Superman who fell to earth', but there had been a lot more about football and a competition for concert tickets. Ten tickets for Barenboim playing Boulez, nice prize.

Lukas Winkler looks Caro in the eye and shrugs, then walks away. He'd known Klaus longer than anyone and they always described one another as friends, though Lukas is a cop, a Kriminale Kommissar, an Inspector who calls and drinks till four o'clock in the morning, whether he's on duty, or not.

The graveyard is overwhelmingly green in summer, compared to Berlin's skull grey winter gloom, the time of year when most Berliners imagine they will die. The mourners pay their respects to Caro and try to express some level of commiseration, but she doesn't care what any of them think and they know it. Katherina Jana Jonson, Fr. von Braun, Rudolf Hanneman, Uwe and Ulrike, Elfie Malzenberger, Dan Daenger, 'Fat' Pete Branitz, Senta Quist, Peter-Paul Prinz, Alex 'Sasha' Schmidt and the rest all stood silently round the hole in the ground and tried to avoid each others' gaze.

He'd made them all money. He'd made some of them laugh and some of them cry. Even Marie-Hélène keeps her mouth shut, which is wise on her part.

Detlev and Franz look as if they're about to start an a cappella duet, but noting Caro's disapproving frown, they desist and Klaus' ashes are spared the indignity of facing the final curtain to the sound of would-be crooners doing a wobbly Frank Sinatra imitation. They look like well scrubbed schoolboys with matching beards and as a sign of respect, they're wearing their very best Rolex' and made to measure suits from Biskeys, the gentlemen's tailer of Goethestrasse.

Despite the divorce, Caro has been cast in the role of grieving widow. Protean charcoal Chanel jacket, a chic hat, a modest veil, sunglasses and ear rings, all black 'Natalie Portman' dramatic. She catches the eye and invites the shedding of a tear. A widow with allure, and skinny enough to bring it off with panache.

The supporting cast included her Dad, Bernhardt, who had always rather enjoyed Klaus' improptu roguish air of urban piracy, the inimitable off-key degenerate charm. He'd turned up at the last minute and stood loyally next to Caro as the ceremony progressed, then ostentatiously paid the undertaker's bill in cash, which wasn't necessary, but was noticed and helped sustain the fiction that Caro was facing hard times and that Klaus might have died leaving her impoverished.

The whole affair is unconvincing, the mourners are respectful, but no-one, Caro included, actually seemed sad, resigned maybe, disappointed, angry some of them, but sad, no, not actually sadness.

A black clad pastor spoke, proposed they pray, muttered rapidly and gave the impression of being completely uninterested. Once he'd completed his prayers, the po-faced Protestant simply turned on his heels and walked away as though he too had secrets he urgently had to hide, or perhaps he just needed to take a leak.

"Ooh, a nihilist, deep stuff. Theologically, I believe that was an expression of what is called Doubt, with a capital 'D'," Dan Daenger said to Alex Schmidt with whispered sincerity and Alex gave an atheist chuckle, "Oi, you lot, prepare to meet thy doom!"

"Maybe he bought one of Klaus' flats."

"God help us, one and all," added Dan with a beatific smile for the whole assembly. He had grown up in catholic Bavaria and equated Christianity with toothache and child abuse.

Klaus' brother Erik arrived late and rushed off as soon as his trowel of sandy earth fell silently into the grave. He'd given Caro a nod of recognition and seemed to be crying. No-one else was, unless there'd been a crocodile tear or two, she'd failed to notice.

By that time, the online edition of the gutter press BZ were on the story, brief and to the point. "Splat!" (two letters shorter than the German 'Platsch!') was their good natured headline and a vignette of the carnage replete with kilted celts, was superimposed over a photo of Klaus arriving at court for his trial, when they'd called him the 'once upon a time man'. They even ran a 72-word story about Caro, the girl who got away (and took the money with her?). A picture taken that morning showed her scowling at the camera as she had been putting the urn in her car at the airport.

She did look grim.

Once the simple funeral was over, most of the mourners left for the Akademie der Kunst at PariserPlatz near the Brandenburg Gate to revive their spirits and enjoy the opening of an exhibition of paintings in the academy gallery by another of their friends, who was happily still in the land of the living, prefers bright colours and likes to drink a lot, which cheered everyone up. Even Lukas Winkler decided that a good cop needs to keep up with the latest trends in art and culture and headed after them in the hope of a decent glass of white, some gossip and a snack of wild boar knackerwurst.

The S-bahn connection got the whole crowd there directly in ten minutes, super convenient, couldn't be better. Most Berlin artists are more accomplished at drugs and drinking than art, which is why they're stuck in Berlin. So are the politicians, which is why they're stuck in city politics and fail to make it on the national scene. 'Bloody Mary', the recently appointed Senator for Finance will be there, as will the Staatsekretar for Planning, Michaela Brandt. She'd skipped the graveyard bit to avoid the media quips about digging her own grave. The other Airport, the infamous brand new BER, still hasn't been completed and she is carrying the political responsibility for twenty years of bungling. Thankfully, it has never been implied that Klaus had anything to do with that.

No-one suggested Caro should join them for the opening. Naturally, Klaus had been on the guest list, but the invitation still lay on his desk, unopened. An ill-informed marketing assistant from hospitality marked him down as a no show, which wasn't actually wrong, just disrespectful. Klaus had given them something to talk about and good reason to conjure up a thirst to celebrate their own survival, so it was expected to be quite a party.

Berlin is getting on without him, and so is Greece.

Caro would like to get over him too. He'd been a big part of her life since her first year as a student at the Free University in Dahlem and much as she once adored him, he'd eventually become an encumbrance.

Once the last of the mourners had sloped off to the Academy Gallery, Caro and her father were left alone, with only the gravediggers patiently waiting for them to leave, so they could tidy up the plot and dig another small hole to prepare for the following day's interment.

Then that was that. It hadn't taken very long at all.

In fact, the whole business of putting a pot of ashes in a hole in the ground had been surprisingly perfunctory, or that was how it seemed to Caro, who felt she should have been more moved than she actually was.

In the days when people had been buried in coffins, the holes in the ground were much bigger and the thought of a recently functional body being laid forever in the box, made the whole business that much much more macabre. She suspects the gravediggers feel that way too, when all there is to bury is a pot of ash and bone.

When they finally leave the graveyard, Caro feels disorientated, but as much as anything, she simply felt relieved it was all over and wanted to go home and get some sleep.

By late afternoon, after they'd been to a meeting with Klaus' lawyer, Caro's Father drove her away from Berlin and the two of them picked up a holiday flight to Cuba from the airport at Leipzig. Caro sleeps on the plane under the watchful gaze of her Dad and a few short hours later they settle into the five star luxury of a shore-side bungalow in the Caribbean, where friendly waiters catered to their every whim.

Bernhardt can work anywhere, as long as he can get online, but Caro was quietly moved that he showed how much he cared by looking after her this way. They swam together, drank a lot, enjoyed good food and reminisced. He told her about the day he met Castro on four different occasions and all Fidel had said was 'You again, you seem to get about.'

He did.

He still does.

He cheers her up.

Ten days after the funeral, apart from the bit about the missing millions, it was almost as though Klaus had never existed.

Almost?

More, or less.

Well, maybe,

.....sort of.

The people at 'Network Check' are pretty thorough and reported nothing unusual, no untoward viruses, serious hacks, latent crisis, or personal threats, so Bernhardt and Caro could sleep easily and they did, soothed by the gentle sounds of waves breaking on the nearby beach.

With thirty eight million registered users and more every day, 'Network Check' are getting better and better all the time. Their systems will soon reach a level entitling them to claim 'online dependability' and the big shift from data mining to personalised social management can begin. People are beginning to wonder whether a take-over might be in the offing. The shares are gaining value, though Caro hasn't checked their price.

Thanks to a minor indiscretion over lunch, her bank manager has mentioned just how many shares she owns and how much wealthier Caro is than she had been just a few weeks earlier, a little nugget of news that is gossiped from one side of Berlin to the other in less than an hour. The bank manager has always found launching new rumours one of the most satisfying aspects of her job. Sometimes they're true, but more often than not, they simply reflect the way she thinks things ought to be and sometimes they're merely mischief-making. She's never been threatened with the sack, or even warned off rumour mongering by her bosses. They find it convenient to make use of her loose tongue, when they want things said but don't want to risk being the source of a quote. Had she known, Caro wouldn't have been surprised.

She'd heard a lot of the woman's more fanciful notions over the years and learned to ignore most of what she said.

People feel irritated by the rumours of Caro's unexpected prosperity, and in bars and offices across the city, eyebrows are being raised in critical surprise, rather than congratulation.

What else might Caro have managed to get away with, while Klaus was busy arranging to kill himself in Greece? The prank with the hang-glider had left them all looking like fools.

Chapter 2

"So what was that all about?" Georg (pronounced 'gay-org' in the German manner) asked, when his girlfriend Dani finished what had been a twenty minute phone call, in which she'd done almost all the listening.

He refilled her glass without being prompted. Georg is commendably pragmatic. He was still sprawled across the bed, while she sat propping herself up against the pillows, as he successfully refilled their glasses without a drop being spilled.

"That was Caro, remember her? The woman who was married to Klaus," replied Dani with a sigh of resignation. "She's back in Berlin."

"Don't get involved, whatever it is she's up to. Klaus was a second rate crook and the chances are a thousand to one that she is too. It's late, come back to bed."

Dani and he don't always agree, but this time, she suspects he might be right. His view of the world is simpler and more benign than hers. He's a bedroom boyfriend, a nice guy and a good fuck, not a partner, not a potential husband.

Georg doesn't get in the way. The wine buyer for a chain of supermarkets, he only gets to Berlin two or three times a year, which from Dani's perspective is quite enough to be going on with.

She also has other beaux in tow.

He'll be off to Argentina in a few days time to sample the latest harvest that's ready for bottling.

Another decade of sipping and slurping samples of cheap red will see Georg's liver expand like a rotting beetroot, then implode from cirrhosis, so she doesn't see him as part of her long term future, or indeed his own. He could be right about Caro though. Her reputation has preceded her, all those scandals with Klaus.

Dani has no great expectations.

People say old Klaus left Caro next to nothing when the businesses went down, so by now, she's probably hard up, unless she cashes in her shares from 'Network Check'. Is she being unfair? Not at all. At least half Dani's clients have problems paying their bills. About one in five don't even bother to try.

She and Caro have already run into each other once or twice without getting to know one another, a brief introduction ages ago in the company of other people at a theatre, then another (Oh hello, smile.. smile.. I suppose we must have met somewhere, haven't we?...smile...smile....turn away.. nothing ventured.. who the hell was that) at a party a couple of years ago. Based on this 'half know' minimal interaction, they seem unlikely to become great friends. Nothing had attracted either woman to the other.

Now comes this late-night phone call and the suggestion they meet. Given a choice, Dani would turn the job down, but like every other freelance in Europe, she can't afford to say no. There is income tax to be paid from the previous tax year and she doesn't want to dip into her savings. There's going to be trouble.

It feels inevitable.

A kind of strangeness is creeping into the way of things in Berlin. It had begun with phrases seeping into everyday chatter that would have been totally unacceptable only a few years earlier. Then came racist attacks on the streets, the terrorist murders at the Christmas market and the nasty Party are racking up the tension as they try to win votes with the age old 'us and them' tactics of intolerance.

Georg agrees with Dani that the city is losing its charm.

Whatever, Dani had agreed to be at a bar known as 'Soph-Am', near StuttgarterPlatz, the following morning at eleven, so being a reliable kind of person, she will be there.

Daniela Mendel, known to some as 'Dani', less often to others as 'Ela', is slender and fit. A year or two younger than Caro, she's turning forty. She likes flying and is fond of dogs, preferably large hairy dogs like Georg. She can growl with conviction and sometimes she howls.

Contrary to expectations, Dani's bite is worse than her bark. There's a new nine millimetre semi-automatic in her shoulder bag.

She does running. She trains hard. She would make a great valkyrie.

Things aren't quite getting out of hand, but it's getting uncomfortably close. It isn't Georg's fault. Nothing is ever Georg's fault, he's too amiable for that, too close to turning fifty.

Anyway, he'd already left for Frankfurt by the time she'd woken up.

She'd slept soundly.

Awoken.

Morning.

Nothing exceptional.

Dozens of bottles of wine in the kitchen, which is nice of him.

At least there isn't going to be a third world war in the next couple of days, not like the one she'd dreamt about during the night, which had all been over in a flash. The Hungarians had been to blame, but it hadn't made any difference. The news from Ukraine is still dire. Trump is Trump. Macron is diminishing. People in a dozen countries are being squeezed and bombed and starved thanks to their governments, rebels and their big power sponsors. Thanks to Trump's vulgarity no-one says twerk any more.

Dani is feeling deflated and gloomy.

Not that she's in a bad mood exactly, just a bit tetchy.

Events are askew. Turkey is a mess. North Korea is a mess. Venezuela is a mess. They needn't be, need they?

It could get worse.

Catalonia comes to mind. Myanmar.

According to DeutschlandRadio there will be a debate in the Bundestag in the afternoon. A minister might resign, but no-one cares which one. An actor is in a play, so is an actress, says the radio reporter. There were people in the audience at the theatre. A director has completed a film. Police are expecting a riot, somewhere or other. Footballers are being paid a lot of money. What else is new?

According to a survey, the Greek economy will soon be booming.

According to another survey, Greece is no longer in recession.

According to a third survey, Greek society is on the point of disintegration and poverty is threatening the well-being of millions.

Dani wonders which of them is more likely to be right.

The IMF disagree with one of the surveys.

For the moment there's no government, just Merkel. 'To Merkel' has officially been recognised as a verb, without anyone knowing what it stands for. There will have to be a new election, eventually. They might even have achieved something innovative, the 'do nothing Parliament' when people were elected and took their places in the Bundestag, but never actually met to make decisions, before another set of elections were called. Scientists claim there could be an earthquake in a far off land and in Baden-Baden there might be some sunshine later in the afternoon, though according to the weather forecasters there's a real possibility it might rain a bit too.

There is laughter in the dark and a mystery is coming to television: 'Black Zero - Curse or Blessing', 'Schwarze Null - Fluch oder Segen', sounds exciting, but is actually a studio discussion about the German tendency to hoard rather than use government money to pay for useful things like schools and roads. Once upon a time there was a Minister of Finance called Schäuble, who was indestructible.

Three large kites are flying from the roof of the house opposite. One is red, one is green and the other deep blue and purple. She wonders if they are Mongolian.

There's a turqoise Audi parked nearby, a study in bad taste.

Dani does a bit of yoga, then stares out of the window for ten minutes, wondering what the kites are for. They're pretty though.

Three cups of coffee and a hairwash later, the 'bio' egg she cooks for breakfast is too small to eat from an eggcup, so she ends up squidging it on toast, which is extremely annoying. The yolk is anaemically pale. Why on earth should modern eggs have become too small to fit into traditional eggcups? Don't the chickens get any proper dinners?

Breakfast over with.

The egg had tasted surprisingly good.

She'd been hungry.

She recognised the face in the mirror successfully. It is her own.

She's in no hurry.

A thorough wash is a pleasure. Her lips are slowly lipsticked.

An eyebrow is given a pluck, but right at the last moment she succumbs to an unusual desire to wash her ears with old fashioned soap and hot water. Super clean ears are one of life's very personal minor pleasures, she tells herself. The lipstick will need re-doing once she's dried her face.

When all that's completed, Dani doesn't look any different, but she does feel better.

She isn't going to try and compete with her client's sense of fashion. Never compete with a client. Caro is known to be chic, decisively chic, incisively chic, intensely chic, assertively chic, whereas Dani has become pragmatic about her looks.

She looks into the bathroom mirror again and decides she looks no worse than yesterday, then quickly smooths in some face cream, on the assumption it won't do any harm to repress a few wrinkles and she finalises the lipstick. A dark green top, moss green it's called, black leather biker's jacket and jeans, her new leather shoulder bag, saddle brown. After years of looking, she's finally found a bag that can deal with all the stuff she needs to carry and not just some of it. The little gun weighs no more than the reserve battery for her tablet, but the bag has a well made holster pocket she can open quickly if she's in a hurry to brandish the weapon and shoot. And with her tablet safely stowed inside its leather and kevlar cover, the bag is effectively bullet proof. She can use it as a shield, assuming a shield might be necessary.

Another glance in the mirror.

She will do.

She's ready to go.

Dani is a punctual person.

She'll be at the rendezvous ten minutes before they're due to meet. Yet another Thursday, sunny, warm, late summer, maybe a hint of rain. Soon it will be October.

She hums the September song.

May seems a long long time ago, surabaya Johnny; then Joe ... a red bandana, plays a ….....mean piana..... down in Mexico. She can't remember all the words, but mimes and sways to the rhythm of the 'The Coasters' and felt it was worth the listen. It's a new genre 'Tex-Mex-Brecht', 'a dance I've never seen before', about as multiculturally politically correct as you'll get, despite being just a little bit ever so sexist.

Dani suspects Caro will be one of those women who judge people by their sense of fashion, which is something she despises. Actually, she suspects this Caro is judgemental in general and that in the negative sense. She has a reputation for being sharp tongued and cynical, which isn't very promising. A sign of the times, though taking the business with her husband into consideration and bearing in mind the way the media went for them both, she has more reason than most to be touchy. Dani hesitates about going to the meeting, but then decides to turn up after all. Don't diss your day-job.

Humming a tune she can't remember the words to, Dani decides she looks acceptable and is at least pleased about the effect of the shoulder bag. Her humming isn't very musical. The way she's feeling, she wouldn't mind a little drizzle. There's nothing wrong with light rain on a warm day.

Summer rain might sound like a melancholic French chanson – love, regrets, men called Yves. Autumnal drizzle doesn't, but it still involves cool drops of mildly polluted water and doesn't do anything for your hair.

Maybe she should head for Paris.

The dinners are usually better than Berlin, even if the romance can be a bit of a let-down.

Soon it will be time to go.

All she has to do is walk downstairs, cross the street and in five minutes a big creamy yellow double-decker bus will arrive on time and stop at the bus-stop.

She can be confident of that.

The drivers do their best to be gruff and rude, but they're also dependable. In Berlin the buses are always on time. Once it sets off, the bus will take her to within a couple of minutes walk of the 'Soph-Am' and that's her journey to work.

Twelve minutes, door to door, including the wait and the walk. There's no point having a car in Berlin and you get wet riding bikes, so on most days the bus is a good option.

This isn't one of them.

She got as far as the bus-stop.

She has her travel pass.

It's valid.

As a distraction she noticed two crows playing with a chestnut, a simple pleasure, both for her and the birds. Crows have been people watching and people have been crow watching for tens of thousands of years and for their part, crows do seem to know they're entertaining. They're very aware of being watched. She took another look up at the three kites, then she heard the bus come around the corner.

Then things got worse, considerably, catastrophically worse.

There was a poignant moment of incipient disaster, as everyone instinctively recognised that nothing was going right, nothing at all, but they felt frozen, motionless, as though the crash was inevitable, impossible to avoid, impossible for anyone to intervene. Even Dani, who wasn't watching the traffic could sense that something terrible was happening out of sight behind her.

Two beats of a rhythm later, there were tears, screams, howls of horrific pain and gut wrenching shock. Dani turned to look, then gasped with horror, taken aback.

The smell of diesel emphasised abrupt physical change.

There was blood.

There were bits of things in heaps and tangles, stuff scattered.

The bus was supposed to have been driven round the corner and slowed to a halt at the bus stop, but it hadn't. It had come around the corner and carried on.

Ten minutes later the paramedics closed the doors to one of the 'Rettungswagen' ambulances and drove slowly away without bothering with the flashing blue emergency lights and siren. Five more ambulances are lining up to receive the injured, with several others still arriving. Stretchers, oxygen, firemen with equipment to prise car doors open, the whole deal.

The old man had been trying to cross the road when he'd been hit by the lorry, which had swerved to avoid the oncoming bus and failed. A Skoda, an Audi and a Fiat were also involved.

The truck driver had been thrown through the windscreen fairly unscathed, but fell under the wheels of the bus that Dani had been waiting for and was fatally injured by the impact of a damaged shock absorber which had broken away from its mount and speared first spleen then aorta. Not much speed, but a forty tonne load means a lot of momentum, so the fully laden truck made quite a crunch, taking out the bus shelter as well as the front end of the bus. The bus driver was shocked but also basically ok, apart from a broken arm and some cuts, until the windscreen came to rest sharply across his belly. A transparent guillotine.

Suddenly, he was much worse.

There was blood, an enormous amount of blood flooding everywhere as he screamed in horror, aghast at the sight of his own intestines bulging like links of sausage through the glass. The rescue guys looked away and grimaced, as he groaned, then sighed his last, the body neatly sliced from side to side to separate top from bottom. Someone from the bus company will inform his next of kin.

He was popular, a nice guy.

The sirens made a lot of noise and in Dani's eyes, the flashing lights were unnecessarily intrusive. There's a large heap of metal near her feet. It could be lorry. It might have been bus. In fact it was a pale-blue painted bicycle.

Some were bleeding, some had stopped bleeding and some would never bleed again.

A camera team from the local tv station, RBB, arrive in a red and white mini-van and begin to film, then Rainer the bald headed reporter puts his story together and does a piece to camera.

Three dead and four seriously injured, all at a speed very little more than walking pace. Seventeen passengers suffering different degrees of injury and shock.

Three more ambulances were full and driven away, lights flashing.

Dani was unscathed, but shaken and relieved to have survived.

The police were unimpressed.

They were hoping for dashcam videos of what had happened, but there weren't any, though there are videos emerging online from people who had heard the carnage and reached for their mobile phones. None of them, not even the passengers, caught the crash itself, just its appalling aftermath.

Dani told the police what she'd seen.

She mentions the crows.

They're dismissive.

She'd been looking at the kites, she explained.

One was red, one was green and one deep blue and purple.

They still are. The noise of their flapping had caught her attention.

That was all.

Then the smell and the screams.

Of course, she'd turned to look, as the crows flew off in alarm.

No, she has no idea how fast the bus was travelling.

She'd tried to help, but she didn't know what to do.

She hadn't noticed the lorry.

Maybe there was a bicycle, she isn't sure.

Despite standing next to the bus stop, she just hadn't seen anything of the accident until it was almost over. She'd heard it, experiencing a series of disconnected sensations for compilation to become her version of events. The images imprinted on her memory are a series of still visuals captured as she responded to the sounds.

First a shudder of emergency deceleration, then the gasps, groans and crunching sounds as metal squealed to crumple and fracture against metal, plastic, bone and flesh, drawing her attention away from the kites.

By the time she turned to look, apart from the oozing streams of anti-freeze, sprays of blood and jets of fuel, everything was still-life motionless, street sculpture, a 3-D installation of an impromptu, rather than conceptual kind, though the kites flew on. A wide-eyed head bounced onto the pavement giving a silent scream.

Sympathetic to people's ills, she might be, but Dani is annoyed by the accident and tells the police she can't describe what happened. She doesn't feel responsible. Hopeless witness, the police agreed and having taken her details, name, address, identity card number, let her go. She decides to ignore the maybe Mongolian kites and calls a cab to take her to the 'Soph-Am'.

The rain starts, quite heavily.

She has a small umbrella in her bag that doesn't want to unfold and open properly, so she throws it away.

Will the rain be sufficient to wash the blood from the street?

She doubts it.

More upset than she realises, when he finally shows up, she yells at the cab driver to get her out of there.

No-one had even noticed the cyclist who had been flattened first by the swerving truck, then squashed under the back wheels of the bus. He would be identified later in the day as someone who was married to someone Dani knows. But she had never met him and now she never will. He was sixty years old and the father of four children by three different girlfriends, though Dani didn't know that either. Details of that kind are worse than distracting, they're the building blocks of nightmares she can do without.

As news of the crash percolated through the local media, there was general dismay, but half a dozen of those who heard the reports were delighted by every detail. You may be alone in Berlin, but you're rarely short of an enemy.

The cab ride took only seven minutes and two of those were spent waiting for a red light to change on the Bismarckstrasse, as a couple of ambulances drove past. The emergency services had flagged the bus crunch as a major incident and 'Network Check' flashed warnings.

"Terrible thing, accidents like that," said the taxi driver, "No sooner have you got used to being who you are, then suddenly bang and all of a sudden nothing works properly any more, and that's if you're lucky enough not to get killed outright."

"Can you shut the fuck up," she says bluntly.

"Oh, like that is it."

She had a feeling the driver had been heading in her direction anyway, probably to one of the taxi ranks near the S-bahn station, so the six Euros he charged her was a lucky if modest bonus. At least he hadn't asked her to describe the crash.

There's Adele playing on the radio. She can sing, so Dani listens.

Once she got out of the cab, the driver simply stayed in the same place as a middle aged man in a calf length raincoat emerged from the bar, gave Dani a dismissive glance, swept past her and got into the back seat.

The cab pulled away, once a mid-blue end of an era VW Skunk had belched past leaving a mucky cloud of diesel fumes in its wake. There's a mild smell of horse shit in the air.

Did she know the guy in the raincoat?

No.

He seemed flustered, but excited and happy.

She wondered why, then concluded he could be forgotten. Who? Him? No idea.

Cashmere loser, probably, from one of those families that don't talk about how they'd made their money? Probably, no certainly. She remembers his name. Peter-Paul Prinz, sort of friend of Klaus, funeral attendee, owner of about 50 apartments inherited from his grandfather who had bought them cheap on borrowed money in the 1930's from people hoping to leave Germany. Actually this meant that for next to nothing, with the help of the Party, the grandfather had picked up the homes of Jewish families fleeing the Nazi's, but these kind of business 'start ups' are no longer referred to in such disparaging terms as they used to be. Vulture capitalism grows its own authentication myths. The grandson thinks of himself as a businessman pure and simple, someone who recognises a good deal and acts incisively. People who know him say he's a worthless parasite, but charming, kind to animals and unfailingly polite. PPP is tolerably well-liked, but were you to ask, the emphasis would be on tolerated rather than well-liked. No-one is entirely certain who his friends are, or if he has ever really had any. He's a boules player, takes it seriously, which Dani finds laughable. 'Network check' send a minor pling to all subscribers warning of yet more traffic disruption in Charlottenburg, because of the accident.

Across the city, people are gathering for meetings.

Some people lie and some will be lied to.

Some people will listen as others try to explain themselves.

Many people are distracted and cannot concentrate however much they'd like too. For some people decisions symbolise devotion to duty. Some people don't give a shit.

That's the way things have always been in Berlin.

Some of the people who should have been involved in making decisions had been on the bus.

Because of that, the decision whether to build a new U-bahn station in the airport building at Tegel will be deferred for yet another year, just as it has been every year since it was proposed in 1977. The airport could well be closed before they get round to building it, but by then it will have become an even more vital element of infrastructure if plans for the future are to be realised and a final decision on the issue could be made in the next ten, or fifteen years.

Berlin City Planning is a mystery unto itself, which is about the only point of resemblance with the Vatican in Rome.

Chapter 3

The 'Soph-Am', pronounced 'so-femme', officially the 'Sophie Amalien Cocktail Lounge', is an agreeably gloomy, medium sized Berlin café with twenty odd tables and an air of comforting semi-permanence.

The clientele are also agreeably gloomy, though they would prefer to imagine they are jovial, the café baccanalial. Being honest with themselves they would admit to being too old for that kind of thing.

The majority are middle aged, married and mortgaged, or suffer the mid-life financial consequences of marital disaster. Multiple spouses, patchwork families, the whole deal and more.

A lot of sorrows have drowned in the 'Soph-Am'.

Some people avoid the place, not wanting to run into someone they were once married to, or even worse to run into someone they still are married to who has run into someone they were once married to and are having second, or third, or however many more, thoughts.

That's just the kind of place it is.

The name was an error, a 'denk fehler', 'thought error', an erroneous assumption. Sophie Amalia had been a Queen of Denmark and Norway, but the original owners of the café had mistaken her for the Duchess Anna Amalia, who gave her name to a famous library in Weimar, conflating her name with another aristocrat Sophie-Charlotte, (born 1668, died 1705, if that is a concern), who'd given her name to a nearby street, a square around the corner, the local Schloss, indeed the district as a whole. She'd been the posthumous

Charlotte in Charlottenburg, who married a Prussian king called
Friedrich 1, who she heartily disliked, nay scorned, yet became the
first Queen of Prussia at the age of 33, four years before dying of a
throat infection in Hanover. Frederick the Great's grannie, she'd
managed her own affairs in every sense of the word, which was
what the founders of the cocktail bar had intended to celebrate.
The founders of 'Soph-Am' had long since turned into little old
ladies and most have died, but their legacy is more or less intact and
for that the regulars are duly thankful.

There are only three people seated at the bar, when Dani strolls
inside and takes her seat near the newspaper rack. Copies of Taz,
FAZ, Die Zeit, Der Spiegel, all still in print. Two men and a
woman, 'regulars', they're the actors who'd been at Klaus' funeral a
few weeks earlier.

She greets them politely without giving the impression she wants
to talk. She's feeling stunned, but doesn't want to show it. They
know her well enough not to be offended. She doesn't care either
way.

There are two flavours of customer in the 'Soph-Am', the regulars
and the play-pals.

Overtly Anti-Royalist, the café was an offshoot of the last century
feminist seventies and a meeting place that announces your
sympathy for old fashioned notions like freedom of speech,
democratic autonomy and independent thought, or a more
contemporary dependence on online dating, depending on your
affiliations, age group and status as a customer.

Play-pal, or regular, one or the other.

You can't be both.

Accomplished drinkers, definitely regulars, the three barflies are
actors simply waiting to be called upon to act. They need an
audience and crave direction. In the mean time, as three muses, they
listen, drink and gossip. Most of the time they're waiting, but
sometimes they do work quite hard. If only life were so simple.
They complain a lot. Some of their complaints are justified, some of
the time and the rest of the time not.

"Madame Daniela is looking exceedingly serious today," says the
taller of the three, the one with the long nose, known as Phil.

She scowls in his general direction, plonks her bag on a chair and goes to the bar.

"I saw Peter-Paul P. looking unreasonably cheerful as I came in."

"One of his tenants has died suddenly, leaving an empty flat and no-one to inherit and take over the lease. He can tart the place up and sell for hard cash. He's euphoric, no more renting for peanuts!" says the woman. "The way the market is going, if his tenants weren't so obliging as to die of old age, he'd probably start murdering them."

"So what are you doing here, Dani? Nico asks. "An assignation? A fresh squeeze among the play-pals? Any of them take your fancy?"

Expert in divorce, Nico is shorter than Phil, but not round.

"I don't think she's going to tell you any of her secrets," says the woman, pushing her hand through the thatch of blonde hair that seems to be annoying her, but is the envy of half the women in Germany. The other half of German women envy her fame, her success and her beauty. The blonde does movies. From time to time, she does television, but only for exceptionally good productions. Despite her talent, she has very few female friends. Women find it disturbing the way men worship her. Men find it disturbing to find they worship her. She's getting cynical about worship, there's far too much of it about. A bit of predictably dull domesticity would be welcome, but anything so seedy as a 'play-pal' is taboo. Her agent had made that clear the minute social media had been invented.

The 'play-pals', who find one another via the dating apps on their mobiles and agree to meet before deciding whether to cheat on their spouses and go for the 'fresh squeeze' option. have made the 'So-femme' a regular haunt for the long married lawyers, fancy-free accountants and over-stressed school-teachers, who don't usually fetch up in bars. Four couples are already doing their best to to be unobtrusive and a man in a leather jacket looks annoyed. Presumably he's been stood up.

A couple of minutes earlier, a woman had come inside, looked around, then turned on her heels and left.

Perhaps he was her husband.

Perhaps they'd never met before.

Perhaps she'd been looking for someone else.

Perhaps she'd taken one look, decided no, without bothering with the thankyou but no thanks bit, which happens more often than people like to acknowledge. His paisley silk scarf is redundant. So was her unread copy of the Financial Times.

Dani smiles. "Well, I didn't come here to chat to you lot."

"I want to devise an alternative to Aperol for the play-pals," explains Ulrike, usually known as Uli, which is common enough, but sometimes at home with her parents in Hamburg, they distinguish her from her brother Ulrich, by referring to her as Rika. She is mixing a drink of her own devising to impress the creative alcoholics among her customers. "The play-pals like to colour code their drinks for purposes of recognition. If everyone drinks the same, they get confused and panic. I want to put some uniquely colour coded cocktails on the website as a kind of self help guide to middle-aged dating. A lot of them need their confidence boosting. I feel embarrassed for them, honestly."

"No one is going to want one of those, Uli, it's a horrible colour, an ugly blue, almost canal green, like one of those backwaters you avoid in Venice, where the restaurants dump their slops."

"What are you going to call it?" asks the blonde.

"Un Macron?"

"How about a 'Happy Hook-Up'?"

"Oh, how about it, I'd love one."

"We all would."

"Indeed? Feeling horny? Fancy a quickie, Dani?" says Phil.

"Oh, horny as hell, always was, always will be, you know me, uncontrollable female passion. Of course, I'd love a quickie."

"We could..."

"No, we couldn't Phil.... I said I'm feeling horny as hell, been ages, well an hour or two and yes I do fancy a quickie, but not with you for goodness sake. God almighty, Phil, take a look at yourself. Give him a shot of the antidote Uli. He's confusing himself, delusion and self-deception."

"How does anyone go about re-educating an aging Lothario," Uli asks herself out loud, "without turning him into a Tartuffe? Before you go any further, Phil, find yourself a better dentist, you grin like Dracula."

"Is that a diagnosis, or a charge sheet?" wonders Nico out loud, as if he can read her thoughts.

"Ker-Pow!" says the blonde, as she laughs at her friend's ego schrivelling humiliation. Phil pretends to ignore them and they turn to next business, if only to humiliate him further.

"And I'd like a manzanilla," adds Dani, giving Uli a smile.

"Did I tell you about the letter Phil got from his insurance company after the Italian earthquake?"

Phil looks like a man contemplating the violent death of an old friend.

"I'm sure you're about to tell us again, Nico, now that Dani's here," says the blonde.

"Dear Phil, Earthquakes, you see Dani, are an act of God, they wrote, and your holiday home is now in the condition God intended all along, so get used to the rubble and the dust. Wave farewell to mortal ambition. In accordance with God's will, your policy was cancelled moments before the quake struck. As an unbeliever, we shall not be willing to provide you with insurance cover in the future as our actuaries are firmly convinced of the power of faith and without trust in the Good Lord, you haven't a prayer. Dear Phil was livid. As a citizen of the European Union, he considers himself to have full rights to insurance cover and equality before the law, even in the small print of financial services, whether he's Christian, Islamic, Pagan, Atheist, or agnostic. Such innocence, touching, don't you agree? Then his lawyer said he didn't stand a chance in court, not in provincial Italy, so he's facing the loss of a house and a bill of twenty five thousand for the demolition and clearance work."

"Nico, Phil is sitting next to you. Don't you think he could tell the story himself?"

"He could, but he won't. And I thought you'd be interested."

"Not really," says Dani.

"And he still owes the bank two hundred and seventy thousand on the mortgage when he bought it. So, in the absence of collateral, he's fundamentally screwed. Old Klaus couldn't have done better."

"Well fuck you too, two too, both of you," says Phil. He's upset.

"Tutu," says Nico.

"Toot toot," says the blonde and drinks down her cocktail.

Dani reflects for a moment. He has good reason to be upset, but no more than the next fool and their dearly departed money. She doesn't sympathise with his sense of humiliation. He's moderately prosperous, but he's always been greedy. One good tv series and a lot of expensive investment management. He has no reason to worry about money. Seven years ago, he'd gotten away with ten per cent of a shopping mall in Santander, tax free, thanks largely to Klaus. He'd never made a secret of that. Dani can remember the celebrations, a party down in Potsdam at a villa on the lakeside opposite the Marmor Palais, Klaus' finest hour! The blonde takes a sniff of Uli's latest cocktail, but doesn't sip and wrinkles her nose in disgust, "Jesus, that is appalling, horrid, it smells of catpiss, start again Uli."

Then a dark green BMW sports car pulls up outside the Soph-Am and Caro has arrived. She comes into the bar, beams a high voltage smile towards Dani and points to a table in the corner.

Phil and Nico take note, appropriate to the moment.

She's chic, exceptionally chic and everyone in the room, including the blonde, compares her appearance with their own. She comes out top. Uli adds her to her wish-list, under the heading of improbables and impossibles, maybe in another life along with Basinger, Blondie and Bananarama all at the same time, which says a lot about her age and what her most recent ex referred to as a retarded sense of retro-development. She doesn't care what other people think. Retro lust is mid-way from street culture to high culture, via a bit of myth, the daughters golden and so on. Uli is a former President of 'Girls like Us'.

"Later guys," says Dani, scooping up her bag to join Caro, who is eagerly checking the menu, having flopped onto a couch by a corner table.

"Hungry?" asks Caro without bothering with much greeting.

"I suppose so."

"Soup would be good."

"There you are. Goulash soup, or Mullygoo spicey vegetable?"

"Goulash, please."

"Yes goulash, mullygoo, yes, no, no. Two goulash then."

Uli takes their order, brings Dani the manzanilla she's ordered, sneaks a look at Caro in close up, leans towards her and inhales sharply. Musky orange, she shivers involuntarily. Then she returns and serves Caro a small glass of bitter Jever pilsner beer without her having had to ask.

"So why do you think we're here?" Caro asks Dani.

"Erm, morals, ethics, the universe, does God exist in Ireland, is income tax necessary, all that – or, no, no idea. Or do you mean why are we meeting? Well, so that you can tell me what you want? You called, I assume about the job you'd like me to do."

"I thought it might be time to overturn a few mistaken assumptions. How about that?"

"You don't have any work for me? Over the phone I had the impression you were giving me a job interview."

Caro giggles and becomes conspirative, whispering, "The play-pals over there think we are about to seduce one another."

"What, that woman with the bright blue scarf and her friend?" Dani smiles.

"Yes, the silk, blue. You can buy them from the Vietnamese shop on Pestalozzistrasse. Quite nice, not expensive at all. I can lip read. She knows who I am, she thinks you're a pick up. We are about to be outed via the internet as lesbians. She's a lawyer and he's telling her about being a drama teacher."

"Courtroom meets drama, how very predictable."

"Christ, that's hot!"

The goulash soup had arrived. Dani put her spoon to one side and licked her lips where the rich brown sauce had scalded. "Microwaved."

"Do you dance?" Caro asks.

"Sometimes."

"Then, lets give the voyeurs something to gossip about while the soup cools sufficiently to eat."

"Foxtrot, quickstep, tango?"

"You sound like an air traffic controller."

"When air traffic controllers dream of crashes, are they horrifying nightmares, or the fulfilment of their wildest dreams?"

"Cannibalism."

"It's a option, but I'll stick to goulash. Ghoulish can wait. You want to dance?"

"Why not! "

"I should have worn my dirndl and tracht."

"Do you have one of those really old leather things?"

There's an edge of fascination in the question. Not every-one still has a traditional leather bodice in the family. They're more like something for a carthorse than a woman, improbable objects to modern eyes.

"No, but you know what I mean, rustic alpine wench meets city slicker in sleazy bar."

Caro doesn't really follow. The Soph-Am isn't sleazy, not really sleazy the way really sleazy places are, so she picks some tunes on her pale blue tablet and lets the tinny speakers do their stuff as they take to the floor. In an authentically sleazy bar they would hardly raise a flicker of interest. Here in the Soph-Am, the play-pals are watching them like hawks. The Network Check AI registers them as subjects of interest and sends a little pling to its subscribers.

Caro and Dani have forgotten to agree who will lead, so their little rhythmic excursion begins with a jolt, then Caro hisses, "I lead, you follow, OK babe?"

"Whatever you desire," answers Dani disarmingly, preparing to shift into reverse, like a valkyrie turning in mid-flight. They move in unison.

The three muses set thoughts of acting aside and pay attention to the slow slinky steps of the two women as they start their first dance together. Two doctors, a tax official and an insolvency lawyer also turn their heads, if not in admiration, at least with mild erotic curiosity and growing anticipation. Maybe the Soph-Am is livelier than expected.

Good dancers need no music. Great dancers make their own. Caro and Dani aren't bad, but they could do with a tune, or two and some practice. Following rhythms of their own is more or less sufficient, sway and turn, a step, a glance, a dance. Soon enough, they're moving better.

This is the kind of bar the Soph-Am ought to be, but all too rarely is. Caro and Dani have brought a new dimension to its attractions, a hint of decadance, which Uli recognises is just what the old place needs. She takes note. Enhance sense of decadence. The play-pals are just a little bit too predictable as they slope about politely hoping to avoid being seen by anyone who knows them. The old place could do with a bit of steaminess, she decides.

Were Dani and Caro surprised with each other? In short, yes, but their dance was something other than the onlookers wanted to assume. This was by no means the beginning of a beautiful friendship, it was a means of conversing securely.

"Do you have a gun?" asked Caro in a whisper as she shimmied to distract any lip readers who happen to be watching.

"Indeed I do," answered Dani firmly, grasping Caro around the waist, content that they'll have foiled any likely barwatching surveillance people.

"And can you shoot?" Caro wanted to know, as she glanced towards the door.

"Oh yes," Dani said, "I can shoot."

And then they turn.

"How did you learn?"

Swivel.

"My father taught me."

Sway.

"A soldier?"

Turns again.

"A pilot."

Arms around her shoulder.

"Can airlines pilots shoot?" asks Caro, gazing into Dani's eyes.

"I wouldn't know. Maybe they do? My Dad was in fast jets, Cold War readiness. Boom, zoom, whoosh and away," Dani side steps to the left, "Not an Airbus in sight."

"Are you American then, Dani?"

Caro to the right.

Next thing, they're dancing cheek to cheek.

Uli is envious – either of them would do, both would be better than a White Christmas.

"No, Dad's French, my mother Polish, I grew up in Tegel. He started on home grown Mirages, the Dassault Mirage, quite a machine. Of course, he had no choice about Tornado's, no-one did, that's NATO, but he ended up on an F-16 for a couple of years before they retired him. He loved his F-16. He says it made his ass tingle."

"I didn't realise the French had an airforce, well not a proper one, not in Berlin."

"Of course, one, two three, four powers. The French sector, Wedding, Tegel, Reinickendorf. My Mum always thought that Poland had as good a case as France to be one of the occupying powers, but she was in a minority and she certainly had no intention of returning to Poland to argue the case with the other members of the Warsaw Pact. Instead of that, she worked part-time as a teacher at the prison."

"What did she teach?"

"Ambiguity and the law."

"What?"

"How to get your lawyer to help you build a defence."

"Oh, what a good idea," says Caro brightly.

"I suppose so."

"When you have to use your gun, do you shoot in self defence, the desire to attack, or the urge for revenge?"

"What?" Dani doesn't like this.

"Motivations," says Caro. "Men and women usually fail to recognise the most important impulses in one another's lives."

"Are you sure?"

"In my case yes, and yours?"

"Possibly, probably, conceivably. Self defence, sure, once or twice. I'm not so sure about revenge. Attack? What kind of person do you take me for?"

"An eternal paradox of conception and misconception."

"Tripping off the tongue too easily."

"They do, don't they, they tongue," says Caro.

"And they trip," Dani replies.

"I've done a lot of tripping thanks to my Dad."

"A thought as we dance?" suggests Dani.

"A question I'd like you to consider. What is there to distinguish the fantasy world of a dolls' house and a model railway?"

"That covers a lot of ground, but boy dreams and girl dreams basically."

"Though they do overlap, I think. Alice through the signal box."

"Maybe, but not necessarily, not always. Trains and tunnels?"

"I think the goulash will have cooled enough to eat," Dani says, adding, " Maybe you should be talking to someone else, not me."

"Yes! That's a possibility. I'm famished. Mmmm, actually this is really quite good," says Caro, as she samples the goulash soup, spearing some meat with a fork and dipping a chunk of bread in the sauce. "Paprika, genuine, fiery paprika. And lamb! You know, the old complaints about men no longer have the resonance they once did. Look around you."

"And?"

"Only a very few years ago, the men who drank in this bar could be depended upon to have lank greasy hair and dress in unwashed jeans with sweatshirts that reeked of personally sweated sweat and occupied themselves to amuse their independently minded feminist girlfriends by composing melancholic apocalyptic ditties between mainlining self-destructive hits of adulterated heroin. And now what? Displaying the originality of an all day breakfast, blokes lounge around suckling on e-cigarettes and cigars, infantile lollipops, perfumed and pampered with skin lotions, preening themselves and combing out their beards like taxi drivers on a wet Sunday morning in British Columbia. And what do they have to discuss? Revolution, rebellion and the collapse of capitalism, or the latest episode of Game of Thrones?"

"Vanity is the lowest form of individualism said Sartre to the mirror and jotted a note to that effect in his little green book of witty aphorisms for putting down Simone."

"Street fighting man succumbs to mobile phone virus."

"You're a cynic, Caro."

"Sometimes. I have good reason."

Dani decides it's time to get serious.

"So, what do you really want? Since we hardly know one another, I'm assuming you weren't suddenly overtaken by the desire to go dancing and eat goulash soup with me."

"I liked the dancing and the food is good, you must agree. You'll help?"

"I didn't say that, I asked what the problem is. I'd like to know what I am getting involved in."

"Oh, well, I don't know, not exactly, which is why I need you. I want you to find out."

"Is someone threatening you?"

"No."

"Is there something you've seen or noticed.

"No. Yes. I don't know."

"Is something missing? Money? Things?"

"No."

"No?"

"Nothing like that, not that I know of anyway."

"Have you committed a serious crime? Because if you have please don't tell me about it because I'm not a lawyer and being a good citizen, I would have a theoretical obligation to inform the prosecutors' office, even if I might think the better of it, just to avoid the hassle."

"No of course not, nothing like that."

"So what the fuck is your problem? Is it tougher being a widow than you imagined?"

Dani isn't sure why her patience is wearing thin, maybe it's the feeling this woman will expect that a bowl of soup is sufficient recompence for her time.

"At the beginning of next week, a lawyer is due to fly into Berlin from the USA. We met after my trip to Cuba, on the way home via Miami. My Dad introduced us, which is the first improbability, then the lawyer claimed to be clearing up some of the legal mess my husband left when he died, which is the second imponderable. Klaus' lawyer has an office on Walter Benjamin Platz. I know his wife, their daughters and his son who wants to become a footballer. In fifteen years he never alluded to legal bods in Florida, or anywhere abroad. Klaus' mate Markus never had anything to say about that either. Thirdly my dear ex-husband Klaus was all of a sudden supposed to have had businesses in three US States, together with Guatemala and the Dominican Republic, none of which I had ever been told about. Accordingly, there are people who want to give me large amounts of money, which I find impossible to take seriously, but maybe I should. I don't know what to do."

It is all unconvincing. Presumably Klaus had been busier than Caro realised after they split up. But Dani thinks she knows which Markus Caro is talking about and assuming she takes the job, she'll go to see him. "Now I see why you wanted to dance."

"What kind of answer is that?"

"I'm just trying to give myself time to think. None of this is very plausible." Caro says nothing.

A think bubble should arise over Dani's head, but it doesn't.

"We can talk as long as you like," says Dani eventually, "but it would make sense if you gave me something to do, otherwise you're spending a lot of money getting me to listen and waste time that could probably be put to better use. You know I am usually employed to find things, that's my role, a finder."

"But do you see what I'm trying to understand?"

"The easiest solution would be to tell them you aren't interested, don't need the money, don't want the money, can't be bothered, better things to do, please go away kind of approach."

"Would they believe me?"

"I doubt it. Actually, when I think about it, that could be more dangerous than pushing for more of the money. People are suspicious of anyone who says they don't need money. Greed is human, altruism divine and commensurately improbable. Yes, tell them you won't sell up for less than ten times their offer. Greed is pre-programmed. Now having said that you should realise not to ask me for advice, but simply tell me what you want me to find."

"There you are then. What might be the most sensible question to ask?"

"Were you surprised that your father was involved in clearing up Klaus' business dealings? "

"Yes. I had no idea they were working with one another. Klaus was property, my Dad is in pharmaceuticals, mainly. People are usually at their best when they are expected to perform a role they know and understand. Set them in unusual situations and only a minority prevail and they are usually people who specialise in adapting to new situations, which was neither true of my Dad, nor of dear old Klaus."

"What's this lawyer guy's name."

"The lawyer isn't a guy, she's a gal, a girl called Maria, with three adorable children who go to weapons training twice a week, then show you stuff on their mobiles of them firing off AK47's and Uzi's, and she has a husband called Lee who claims to have studied philosophy under Richard Rorty at Stanford, before deciding to retrain as a hit-man. He works for the mob, or anyone else with enough money and he told me he enjoys his work, likes to achieve a clean hit, a good result, a phenomenological identifiable moment of being and nothingness, he claims, depending on the timescale of your system." "Oops. Can't be real though, can he?"

"Well hell yes, who knows, oops, you took the words right out of my mouth. OO.oo.oops, what the fuck, which is approximately what I said to my father after he introduced me to these people. The children had been to their shooting practice and returned home hungry for burgers, so we all barbequed in the garden of their eight bedroomed art deco mansion."

"So what is your father's standing in all this?"

" I do not know, he has all kinds of people running around for him. They're his crew, his équipe. My beloved Father is a recreational drug designer, happy highs. He got into honey when he was young and made enough money to do as he pleases. Now he's getting keen about online games. He spent the whole boat ride from Havanna to Miami talking about something called 'Gaming with Attitudes', which in his version of the concept involves getting gamers to become heavy drug users in order to gain a minimal advantage within the universe of the game they're addicted to. Attitudes become assertions and are expendable. Game addict meets drug addict, what a world!

When I was a kid my Dad was a walking laboratory for anything hallucinogenic. He was a precocious genius, the Steven Hawking of narcotics. He used to make jokes about sending his children, ie me, to 'high school' and as a teenager, I spent a lot of my weekends locked in the attic with a brainful of Bernhardt's alchemical doodles. He would concoct something in the lab, then use me as the anything but clinical trial. My childhood memories are littered with nebulous impressions of long Sunday afternoons spent tripping under the roof beams, after sampling Dad's extra-special pharmaceutical delights. Sometimes I was Alice, sometimes the rabbit and just once I was Janice Joplin, but by tea-time I morphed again into Paula Kelly and shocked him with a raucous rendition of 'Hey Big Spender' as he walked through the door to see how I was getting on. He's still at it. I'm surprised I got through adolescence with my mind intact. I wasn't the only one, of course. My successor was a girl called Allegra. Luckily her parents recognised the warning signs, so they removed her beyond his reach. Thank goodness for her, where-ever she is."

Caro explains she has only the haziest recollection of having met Allegra at a concert. She can remember the evening quite distinctly for a different reason.

Bernhardt had subscriptions to the Berlin Phil, and Caro had been treated to an evening of Hindemith, Strauss and Arnold Schönberg which accidentally comprised a programme of works they'd completed while living in Charlottenburg's West End. Schönberg lived at Nussbaum-Allee 17, Hindemith at Brixplatz and Strauss on the corner of the Heerstrasse and what is now Theodor-Heuss Platz. Caro had been struck by this odd geographical coincidence. The concert had been a success, good performance, appreciative audience. The pieces could have been programmed together at any concert hall in the world without reference to Berlin, but there it was, she'd been listening to the fruits of local labour and a major chunk of 20th century culture all rolled into one. After that, Caro liked to imagine you might have overheard the composers at their piano's, as you walked to and from the local shops in the days when the 'West End' had been a newly built and rather flashy suburb for Berlin celebrities. The other reason she's remembered the evening was the skinny little thing in the seat next to her had been unusually fascinated by the music, which Caro had assumed was a sign that she was going to be exceptionally talented. That skinny little thing must have been Allegra. They haven't seen each other since. She must be in her late twenties by now.

"Couldn't he have been sent to jail?" Dani asks suspiciously, watching Caro's face for signs of stress as she explains.

"I'm pretty sure he was sent to jail, at one point, though not for abusing children. All that happened in jail was that he made some very useful contacts with the Colombian drug barons. It was one of those countries where you get out of prison by bribing a judge and not before. They forgot to tell him that until he'd been inside for a few weeks. He told me later, they taught him a lot. He never dealt in illegal substances, he invented not yet illegal hallucinogens. Never forget, he started out with honey and adulterated that."

"Ah," says Dani, as though that might have been self-evident.

"He may have had something going with Klaus, I've no idea what, probably money laundering, Klaus wasn't a dealer," Caro says.

"Drug money becomes property?"

"Why not, it would make sense to a lot of people, they'd accept it as an explanation. Especially if there was a profit to be made on the property too. I can imagine Klaus being tempted."

"You know, now I recognise you. You're, weren't you the little girl on the label of the jar of that breakfast stuff, I can even remember the words -"Bernhardt's Hilberg Honey Spread" blended from 'sustainable' corn syrup, purified molasses and the honey's of many a hundredfold artisan producers around the globe."

"And marketed using me in a variety of 'english summer's day Lolita glowing at the gates of dawn' pictures."

"My brother used to fancy you."

"Half the men in Europe started their days staring into my badly printed eyes and even now, about half of them half recognise me in the street without knowing quite why. I'm lumbered with it, too late to change anything now. A lot of them confuse me with Alice in Wonderland. I tell them I'm the Alice from 'Through the Looking Glass', then tell them to get a life, or chase a different rabbit. Erotic spread, Alice and buttered toast, so english, le weekend, not nine and a half weeks. The full english. More tea with the toast? I ask you! I might just have well have stuffed a tennis ball in my knickers."

By this time, they've finished their soup.

"So what do you want me to do?"

"They claim that I am going to be paid a lot of money."

"How nice."

"But for what. Where am I leaving myself, legally I mean, if I accept the cash, then it turns out to be unlawful money, I don't know, drug stuff, stuff Klaus should never have become involved in. Am I making myself liable, would one of these guilt assessors come along and pin the blame on me? I want you to find out."

"But I shall need something to assess, if you want me to work on your guilt. People are checking out Klaus' affairs and I could take a look at your stuff, but I don't see how I can work out where your stuff and his overlaps without going right back to the days when you were working together."

Caro considers Dani's remarks for a moment, then she suggests what she could do.

"Come along to my meeting with this Little Miss Muffet from Miami and tell me what you think about her."

"That isn't supposed to be guilt assessment, nothing official, just an opinion."

"You're right, but do come and we'll see where we go from there."

"A start, then, you have to start somewhere," Dani said.

"Easy money, then, hard to say no.

"Never assume anything is going to be easy."

Caro finished her soup. She felt more relaxed.

Dani finished her soup. She felt full.

They both decided to have a brandy with their coffee.

Why not?

"You're driving," Dani pointed out.

"I know," said Caro emphatically and drank down her brandy with a determined glug, then signalled to Uli for another.

Unconcerned by the impression she's making, Caro failed to mention that her office is only a couple of minutes walk away. The car can stay where it is overnight. She can be economical like that, but she did pay the bill by credit card then gave Dani a padded envelope. Inside it were fifty one hundred Euro bills.

"Don't spend it all at once," she said with a smile. "Keep a tally, but I don't want a detailed paper trail for this job, alright?"

"Do you expect to be sent to prison."

"Maybe, I don't know. Not yet. I'm worried. Maybe someone will kill me before it gets that far. You can never really be certain about such things, can you?"

The two of them take stock of the conversation so far.

Just a spoilt brat assuming that someone somewhere would take on the risk and the cost of a killing, says Dani to herself. She isn't convinced. Thoughts of murder rarely go further than muttered threats and contract killings are almost unheard of, despite what you see in the movies. Berlin doesn't have many murders at all, more than Lisbon true, but half the rate in Amsterdam, or Glasgow. The problems seem real enough however. Klaus and his escapades are hardly ancient history. Maybe Caro is right about needing help. Dani has nothing to complain about. The bulky wad of banknotes feels snug in the inside pocket of her biker jacket.

A willing subject, good enough to be useful, not so good that she'll become a danger, Caro concludes optimistically about Dani, an unwitting agent of change, someone who can hopefully be used to nudge a reaction from people. It will be interesting to see how far she gets on her own.

Caro isn't at all clear that Dani has really understood the seriousness of problems she could face. Apart from that, she has no particular expectations. She'll wait and watch, see what happens.

Dani is being a bit too glib, but that isn't very friendly of Caro either. She isn't shelling out a thousand a day for the fun of it. She's actually extremely nervous about the ways things are going and is very uncertain about what will happen next. Klaus has left a can of worms half opened and those people in Miami have frightened her, partly because they'd been so charming and friendly, partly because they seem so certain about knowing so much more than she does about the current state of affairs.

Dani left first, then Caro scowled dismissively at the three actors as she was on her way out. They didn't scowl back, they paused, primed to gossip away the rest of the day and wondered aloud what the fuck that was all about. Dani finds and Caro floats. The actors decide they're not just odd, they're a destructively incompatible couple, but they won't let it bother them. The next subject of their attention was an even more improbable but entertaining impromptu meeting between a pair of play-pals, one of whom had been a Liberal politician, a rising star until she wasn't, when some-one pointed out politely that she'd cheated her doctorate (like ex-Dr Karl-Theodor von & zu Guttenberg and various other political academic fakes). The other is a tv reporter, who used to be head of something or other for ARD, German State Television, but had left to join Al Jazeera and was assumed to be based in Moscow.

"So what the fuck is that slimeball up to," said Phil.

"They're talking about Gerhardt Schröder, the Kremlin creep, he just called him."

"Mrs. Merkel's predecessor, remember? The man that time forgot."

"Schröder, the man we all forgot."

"I find it difficult to recall there actually was a time before Merkel, even when you try to think about it," Nico said and Uli nodded,

"Yeah, we forgot. Never underestimate Helmut Kohl's prescription for political success in Germany – do nothing and see what happens. You, Nico, were little more than a babe in arms, when Kohl ruled the roost, the only cabbage in town."

"Ui," Nico replies, "How much I wanted that role, Arturo Ui, but they gave it to Martin Wuttke."

"They were right," says the blonde, "he's brilliant, he's made it his own."

"I know, that's what hurts."

Uli is wondering what to do about the light dusting of cocaine that covers every surface in the Soph-Am. There isn't enough to be worth recovering, but just enough for people to wonder why the place isn't more polished.

Then two Turkish boys come in and offer to work for her.

Uli thinks for a minute, asks them their ages, then when they tell her, sixteen, seventeen, she turns them down. Too young, even as cocaine sweepers. Anyway what would their no doubt devout Muslim parents say if they knew they were working at a place that is dusted with drugs, sells alcohol, where the boss is a woman?

Uli decides she was probably doing them a favour by saying no. The boys don't agree, but they can't be bothered to argue with her, because she seems like a nice woman and they wander round the corner to pester the people running the other bars, first Lenz, then Dollingers.

One of them threatens to burn down one of the cafés, then offers to burn down the other, but the bar owner they're talking to says he isn't willing to pay for them to do that, so they wander away thwarted once again.

They consider burning down both cafés simply out of boredom, but they aren't going to make anything from that, apart from a mild sense of satisfaction.

"All I actually want is some fucking money," the older one says sincerely to his brother, as they head for the S-bahn, and he wonders whether it's time for plan B and he should take up the chance to study for a degree in Chinese Literature at the Humboldt University. He decides it makes sense to qualify for a student loan from the Bafog, so he can stop mugging people for a living.

The younger brother wants to be a dentist, but his hands shake and he has problems with reading and writing, so it probably won't work out and he'll have to be settle for being a professional footballer, something he's good at, but doesn't enjoy. He already has an offer from a club in France that he'll accept when he finishes school at the end of the year. He knows they don't want him at Barcelona, but there's just a chance he might get a contract in Italy. If he does ok at football, he thinks he might get into dentistry later.

Once she's home, Dani puts the cash in an envelope with Caro's name on it and logs the sum in her book-keeping system as a 'pre-payment' against expenses and as yet undefined future bills and sends a text to her accountant. That should be sufficient to keep her out of trouble if anyone comes to ask. Cash has become unfashionable in banking and accountancy. Soon it will be impossible to use money to pay for much at all.

Anything over five thousand in cash already feels like money laundering, unless you're a money launderer, in which case it's peanuts. Just ask the guys at the Italian restaurant round the corner. The tax office blindly accepts that they sell one and a half tonnes of pizza and pasta a week, more than anyone could possibly cook on a four flame gas range and simple electric oven.

Their paperwork is immaculate. The luxury €50 pizzas are delivered complete with little bags of cocaine, or MDMA as a thankyou from the chef. If anyone ever gets caught, the delivery guys get the blame. They're self-employed, slipping something into the pannier, disgraceful, nothing to do with us.
Fresh deliveries by courier from Wuppertal, every second Thursday.
'Bye-Bye suckers. Enjoy your supper'.

She half watches the television news, an excuse to relax as much as anything. After half an hour of media woe, she'll get on with some more work. There's not much that would surprise Dani.

People in Aachen are being given iodine tablets in anticipation of a nuclear accident in Belgium. That didn't surprise Dani, either. Belgian reactors have already been recognised as leaky vessels. But it does worry her. What the hell do these people think they're doing?

Where are the Greens when you need them to say Nuclear Power, No Thanks? Too busy running supermarkets and selling windmills to the Irish, or wrangling with Merkel for nice little jobs in the government, until they aren't and the other party can have a go. They're all scrambling for preferment, except for red haired Eva from Adenauerplatz, who'll be a radical forever, but she is a voice in the wilderness nowadays and Dani hasn't run into her for a while. Maybe its all over for the Greens, who seemed to have compromised themselves into oblivion. As to the woman herself, the Merkel era was evaporating around her, but she seems impervious to change. She's patient, simply watching as she always has, while her rivals burn their boats. But this time there's a feeling she too will be gone before long. Dani can't do much about any of that, but she has other problems to deal with and if she doesn't pay attention they'll also drift out of control. Two of the current bunch of cases worry her even more than the lack of a government. She thinks a dose of anarchy might do the Germans good, but the parents of a fifteen year old concerned that he is nightclubbing have admitted it is their fault that he's started dealing. He's too young to go to prison, but he'll officially become an adult soon and then he's facing instant incarceration unless he mends his ways. She doesn't know what he's using and she can't find out where he's picking up the dope. The situation is pretty hopeless. Dani doesn't know how she can help. Maybe he should run away.

And there's the old lady due to be deported to Canada for breaking all kinds of laws in Denmark and Holland, but she was caught stealing a Porsche in the Bismarckstrasse and wants Dani to find a witness to the arrest who'll back up her claims of police brutality. Despite her optimism, the old lady is in deep trouble. Dani sends an e-mail to the woman's lawyer explaining that she hasn't come up with anything that might help and isn't likely to. A plea of insanity might be worth thinking about. Would Canada be better or worse than Germany, when it comes to psychiatric hospitals?

The other cases are trivial, just the usual mixture of money and narcissism, betrayal and sex. She isn't going to lose any sleep over them.

The daily phone call is a legitimising ritual even when there's nothing to report. Dani has to talk to six clients for five or ten minutes every morning before she can concentrate on whatever it is she's planning to do with the day.

It pays off. The clients are reassured. She is reminded to take them seriously. Now, they can be reminded to pay their bills.

Quite early next morning, five calls done, then it's Caro's turn.

She's still sleepy when Dani phones.

Neither of the women are very informative.

When they talk to one another it's as though they are reluctant to tell each other anything that might turn out to be important, so their conversation stalls.

They don't seem able to communicate.

Dani says she's about to meet someone who should be a real help.

Caro answers that she can't actually remember the last time she met someone who turned out to be a real help. Most people seem to get so far, then screw up, or get stuck – the old 'typische Berlin' thing again. So that was about all, apart from agreeing to talk later.

Still Caro wishes Dani luck and says she needs to blend the paint for her window frame. Just they're about to hang up, Dani asks if there is a particular crime that Caro is concerned about.

She says no. Then she says the issue is one of prevention, whatever that is supposed to mean, and rings off.

Chapter 4

Dani has never considered herself to be anything so exotic as a 'private eye', or one of those fast and fancy fictional female detectives who rescue damsels in distress from burning boats or beds, or worse.

On one occasion, a foolish American had referred to her as a 'private dick', but quickly wished he'd chosen his words more carefully.

He hadn't hung around for long.

If Dani does have one distinctive talent, it is this. She is quite simply good at finding stuff when people need help, a line of work she'd begun when she was still a student. She doesn't snoop, she doesn't spy and she doesn't speculate. People will say they've looked everywhere, when something is lost, or someone is missed, but looking everywhere is time consuming and more often than not fruitless.

Finding stuff is usually the result of knowing where to look, rather than the 'looking' for its own sake, so that's what Dani does. She works out the best place to look then goes off to check. Sometimes it works and sometimes it doesn't, but she wins more than she loses and that helps.

Sometimes it's fun, sometimes it's dull.

The other kind of searching comes from being asked to solve a problem and the most important criteria then is to decide what exactly it might be useful to look for, once you've worked out what the problem really is. The problems people want to talk about are rarely the problems they ought to be facing up to, which is Dani's expectation of the situation with Caro. Sooner or later the truth will begin to make itself plain and then she'll know what she's after. Till then, Caro's little litergy of problems falls into the category of interesting confusion.

Just a job, just a job, Dani reminds herself.

Any resemblance to 'Network Check' is quite coincidental and the similarity to Caro's way of looking at the world is not only superficial, it is basically incompatible with Dani's approach, which sets them apart from one another, even if they wanted to collaborate, which they don't seem to, at least not yet. Caro and co expect to reveal structures and relationships. They'll build some kind of framework then see what might work out. Dani sees events and circumstances. She starts out with what happened. They are altogether different.

As a student, Dani had known from the beginning that she wasn't going to make an outstanding scientist and working as an assistant in a lab was not they way she intended to spend her days on the planet, so she'd pocketed her degree and taken to working as a 'finder', getting started by putting an advert in the window of the community project office on Seelingstrasse under lost and found. 'Let me find what you have lost' sounded quasi-religious but was general enough to attract one or two folk with problems she could solve.

A couple of early successes meant people got to hear that she's useful. Then lawyers started asking her to do stuff and she'd soon begun to flourish, though she had to accept that lawyers have their own expectations of how and why things are done.

So, what began as a vague desire to make a living by being helpful, fairly quickly changed, after a series of situations that began to feel like 'cases'.

A lot of the people who approach her seem to be expecting help to build stories that will convince their lawyers. Some were witnesses at other people's trials, who needed to firm up their stories.

There were those she suspected who were probably the accomplices of the people who'd been charged and didn't want to be found out.

She tries to avoid the defendants themselves.

If it's going to court, they're almost always guilty. If there's one thing that's certain anywhere it in the world it is that public prosecutors don't waste their time going to court with being confident they have a case. If they don't have the evidence, they'll look for someone who can make it up.

A couple of decades later, and Dani knows the local authorities, the archives and records, the data bases. She knows thousands of names and has knotted all kinds of working and social connections into a mental tapestry of the city as an abstract space where people go about their business from day to day.

Hers is an unofficial picture of the city that includes the crooks, the saints and lots of people who are in between and it's a richer mix than the official PR version of Berlin would embrace, but she knows she's only been scratching the surface. There are other forces at work that rarely reveal themselves at the level of daily experience.

She would accept that might be where Caro's kind of approach comes in, but it's all too imprecise and speculative for her liking.

Sometimes Dani works by the hour, sometimes she'll work for a fixed amount, but once or twice she's had the luck to be given a finder's fee of the kind they accept in the world of finance, five per cent of the value of the job.

Thanks to a land deal in Ludwigsfelde back in 2009, she has enough in the bank not to panic when new work seems thin on the ground, but not quite enough to retire.

She's always mildly embarrassed when people like Caro ask her about the pistol, but the truth is people have pointed guns at her from time to time and she knows the effect of blind panic, when unarmed, you stare down the barrel of a loaded weapon. So, some days her pistol is security, some days a frightener and there have been three days when it saved her life and one day when she'd shot the top off someone's head from a distance of twenty five metres, when she'd expected to miss.

She hadn't been seen.
She hadn't been heard.
She hadn't been found.

And she hadn't left any evidence.

So she got away with murder in broad daylight not far from the Brandenburg Gate in the wooded parkland they call the Tiergarten.

She knew it was her lucky day when it had taken two weeks for the corpse to be discovered. By then, foxes and wild boar had done their worst.

Even the cause of death remained undefined. The bullet that did the damage had ricocheted off into the woods never to be recovered.

No-one even looked.

The crime scene reverted to picnic area.

You can always get to the bottom of things, unless they get to you first, by which time it will probably be too late, but that is merely to quibble over the sequence of events. To navigate the depths of a city made murky by cul-de-sac confusions of blank walls and shadows is a challenge, even to those who claim to be expert at exploring the urban deeps, or imagine they understand the quirks and echoes of the people who live there. Search and you will find. Finessing people's fetishes needs both sense and sensibility. Recognising people's true desires can sometimes bring very unpleasant surprises.

There's only one more point about search and find that sets Dani apart from the rest. She is always very careful to ensure that whatever it is that she's sought is the thing they really needed finding and that isn't always the thing they'd said they were looking for at the outset.

The banal reality is that there are very few genuine mysteries and the solution to most problems is blindingly obvious except to whoever it is who has forgotten where they left something, mislaid an address, or a relative, lost a slip of paper with a phone number on it, accidentally thrown away a document worth millions, or simply found they're tormenting themselves about something that slipped their mind that doesn't matter. There's no shortage of nonsense. People argue over irrelevances. They fall out over trivialities. Much more important are the things that people suppress among their memories and are reluctant to recognise. That's when it gets dangerous and they start thinking of killing each other.

With respect to the Caro job, Dani is tending to think it's more important to ask herself why she's being asked to do anything at all, rather than sweat the details. Dani wants some backup, so she's off to see someone she hopes might make sense of the messages Caro has been flagging up about her Ex and her Dad.

She suspects Caro is either bluffing, or lying, maybe both. If she's lying about Klaus and her Father, then she's probably lied to Dani about everything else. Nothing is implausible in a place, where almost everyone is either foolishly optimistic, or optimistically foolish.

The name Markus Sonne had come up as they'd chatted at the Soph-Am. Klaus' mate Markus. Dani thought she'd make a start by talking to him. He's one of the few people Dani and Caro know in common.

She doesn't know what to expect from Markus, but he has always had a good nose for bullshit, whereas Caro is highly suspect. He agrees to see Dani as soon as she wants. He also says he wouldn't eat at 'Last Supper'.

Markus sells used cars at reasonable prices to people who think they know about cars. He works out of a more or less anonymous yard in Schöneberg, which doesn't seem to have a proper address, just a vague plot number on an industrial estate, next to the Reichsbahn area, where the trains no longer run. Dani had found it at the end of a long lane skirting the old railway land behind the S-bahn station, neighbouring a row of scrap dealers and an auctioneer's warehouse.

There are yet another pair of Mongolian style flags fluttering among the lines of pennants strung over the entrance. This time they're brown and magneta. The pennants are mainly red, though some are green. There are silver streamers attached to the radio aerials of some of the older cars. All the flags and flaglets are flapping in the wind.

Lulled by the mechanical nature of his business, Markus' customers are softened up by the confidence of getting a fair deal for the car, often a genuine bargain Markusmobile, then as an afterthought, he sells them the insurance they don't know anything about at all and makes a lot of money from extras defined via paragraph after paragraph of small print and indecipherable technicalities. Thanks to Markus, a surprising number of Berlin drivers are already fully insured to drive their cars in Mozambique, the Seychelles, the People's Republic of China and Uruguay should they ever be going that way.

The people who buy cars from Markus pride themselves for being 'in the know'. He's their guy. It never does any harm to feed a myth that works in your favour, so he never disabuses anyone as people pride themselves that they're one of a privileged circle of elite customers who'll pick up a genuine Markusmobile and not a cheap imitation via the internet.

The truth is he'll sell anything to anyone, if only they can tell him what they actually want. All they have to do is ask, say what they can afford to pay and he'll do his best. He isn't choosy, not the way people imagine. And he works quite hard, enjoying the business of tracking down bargains and selling them on. Markus, back then known as Marky, or sometimes as Kussi, learned his trade via the back door to the PX, when the Americans had their garrison in the southern sector of West Berlin. He misses the Americans. He misses stealing their cars and their wives.

He would be choosy about women, if that was at all possible, but he'd recognised long ago that it's the girls who get to do the choosing. Boys just hang a sign around their neck to say they're in functioning order, ready and available. They get interested in cars, as a distraction from superfluous male syndrome, A lot of them never recover and love to give their motor a kiss and a polish as they tweak the tuning.

His biggest profits are made from men who've recently divorced and decide they need to impress with new wheels. Where once they had a wife, now they'd like a McClaren with a bit of throat.

Dani waited for twenty minutes before he could talk to her, during which time his sidekick had tried and failed to sell her a car. She deflects Markus' entertaining sales patter, avoids buying a much used Lamborghini with commensurate insurance (including Nicaragua and Nepal) and tells him she needs to discover the ins and outs of Caro's situation.

"Situation? About what?"

"She seems to think she's being stitched up, by her father among other people, the other people including people who claimed to have worked with her Ex and are tidying up after him." 'Typische Berlin', Markus told Dani, blue eyes a-twinkle, after she's told him more about the Caro business, "What the hell does she expect, sympathy? Out of her depth and out of her league."

"Her league being?"

"Come with me," he says, and leads her over to a freshly renovated Aston Martin.

"Get in, this old thing needs some exercise and we can talk. And you get to feel like a Bond girl as an extra treat."

"Markus, that isn't a treat."

"Never mind."

He drives towards the motorway then whisks the classic car south on the new autobahn heading down to Dresden, before turning around to dive past the old Tempelhof airfield on the road to Hamburg, Konstanzerstrasse and Charlottenburg.

"Look at all these buildings," he says. "Each and every one of them has been sold at least three times in the last ten years and every time they're sold, the costs for agents and lawyers and the tax man are anything up to ten per cent of the price. So what does the property business do for Berlin. This how our city cashes in. This is the lifeblood that keeps Berlin alive. One third of the value of all the property every ten years. That's what Klaus was about. That was why the politicians loved him. Property, tourism and government administrators, that's it, the fucking economic anatomy of a metropolis that has to pay for all the rest. You don't think anyone in Berlin pays income tax, do you?"

Markus sticks to the autobahn and makes a lot of noise going through the tunnel under the airport at Tegel, then heads out into the countryside, where there's no speed limit. He gives the car its head. They hit two hundred, but not for long. There isn't enough road before the speed limits are back again.

"That was fun," he says with genuine satisfaction. "Better than sex!"

"Sure, better than sex with you, anyway," says Dani.

"OK, so now sex is out of the way, what about dear old fucking Klaus, god rest his soul etc? He cost me and three of my friends, a lot of money, that one. As for Caro, her father probably tries to stitch up everyone he meets, nothing new there. What makes her think she's any different? Bernie Hilberg would rob his own grandmother, never mind his daughter. Is she sure the new faces aren't just legacy sniffers?" "Perhaps," says Dani. "Caro claims she had never heard of any of these people before she went to Miami with her Dad after Klaus died. She's looking for someone to blame. Now, Markus, please don't tell me blame is the opposite of praise. You can praise people any time you like, whether they deserve it or not, no-one minds being praised, but try blaming someone who isn't to blame and you're in the biblical shit end of deep trouble. And if they really are to blame it can be worse."

"Sure, so what. She is obviously responsible for her own predicament, so tell her she's only herself to blame and that's that, which is almost certainly the case.

Then you have to tell yourself that whatever she expects of you has nothing to do with apportioning blame. She may be at fault, but what she needs right now is someone who can help her get out of a fix, which is why she came to you. So that's what you should be trying to do, find a fix to whatever it is that's troubling her, but first she has to get over the blame business, or you're wasting your time. If you can manage that, then you'll have earned your daily bread."

During the brief pause in his speech, Markus looks closely at Dani, "You don't like her much do you?"

It wasn't much of a reply and it was true Dani didn't have a lot of respect for Caro, so she told him about Caro's Dad with his 'Gaming with Attitudes' preoccupation and the phrase that had cropped up more than once or twice - 'guilt assessment'.

"They aren't the only people looking in that direction, 'Attitudes and Guilt' delicious mix," says Markus about the gamers. They chat about Markus' fourteen year old son, who Dani has known since he was a baby. Markus says his only concern about the boy is the excessive amount of time he spends online and the threat from 'Game-a-dope', who are a bunch of Burmese-born Indians who want to spice up the gaming community via the dark net with drug enhanced play modes the kids call curry powders, logic blockers, which could be the same order of nonsense Caro's Dad is messing about with. Some people call it 'gaming with platitudes', he claims. There are others who talk about lobotomy online.

Dani has never heard anything about this, so Markus curtails the discussion and gets to the point. 'Game-a-dope' are aiming at kids in their early teens and he suspects they're a slippery slope to the heavy duty addictive stuff, dope a gamer, so to speak. It would only take one in a thousand to succumb and soon it could be an epidemic. The economic consequences are immense.

Having given himself time to think by meandering through the theme of drugs and gaming, he suggest there's someone she ought to see. "You ought to be talking to Dietmar, but he won't have anything to do with Caro, for good or evil; so go see this woman instead and tell her the story you've told me, just as you've described it. She's in human resources, a kind of a head hunter, head shrinker too, though some people think she might be involved in trafficking refugees from the afro-middle east debacles. The same as the rest of them, she's a sort of a crook, but nothing proven, based in Steglitz and used to know Klaus. She certainly does blame, that's for sure. The woman is a compulsive complainer and blamer. They call her Elfie Malzenberger. You needn't be afraid of her, it's mainly hot air, she's an intimidator," Markus said.

Dani hopes that he's right and asked him to set up the meeting.

"So who the hell is this Dietmar that doesn't like Caro," she wants to know.

"Wrong, he adores Caro, infatuated. Dietmar is an extremely bright guy with some personality issues, major disorders in fact. He stalked Caro for years, broke into her apartment, stole stuff, left love letters under her pillow, threatened suicide, attempted suicide and ended up in a psychiatric hospital for his pains. He'd been Klaus' best friend at one time. As you might imagine, once he was identified, there were all kinds of court decisions. If he gets close to her again, he'll get locked up for good in the klaps mühl, the funny farm. So he does his best to keep a distance. If I were you, I would stay away from him for your own good. You don't want him turning you into an obscure substitute for the object of his fantasies."

"That almost sounds like a threat."

"No, no, no, a friendly warning, fingers off. His name is Dietmar Marschal and he lives in Alt-Lutzow, near the Schloss. If you have any kind of contact with him, let me know and I'll see what can be done. Maybe I'll see you in Soph-Am tonight. I haven't been there for a while. Do those actors still do their lurking at the bar?"

He dropped her off on the Kaiserdamm, not far from her apartment, which was kind. She's actually enjoyed the fast old car and she heeded his warning never to buy one.

"A supercar like this is a delight, but it is important to understand that after two or three hours on the road, they spend three or four days in the garage as one by one the original parts succumb to metal fatigue. So unless you are a competent and dedicated mechanic, the bills will simply be enormous. I'll sell you this one if you really want, it isn't expensive to begin with. You can help make me rich."

Dani leaves Markus and wishes they'd stuck to discussing car insurance and other stereotypes. Stalkers and their kind are beyond her experience and she wants it to stay that way.

Late afternoon, he called back to confirm the Malzenberger meet and gave her the address. "And Dani, just don't give her the chance to intimidate you. Oh, and avoid wearing leather, unless you must. She gets her kicks that way."

Meanwhile, Caro has been chatting to a drummer she's known for the better part of a quarter of a century. He's less vibrant now and considerably balder than he once was, while his tail has less sting than an asiatic scarlet swamphawk. Twitchy Martin's powers had peaked young, then his rhythm went after he broke an ear drum in Istanbul. Born in Delft, brought up in Hoboken, stranded in the Berlin music business, he has also ended up dredging in human resources. His office at DissCo has a view over the comically gothicke red brick OberbaumBrucke looking in the general direction of Kreuzberg and an ever changing supply of sunsets.

Caro lays claim to the couch and smiles, considerate as ever, attentive, ready to listen. The walls of his office are a strange disconcerting, coloured something between mustard and chrome yellow, then pin-striped with aubergine in op-art swirls. In among the stripes, there are blotches and a portrait in ink of Nick Cave. These are walls to conjure after images. There's a big ornamental mirror to impress and another one on the big grey desk for cocaine.

"Did you see the article in 'Rolling Stone'?" A gnarled fist taps emphatically backbeat against the slate-grey desk and the Ray-bans glint a rainbow of colour in her eyes. Martin doesn't notice. He wears his shades high on his forehead to protect his bald patch from sunburn. "They described me as legendary!" he announces with pride and crackles his fingernails on the desktop. "Means they were surprised to discover you're still alive. Courtesy title."

"I know, I know, but every mention counts in this business. Don't spoil my moment of renewal. Born again, what could be better."

His false teeth glow in the sunshine, as he grins. He's a grain of truth type, as well as a grain of opiate afficionado.

"My boss was ecstatic. She said she'd heard one of the other passengers talk about me on her flight from Buffalo to Charlotte, which is North American for parochial. They thought I'd done things that were the work of other people, but who cares, they know my name. I'd like you to meet Hayley before you go, she loves your stuff too. She found a file about you in my archive. The photos were monochrome and faded, which seemed to spellbind her, you, the Katakomben, CBGB, even Amos Poe and his little silent 16mm movie camera. Classic. You seem to have awoken some kind of ghost in her mental machinery, an echo of pre-techno, post-punk ravenous fusion - the LA Woman of Berlin Charlottenburg."

Caro assumes Martin spends too much of his time staring out of the window as he listens to music and fades to his own kind of nostalgic monochrome. Ravenous fusion had been one of her subcults that persisted for a few weeks then blended in with the rest, though Martin seems to have forgotten about her place in its discovery. That was the time when she'd been the 'anthro-chick', before she became 'that woman with Klaus'.

Martin is assertively bearded, cheerful as only a determined Dutch survivor can be and has an unrivalled collection of other people's skeletons in music business closets. He'd have been fired decades ago, if that wasn't the case. Hayley must be the latest in a long line of nearly but not quite top managers whose careers flounder on the rocks of DissCo. They last four months on average. He says the experience does them good, then laughs his mephisto cackle. They flee Berlin for centres of cultural intensity like Rostock, sometimes Kiel, where people seek penance for their sins. "Grim is grim, grime is grime and Grimsby is Grimsby," he groans contentedly. "Rostock, rock and rollmops, what a place!" Martin chortles in sympathy with his own sense of humour.

"Fuck 'em all, Caro, that's what I say, sod the bloody lot. They used to call me an A&R man, artists and repertoire, music and musicians, dangling the prospect of recording contracts in front of snotty nosed thrashers and stitching up the copyright on their slender talents and minimal creative output. The number of songs I wrote, or gave titles to, not to mention the composition work, fleshing out sketchy improvisations to create something that could be considered copyrightable. The world of music and dance is a battlefield of broken promises, lies and extortion, aids, theft and fraud. It's part of the fun, if you like that kind of thing and some do, dodgy businessmen, even dodgier agents and managers, the legal and litiginous. The music business and guilt go hand in hand. I invented whole sub-genres of creativity to satisfy the copyright lawyers. Remember 'Blissrock'? Not many do. Ask Kwietniowski. Who wrote what when, played with, dreamed up, signed, copied, sold, denied. The permutations of deceit are legion. Session musicians, for Christ's sake, talk about self-selecting victims, worse than boxers and their sparring partners. Boxing has a pretty bad reputation, but the music business is ultimately inimitable for sheer gloves-off bastardliness. Don't you remember Venezuela?"

Her visit has put him in a good mood, there's vim in his exuberance.

"Of course I do Martin, we nearly died."

"We did indeed, bliss out. There's talk of a movie, 'Dodgy Liaisons' with Malkovitch playing me, or you, could be either, one of us anyway, or it might be Sean Penn doing his Ezra Pound. Oil rigs and white powder, remember? Bananarama too, to give it all that unique contemporary feel. In those days when I could present myself as a well oiled Bananarama boy, if you recall the style, south London girls with muscular models in their sights, as men with minds went out of fashion. Post-punk, pre-Spice, gorgeous, I was. George Michael told me that."

"No he didn't"

"Well he would have done if he'd met me at the time."

"Well, if that's how you like to remember yourself. But Malkovitch and Penn are older now and so are you. Old Ezra died long ago, when even you were still at school. The only thing you and Malkovitch have in common, Martin, is a lack of hair. He is a dandy, while you are, at best, ambiguous. Talking of which, have you ever tried using a 'guilt assessor'?"

"I've never equated guilt with baldness. I expect they'll squeeze Tilda Swinton in somewhere, too. She could play me, or she could play Suzanne Vega and I'll be her brother Vincent. I could manage her band. If you ask me about guilt, of course, we're all incredibly guilty, ask anyone, but we all also had a hell of a good time before the doubts set in, except for the ones that didn't, or were too busy working, or were too tight zipped shy and stayed at home. That's the difference between music and politics. Politicians never have fun, nor do business folk, not the ones who succeed. You can ask them that and they'll agree, eventually. Maybe that's Tilda's part. Politics is a guilt trip, guilt and self-abasement; business is for workaholics who can't face up to the inadequacies of their personalities. Tilda would make a great businessman with political ambitions. That was the problem in Venezuela, remember? Businessmen, policemen and politicians, shit, lethal incompetence. Coke, Colombians and ammunition are like guilt and blame - far from interchangeable and the courts usually get things wrong so you can't look for any help from that direction. Do you remember Rudiger the defence lawyer? Old pomposity himself, remember the plummy vowels, 'Meine leibe Martin, I never realised diet coke came as a powder.' 'Take enough of it and you'll slim down fairly rapidly,' I replied. 'Well, well, maybe I should give it a try,' he prattled fatuously. He always prattled."

Martin rounded off his mimicry, to continue the narrative in a more or less normal voice.

"Complete idiot, Rudi was, actually he was worse, he was an incomplete idiot. Ask a judge, they'll soon put you right. None of them have a clue when it comes to drugs and music. I'm not attuned to these guilt assessors, though I suppose you never know when you might need someone like that."

Martin's concentration seems to be drifting, but he ploughs on in the vague hope of turning up some treasurable nugget of wisdom about guilt assessors. " The pay is good, so I've heard and I'm sure we must have one somewhere, probably in Toronto, you know, friends and family, friend of the Family and all that laundry business. They're fashionable, but only for the moment if you want my opinion. Did I say Toronto, maybe I meant Taormina."

His mind is beginning to wander as the sun shines in.

"Some like it hot?" Caro asks.

Then he starts getting expansive again.

"More or less, but that was Chicago, don't forget, a city of streetwise creatives and corrosive repression. Filled to overflowing with lawyers, Toronto has an office based lawlessness all unto itself, the heart of administrative darkness. The closest North America has to Kafka's Prague. Toronto and Chicago are worlds apart. The Canadians would never machine gun a bass player; they'd send a letter to the bank. Another constellation, Taormina, oof!"

"Stars are born."

"And I discovered most of them!"

"Bullshit, Martin. You said Phil Collins was a wanker and Sting a talent free poseur, Robbie Williams a whinging warbler with the sex appeal of a mouse, Madonna a wizened old witch and poor old Björk a jabbering grandmother. In fact you haven't really liked anyone since Joni Mitchell. And you wrote off Kraftwerke as passé in 1975, which you must admit was premature. And I'm not going to remind you about what you said to Laurie Anderson after that concert in Kreuzberg."

"But wasn't I right? You have to admit Joni was better than the rest and she has teeth, or she had teeth, great teeth. I wonder if she still has them. I like teeth on a singer. They bring the promise of throat and good throat means laryngial bliss and a better voice. Joni's teeth have more character than most people's autobiographies. Remember, Carly, the very peak of orthodontic singer songwriting. You know when I was young, toothsome was an adjective. Haven't heard of anyone being described as toothsome for at least thirty years, or did Woody Allen say that about Susie de la Riva, you remember her. 'Shagging in Sorrento' wasn't it, or 'Old Memories and other nightmares'? I may have under-estimated fresh talent, from time to time, but 'Sponge Magic' were mine, and so were 'Odd Lozenge', who made more money than sense. 'Barbados Blues Breakers' meets 'Blood Lettuce', they were, without forgetting the influence of 'Throbbing Gristle', as so many do."

"I liked 'Crunchy Water'."

"So much better than they were as 'Splash', same guys, different trope."

"Cooler. It was sad in Posnan."

"Two concerts and an inquest, what a sorry tale of a career. Five fat guys playing 'Hunkyfunk R&B' and overdosing on crystal meth."

"Sad story, yes, especially for the drug dealer. They caught him in Kiev. He went down for twelve years in a Ukrainian jail. There was talk of a revival band, 'Thin Ice,' but the name has gone, there's a band in San Antonio and some other guys in Denver call themselves the Thin Ice Band, so it's clearly not open for adoption."

"You know the odd thing about drug dealing is that the mark up from wholesale to the street is about the same as all the other stuff that's bought and sold totally quite legally, fruit and vegetables, or tea and coffee, a lot less than selling coffee to go, which is amazing profitable, believe me, a businessman's dream. It's a calling of a sort, drug dealing, though the risk of being jailed is a fairly absurd thing to accept as a workaday downside. If you buy coffee direct off the tree, it's sod all a tonne, but thirty cents a 5 gramme capsule for one of those posh machines, so 6cents a gramme and there are a million grammes in a tonne. Then people pay how much per cup for a paper beaker to drink as they walk down the street? So you're going from two or three thousand a tonne for the beans to three or four hundred thousands worth of coffee's to go. But enough of that. Despite the ups and downs, dear Carolina, I do think I played my part in the development of our global musical culture, and an honourable role at that, as in the Bob Dylan Nobel award. Did you read about it? Was I mentioned? Never mind, at my age modesty becomes one. As to guilt? I don't subscribe to it. Revenge yes, guilt, forget it. There's a woman in Brussels we use, Sally someone. She's not so much guilt assessor as avenging angel. Very expensive. Maybe you could talk to her. You point, she shoots. Would you like to meet her? I could set it up."

Caro wonders what he's been smoking. "I'll let you know?"

"On second thoughts, seeing sister Sally probably isn't a good idea. With people like that, generally a better bet if she has no inkling of your existence, ever. You can never be completely sure that your profile might not be dangled in front of her by one of her other clients and she picks up on your name and thinks hey I have the address, easy peasey trigger squeezey. There's a guy in Miami too, Lee something, but I never needed to ask."

Martin falls quiet for a moment and his mood changes, the glibness has gone.

"Caro. If I'm honest, I don't concern myself with guilt. Our world is so extraordinarily complex that hardly anyone, in practice no-one, no-one at all, not one of us, including you and me, can really understand the detail of events as they unfurl, so who is to decided between truth and lies, innocence and guilt, counterlies and contrary opinion, not me, for sure. I do songs and raps, trip hop, house, whatever, music, that's it. Politicians, policy makers, business specialists, we all carry on regardless, then swerve to avoid collisions at the last moment. Politics is like driving down the autobahn to discover it's actually a three lane highway and half the drivers are racing in the opposite direction and you're going to be dodging them at full speed. That's all, the rest is wishful thinking and election promises. If it weren't so important it would be laughable. Ask the SPD where it all went wrong and they'll tell you it's because of wishful thinking and the misplaced conviction that they'll do the right thing by saying they want to be nice. They don't, they aren't and they know it, because they don't know what they're doing half the time and the other half of the time they don't know which half of their time it is and nobody believes them anyway. What did I say about neo-Nazi's leaking into governments all over Europe? Look at Austria."

"That was convoluted."

"Yeah, it was a bit, wasn't it. But you know what I mean?"

She doesn't and wonders whether he's right. He might not be completely wrong.

"So, Caro, what do you want? You owe me an explanation We've known each other a long time and this is the first time you've been here to ask me for something. There must be a reason. Would you mind coming to the point? What is the problem? Who is the cause? Do you have a solution in mind? How can I help? Question, question, question, question, question, answer me please in that order, answer, answer, answer, answer, answer."

"This guilt business," says Caro.

"Yes?" he says, inviting her to be more forthcoming.

"I was wondering, that's all."

"Have you never asked yourself about the consequences of being Klaus' paramour? Not that anyone resented you taking on the role, someone had to, he needed a wife, not just a girlfriend. The bankers insisted and you liked one another, so why not, but there are a few folk about town who might be waiting to have a chat with you now that he's snuffed it. You can't pretend it never happened. He was a tricky little bastard, you do appreciate that, I hope. Some would say a complete shit and I would not contradict them. You gained some credit when you ditched him, but enough of the questions go back to the time when you were together. People do wonder how much of a role you played."

"Do they? Once we split, I wasn't involved in the business."

"The good wife knows nothing that might incriminate the dearly beloved spouse. Are you sure? Questions have been asked."

"Not at all. For the last five years, I never went to meetings, I didn't draft any documents, I didn't even get to check the finances, which in retrospect, might have been a very good idea."

"There you are then. All that and particularly because you were involved with a guy who claimed to have had the ear of at least one US President and at least two of his predecessors, which impresses people even if it wasn't true. You've succeeded in answering your own questions. We have a Construction Industry Presidency after all, which makes a change from the Intelligence Community Presidents and the Chicago Elite Community Presidents, or the Dynastic Presidencies. It's a dirty city, Berlin, a supremely dirty city. Sometimes I think Berlin patented dirt, it's so dirty. Who the hell do you think are running the migrant trade across the Mediterranean, who are running the gangs behind these slave traders and their sinking ships. Do we think that the Luxembourgers invented pan-European tax avoidance as an incentive to assist their redundant steel-workers escape the consequences of unemployment? Just because the slave ships set out from Africa doesn't mean they're run by Africans. You might be able to trace the tax avoidance back to dear pliant loveable Ireland and their little green men, or the micro-world of accomodative Luxembourg, but wake up please, where do you think the grown-ups are? In Connemara? In Luxembourg City, population 115,227? Where do the real Mafia bosses live, Palermo, or Long Island, think about it. Have you seen the places people call home in the Hamptons? And you beware Greeks owning ships."

"Martin, you aren't going to suggest I phone the White House to talk about illegal migrants, are you?"

"Eventually, why not? They're just people, after all. Ask the right question and they might decide to help you. All they can do is tell you to fuck off, or send you to Guantanamo for corrective treatment, or have you blown off the surface of the planet in a drone strike."

"Has anyone ever suggested you are totally deluded?"

"Regularly, but they also get back to me and say how surprised they were to find out I was right all along.

Trump is a property developer, New York construction industry, you know what those guys are like, it's a tough city, a tough industry. They bruise. They get sensitive. They imagine they're being insulted.

Your Klaus was Berlin property, Berlin construction industry. Do we, or do we not live in a global economy? Construction industry is construction industry, it's all the same shit, contracts, credit and concrete, and these guys stick together, don't they.

Now what do we await of a construction industry Presidency, subtle innovations in international relations, constitutional reform? No, what we await are contacts, contracts and concrete, more concrete, more contracts, more contacts, roads, walls, roofs, bridges, runways, more runways, pipelines, in a word - construction. Why on earth should anyone expect anything else?

Donny Trump is not going to be remembered for finessing the moral basis of administrative ethics. It's an innovation.

Even Nixon came from insurance, not construction.

OK, Berlin doesn't do high rise, I know, not real high rise, it doesn't need to, we have the new airport to soak up the slack. But there are similarities, you must admit, like investment funds and tax avoidance. The wise guys pay no tax; they're smart, they're sharp, like cards. We live in a global economy. Do it in China. Do it in Russia. Do it in Iran. Get rich, stay rich, don't blink. Do you think for one moment that the Great Wall of Mexico has anything to do with migration, or do you think of it as a massive bundle of lucrative building contracts for friends of friends and their friends?"

"But Klaus was sophisticated and thoughtful."

"Don't you think a guy like Trump would appreciate that?"

"You aren't trying to imply that Klaus was in cahouts with Trump, are you? Please, stop it, that's silly."

"Then look around you and learn what it is that's going on that makes it worthwhile for people to suggest you start assessing guilt. Some people might think it was a good idea to talk to Simon Schmidt."

"Oh for Christ's sake, not Simon fucking Schmidt the pretentious shit. I can't stand the guy. Even Trump wouldn't get tangled up with slimy Simon."

"Then it might not be such a good idea for you to talk to him."

"No fucking way. Martin."

"Good luck, Caro. Let me know how you get on. And if you need any help, just call."

"There's lawyer coming over here, from Miami, claims to be tidying up Klaus' leftovers. She wants to talk to me. I wish I knew what kind of a mess we're in. "

"You are in, delete the 'we'. The rest of us have our own little piles of excrement to deal with and I'm not sure we piss in the same boat."

"I suppose you could put it that way, though I'm not sure why. I'll see you around, Martin."

"Ask yourself how the city works, Caro. Berlin is a squalid teeming morass of semi-competent tricksters, dung beetles each with their own little ball of shit to push around, always has been, not so different from New York as people in the Bundestag committees would like to believe. Till the next time, God willing, oh, and good luck with whatever you're fucking about at. Talk to Klaus' old lawyer. I don't believe a word about this guilt assessment crap."

If she was being honest with herself, neither did Caro.

"And I don't believe a word you've said about Donald Trump."

"Neither do I, but I don't know what to believe any more," said Martin. "You could do worse than to make it clear to this lawyer woman that she is in a foreign country, not an overseas territory of the USA. Americans tend to assume that we all play by the same rules."

"How would you suggest I go about that?"

"Get her settled in at the hotel, are you still using the Savoy?"

"Yes, it's convenient and lawyers are at home there."

"Good, then take her for dinner at 'Last Supper', but explain how the food is prepared when you're half way through the main course. People have a way of re-examining their sense of exquisite cuisine and their attitude to fine dining once you tell them that!"

"Have you had their caviar specials, or the adventures with truffel haggis?"

"No, and I wouldn't dream of being persuaded to try. 'Last Supper' requires an especially honed sense of taste, not to mention a strong stomach."

At last they agreed about something.

She's ready to leave.

His pomposity was only exceeded by his verbosity and she'd heard enough.

But he had one more remark. He said he didn't believe in suicide. Then he asked her the question no one else had posed.

"No," she answered firmly in answer to his suggestion that she might have been responsible for murdering her husband.

She sounded so insistent that he wasn't sure he believed her.

When Caro left, she drove north through Friedrichshein and Mitte to Pankow, met someone she didn't know very well for twenty minutes, decided she wasn't interested in what they had to say and wouldn't be going to the 'Schwelle Treff' with them over the weekend. She'd had enough of tantric groping in the days when orange was by no means the new black and indicated that you went to the Baghwan's ashrams for the orgies in the days before HIV made its ugly appearance and caution was no longer thrown to the wind.

Stop start, there seemed to be more traffic signals than ever, stop start, left, right, stop, go.

She bought a paperback of Swedish love poems at the Scandinavian book store near the park, then drove herself back to

Charlottenburg via Moabit. A message from Dani said that they should get together once she's had a meeting the next day with someone called Malzenberger. Caro sends a quick ok back to her, with a question mark, where, when?

The answer was, 'Soph-Am, 16.00'; the reply: 'OK'.

Malzenberger - she can half remember the name, but can't tag it with a face.

Maybe she'd been at the funeral.

Probably.

Caro can't recall. She can't remember the details of the funeral too well.

At home in the Dankelmannstrasse, there was a bottle of Aldi white wine in the fridge and one of Klaus' bottles of plush Argentinian red on her bedside table, half empty, half full.

To hell with housework.

A message on the answering machine from Frau Hedwig Trautmann calls. "Fuck my knee," says the woman, "Fick mich am knee".

She'd phoned at nine fifteen, as she does every day.

Caro grilled herself a steak sandwich, poured out the red and polished off the lot. As an afterthought, she enjoyed a supermarket lemon sorbet out of a plastic pot with the white wine and watched some film on tv, Joachim Phoenix as a doped up private eye in LA vaguely clutching at straws.

She can empathise with his predicament.

It felt good to relax.

There's nothing from 'Network Check'.

There was no time for Soph-Am tonight.

Then she slept, but awoke after half an hour and stared at the ceiling.

A man might have made a welcome distraction, but Caro settled for sweet dreams and her little electrical gadget that encourages them and reminds herself to contact the occasional Spanish Professor, or the enthusiastic surgeon about their plans for the coming weekend.

Then she slept deeply till morning, dreamed a full and entertaining programme of dreams and her snoring alarmed the cat next door, as it settled to sleep after a night on the tiles. The things they expect you to put up with. Not even a saucer of cat-a-tonic to help you sleep despite the incessant rumbles, groans and spluttering snorts in the background till the alarm clock finally brings it to a halt.

Chapter 5

The following morning there are no unexpected interruptions, or disasters, though there are large numbers of ladybirds wandering everywhere. This is good news for the frogs, who enjoy them as food. The swallows are already feasting. Kites still fly over the neighbouring rooftops and the sun is shining.

Dani takes to the city streets and goes by U-bahn to the shopping centre in Steglitz, U7 first, then the U9 from Berlinerstrasse, less than half an hour. From the Forum, a dumb name for a shopping centre if ever there was one, this isn't Rome, she heads down one of the side streets to find the Malzenberger woman.

In one direction, there's the Botanic Garden and Dahlem. In the other, not far away, is the main south Berlin hospital, the Benjamin Franklin Klinikum, so in theory the area is prosperous, filled with well-paid medics and bureaucrats, a smattering of academics from the Free University, managers of one kind and another. But a lot of the locals are pensioners and the familiar influence of property developers in search of higher rents is taking its toll, so investors are wondering why their apartments stand empty. After a few months the city can insist they're rented out, instead of being left unoccupied, but that isn't enforced very often for want of motivation among the bureaucrats.

The town hall has been closed down and is being turned into flats. No-one Dani knows can imagine who might pay €10,000 per square metre for somewhere on the top floors of a former high rise office block, but 10k per square metre sounds like a firm foundation for the investment economy dependent on phrases like 'values up to....'. Maybe the developers imagine a rooftop nightclub drawing the chic and wealthy to this unremarkable suburb. It's a stretch.

The German economy is booming, that's official, everyone agrees. Yet, in Berlin it's a funny sort of boom. People are going bust at the same time, without waiting for the boom to burn itself out. In truth, the fact that people are going bust is feeding the boom, which is a contradiction based on the availability of loans with close to zero interest rates.

And what is the point of a city full of newly renovated buildings being left unoccupied, or shops that are merely refitted because the previous tenants went bust, closed down and got themselves evicted?

It breeds resentments, like restaurant rubbish bins breed bugs and there are plenty of those to be found, if anyone actually decided to look. The underpaid and the over-optimistic outweigh the folk in safe jobs and that is slowly festering and fermenting to become a destructive issue.

Dani is looking forward to meeting this odd woman Markus had suggested. She has the feeling she should have known about her already, but she hadn't.

Cairo of kites fly over the rooftops almost everywhere in Steglitz. She'll ask Caro her anthropologically informed opinion. 'Network Check' hasn't reported any warnings about the things, so these kites must be harmless. Anyway, Dani likes them. Isn't that enough? When she finds the house, there's a heavy dark green double door at the entrance that looks as if it's made of metal. To one side is a panel of bell pushes for each apartment, name by name. She doesn't recognise anyone she knows. Pale pink and lime green kites this time, which reminds Dani of fairground candy floss set against the gloomy streets.

Is it just fashion, or a sign of some significance?

Dani rang the bell for 'Hinterhof - Gartenhaus Malzenberger' as instructed and was buzzed inside. The small single storey building where she's been told they're to meet is tucked away in the garden behind a typical five storey 'Altbau' apartment house. They're an odd match, the main building was probably been built just before the first world war, whereas the newer place had been hurriedly thrown together from breeze blocks as an improvised workshop soon after the second. Painted bomb flash white in anticipation of the third world war sometime around 1957, but not at all since, it hosts a subtle array of lichen, mosses and anonymous funghi. There are greenfly on the rambling roses near the multi-coloured rubbish bins, green, yellow, white, brown, blue and orange.

This white place is definitely a cat killing curiosity trap. A couple of security cameras front and back fail to cover all the angles. They're just for show.

Whenever you see a single storey building like this, it is safe to assume that rather than being an orphan it is simply the top floor of a structure that descends below ground into catacombs of basements and cellars.

Dani can remember being taken to a club a few doors away. The 'Dark Place' had played host to people with very different tastes to Dani, the bondage, dominance, sado-masochist brigade. Quirks and failings are the city's first line of defence, but people's secret foibles are it's strength, the realm of the hinterhofs, the back yards, in stark contrast to the deceptively conformist world of the streets.

As Dani walked across the gloomy yard, a big woman, tall and tough, came towards her, rasped a ripe tobacco cough, spat into a rhododendron bush, then welcomed Dani personally. "Komm 'rein, madel; come inside, lass."

She's clad in leather, a suit of soft white leather that masks her bulky figure, but gives her presence emphasis, like a heavily loaded cargo ship under sail.

"Mendel," said Dani, to introduce herself, wondering if there's such a thing as a 'white leather club'. The people next door had been leathery, but of a black, buckled and studded, metal zipped and chained variety.

"Malzenberger," said the woman, who offered an arthritic hand to be shaken, waved Dani to a seat and started talking. "If Vienna was once a mecca for psychologists and doctors, where people arrived in search of therapy, then this Berlin of ours is a city of fantasists and megalomaniacs fruitlessly exploring their fears and obsessions to the general detriment of humanity, and that includes you and me, leibling, so forget your fancy aspirations."

The woman monologuing Dani runs a 'human resources' consultancy and without her knowledge is being investigated for involvement in trafficking migrants from West Africa to Europe. She expects to be listened to for so long as she chooses to talk and talk she does.

Elfriede Malzenberger, known as Eli to her Dad, Elfie to her mother and Frieda to her husband, (or sometimes a Russified – Friedotschka to her enemies) is stout and a cosmetically surgeoned fortyish going on late fifties/nearly seventy, with a smear of ruthless red lipstick to underline her undiminished ambition.

She had the chance of reaching the top in Berlin politics, but the CDU had made it known she wasn't required once they'd found Helmut Kohl his East German 'madel'. Angela Merkel had won on malleability, determination and lack of personality. Things had only gone pear shaped later, though Kohl had been that shape for donkey's years.

If Elfie Malzenberger has one real talent it is to be good at sifting through people's principal characteristics. Then she filters out the ones that won't be wanted by employers to see if there's anything left over. If there is, the lucky few get recommended for a job. It's a simple, but valuable procedure. Frau M. is only impressed by doctorates, professional exams, and breeding. Being a femme fatale who gets people in and out of trouble wouldn't win you anything and in this city, femmes fatales are two a penny. Among people who know her, whenever someone talks about 'that old witch from Steglitz', everyone knows who they're talking about.

The moment Dani had walked into the room, it was clear she wouldn't be offered anything apart from a courtesy mineral water.

Dani notices an elderly man is working at a desk in the adjacent room, but he isn't introduced and he shuffles away as they begin to talk.

"Look what happened to the new airport, the Museum rebuilding, the Opera House refurbishment. You name it, it's an embarrassment. Nothing ready on time and when it is finally complete nothing works, useless tossers, the lot of them. The last good buildings in Berlin went up fifty years ago and the best of them have already been demolished. Just ask I.M. Pei about the Japanese Embassy."

"Isn't he dead already?" wonders Dani.

"Not the last time I looked, he's the world's best hundred year old architect. "

"Sounds a bit like one of the eggs you get in Chinese cooking."

"There might not be that much difference."

Dani realises that the once mousy, then grey hair is chestnut now, thanks to Wella, and there are contact lenses to give her eyes an enigmatic deep green gaze. To imply she is ugly would be unfair, but no-one could challenge the view that her looks are disconcerting. At one time she might have become a Red Army recruiting sergeant, or a Catholic mother superior.

"And I do wish we had some decent restaurants. The bad lunches I have to chew on in the cause of work merely serve to double my sense of fruitless toil and provoke a further round of indigestion. It isn't enough for food to be chic, it also has to be edible! The pretense of eating well. 'Last Supper', ha! What is a curry wurst made of? I hope we're never told."

Frau M. has mastered the dismissive shrug and makes it clear that she is only talking to Dani, as a favour to her old friend 'Lina', as she refers to Caro, having conveniently bipassed the introduction via Markus. Is that the glint of a smile, or a glower? "So what can I do for you?"

Humming to the conclusion that what Dani wants to know is how they check up on people, hum, she goes into detail to describe some of her methods, hmm, especially if there's some suspicion that their description of their talents, hmm? and abilities, hm, or their qualifications are askew, hmmm.

"You mean when they've lied?"

"Of course, don't be naïve, don't be silly, I have never seen a CV without at least one lie. I sift. I eliminate. A vital aspect of human relations. Do try to learn to enjoy the pleasures of elimination."

There are credit ratings, she explains, court records, private archives, police databases, even newspapers, that all help build a framework for the metadata you can pick up on the net and gets used by people like 'Network Check'. From LinkedIn to LockedOut, it's a spectrum, she claims. Those special reports that she mentions as though everyone spends money on snooping, are usually enough to finish the job.

A lot of people, she claims, have little lies in their vita's that have been there so long they start to believe them. With men it's usually about sport, while women forget that they were an assistant rather than a manager, clerical worker rather than executive, foot soldier not officer. No-one ever admits to having done physical labour of any kind at all, ever. Digging is degrading.

"What brought you to Berlin?" she claims is always a good question to fish out the fakes, more or less foolproof. "Apart from people who work for Bayer and the politicians, who have no choice, the truth is that almost every outsider comes here for sex, even if they're students, or in business. As for the rest, a lot of them are simply running away. So many people pretend to have studied something when they just have some on the job training and a year or two experience. Ironically, that is often all they need, so unless they get caught out everything goes just fine. Either you know what you're doing, or you don't. Ask the people at Volkswagen."

Dani tries to look impressed at that double edged comment, as Elfie continues without stopping to draw breath.

"Men hide unacknowledged offspring, children from youthful liaisons, or the marriage before this one, especially if it happened in another country. And women, almost universal this one, women lie about their age. So, you see, I work in a sea of lies. Sometimes it's the other way around, but less common. I know of women who've hidden unacknowledged offspring and the there are men who lie about their age to avoid retirement mainly. Ask Caro about that, her Mother was a mystery to most folk. Party membership, political affiliations, you don't need to worry about that with Caro's people, but the other falsehoods. The I did, I didn't, I never, of course, I was. Oh that! It was all a very long time ago and times have changed. A great deal of that. Shall we write a book together? People don't change though! Ask anyone about someone they knew twenty years ago and the crevices are revealed as great yawning cracks in their credibility. That's what would think about if I were you."

She laughs and reaches for a cigarette.

"Ever heard from the security people you said you've never heard of?" she asks Dani confidingly. "Have you ever met anyone who could be described as lovable, or adorable? Dogs, yes, babies sometimes, people no and that also goes for claiming to have a 'sense of humour'. Did you know pandas use bamboo shoots as toothpicks after they've finished their favourite dinner of puppy dogs and kittens?" She laughs a cackle, lights the cigarette, inhales, exhales, coughs and splutters back into life.

"Health, or the lack of it! Don't ask me. Short sighted, why not, just don't try to be a pilot. Deaf! Astronauts should be able to hear, to read, write and do maths.

As for inadequacies, aren't we all. At another level, driving bans, arrests, assaults, forgeries, insolvencies, alongside priests thrown out of the Church, doctors banned from practising, lawyers who're disbarred. Drunken sailors and sinking ships. Ferrymen who stole the pay. Alcoholics and drug users, gamblers, and yet more and more alcoholics, nevertheless, the big one is sexual orientation.

I've never worried whether some-one wants to be plunged, or does the plunging, so long as they don't upset their colleagues. We all enjoy the search for erotic ambiguities, don't we? I know I do.

Nothing that you can write on an application form will make you likeable. However there is unanimous agreement that old fashioned philanderers do much more damage to a business than the typical deviant."

 "Are there 'typical' deviants?" asks Dani risking a question. "Isn't that a contradiction?"

 "No, but people do come bundled in latent clusters of unusual preferences, which is more than enough for most purposes."

 "Does anyone actually behave the way psychologists claim?" Dani doesn't like the notion of people being 'clustered' as though there could be little clumps of bodies strewn and corralled in odd corners of the city. Though based on her experience, that does seem to be the case.

 "You should ask Lina about all this. She's the anthropologist. There are clubs....."

 "We all know that, but are they clusters?" says Dani and smiles, wondering whether they might be clutches like eggs in a nest, a dragon's nest?

 "Never mind. What was it you wanted to ask me about?"

"Oh, I think you've covered enough ground for one day."

"You can never cover enough ground without unearthing a victim. Who is out to get young Lina?"

"I don't know. I'm not even sure if there is anyone."

"Then that is the first thing you need to find out, otherwise you don't really have a job to do, do you?"

"This lawyer woman we talked about over the phone."

"What about her?" asks Dani.

"I'd like to meet her," Elfie admits.

She is curious about the midset of a legal brain from Miami. "Let's make a date, we can take her to a club or two and see what kind of a girl she is."

"Isn't she likely to be a bit old for the Berghain?"

Malzenberger laughs in agreement, "And we are too, but there are addresses we can find that will be just perfect, if she wants to discover her true self. She wouldn't have come to Berlin in person, unless that was the case. She's on a quest, of that you can be sure. Mention that to Lina, if you will and she can propose the idea when they meet for dinner."

Elfie notices that Dani is glancing towards the old man working at his desk in the next room.

"Ah," she says. "You're wondering who that is. His name is Helmut and I have recently grown to accept that that podgy little fellow with the bald head is the love of my life. At my age, you can work these things out retrospectively without too much difficulty."

As she about to leave Dani asks whether the name Dietmar Marschal rings any bells?

"Sort of. If it's the same one, he's rather sweet and caring, but he got a bit carried away when it came to Caro. Boys can be like that. Diffident at first, then rash and impetuous. He's still on various watch lists, I think. There was a lot of gossip about having him locked up. But I don't think it came to anything. People interceded before it got that far. His friends in high, but slippery places. But with Caro, her Dad's the one you want to watch. I'm not altogether convinced that the old adages hold in this case."

"Which are they?"

"Number one, follow the money. Money is always an issue, but not necessarily the primary issue. You should certain pay attention to funding and incentives, however. So that's money. Caro's Dad adores money almost as much as he adores himself, though I'm sure he would deny it."

"And"

"Number two, who benefits, cui bono. Whoever it is, you can rest assured it won't be me. Of course the boys and girls at 'Network Check' would place great faith in connectedness and the power of the network, our old friend big data. And who am I to say they're wrong? Maybe the world is being run on electronic wisdom."

"Then?"

"What happens next, followed by who can you believe and should I be taking any of this shit seriously at all, or should I be sitting at home watching tv? Then again, keep a close eye on young Caro, she's another little scorpion scurrying here and there. Oh, and one more thing..."

"What's that?"

"Don't ever say that I didn't try to help you."

She doesn't have any more to say, about that, or anything else.

Time to go.

No-one shows Dani to the door, but she makes a polite exit and once she's outside she realises that similar building in the next yard actually is the nightclub she had remembered. Grape vines almost hide it from view at ground level and it is invisible from above. Rot has reached the rafters. Wet rot, dry rot, every kind of technicolor rot you can imagine.

Consequently it's one of those places that no one thinks to check out. She can remember being with a couple of friends who suggested they see what was what so she'd been visiting by accident and got out as quickly as she could to avoid the slings and arrows of outrageous behaviour when she'd asked an unwelcome question. Dani isn't a prude, but she finds no pleasure in pain.

Everyone else had seemed to be having a great time, but that is sometimes the way of things. Dani accepted that without question.

Assuming Elfie Malzenberger been telling the truth, what then?

Maybe she tries, Dani concedes, then reminds herself the woman is probably concealing ten times more than she's revealing.

As she's walking to the U-bahn station, Dani realises that in the course of a ninety minute discussion the Malzenberger woman hadn't really told her anything she didn't already know. She hadn't even confirmed Dani's doubts, or allayed her suspicions of Caro.

Elfie is one of those women steeped in the belief that truth is hard to define and somewhere along the line she's become firmly convinced that whatever she says must be correct and the truth springs into her thoughts of its own accord.

She isn't quite infallible in her own eyes, but Elfie would contend that she's almost always right. Maybe she is, some of the time.

In Berlin, madwomen get to enjoy the cellar, not the attic.

The archaeological record is inverted.

There are rivers and streams, stores and shelters.

Sewers gurgle and flood, ignored and be-ratted.

Pipes and cables underpin the rest like a mat of wire and plastic.

The city is a survival machine for rodents as much as for people and there's room for everyone, one of Berlin's abiding charms.

Chapter 6

Making her way back to Charlottenburg, Dani steps off the U-bahn at Adenauerplatz and wanders down the Wilmersdorferstrasse towards Frau Behrens Patisserie, where she can enjoy a hand-made croissant and a large cup of aromatic coffee. She likes watching the bustle of bakers as they go about their baking and decorating. Comforting and colourful, an elite address for cake.

She found 'Fat' Pete bidding farewell to a well spoken middle aged lady who will be off to meet a potential tenant for one of the shops he's arranging rent out. "Good luck, Julia, remember nothing less than €140 the square metre a month. You're the proud owner of an address a fashion house can list on their shopping bags."

He is contemplating the potential of another slice of apple and walnut tart, having calculated his diabetes will allow him that much and no more.

Like Klaus, he's a property developer, but unlike Klaus, he's still alive and specialises in a narrow band of buildings within a hundred metres either side of the Kurfurstendamm, from its beginnings near the Gedächtniskirche and Berlin Zoo to its dissipation a mile or two further west, as it seeps over the railway bridge towards the roads down to Grunewald. He knows the layout and the structure of every apartment, every office and every shop in six or seven hundred buildings. In twenty-five years he's bought or sold most of them, sometimes more than once. He knows who are looking to buy and he knows who are looking to sell. All he wants is a fee from both parties to a transaction and then he's satisfied. It doesn't have to be much. He doesn't try to own things. He has a reputation for fairness. As an old fashioned Marxist, he considers private property immoral and he's trying his best to be subversive, to insert a fatal virus in the system. He wants the theatres to survive, too many cinemas have already gone. Charlottenburg needs its cinemas back. The city is overflowing with shopping malls and has no need of more. He doesn't touch shopping mall deals, not any more. He's done quite enough of that. Apart from the paperwork, which is a tedious necessity, what he does is a very simple business, intellectually undemanding and in Fat Pete's hands a one-way bet. In the long term, he is committed to inflating prices to the point of becoming unpayable, when buildings will end up unoccupied, unrentable, their value undermined, no longer financeable within the remit of the finance system and burdoned with taxes reflecting the developers' exuberant over-optimism.

 Once that point is reached Fat Pete will encourage people to go liquid, sell for cash, take their profits, stimulate the rot and watch the crash that follows, at which point he will buy to help the local market recover. Until then, he ploughs on, banks the profits and eats. Sometimes he does sex and sometimes he reads 'The World as Will and Representation' for the umpteenth time. He's a Schopenhauer fan. He also goes to gallery openings and trashes the inadequacies of conceptual art, which isn't much of a talent either.

 "How can I be of help, Ela?" he asks Dani.

 "How big a crook is Carolina, you know the one, Klaus' Ex."

 "That depends on what do you think of as big. Our Lina probably imagines Klaus was more of a player than he was. How much would you guess he was worth?"

 "I haven't a clue."

 "A good deal less than a hundred million, if that's worth knowing, I don't know. The net was a minus, but then it always is when the music stops. I'm worth nothing at all, or so my accountants tell the tax people every year. I have friends who say I'm worthless. Isn't that reassuring. To make worthlessness an asset. I am worthily worthless, how about that!"

 "Nothing to lose?"

 "Have you selected a cake for yourself, Daniela?"

 "Not yet."

"I would suggest something lemony to augment the bitterness in your heart."

"What bitterness, why did you say that?"

"Are you implying I'm incorrect?"

"Totally, completely, I'm not bitter."

"If you so insist. Then try the orange surprise. You might be cured....."

"Pete... ."

"like leather," he adds.

Her voice dwindles as he leans forward, rests his arms on the table and stabs the air with a twirl of cake-fork. The gesture is impressive, yet futile.

"Dani, what is Carolina asking of you?"

"There's a lawyer arriving tomorrow from Miami. Caro wants me to be there when they meet and I think she wants me to dig around this woman's connections to see what there is to be uncovered."

"Couldn't she handle that on her own, or get her own lawyer to be there. My advice? Now? Just hand the whole business over to the lawyers and accountants, let them bicker among themselves and ask them to bill Caro once they've finished a deal. That's what I would do. These things are far too bothersome to handle yourself. There's nothing to be gained. Do you want to buy a house?"

"Fr. Malzenberger told me something similar."

"Oh, Dani, dan-ee-Ela, don't listen to that woman. She's a fake and a fraud."

"More, please?" Having met the Malzenberger woman for the first time only a couple of hours previously and that only because she was recommended by someone she trusted, this attempted demolition of the woman's credibility was as unwelcome as it was surprising.

"Cake or indiscretions."

"Both, please."

Fat Pete waves expectantly for service and orders more cake, "Noch kuchen, schatz,", then returns to gossip as the tall waitress scowls at his presumption. She's nobody's 'schatz', the derogatory version of 'treasure' usually employed as a put down by irritatingly arrogant males, which is what Fat Pete is. The waitress considers flipping a plate frisbee style for him to catch with his teeth, then decides not to, but clunks the plate with the cake on the table, to demonstrate disdain.

As he's talking with Dani, Fat Pete spends most of the time staring at two pencil thin girls who are sharing a single slice of ginger cake and drinking tap-water. It would take both of them to balance the scales with him. He and Dani are drinking satisfyingly rich coffee, Weiner melange, which is served with a glass of very cold water.

"And darling Elfie informs on people, so be careful."

"Informs?"

"She rats, regularly, makes a living out of passing on gossip to anyone who pays. She'll rat on you, rat on me, rat on anyone at all. She'd rat on herself if she thought it could do her some good. She's quite cheap too, so don't imagine her stuff only goes to the rich and powerful. Put a glass of white wine in front of her and you'll set her off. She a compulsive ratter, sharp teeth, four legs, fur and a tail, and she'll rat on you whether she's telling the truth, or not. She's a panda in rat's clothing. Eight in the evening every Friday night, you find her at the Fehrberlinerplatz for her regular meeting with the police and on Tuesdays she has lunch with Major Nadja Reiker from the military security services. I've heard it said she's involved in financing the AfD. Rest assured, your name will now come up in half a dozen contexts, that may or may not be relevant."

"She isn't very nice then."

"No, I wouldn't say that. She can be delightful if she decides to like you, though I'm not sure it's worth it, because she is equally well known for the vindictive and venomous contrariness with those who fall out of favour. If the AfD take her money, they're totally fucked. She leaks politically. Our Elfie is a bit of an omnivore. PPP called her an unremitting harradan, the last time her name cropped up in conversation, but PP can also be vituperative in his own way. He was husband number one, you know."

"Were there more?"

"Yes, but they're all dead, bar Helmut and he is nearly. She's a bit of a black widow."

Dani wishes she hadn't heard that, then she's glad she's been warned before too much had been said. Vindictive, venomous, vituperative, and black widow. Hardly commendable. Rat, ratter, rattest, most ratty, comparative disgust. When in Berlin, never

92

forget the police files that went astray about the guy who drove a truck into the Christmas market and killed a lot of people. Ask a bureaucrat for someone's files and they redirect you to the 'lost and found'. It's typische Berlin. Always blame the informant. Stands to reason, really.

 "Just think, Ela, if Malzenberger can get information for you about other people, she will do the same for people who ask about you. And the other people she does things for includes some extremely 'other' kind of others, not to mention the French, which might concern you given your Dad's situation and some funny folk from New Jersey who seem to get everywhere nowadays. She's a dangerous person to know. She also eliminates and sifts, I'm sure she'll have mentioned that. Now ask yourself what is implied about an eliminator? In France they would call her an eraser, the 'gomme', she rubs out, hiring others to do the dirty work when she can't be arsed to do the job herself. You've read Robbe-Grillet of course, after Schopenhauer, he's really the best for any who likes hard edged existential ambiguity with a romantic twinge of optimism."

 "And what about Caro and Klaus?"

 "Nothing Klaus ever did was simple or straightforward. If it was in any way possible to tangle a web of confusion, he would do the tangling, but there was usually a fairly clear sense of purpose behind his ploys, until they fell apart. He never ratted, however. And he wasn't dangerous, not to life and limb. He was lethal for bank accounts, financial cyanide, but who cares about that. Remember the Berlin banking crisis in the nineties? Ah, he was proud of that. He said it was like pouring beer from a barrel. How many hundred millions a month and how many months? Whether Caro understood any of those things is debatable. This cake is excellent. Try it. Take a forkful. Delicious. Fattening of course, but who give a fuck about fat any more?"

 Dani prods the cake, separates, scoops and slides a forkful into her mouth.

 "If she did, what then? Mmm, you're right this is good."

 "Better than good," he corrects her, "the flavours stay on the palate like fine wine. For Caro, Klaus represented the antithesis of her notion that people are most effective when they adopt a particular role and play the part like an actor, whether doctor, or nurse, prince or pauper. Some of them, Presidents and Generals, Admirals and policemen even need uniforms to bolster the conceit and convince people that they are fit to perform as required. Would you fight for a General who presented himself in dressing gown and pyjamas?" "Caro is very structured in her thinking," agrees Dani.

"Increasingly, it looks as though Klaus was right. Anything goes in Berlin, so long as someone claims it to be legal and there's a daunting heap of paperwork to go with it. People don't like doing diligence in Berlin, they don't live out their roles. Berliners don't check, they pretend, they smile a lot. Call it laziness, call it cheating, sometimes it's dangerous as well as pointless. They might eventually apologise, but more often they'll hope to be forgotten. The documentation is often a mere cypher for reality. Klaus recognised that long before the rest of us. Land, factories, apartments, office buildings, airports, canals, needed or not, useless, or essential, who cares, fitness studios for arthritic old aged pensioners, rooftop swimming pools, bars with no name, people without shame. No-one gives a damn. Some people even want to lose their cash in movie production. At first, it all sounds reasonable enough then you realise that nothing has actually been justified. Old fever hospitals become housing developments. Shopping malls mushroom, then turn fungal. All kinds of things get done for accounting purposes, but it really is blind luck whether they're actually what the city needs. That was just the way Klaus had been, charming, rash and dependably irresponsible, courting disaster and evading trouble by the skin of your teeth, if his own weren't up to the job.

He'd been among the first to recognise the corrosive power of purposeless finance and he leveraged his perception with considerable aplomb, I do admit. He is to be admired for that, at least. His greed was visceral, instinctive, an inborn talent.

If Caro understood, she's likely to be an extremely wealthy woman by now. There were enough deals on the table, there were, right from the beginning, when it was South Koreans buying art in the 1990's and a hatful of accountants punting for profits in Prenzlauer Berg. Klaus cherry picked. He pulled the wool over the local politicians' eyes whenever they asked him to. Professional politicians are people who confuse sitting on Committees with doing things, you should learn that. More often than not they're crafty wanglers who make dinner date deals and end up having to resign. Tediously predictable. Klaus understood that. He watched what they were up to, then offered to help. You should think that way too when you hear what Caro has to tell.

Klaus made them feel as though everything was being handled correctly, because the forms were neatly filled out and complete. He was an exemplary form filler. God help our future historians when they sift though the archives and hit on the comprehensive and convincing array of lies. The nonces thought they were getting free dinners, but he was taking them for a ride, on a hiding to nothing. He was very very good at it.

So, tell me Dani, do you imagine he was any good in bed? Finance people don't usually have the energy for a fruitful sex life, which requires selflessness rather than greed. So whatever Caro saw in him, it wasn't sex. Therefore ask yourself what it might have been. Now, listen to me Ela, I do suspect Caro has been tidying up behind him, then cleaning up on her own behalf without informing anyone. Those insolvency guys were too lazy to challenge her. All that interested them was their fees."

Pete lets that thought sink in and shovels another forkful of cake, the takes a sip of coffee.

"And, even a percentage or two of what Klaus was playing with was more than most people earn in their whole careers. Acting dumb comes easily to the recently bereaved. Believe me, I know that, I've been there and back. Remember my Richard, do you? Seventeen years since he got the virus, twelve years since he died. Surprised? Long time, yes, a long time now. Yes, well. So who is Caro trying to kid? You should ask her straight out. She isn't the only widow in the web. So there you are, you have my opinion, you have my advice and you've had a bite of my cake, as well as that lovely orangey torte of your own, so off you go. Grand Marnier, good with coffee, delicious with cake. If I promise to pay for the 'kaffée und kuchen', will you promise to keep me updated on the progress of your case. "

"I'm not even sure I have a case, anyway cake is cheaper than blood, you'll have to do better than that."

"OK, Dani, keep me informed and I'll back you up with whatever I get to know. Mutual backscratching, you know the drill. Good advice has no calories. And remember, there's no kind of loss like a tax loss!"

"That's better."

"And we can split the profit."

"Sounds reasonable."

"Good, you should never ignore the prospect of a deal, my dearest young partner in crime." He sighs and stretches, "We must all be grateful to grandpa Freud for making the invention of the wellness industry possible, that happy boost to any flagging economy. From Saudi to Singapore, Sligo and Stockholm, we're mired in an ocean of slithery sins and massage oil. You know a properly trained masseuse can make a fortune hereabouts. Try it some day. You'll be astonished." He smiles benevolently. "This is a city committed to addressing neurosis through flattery and self deception. Smooth and soothe, as profitable a tactic as any, even if it isn't quite a strategy. The downside is that outside law and psychotherapy, it is incredibly difficult to find anyone in Berlin who is half-way competent for any of the other jobs that need doing. Professors, crooks and cranks galore. Bus-drivers at a premium. Who can say which are which? Not I. Say hello to Georg for me. Tell him we are all eagerly awaiting first news of the Argentinian vintage."

"Georg tells me the Argentinians are pleased, so buy some."

The man's a pain, Dani told herself. If she'd said it out loud, he'd probably have agreed. Fat Pete no longer deceives himself about himself, or anyone else.

"Lovely, Malbec, Je t'adore."

Then as an afterthought he asked if she'd like some cocaine.

How much, she wanted to know.

"Not a lot," he replied, pursing his lips, "A kilo, two kilos, not much more."

She declined. He doesn't seem surprised, "Oh alright, but let me know if you change your mind. I found it in a box of bananas at the supermarket, €1,30 per kilo, which seemed like the bargain of a lifetime till I realised that was the price of the bananas, the coke wasn't priced, so I thought it better to give it a new home. It would only have been wasted otherwise. But I can't use all that myself."

This was true enough. He didn't have twenty years to live, or even ten. He never needs more than a gramme a week for himself and his boyfriends. He needs insulin, not cocaine. Eventually he'll give most of it away as Christmas presents, cocaine laying round about, winter fuel, deep and crisp and even.

"I think I've said as much as I feel able to tell you," said Fat Pete, looking around. The café had begin to feel crowded and it was time to go, so Dani left.

"Later, Dani girl," he said as she strode out of the cake-shop, then he smiled a corrosive leer towards the slender young women who had caught his eye earlier. What would they be willing to do for money, he asked himself pragmatically. Then he asked them, paid for their cakes and shortly afterwards the three of them left for a nearby hotel. He ordered prosecco, ham sandwiches and some clean glasses from the concierge and swallowed a little blue pill.

Half an hour later, the girls told him he reminded them of a slug and went away as soon as they'd enjoyed a glass, or two of his fizz and pocketed the little bags of powder he gave them for good luck. Twenty minutes later they were arrested for shoplifting on the Ku'damm, then released with a warning on the grounds of stupidity. Then they went to the University for a lecture. Derrida, Kittler and Confusion Theory. All of a befuddled muddle, it didn't make much sense to them. It made no sense at all to the other students, who had paid much closer attention to their overly serious Professor and found him profoundly unconvincing.

Cake shop to Soph-Am isn't as far as it looks, follow the Wilmersdorferstrasse as far as TK Maxx, then turn left and walk past the S-bahn station towards Stuttgarter Platz and you're there. Try to avoid temptation, take a deep breath and pretend you haven't seen the Deli on the corner of Windscheidstrasse, and don't get sidetracked toward a Windburger, or the Spanish Cat before you reach the Soph-Am.

Caro may have promised to pay the bills, so Dani does get to Soph-Am on time, but Caro has yet to do enough to win Dani's loyalty. Maybe she never will. Fat Pete has dented Caro's credibility in her eyes. Then Dani has to remind herself that undermining other people's reputations is what Fat Pete is famous for, so maybe the jury should still be out. He's no kind of an arbiter. She wonders whether he used to hang around the sleazy old clubs and gambling joints that once lined the street from Kaiser Friedrich to Windscheidstrasse. Now the brothels and clip joints have been closed down it's all fairly innocuous, just food fetishists at the deli and hostel style hotels for students in search of cool. Even the gun dealers have lowered their profiles, once upon a time it was gas pistols in the window and a choice of M16's or Kalashnikovs on delivery, but those days are long gone. So have the memories of the Baader Meinhof gang, now the old commune has been gentrified. Almost twenty years ago the old 'King of Stutti' took early retirement in a prison cell. When the British and American soldiers left town, his camouflage faded in the wash. So far as it went, his successors were more or less legit. The local colour had leached away. Nowadays the graffiti has gone. All you get is a coat of paint from a company that does exterior decorating and shopfronts. The primary question for Dani is what all these people around Klaus and Co, thought they were up to. Nothing Dani's heard so far is particularly edifying. Scruffy money-making gambits and little deals. A ten minute drive away there's a government that measures everything in billions and some things in thousands of billions. Shouldn't that be where they're concentrating their attention? Why aren't people like Fat Pete and Elfie M., Bernhardt and Caro milking the government for all they can get.

There are major crumbs being swept under that particular table, yet for most of these people, the height of their ambition is to part dentists, accountants and each other from their tax avoidance windfalls, then use the proceeds to buy themselves somewhere nice so they can bask in the Tuscan sun. It isn't a lot to ask for. You could manage the basking thing much the same by going to live somewhere sunny and finding yourself a job as a goatherd. Maybe building bridges, or moon rockets is too much like hard work for entrepreneurial Berlin. A sizeable chunk of all the new businesses are hobbies for tax avoidance, vanity projects and money laundering. Look at what people do and it rarely adds up to a profitable living, yet a nice family home is cheaper in Los Angeles.

The three actors are posed and ready, when Dani arrives to join Caro, who is sitting comfortably at a corner table by the window looking along Leonhardtstrasse. Pleasingly chic, Caro is in a dark blue linen dress, one of three from Ilke the dressmaker, all cut to the same pattern but in different colours. Dani is reminded of the kites flying from the house near her apartment. There's a Turkish woman talking to the three actors. She's a tv star, famous throughout the middle east, a garrulous Auntie in a long running soap opera about her kindly nephew the Iman and his commendably devout sister. Nico is being provocative, "Don't bother dieting dear, just relax and learn to love your flab, like so many million others."

Dani ignores the actors, sits with Caro and begins. "I had a chat with Fat Pete about the Malzenberger woman. He has a low opinion of her."

Then Caro said, "We should be more concerned if he said something nice."

"She told me she'd like to meet your lawyer from Miami."

"Is that all she had to say? Nothing more concrete?"

"More, or less. Apart from reminding me in a thousand ways how people rarely tell the truth. "

"So you haven't actually learned anything at all," Caro says.

"Not really, no."

"Nor have I," admits Caro.

"Then, the only sensible thing is to meet with Bernhardt's lawyer and see how things go." Dani tries to sound bright and positive. She isn't sure why.

"Alright, but sometime in the next couples of days, could you check her credentials? Make sure you get her business card, then ask whoever it is you have to ask. I never saw anything in Miami to confirm that she is who she says she is. We didn't meet at her office."

Caro wonders whether Dani has something to hide, then dismisses the thought as a foolish irrelevance.

Far from wondering about Caro's dilemma, Dani is wondering what to cook for supper and what she will have to get from the supermarket.

She doesn't feel up to facing Soph-Am food.

She'd like scallops with a bit of cheese sauce and salad to eat in front of the tv. Simple enough, ready in twenty minutes.

All she needs are tabs for the dishwasher.

There are shellfish in the deep freeze. Since Georg is gallivanting over the pampas, after scallops she will watch an old movie, then just maybe drift round to the 'Spritz' club for a drink and some distraction later on.

She doesn't know whether 'the distraction' is going to turn up. He can be very unpredictable, but in the absence of Georg, he'll do. They try their best to meet as if by accident. It brings a bit of zest to their flirtation. She knows he's been in Hamburg for a meeting about cables and connectors, but he should be back by now.

If he isn't, he'll be in Magdeburg, which is boring.

In an age dominated by talk of software, people tend to forget it's all dependent on hardware and wetware has its place too. The distraction doesn't talk much about technology, people get bored by cables and connectors, unless they need to buy some, so he sticks to seduction and he's good at that, a wetware connoisseur of female psychology and that keeps Dani happy when Georg isn't there.

As well as cables and connectors, the distraction is into bondage, a healthy work life balance, as he describes it, but Dani doesn't like being tied up. He accepts that with good grace and leaves his ropes in the car.

Oh, what a pragmatic life we lead. She thinks of him as a benefit with friendship.

And as things go, they came and then he went.

By the time Dani awakens, the distraction is well on his way to Eisenach, which is a feat in itself to most Germans, the majority of whom have never visited the place and probably never will, though Bach was born there and Martin Luther translated the bible into German in the local castle, the Wartburg, a fortress built by a minor princeling catchily named 'Louis the Leaper'.

The distraction also has customers near Erfurt on the road to Gotha, but he never needs to visit them. They do everything by fax.

Dani is in a good mood.

Once she'd heard the distraction leave, she'd snuggled down for an extra couple of hours sleep and now she feels doubly refreshed and is looking forward to meeting the lawyer.

Chapter 7

The Fasanenstrasse is an extremely useful side-street, long, quiet, narrow, not far from Zoo, it crosses both the Kantstrasse and the Kurfurstendamm, boasting a string of restaurants, the Berlin Stock Exchange, bits of University, a major Synagogue, hotels including the Savoy and the Kempinski, various 'pension', art dealers, at least one Cinema, the Kathe Kollwitz Museum, some posh clothes shops, fancy jewellers, a couple of sleazy clubs, a bordello or three, and the Literatur Haus, not to mention a shoal of lawyers' offices and assorted apartments. A selection of posh people and a smattering of notorious Nazi stooges have lived there over the years. At one end there's a borehole reaching down through aeons of geological history, at the other fancy houses where the 'hoch bourgeoisie' used to graze in the days when the 'hoch bourgeoisie' still considered Berlin to be an acceptable place to visit, which is a long time ago, part of the holocene, or perhaps the more recently defined Anthropocene. Look at the street and ask yourself - Is this place more about the future, or the past?

Easy to find, the garden café at the Literatur Haus is as neutral a place as you'll find in any big city if you want to make a good impression on newly arrived visitors and this is where Caro has arranged for Dani to meet the lawyer, who has been booked into the Savoy, a hotel acceptable without being overly extravagant.

No point drawing overt attention to oneself, is there? Caro had met the lawyer at the airport mid-morning and ferried her to the Savoy then promised her a light lunch nearby.

There having been an evening in Florida when Bernhardt had taken Caro to see Maria, they both agree, politely, that it was lovely to meet one another again. The exchange of kisses was aetherial. Caro was amazed by the pile of luggage that accompanied the woman through 'Arrivals', where a group of adolescent gamers and their parents were also hauling baggage off the carousels.

Maria is far less tired than Caro had been at the end of her own frustrating west to east odyssey via Frankfurt-am-Main across the Atlantic. Either she's excited by the prospect of her first visit to Europe, or she had dosed herself with something to boost her energy and wakefulness. If she has, she'll crash soon enough. Caro gives her till four o'clock in the afternoon, then it will be a stretcher bearer back to the hotel and time for bed.

They were lucky to find a table away from the crowd and managed to order. Maria can relax a little. 'So this is Berlin and these are Germans,' she says, playing the ingénue and watching the ladies who gather to gossip away their afternoon with tales of culture and adultery.

The Literatur Haus is a small villa that predates the rest of the district and has retained its garden, so there's ample space for twenty or thirty tables resting on the white chippings that contrast with the fresh greens of trees, the flowers and the well tended lawns. This wasn't at all what she'd been led to expect.

She's sipping a glass of green tea, pale as the sickly sunshine, and is threatening to nibble a lettuce leaf, while several sparrows hop around at her feet, no doubt intrigued by the sweaty scent of North American shoes and stockings. Maria Valdes-Hartman had studied at Northwestern, at Madison in the wintery wilds of Wisconsin, picked up good grades in law school, qualified as an attorney almost twenty years ago and is nobody's fool.

She'd given Dani a friendly grin as they'd shaken hands and swapped cards, then said she's glad to find they're to work as a team and she isn't being left to go it alone. She's not proposing to read anything in German having heard that German law is dominated by the notion of paragraphs in a legal code, not her style.

"I'm more of a lets get that down in writing and see what's right and wrong, then work out a deal that won't be challenged in court kind of person," she declared and smiled pleasantly.

Caro didn't believe that for a minute.

"I like making lists," she added,

That, Caro did believe.

"I hope my english is good enough to keep up," said Dani quietly, as she overhears some-one at the next table say that Turkey has never had much luck with politicians and now the situation has taken another turn for the worse.

"Erdogan will be forgotten soon enough once he's deposed. And the sooner the better. I'll do it, if no-one else volunteers." The speaker was a handsome young man with a lapel badge based on the Turkish flag. "Stand in line," laughs the middle-aged woman in Ankara, who he's chatting with via his tablet. "All you need is a wall and a machine gun," says another voice. "Why bother with the wall, a waste of good bricks. One shot should suffice."

Maria may be enjoying tea, but Dani has her nose in a glass of white wine.

Caro notices Doro the slender yoga teacher is chatting to one of her friends. They're sitting at a table on the patio.

Dani and she exchange mild smiles of recognition.

Caro notices that too. Who is the guy she's talking to? Could it be Paul, the local contortionist?

Dani takes a sip of the wine. Not great, but a modest hint of something like peachiness, as well as a mild mist of alcohol.

"There's a question I've been waiting to answer since we met in Florida," Maria said to Caro, "But you haven't asked. Now, I'm beginning to wonder why."

Dani is watching her attentively, but turns for Caro's reaction to the comment.

"Then I had better ask you what question you have in mind."

"Simple. Why on earth should your father be showing such a lot of interest in your ex-husband's affairs?"

"Well, he's my Dad," says Caro, as though this is self-explanatory, "Wouldn't you expect him to want to help me?"

"He seems to be going a good deal further than mere paternal concern would require, wouldn't you agree? I mean this trip is costing him several tens of thousands and no-one is suggested anything untoward has happened to you, either materially, physically, or financially."

Without saying a word, Dani agrees. If he's covering the cost of the lawyer's trip and she's billing him at the full rate this is a great deal more than parental interest. Dani has never met Bernhardt, but he's reputed to be a mean bastard when it comes to parting with money. Maybe business is different. Maybe he's changed with age, people do, sometimes. The word that gets used is mellow, but the implication is that they're going soft, rather than maturing.

Caro looks a little puzzled, but doesn't seem concerned. "My Dad is impossible to second guess, so I wouldn't bother trying. I don't. He'll have a reason, but don't confuse reason, motive and logic, ok?"

At that moment, Katharina Jana Jonson, one of Klaus' former assistants, who Caro hasn't seen since the funeral wanders into the garden. She's wearing an alarmingly maroon and orange ice cream cone striped jacket and waves gaily to Caro and Dani, then settles herself on a chair a few tables away. Her loud voice can be heard commanding a waitress for something calorie free, organic and nutricious that tastes good. The waitress says they only have what's on the menu. The woman decides she wants bratwurst, fried sausage, and potato salad, which confuses Dani for about half a second, before she recognises the sign of a native Berliner. Vegetarian or vegan, they still revert to bratwurst whenever their judgement is challenged. Even the KaDeWe will manage a reassuring sausage for you up on the sixth floor where the gourmet foods are to be found.

"Is she out of earshot?" Dani asks.

"More or less," says Caro.

"Is she someone who might....? " enquires the lawyer, who has of course never seen the woman before and is wondering why she's caught Caro's attention.

"Katharina was Klaus' assistant for a couple of years," says Caro. "She married a gallery owner and switched to selling paintings for a living. Then she walked away from art and started a piano shop, second-hand Steinways and reconditioned Bechsteins. Effective to offset against tax and the 'salon' opens up the chance to hold little soirees to impress friends and acquaintances, so invitations are reciprocated without much bother. Easy to inventory and rarely if ever stolen, so easy to insure. They're one of my anthropo-business trends. You know how accountants give their wives little shops to keep them amused and reduce the tax bill. Only harp shops are comparable and I only know of one, so selling harps must be a legitimate specialist business, rather than a hobby. "

"Oh sure, so you do hobby businesses here too? And I thought it was a Florida ploy. Do we get invited to these soirées? I'd enjoy a little local culture while I'm here."

"Oh, any time. Dani why don't to take Maria along? Anyway," explains Caro, "even I can see that a beautifully made piano is going to be worth more as an investment than some crappy dribble of German art. Actually, I find it fascinating the way tax avoidance and accounting tricks can be genuine precursors to commercial innovation and social development. Lock up cash as investment in piano's, write down the value against tax, start a shop, or two, organise soirees and recitals, encourage musicians and new music, kick start a community and provide the seedcorn to encourage a new sub-culture. And all because they want to pay less tax. Marvellous ingenuity, such creativity! Such a heap of bullshit, if you'll excuse my prose. Actually, I think she earns her pocket money as an event manager."

Maria doesn't seem very impressed by Caro's mild pomposity. There's nothing wrong about earning your living as an event manager.

"Were she and Klaus on good terms after that?"

"Sure, I think they fucked each other twice a week till the husband found out, after which she got divorced and Klaus immediately dumped her. Actually, all that piano playing got on his nerves. Klaus was always a four beats to the bar rock and roller at heart. He told me that. What he told other people is anyone's guess.'"

"Oh, she has motive! Do you think this Katharina could have murdered him?" Maria asks melodramatically. This is almost as good as gangster and moll spotting in Miami, though were Maria honest with herself she would have to accept that the only gangsters she has met in Miami are her clients.

She turns to get a better look at the Katharina woman. Is this mousey lady with an orange cocktail a potential murderer? They all are, but suddenly, this one is candidate number one for a charge of homicide and her name will soon be tagged for addition checks by US customs should she decide to holiday in the USA. All that inside six hours of Maria's arrival in Berlin! What a city!

Then she's reminded that she's going a little too far.

Caro gets another turn at explaining.

"Unless looks can kill, I doubt she's capable of homicide. Her husband might make a better candidate. Katharina lived in one of Klaus' first apartments, a nice place around the corner from here. The husband bought it via Fat Pete without too many questions. Bad tempers all round though, when the truth came out, especially the husband. He felt betrayed by both of them, but the venom was reserved for Klaus. Klaus got the profits, she got the home, Pete took his cut. The husband got taken to the cleaners and was seriously annoyed. "

"Understandably, wouldn't you agree?" said Dani. She could remember the rucus. The husband had done a lot of public seething, much of it within hearing of the Soph-Am regulars. Served him right, she thought. He'd gone to live in South Africa and that had been the end of him, so far as Berlin was concerned.

The lawyer is busily scribbling notes, "I have never come across a situation where the lover sells the husband the place the lover is using to meet his lover, the wife. Takes some nerve to bring it off. Determination even. Was your Klaus always equally unscrupulous?"

"He was always very motivated when it came to money, very motivated, you might say. Some people said he was excessively greedy, truly voracious. He couldn't care less about who screwed who, unless he was involved personally."

Dani represses a guffaw.

"So it seems, and Mrs Whatsit over there, what gets her out of bed in the morning?"

"She sold the flat, I think, after Klaus let her go. Made a significant profit considering she hadn't had to pay for it in the first place."

"The wages of sin," says Maria with a giggle.

"Apart from that she's fairly average."

"He 'let her go', you mean from the job, or once he ended the affair?" This Maria is very inquisitive. She thinks there might be enough material here for an article in the chatty section of the Miami lawyers' monthly.

"We had split up long before, so I didn't ask too many details," Caro explains. "His subsequent amorous exploits were none of my business. It's only sex, after all. I never knew the exact order of events, one doesn't in such circumstances, does one? "

"I suppose not, though why not? Always a good idea to pay attention in my view," says Maria, casting a suspicious glance across to Katharina to check if she's overheard what they've been saying.

   "After that he moved on to Kirstie, the Dutch girl," said Caro, "She's nice. Everyone likes her, open, friendly, easy going. She left town the day after Klaus took his dive. Can't say I blame her."

"Yes, she's lovely," agrees Dani, who has known Kirstie since she was a trainee assistant at the dentists' next to the Bel Ami bar on Leibnizstrasse which had been opened after they closed down the big bordello where the horny footballers used to spend their money and sweat away their afternoons after training. Kirstie is in Liege now, a most peculiar decision.

The lawyer then steers them back to the subject of Caro's Dad who'd never paid for sex, but spent a small fortune on divorces in many parts of the world, mainly defending himself from accusations of having wrecked other people's marriages. An economic inversion, if you enjoy market based conundrums. He's another one who collects musicians, his latest, she reminds them, the 'Juniper Willow Ash in Colorado', is a celloist.

Then Maria began to tell things from her side.

Bernhardt, she claimed, had rung her husband up in the middle of the night about six months ago and talked to him for at least three hours, then asked to talk to her, which was the first time she'd spoken with him. "Marie, he said to me, he still gets my name wrong, never Maria, always Marie; Lee, he says, thats my husband, has just told me that you know a lot about checking patents."

"Misleading to claim I was an expert, I told him, but I have done some checks about patents that are supposed to cover different parts of the world, but don't necessarily conform to local law. Those requests had been from people who wanted to find a country where the patents wouldn't apply, so they could start producing unlicenced, but legal, copies of things. They usually ended up hoping to go undiscovered in some distant Chinese province without bothering to ask any questions. Presuming Bernhardt was interested in the same kind of information. I went along with it, so far as it went. That was all it amounted to, to begin with, then they'd had a couple of meetings. He'd given Lee a job. My husband Lee is in human resources and works in sifting, as an eliminator."

Dani toys politely with her food, orders another glass of wine and merely noted the use of the word 'eliminator', which was also the job-title Elfie Malzenberger had used of herself. What had she said, something about three main approaches perforative, sectional and expansive, though she hadn't elaborated and Dani hadn't wanted to know, though she assumed this meant bullets, knives and bombs. She decides it could be a good idea simply to play the silent witness.

Dani only half listens, trying to seem polite as the lawyer explained herself more plainly for Caro's benefit. A jackdaw struts and hops along the garden path looking for titbits without finding anything meaty. Then a stray bottletop glints in the sunlight and distracts the bird. Dani returns her attention to the conversation as a sparrow tries to land on the table and needs shooing away. Then crows caw.

"Just for the moment, Carolina," Maria said, "I would like you to stop thinking of me as a lawyer of the kind who will represent you in court, or sort out the wording in a contract. I have travelled a very long way to meet you and so far as I can tell, there is no practical or legal purpose for my being here. Any questions I might want to ask could have been answered by phone. I know nothing about the law in Germany, or anywhere in Europe. You do things differently here. Which is fine, carry on, it's your country, do whatever you please. If it works, great. Who am I to complain?

So why has Bernhardt arranged for me to come to Berlin? Let me be frank, I don't particularly like the guy. I know he's your Dad, but I don't trust him, sorry. We have all kinds of issues with drugs in Miami, and he isn't just a dealer, he's a drug designer, a rogue chemist, a real and present danger to our young people and I have three young children who are approaching the age when drugs become an issue. He's someone who spends his days dreaming of brain chemistry, then makes things happen, engineering ways of fucking with the minds of millions, while he makes a heap of money. He taints the globe with new highs!

Excuse me, but your father, my client, is a seriously dangerous motherfucker, so why this chickenshit in Berlin, if you'll forgive my phraseology. I am perplexed. Why I am supposed to be here, please, unless it is to check up on you?”

What on earth could have provoked that outburst? Perhaps she's just exhausted after the journey.

“I'm wondering whether Bernhardt made a mistake in hiring you,” said Caro calmly. “But for the moment lets assume there's some logic behind your doubts. I didn't invite you, nor did I suggest you should pay us a visit. You're here because of my Dad. He's the organ grinder, you're the monkey. You should just do as he's asked, I'd have thought.”

Dani and the lawyer sat back patiently as Caro tried her best to come up with a more credible answer, or at least a reasonable explanation.

When she finally does, it goes like this.

“On the first Thursday in July, when we were in Cuba after the funeral, Bernhardt told me he wanted me to meet someone, so we packed, left the hotel and picked up a ride on a private boat that would set us ashore in Miami. We were on our way to see you.

I wasn't sure why the trip to Florida was necessary, until Bernhardt admitted that Cuba no longer excited him now that Castro is dead. The simple fact of his presence had always given visits to Cuba an added kick. After all, the old man had defied the USA for two generations and escaped assassination attempts by the dozen.

Emotionally an electoral victory in France by Marine LePen would have meant nothing by comparison, though Bernhardt said the Macronite disaster might have more significance in the long term and LePen still might happen. Berlusconi and Putin to Macron and Trump is a progression, which no-one should claim to call progress, he declared. A lot of people here would agree with him.”

“So would a lot of people in the USA,” Maria adds.

“OK, I thought Dad was getting bored in Cuba, he's been there so often, done the gunsights, stared down Guantanamo, the whole deal, so I accept that this is the first leg of my journey home, but he's bringing us down lightly, holiday over. Bernhardt can be very subtle like that and he does try to be kind. Tyrants nearly always have a tangential kind of sincerity and he's no exception.

He told me he was thinking of buying a house in Antibes, which I considered a waste of time and money, and told him so. He would never use it. Reluctantly he admitted I was right, then made a phone call to France and jettisoned the proposal, so I saved him a lot of Euros that afternoon.

The short journey to Florida was a beautiful day trip over a calm sea and clear water so blue it sometimes seemed like violet. There were dolphins, flying fish, probably shark and tuna, maybe a Hemingway or two, certainly gulls and an assortment of US Coastguard vessels and smugglers. Huge container ships and tankers cast a dark pall of stinking pollution ploughing their way to and from the recently enlarged Panama Canal, but they couldn't spoil the journey for me. We were flying. My Dad gave me a little boost to enjoy the spray. A thousand prisms of sparkling sunlight dancing before my eyes.

I lounged in the sun, drinking Daiquiris and enjoyed the mesmerising splosh and splash of the boat as it sliced through the water, creating a fan-like wake of white foam spreading and splashing over and again. The spray made a rainbow in my mind. Mesmerising. I can see it now. Actually, I can feel it too, whoosh!

Dad spent the whole trip shut up in the cabin making calls on his satellite phone. He even flew a pair of kites from the radio masts, orange and pine green, floating steady in the breeze as we sailed along. There were succulent shrimp to be eaten straight from the galley grill, but Bernhardt had bigger fish to fry. He didn't tell me anything, but then, why should he? I'm daughter, him Chief. I'm girl from Berlin, he's man of the world, global player, or so he likes to imagine. Sometimes he's a real dickhead."

Caro laughs with pleasure at her father's pretentions, his notions of grandeur, his daily day-dreams.

"I accept that he's busy. I also accept that he's an egoist of the first order, a potentially dangerous freak and so should you.

He's always been like that, so it would be odd if he was suddenly any different.

Equally I was relieved that the new wife wasn't travelling with us. The Juniper is a highly opinionated musician who lives a long way from anywhere in Colorado, which is itself a long way from anywhere, unless you're already there, so she really is a very long way from everywhere except where she is. He claims to like the way she plays alone in the desert nights, naked except for the moonlight. She harmonises with the coyotes. As long as we meet only once or twice a year, I supposes I don't mind, especially since Erda, my mother that is, has developed an aversion to Bernhardt of biblical intensity.

That little triangle of love and hate has all the makings of geriatric Hollywood soft porn. Eventually there must be a revenge movie – 'Three in a Death Bed' or something like that with Kim and Michelle as the old hags and someone like Richard Gere eyeing his Lotharian wrinkles in the mirror of old age. You get the drift, nothing stiffer than rigor mortis, Caro emphasised before returning to her narrative.

Bernhardt has a way of being disconcerting. As we were disembarking at the marina he suddenly asked, "Is there anyone planning to do away with you?"

"That wasn't a question I've been expecting," I replied, "But so far as I am aware, the answer is no."

"Just so, just so. What with Klaus being gone, I had wondered if you might be, what shall we say, exposed?"

"No, Dad, no one is planning to murder me, OK?"

"Good, well, that's all right then," he replied with a flash of teeth and his family man grin, "Now let's go meet the enemy." By whom I assumed he meant you, Maria, and Lee. He told me about you both the night before.

Caro explains she was more concerned with their baggage than the chances of being shot, but once they were in the taxi, she did ask the same unplanned exit question of him.

The answer was predictable, rather than precise, "Oh, I don't know, you never do, do you? No-one tells you in advance, do they, unless they're just trying to scare you, putting the frighteners on, which doesn't count, isn't the same thing at all. No, a proper professional assassination is over before you have the chance to notice anything, assuming you're the victim. You're out, it's over, that's it. Oblivion, not even shock. You, the universe, finished, gone, happens all the time, as though you've never been. Death. The big D. Different for witnesses, of course. They get a dose of astonishment and the chance to bewilder themselves when they discover they're under suspicion of having done the deed, which at first they all are, till they're sifted out and eliminated from the enquiry. Plenty of media interest too, assuming the victims are reasonably well-known. A lot of fuss all round, except for the deceased."

He sounded cheerful enough.

I wondered what he would have said if I'd told him I did in fact feel threatened – by him! I like being with Dad. He's good natured, generous and respects me for who I am rather than any resemblance to the other women in his life, who tend to combine esoterics and stress in a way that he finds entertaining. And he does treats, the way a good Dad should, despite the fact that he's getting on for seventy and I'm the wrong side of forty. We are very much father and daughter. But he does have his scary side. I hadn't said anything, but he has always seemed to know exactly what I'm thinking and this time it was no different. He can tell!

"What?" he said.

"Why are you being so nice to me?" I asked.

"Well, you're all I have really, apart from the houses and the farms and you know all the rest, all the rest you know about, and I thought you needed to get away from things for a bit after the Klaus business."

He was utterly convincing, Caro declares, as she wipes away a tear, while Dani calls the waiter over and orders more drinks for the three of them, confirming a shift from green tea to white wine by asking for a bottle.

The waiter offers Caro a handkerchief to dry her eyes and sometime later that afternoon will suggest he can do much more than that if she's so inclined.

As a reward for his impudence, on her way back from the bathroom she sprays his hair with clammy cheap perfume from a sample she'd picked up next to the handbasin, so he'll smell like a grannie on the bummel for the rest of the day.

When the fresh bottle of wine arrived, Maria seemed surprised, as though American lawyers no longer regarded daytime alcohol as an acceptable option, but what the hell, she's on a trip.

There are clean glasses.

When in Rome, don't offend the natives.

When in Berlin, forget about the time of day.

She drinks.

"This is nice."

"So there you have it, Maria. Bernhardt is worried that someone is out to assassinate him and me too. And that's why you're here, to do the homework and make sure we are safe. How about that for an explanation?"

It is a reasonable view, Dani has to concede. She realises something has bitten her leg near the ankle and wants to scratch, but won't. Probably a dog flea. A woman at the next table has a dog with her, one of those long haired mini beasts with a ribbon in its hair that are supposedly 'adorable', but yap, bite and smell. This one is infested. She'd like to tell the owner to have it treated, but she feels obliged to suffer in polite silence as the flea progresses up her leg, hop hop, bite bite. Maybe the doggie should be put down. The pistol is in her bag, but no, not in the garden of the Literatur Haus. The fleas seem to be spreading throughout the garden, judging by the numbers of pained expressions on women's faces and their surrepticious attempts to scratch leg and foot without attracting attention.

Then Caro explained that Bernhardt's latest preoccupations are a variety of ideas he's discussing with people from the games industry about the whole 'Gaming with Attitudes' movement, which Dani recalled she'd already mentioned at their first meeting.

In Caro's version of events, even as a student, before he arrived in Berlin for a job at Bayer's predecessor Schering, Bernhardt had dabbled in the synthesis of psychotropic drugs, partly because he was at University in Basel, the city where Dr. Hoffman had been the first to get high on self-administered LSD at Sandoz and partly because it was one of the things he was good at and partly because he was paid a lot for his efforts. Caro told them he also thoroughly enjoyed mind-bending hallucinations and still does, sometimes for weeks on end. He's been made Timothy Leary Retro-Professor of PharmaFun at a newly founded private online university, which is supposedly in New Caledonia, but doesn't have a campus, just a mind-space, some labs and a string of bank accounts in multifarious currencies, a true work of the imagination, as Bernhardt described it. He's proud of a lecture he gave for them online covering the theme of 'recreativity', combining recreation and creativity in world of passive experience. New minds, new mindspace, what else could be more satisfying? Bernhardt blows minds like Venetians blow glass.

Maria sighs as though this is the kind of biography she's heard a dozen times before, though this isn't the case at all. Very few people in the world have built their success on the kind of self-destructive recklessness that Bernhardt manages to embody. His notion of recreativity is only the latest selfish exploration of extreme individualism. That said, Maria could do with a bit of recreativity herself. In this perpetual search for new and confusing terminology she wonders whether sex will end up being branded, as repro-recreativity.

She and her husband work much too hard, if she's honest with herself and children wear you out. At that level, for some of the time, at least, thanks to Bernhardt's generosity, this trip is going to be a present to herself. Recreativity, procreativity, distraction, or something similar including a recreative hiatus, as people are starting to claim, instead of saying they're having a little rest.

Since Bernhardt's reputation as a hyper-committed immersive user-developer precedes him, Caro claimed there have always been a steady flow of requests for him to come up with new and not yet illegal highs for the eager cohorts of users and addicts, or his most loyal acolytes - the dealers. Doctors and other medics had been early adopters back in the old millenium, then the whole rave culture flattered by imitating his lead. There had never been a parade like the Love Parade, before, or since, half a million strong, an acid house Woodstock on the streets of Berlin for the techno and ecstasy generation. Now the gamers have come to call.

We need dope!

Hardly a surprise.

Every succeeding generation needs to convince themselves they've invented amphetamines and opiates, when generally speaking it was chemists working for the pharma concern Merck.

As well as medicine, Bernhardt has done government, car-makers, airlines, even banks, some of the military, so interest from the games industry was almost inevitable, she suggests. Bernhardt is a great cycling fan too and always tries to be at the George V in Paris for the final day of the Tour de France. He is reassuringly expensive.

Dani is impressed.

Bernhardt proffers ideas willingly without going so far as to put them into action. There's nothing illegal about ideas. His entanglement with the games business had begun in a hotel bar in Baden Baden. In urgent need of a fresh squeeze, he'd been people watching, as well as looking for someone to seduce, when he had a fairly simple idea that the gaming industry people have said they like.

Do drugs and games mix?

Of course they do.

In Bernhardt's vision for the world, they are inseperable, in the long term inevitable and in the short term so illegal as to be impossible.

The trip to Miami was so they can meet a lawyer, he'd said. He hadn't just meant you, she explained, nodding to Maria. He called you 'the babe from Fuller Laing'.

Caro had been disappointed. Her finances and things like honey and patents for designer drugs were what this was to be about then, which is boring, though she does remember to say it was a pleasure to meet Maria and Lee for the first time and of course their children, who were charming and unforgettable.

"Though, I admit that I freaked when the older girl showed me that video of the three of them at weapons training. The AK-47 looked huge in the hands of such a little girl and the Uzi fired such a lot of rounds in such a short time."

"That is the whole principle of splatter," Maria reminded her and took another appreciative slug of the wine. She's relaxing. Soon she'll be relapsing, comatose. It is three thirty in the afternoon.

Bernhardt, Caro continues, had no intention of letting her get roped into the gaming thing. It is lucrative bullshit, that's all and he hardly thinks about it. They need privacy, a space to work without interruptions, or concerns like being raided, a place beyond borders and bureaucracy where they can experiment. By the time it looks like being marketed, Bernhardt will have cashed out, moved on and broken off contact.

There's nothing at all she can do about her dear old Dad and his machinations. If Bernhardt aspires to unpick the fabric of the universe, that is just fine by Caro, so long as there's no chance of him succeeding outside the monitor of a computer game.

At the time Caro hoped this would be enough to keep Bernhardt happy, convincing him that all her links to Klaus' failures were about to be well and truly buried. Now she's re-telling the story, she hopes it's enough to put Maria on the defensive and Dani at her ease.

Caro has never minded a bit of luxury; so long as Bernhardt's paying and she hadn't been to Miami for ages.

He's assured her the lawyer is someone she can trust and at his request is due to prepare a report about some of the mess Klaus has left behind him, with some recommendations about how best to clear things up. Caro is there to help clarify some of the detail. That's all, he said, which seemed like a bit of an understatement.

"The thing was, you weren't the first lawyer on our itinerary. Before we got to your place, there was another meeting, 'Morgan, Witherspoon and Blenheim'.

"Can't say I'm surprised, they specialise in setting up offshore companies, good work, perfected tax arrangements in the finest detail. Not my line of work at all."

They had met Mal 'Big Mitch' Mitchel on the terrace of a many starred hotel overlooking the Atlantic. Seven hundred rooms, six restaurants, eighteen bars and enough swimming pools to train the US team for the Olympics. The alligators are kept at bay by stun gun wielding 'environmental controllers', but the sharks dress in cashmere and silk to come and go as they please. A thirtysomething couple are having a row a few tables away, but the noise soon died down, then the man stormed out in a huff.

Bernhardt found the scene hilarious, which Caro and the lawyer found embarrassing.

"We need to clear the decks. There are things that only you can interpret," explained her Dad for the lawyer's benefit, "Klaus did have some peculiar habits, as everyone is aware." Bernhardt shrugged, "there, I've said it", for Caro's benefit.

Then the lawyer took over and Caro began her answers. "The guy wanted to know about Klaus' early days and he seemed quite happy with what I had to say. I think they were trying to work out whether Klaus had been set up by someone needing money laundering via property in Berlin. Oligarchs and sharks, you know the kind of thing, Russians, Arabs, Chinese, Malaysian gamblers? Predators in general. It's a reasonable question. There are plenty of options."

After an hour of discussions they took a break, then Mitchel took his leave. Dani and Bernhardt were alone and just had a drink together, recalling some of Klaus' successes.

An hour later they were on their way to see Maria.

"Actually, I had assumed the first lawyer was your boss, then it was obvious you had no idea where we'd been and he'd failed to mention 'Fuller Laing' at all with the Mitchel man, so I realised my Dad was doing his best to keep you both in the dark. He's always been extremely annoying like that, even over trivialities. But we got to meet Lee and your children and thoroughly enjoyed that super dinner, so it was all very lovely. Great evening. Everyone had a good time, Bernhardt included."

For Maria's benefit, Caro recalls the precarious situation Klaus created for her. "I don't know what else anyone might expect to find," she says.

She and Klaus met in Berlin and that was where they'd built their careers, 23 years of it should anyone forget and half of the time married. She still lives in the apartment they once shared. I mean, what's mine is mine, right? He'd taken what he considered his, when she'd thrown him out.

The dark green BMW sports had been a joint decision, though it had always been registered in her name. Most of the paintings are by local artists and wouldn't bring a lot at auction, nor would the carpets, though they'd cost the earth to have fitted. I've never spent more than ten thousand on a painting and even then most of the stuff we bought was so the artists could carry on qualifying for their health insurance and pension contributions.

All the seriously bad art ended up being packaged with the apartments Klaus sold, syphoned into hotel corridors. He was a major supporter of the arts, when you think about it. His acquisitions drove the local art market. There's nothing encourages higher prices than rows of little red dots next to paintings at exhibition openings. The Malo Twins and Hector Malwitz owed their success to his purchasing power, not to mention Monika Nulle, the big 'O' no, no talent and no underwear that one, though I suppose she should count as one of my oldest friends, nowadays.

No, there was no good reason for Caro to have sanitised Klaus' affairs.

The Merc had gone with him when he went.

The Cessna had been leased anyway, so it didn't count and the old catamaran had sprung yet another leak and sank with all hands somewhere south of Suez.

The house in Potsdam had been a mistake from the word go, so it was no loss and went straight to the creditors.

Klaus' office in Walter-Benjamin-Platz was over-run by the insolvency people, emptied and locked up right away.

He turned his back on them too.

"I was astonished," Caro tells Maria, "when you started talking about these business interests in the US, the companies in Texas. We split up a couple of years before he died. He'd obviously been spreading his wings. I didn't even know there'd been a 'West African' thing, whatever that was supposed to mean."

Dani sits and sips. She isn't taking notes, but she's doing her best to remember the details.

"Happily, I can set your mind at rest at one level," says Maria. "There's no implicit, immediate, or present danger. When you told me you were coming, I asked around and mentioned Klaus' name, but no-one knows of anything we can't solve fairly easily. A Frenchman has been advised to forget some claim he was thinking of pursuing in Cairo, not worth the bother and the Russians have said they never did business with him anyway, which is a convenient lie that everyone has agreed to accept as the official history. The same goes for Ireland, though it's trickier to deny. The videos of Klaus in Moscow are all now officially designated as fake and the authorities have been informed they were actually recorded in Berlin, somewhere called Karlshorst, if I recall, by renegade former members of the KGB. Please don't ask me whether I believe everything I'm told. I have to work with the information I'm provided with. Lawyers have no alternative, we have to work with what we're given. We only challenge inconsistencies."

Maria pauses apologetically, as if asking them to be patient.

Dani listens with some admiration to the increasingly elaborate explanation

"I was also told there were also errors in the passport tracking system that needed correcting, which have now been completed. This required the payment of a variety of fees in several currencies, including Iranian 'rials' and Saudi 'riyals'. Most of Klaus' international associates are profoundly amnesic and after certain payments were confirmed we have written guarantees that that is a permanently incurable condition, call it the bureaucratic equivalent of dementia, take the money, file, shred and forget. Now we have social media, the notion of a paper trail is becoming redundant. So the official position is that you can relax. No-one is looking for trouble. We can do a little smoothing in the archives. In a couple of years it will be as though Klaus never even visited the States, or Mexico. I think we can safely assume that Belize and El Salvador have never heard of the guy. You aren't interested in the house, I suppose."

"House?" asks Caro, bewildered.

"It isn't really a house, as such. He owned a two thousand dollar shack on the Bahia California. It gets used by illegals and the drug mules. My advice is to keep well clear."

"Two thousand, not two hundred thousand?"

"No, two thousand, seven feet by ten, about two metres by three, no water apart from a few bottles, minimal power, just a garden shed on the outside with enough space to hide half a tonne of cocaine securely and keep six people dry in a rainstorm. If they aren't good friends when the rain starts, they will be by the time it stops, either that, or dead.

Inside, the design is based on a restaurant cold store, an entry code on the door and some armour plating, solar panels for the roof. Enough battery to charge a laptop, or boil a kettle. The downside is a snake problem. They curl up where you can't see them, then rush at you when the door is opened. Lethal venom and all that. One bite down Mexico way and you're out. They're solitary beasts, neurotic and easily provoked."

"OK, then we'll forget it. Why on earth did he buy it?"

"Whale watching, it overlooks a bay, he wanted to put a camera in there and stream 24/7. That's what he told me. Alternatively, he was trying to get illegal migrants over the border from Mexico, a little freebooting on the mistaken basis that the border guys will overlook

119

a foreigner's sins. Maybe he was dealing in cocaine. I didn't ask, nor should you. There was one regular visitor from Acapulco, who would turn up, get stoned and watch whales for a day or two, then go home, but she was an exception, a games designer, known as the girl with green eyes."

"Oh, you mean Celestine, brilliant mind that one," said Caro quickly, hoping to avert more unwanted detail of Klaus' affairs.

"You know her?"

"Of course, she's from Strasbourg, worked for Siemens, Microsoft, then went freelance, taught at the Technical University in Hamburg for a couple of years. We used to go to the same dance classes. She and Klaus always flirted, even when he and I were still together. She has bone structure where most of us have curves. Built like a dog kennel, a bone in every corner."

"That's the one," confirmed Maria. "Angular momentum, if you follow me. Celestine assumed she could charm the snakes. She tends be naïve about the real world, which could explain her skills with code."

"Men adore her, she likes to romanticise whales, small furry animals and other cuddly endangered species," says Caro for effect. "She almost believed me when I said pandas only used bamboo as a toothpick, once they've finished off their favourite dinner of fresh kittens. She was almost at the point of sending letters of protest to the Chinese for misleading humanity." Dani is forced to smile at the thought of pandas placidly getting their jaws around cuddly little cats, then getting bits of fur caught between their teeth after biting their heads off. Then she remembers she's heard the joke before. How many more times is she going to have to hear it before the novelty wears off.

"I read, there's a poor bloody panda in the Berlin Zoo which spends all it's time walking backwards. What do you make of that?" said Maria.

"Typische Berlin, sounds as though it has been traumatised," answers Caro.

While Maria and Caro swap details of the games designer, Dani has realised there are another two mongolian style kites flying over one of the buildings opposite. One blue, one red and purple. Berlin is susceptible to fads. Either that or someone is praying rather than playing, though they could be practising a very slow version of semaphore.

Maria needs Caro to sign some papers relating to a project Klaus had started, but never finished in Tennessee. Caro's name had been included in the project documentation, which had been drawn up when the were still married. He'd never mentioned being interested in Tennessee, or the oil and gas industry.

The US tax people, the celebrated IRS knew all about it however, and there was a bill to be paid, which had been done by the people Maria had arranged for it to be sold it to. There will also be some cash for Caro, she explains, though not yet.

She's been given a key that will fit a safe deposit box somewhere, which she passes to Caro. Maria also says there will be a postcard of the Acropolis signed by Klaus which will delivered in the post once the deals are complete and will inform her where to find the lock that the key will fit. All she must do is sign the documents and be patient. She doesn't have a choice. Caro suspects she may be being cheated out of a pot of gold, but who could say? It all sounds completely implausible, but one thing is certain, the landscape of Klaus' business deals is being gently reworked until it will be impossible to recognise for what it was. First his businesses were painstakingly weeded, now he's being raked over, like a molehill in the middle of a well-tended lawn. It won't take long before he's completely ploughed into history.

The USA is another country and sometimes it's better not to pry.

So what if Bernhardt had seemed to have commissioned two different lawyers to do more or less the same job – Maria from Fuller Laing and the man who called himself Malcolm Mitchel at 'Morgan Witherspoon'. Isn't that his business? No-one is going to stop him.

Before they leave town, there'd been meetings with one of the accountants from 'Paltrey, Peacock, Würzelmann'.

Caro never challenges the way Bernhardt handles his money.

The three women got on well enough, but soon the light lunch and the white wine tipped Maria from attentive to comatose as the jet-lag kicked in and they had more or less to carry her back to the hotel.

Then they put her to bed.

The hotel staff are asked to let her sleep for ten hours, then to take her a light breakfast so she can reorientate gently and acclimatise. Once she's had something to drink and a nibble to eat, she should go back to bed again and enjoy some more sleep, by which time it should be seven or eight o'clock the following morning and she should be refreshed.

Caro left a note asking her to call when she eventually wakes up.

She tells Dani to go home and they agree to meet the following day. "I'll pick you up outside your door at ten." Caro wants to have an excuse to check out the site of the by now infamous bus crash.

That night, all over Germany, there are election meetings attended mainly by old people and candidates, who want to talk about money and migration, crime and terrorism, but in every Berlin building people are playing online games in preference to reality.

More than seven hundred thousand are logged in to the main gaming platforms simultaneously and a couple of million batteries are on charge as the rest are asleep. The late night decline in power consumption is a thing of the past as laptops, chargers, routers and servers soak up millions of kilowatt hours of power.

Soon enough, they're due to be joined by hundreds of thousands of electric cars and lorries plugged in for overnight charging. A million tonnes of petrol and diesel fuel a week might seem manageable for now, but where is all the power to come from that is supposed to take the place of even half of that?

By the time Maria awakes next morning, none of the politicians are going to be any closer to an answer to that question, for which the only reply right now can be 'don't know and we aren't going to find out any day soon'. That is a simple truth for a greedy society, that fails to recognise its own voraciousness.

The election looks like missing the point, as the politicians fail to understand how the world is changing and turn to arguments of hate as a bankrupt substitute for thought.

It's what they call regression, but at nine fifteen, in the evening just for once, Frau Hedwig Trautmann called Caro, who confirmed she is busy. "Fuck my knee," says the woman, "Fick mich am knee".

"Fuck you too, dearie," says Caro and never call this number ever again.

Chapter 8

They're going north up the Leibnizstrasse, the sky grey, the road dry, before it turns into Cauerstrasse, past the BundesBank Euro Co-ordination Centre, towards the 'Network Check' data centre.

There's not a lot of traffic. Further along a bridge has a weight restriction, so the heavier lorries take the long way round.

Caro is driving a little hybred Lexus, a pleasantly quiet unadventurous car she's picked up from the hire firm on Kaiser-Friedrichstrasse.

Dani is in the passenger seat amusing herself by watching the charge level of the batteries rise and fall as they play stop/go from one set of lights to the next. She is patiently awaiting the next turn of events. Dani assumes the green BMW has lost its place in Caro's affections, though actually it's in the garage having a part replaced with expensive dedication to technical excellence. Before they finish the overhaul, the mechanics are bound to discover other components that need attention, of that Caro can be sure, something wrong with the suspension, brakes, the soft top mechanism and an issue with the software. Maybe it will need a re-spray, though no-one will be sure the reason why.

"Did you mean any of that stuff about your Dad worrying about the two of you being assassinated?" Dani asked Caro.

"No," she lied.

"Then why did you say it?"

"I had to tell the bloody woman something. She isn't here because of Klaus, you know, or safety deposit boxes with mysterious little keys and postcards in the post."

"So your Dad was talking complete and utter nonsense."

"Not for the first time, so was she," said Caro sincerely.

"How long is it since you talked to him?"

"A couple of days, why?"

"Did he say anything about Maria?"

"Not directly. What would you expect him to say?"

"He might have given you a few clues about why she's here."

"I wouldn't necessarily believe him, if he tried. He knows that."

"Maybe next time you should ask."

"I can't believe a word I'm told. Why do you think I need you?"

Dani expects they'd end up at the Soph-Am, but instead of turning left, Caro drove through the Otto-Suhr Allee junction and for the moment they seem to be heading in the direction of dull grey Moabit, an indeterminate district to the north of the Tiergarten, beyond the railway that stretches across the city east and west, linking Paris and Amsterdam with Warsaw, Minsk and Moscow, but not a lot in between.

"Then what is she doing?"

"I suspect Maria has told us less than the truth."

"I have checked her credentials, you know that. She's well qualified, busy, works with some expensive colleagues in a thriving partnership at 'Fuller Laing'. Her career is flourishing. She has it all, the job, the family, the respected colleagues, the whole rigmarole. Having said she's very good, the people I asked seemed a bit nervous about discussing her. They take her seriously. She has influence. Judges listen to her arguments and take notice. She writes articles for the regional law journal about state law and legal precedences. I was left wondering if she's connected, you know, 'connected', Mafia, Goodfellas, Martin Scorcese, Sopranos. They all love top class lawyers."

"Your Dad seems to have a special knack when it comes to choosing people to work with."

"You should have seen the people he had in Romania, oof! Everyone was relieved when that was over. Solar power for mountainous countries."

"What?"

"People in isolated valleys spend huge amounts on generators, or power lines. Bernhardt's team came up with a cheap alternative."

"Sounds good."

"It was. Then the other stuff messed it all up."

Caro doesn't elaborate, but drives slowly into an area dominated by brand new apartment houses. This used to be an industrial zone, now it's a place where people buy property without bothering to ask themselves why there are so few local amenities, no shops, no schools, no public transport. Sooner or later there'll be a shopping mall close at hand, but that's the last thing people need to build a community. For years, now, the city administrators have been all too eager to sell off land with permission to build expensive apartments as a way of staving off a little local Greek style economic crisis.

There's something incomplete here; creepy, an investor made wasteland of squared off architecture and anonymous plate glass windows, typische Berlin. If there is any kind of a community it consists of people who depend on internet delivery services for everything and more. There are too few boats on the water. The car parks are empty. A lot of the finished buildings are unoccupied, but semi-furnished, as though there might be people who live there, but they've yet to show themselves out of doors. It feels like anywhere except Berlin, the city it is and it isn't both at the same time.

Caro parks close to the canalside waterfront and shows Dani inside.

"I don't live here, but it's useful to have a fall back. No pain, no packdrill, no communications, no network. If you want to use your phone, go on the balcony. These rooms are Faraday cages, no radio waves. Only the elite are offline nowadays. Privacy is invaluable. 'Network Check' gave this place a grade A seclusion rating. I've added a few little tricks of my own."

Once inside, the apartment is small, anthracite and full of greys with sterile hints of beige, a picture of hard-edge monochrome discretion. Modern, well equipped, a perfectly formed cold blooded machine for living. A couple of grey sofas and geometric patterned monochrome rugs. Corbusier had won and lost.

"Get yourself a drink. Give me a minute or two."

She has gone to change.

Dani checks her mobile, no signal, no wi-fi, no connection with anything beyond the four walls of the room they're in. There are papers strewn on a desk. A lot of them are on La Touche Mandeville headed notepaper, whoever La Touche Mandeville might be. Management consultants Dani thinks, but isn't 100% certain, maybe auditors, maybe debt collectors. Maybe one of Caro's clients.

She pours herself a beer and glances at the documents without touching any of them. No-one has yet created a convincingly grey drink that would blend in with the furniture and the paperwork. Bramble egg-nog anyone? She'll mention this in the Soph-Am, see if Uli can come up with something drinkable in shades of carbon black that doesn't taste of squid with milk. The beer is cool, clear and amber, bitter clean on the tongue.

"I don't have any secrets," says Caro as she reappears, "read whatever you like, even the electricity bill can say something about someone, I suppose. La Touche Mandeville have been keeping track of the wreckage that Klaus left behind and tidying things up, as required for the insolvency people. They keep me up to date. They've denied all knowledge of Maria and friends. If you want some entertainment, take a look. I didn't know whether to laugh or cry when I saw the final trail of fiscal disaster. There will just be enough left over to pay their fees and some of the tax."

They flop on the sofas, almost relaxed.

"Well that's what I was wondering about. You see, I think we can agree that although the lovely lawyer Maria is here on your Dad Bernhardt's instigation, I doubt whether she is representing his interests alone. I suspect she's serving more than one master."

"What the fuck are you trying to say Caro? Would you mind telling me?" They've been circling around the theme for hours, without getting to the point.

"My worry is this. Why should this lawyer woman be at all interested in coming to a foreign country to explore the circumstances following the demise of someone with whom no-one in her circle of contacts, colleagues and acquaintances has any interest whatsoever? Particularly, when there are well established firms of professionals and the public prosecutors already poring over each and every little detail." "That being the case, Caro, it could be personal."

"Tell."

"What was it she said, that she didn't believe the reasons she's been told for being here. While she's about it, maybe she's assuming that your father's liabilities include you or whatever, or people, or organisations unknown to which she is probably not a party to, but requires both you, him and the dearly departed Klaus to be of no danger or threat what-so-ever. And if he's so keen on 'gaming with attitudes', what about that lot?"

"That is one too many whatevers and what-so-evers to make sense."

"Maybe."

"Caro, you can certainly forget about the gaming people, games with attitude, all that. The games industry uses money, decisively. They decide what they need and if you've done your work and you have what they want and it would be expensive, or time consuming to re-invent, clone, or copy, they'll buy licences, give you the cash and tell you politely to fuck off. They don't do personality tests on their suppliers. They check code for bugs and spelling errors. Oh shit, could this be your mother's doing, getting her revenge in on Bernhardt by attacking you via Maria?"

"My Mother, Erda is a fantasist of an intuitive persuasion. She offers praise and condemnation without recourse to evidence, but she doesn't mess about like that. She dreams knowledge."

"I thought you said she was a cabinet maker."

"Sure, that too. She makes decorative boxes and small items of furniture. Actually, she is an exacting obsessive perfectionist. Her boxes are very much in demand. She drives people crazy. You should see her trying to decide which piece of wood should be used for what."

"If you say so."

"I do," says Caro, "We should be thankful she doesn't make bows and arrows. Take a look at me, then take a look at that."

"What is it?"

"A catalogue. Her stuff. Strange seats and unusual cupboards. Repositories, boxes that is."

"What do you mean by repositories?"

"Before she makes anything, she will talk to the person who going to buy it and find out what it is they will want to keep in the box. Then she will design and make it."

"Is that really so unusual?"

Caro opens the balcony door and steps outside to smoke a cigarette. Dani follows and sort of admires the view along the old canal, which so far as it goes is moderately pleasant. She suprised how deeply Caro inhales and obviously relishes the tobacco.

"Unusual? I suppose so, nowadays, but for centuries people lavished great wealth on boxes for their jewels and treasures – reliquaries, ossiaries, shrines. Rock crystal boxes for splinters from the holy cross. And twenty or thirty years ago there was a shamanistic feminist fashion for making boxes among the women like her who became artists. Some of them were votive offerings, others little more than introspection, the products of creative self-indulgence. She continued to develop when so many moved on. You could call her a fetishist. She also provokes. She did pill-boxes for designer drugs, when she and Dad were young. Last Christmas, she sent Donald Trump a solid block of wood with a tightly fitting lid labelled 'Donnie's Brain Box'."

"That wasn't very chivalrous."

"It certainly was not. He sent her a thank-you note, as Presidents do. Anyway you can rid your mind of her. She only plays the kind of games where she gets to be god. Mothering was beneath her. They left me to fend for myself from the age of six, except when my Dad wanted to get me high. I expect she'll start on coffins soon."

Dani can imagine the sales pitch for this woman to her oldest friends – hi darling, we've known each other for almost half a century, so how about commissioning a bijoux coffin for the day of the dead that's on its way to you soon. Happy Death Day!

A small boat has been chugging along the canal, as the women are talking. A simple little cruiser with a small cabin and a bit of deck front and aft, a couple of outboard motors, typical for Sunday afternoons on the lakes around Berlin or cruising the German rivers and canals, going fairly slowly, leisurely, no rush.

There are three people on board.

Then there are only two.

"Fuck! Did you see that?!" says Dani.

"I did," says Caro.

"They just...."

"Fuck, they did..."

"What should we do?"

"No comment."

"I mean she just hit him over the head with an oar and pushed him into the water."

"It certainly looked that way."

"He went under, plop, like a brick, straight down. "

"He's gone, and he's not coming back up."

"Do you think someone will ring the police?"

"Good question. Can you see where he is?"

"No."

"He's gone straight to the bottom. Murky waters. Bottom feeder food."

"Shit."

"The boat has turned onto to the main canal."

"Did you see what it was called?"

"No, did you?"

"No, did you notice the registration number?"

"No, I forgot to look."

"Me too. So what do we tell the police? Was the boat German?"

"I don't know. They've gone. Not even a ripple. Do you think the police would believe us if we told them what happened?"

"Only if someone else also called them with the same story, or once the body floats to the surface and they start asking questions of their own accord."

"If someone else is going to call, then we could keep ourselves out of this."

"I have no desire to become entangled as a witness in a murder enquiry."

"Me neither."

"OK, another beer?"

"Sure, hell yes. You could pour me a glass of that calvados too."

"Settle your nerves."

"Something like that. Jesus, she just hit him and that was it, incredible."

"I wonder who it was."

"You didn't recognise them, did you? I certainly didn't."

"No. Do you think we saw what we think we saw?"

"I'm not sure. There's nothing to see there now."

"Maybe we were mistaken, an illusion, a misleading impression."

"Easy to confuse ourselves over nothing at all. But we both saw it, both at the same time, from the same place."

"I think we've enough to think about already, without getting involved in other people's problems. Maybe it was a trick of the light. The worst thing about Berlin criminals is their stupidity. They're probably feeling quite pleased with themselves. Lots of people get killed around here without anyone noticing, it's sort of the way the city works."

"There was a splash, that much I saw, but I don't know, the rest?"

The two women turn away from the window and shut the balcony door, agreeing to concentrate on the matter at hand rather than explore the serendipities of sudden death.

"Anyway, you needn't bother yourself about my Mother, I'll do the worrying about that set of scenarios."

"If you say so."

"You know something?"

"What?"

"Bang, splash, gone. Two seconds, beginning to end. A great way of killing someone."

"That's probably true, so long as there aren't any witnesses. It's certainly fast, but is it anonymous?"

"Or security cameras."

"That's it."

"What is?"

"If there really was a murder then the security company will pick it up via their cameras and send a report via the insurance companies. If they missed something like that, there'd be trouble."

"So we needn't concern ourselves."

"Correct, if anyone ever asks you didn't notice anything, ask which day they're talking about, when, all those kinds of I don't know answers, unless they have us on video, in which case what, I would say neither of us noticed anything, I certainly didn't, and you didn't did you, no, nope, nothing.? " "No, nothing at all, no.."

"Ok. That's settled, we didn't see anything.

"But it's neat. So fast, so little mess. Moveable feast stuff, an off chance, a happy accident if you're the killer. You have to admit, it's a neat trick if you can manage it."

"Like that traffic accident. You're going to get a reputation as a useless witness."

"And if there wasn't a camera?"

"Maybe someone else will come forward."

"Sooner or later the corpse will surface, but where, could be miles away before being found. Then there will probably be a recording showing three people getting onto a boat and another one showing two people getting off and that will be that, throw in some data, gps, mobile, QED, all over. Search, arrest, trial, prison. If Maria's husband turns up, it's a topic of conversation. We can pick his brain about opportunist assassins."

Dani thought for a moment, "Alibi's must be getting much harder to rig up nowadays. Not so long ago, I expect all you needed was an old lady to agree you'd been at her place having coffee and cakes and so long as she wasn't actually suffering from dementia, you were covered. But with mobiles, gps, security cameras, well, they can tell where you've been, or at least where your phone was."

"I think that was one of the reasons for going to Cuba. We were where we were, beyond any doubt. Plane ticket, passports, hotel bills, surveillance cameras, checked in checked out, online stuff, text messages, phone calls, eye witnesses. They knew we were there, but once we got there it wasn't so precise. Was my Dad there, asks the inquisitor. Yes, yes, yes, says the torture victim. Usually Bernhardt could be on another planet, so far as anyone can tell, Spanish speaking cops in particular. Bernhardt speaks Spanish like a goose on hot coals."

"But why? Couldn't the trip simply have been a holiday?"

"In most ways it was."

"So stop pretending it wasn't, Caro. You had a good time holidaying with your Dad, admit it, end of story. I'm beginning to think we've been spending too much time talking about your father, your mother, your dead Ex, whatshername the lawyer and not enough about you and what you are actually trying to do with your life. Why do you expect me to be interested in what is happening around you, rather than what you are up to yourself?"

As she said that Dani admitted to herself that the question she really wanted to ask was why this woman was lying to her. Revenge in first was the phrase that came to mind. Could be that having established that no-one is gunning for her, this errant Father has decided to set someone onto her himself. Had anything suspicious happened in Berlin while they were away? Everything is sufficiently improbable already. She sets her doubts aside. Dani's main concern is to get paid.

"So, why are we here?" Dani asks.

"I think someone wants to know whether I am an emerging threat, or just a reminder of things past, a woman without qualities. I would like to know who they are and what they imagine might be dangerous. Before we meet Little Miss Lawyer again, I want you to take a look at this," she says, popping a memory stick into the tv and selecting one of the video files to play.

The pictures are nice crisp high definition stuff, probably from a mobile, or a Go Pro.

"This was in Cuba, before we went to Miami. The big guy who looks like a guppy with a grin is my Dad. He enjoys watching kids having fun and this was a games convention so all the youngsters were having a great time watching their idols play each other. It wasn't a big meeting, just two or three hundred youngsters, but they were all kind of elite players according to their own way of rating each other."

Dani takes a good look at the way the old man was glancing from one part of the room to another. He'd been on the lookout for someone, not taking a look at the crowd. "Are they one of your sub-culture groups," she asks.

"Sure, they think of themselves as a tribe. Clearly, they conform to the mores and expectations they have of one another, so yes, they're anthropologically legit, spoken and unspoken rules, a hierarchy, neo-priesthood, shamanic tendencies and rituals, so right, it's all there. Not a lot of mating and child rearing, but never mind. A lot of them are Canadian, or Finnish, places with dark winters, unsolved mysteries and long cold nights when no-one ventures out of doors, or get to meet each other face to face without the risk of homicide."

"Did you enjoy it as much as your Dad?"

"Probably more, I'm writing an article about them for the Journal of Anthro-Analytics. Big data is a godsend for anthropology. My Dad didn't enjoy himself for long. See these guys?"

"Men in suits. Well turned out women. They're too old to be gamers. Are they the money men, the bankers?"

"No, I don't think so. Maybe one or two, but they were speaking German. They're from Berlin, that's the point."

"And your dad doesn't seem overjoyed to see them. What happened?"

"They went off for a couple of hours and I enjoyed convention watching. When I asked him where they'd been, he just said drinking beer and jawing. Do you recognise any of them?"

"No, I don't know many men like them, not that kind of thirty five-ish, under forty, ambitious and tanned, but old looking for their age. More your kind of client than mine."

"How would you go about identifying them?"

"Ask people. And online facial analysis."

"Without the online bit? 'Network Check' said there was no coverage."

"I could try the police system."

"You watch it through and I'll run off some prints for you. I'm staying here tonight. Will you go to the Soph-Am?"

"Probably."

Once the photos have printed off, Caro gives Dani an envelope with the pictures and another stick with digital versions and some more anonymous stills from the video.

"I'll call a cab."

"Sleep well, Caro darling. I'm on my way. Guilt and responsibility, that's your theme. Let yourself think about it, but don't let it spoil your dreams. The thinking dream, the best sort, a place of delicious contradictions. Sleep well and enjoy! I need a man."

"A good one is hard to find."

"Unless you know where he'll be. Once you know that, the rest is easy, just yes, no, or maybe," says Dani.

Caro doesn't let on how difficult it is for beautiful women to get themselves seduced by men they find attractive, most of their suitors are small, hyper-ambitious nerds loathsomely desperate to prove their manhood. For her, Klaus had been a lucky find. She doesn't expect to hit on another any time soon.

Berlin likes to present itself as an intense and raucous metropolis, but the everyday reality is one of quiet diligence. Germans get more pleasure from saving than spending, so shops tend to be deserted, unless they're offering bargain basement prices and people certainly don't drink the way they used to. In the city centre most people either work in government ministries, or various bits of local administration, apart from the students and University folk who worry more about grades and research funding than bringing revolutionary mayhem to the streets. The last time there was a revolution, it had led first to Helmut Kohl and then to Mrs. Merkel, so there isn't a great deal of enthusiasm for anything bordering on risky. Germany is increasingly unadventurous.

Demonstrations are of course a necessity for the tourist industry and are usually held on Thursday evening between seven and eight thirty near the HackescherMarkt S-bahn station by anarchic radicals, who are always outnumbered by riot police enjoying the overtime. The radical right prefer to hold their gatherings in the provinces where ignorance prevails and they can moan as much as they like. The AfD is a party of moaners, who don't seem to like anyone, or anything at all, not least, each other. The taxi driver talks through that little agenda, but Dani doesn't listen to a word he says.

Once the taxi leaves the motorway for the quiet streets of Charlottenburg and crawls down the Knobelsdorfstrasse, sloping over traffic calming bumps, Dani looks up into the windows of people's apartments, trying to imagine the contrast with Cuba and Miami, which are cities she has never visited. Architecturally, Berlin is a pale imitation of art nouveau Vienna, but it has better modernist buildings from the nineteen twenties if that is cause for celebration. Nevertheless it is a city that is still becoming, so there's a dynamic of sorts, recreating itself again, building on the strange transition some called the fall of Communism to turn into yet another version of itself. This time it's neither socialist, nor particularly democratic. The approach is timid, yet greedy, aesthetic ambitions limited, investors and developers seemingly scared of their own potential to make better decisions. Even the bureaucrats have abdicated their privileged role in decision making and handed it lock, stock and barrel into the hands of speculators and opportunists who don't give a damn about anything, or anyone except their balance sheet. Shits like Klaus. Bubble economy. Dani reminds herself that corruption is implicit in Berlin, whenever it isn't mandatory. Hardly anyone involved in rebuilding the city actually intends to live there, the same story with new companies. Interest rates are less than nothing.

She hopes the Americans tracking Caro and her Dad aren't getting excited about the Berlin start-up scene, which so far as she can tell is more about 'place' marketing than doing and making things that people need.

Just as before, when she was getting out of the cab, a middle aged man in a calf length raincoat emerged from the bar, swept past her and got into the back seat.

Did she know the guy? No, it wasn't PPP, but she'd seen him once before.

Another cashmere loser, foiled again. Somewhere a disappointed play-pal. One a penny, two a penny, like hot cross buns.

Then she remembered his name, Schroeder, that was it, Tim. He had been a 'new economy' accountant with a genetic engineering company specialising in EU research grants and Estonian case studies. They hadn't lasted long. Now Schroeder teaches two afternoons a week at a local college and goes to Conferences the rest of the time, fishing for work. Thankfully, his wife has a steady job in state pensions admin to pay the bills. He prefers game theory to book-keeping, which he has recently discovered is a serious mistake in the real world of lies and lost illusions. No-one in Brussels has done enough work on the econometrics of institutionalised theft and embezzlement to justify paying for his skills, so Tim is a man ahead of his time, whose competences are unmarketable, which impresses no-one, in particular his wife. His marriage has six months to run, before his wife disappears with an Assistant Deputy Head of Department from the Berlin North Job Centre.

When Dani arrives, the Soph-Am is refreshingly gloomy with a welcoming aroma of top quality cannabis and vintage french tobacco scenting the air. Most of the regulars are already there. Play-pals are readying to depart, returning for the most part to their respective spouses, though one or two are heading hotelwards for skin on skin. A petite drunken schoolteacher is grumbling loudly to her boyfriend about the parlous state of Berlin schools. "How the hell am I supposed to teach genetics in a classroom equipped with no more than a blackboard and some sticks of chalk? And come to that, why am I, a historian, teaching classes in biology to begin with? I know more about the conquest of Mexico than I do about bacteria. Scheiss auf die Demokratie." She'd been brought up in the East.

Dani skirts the couple and reaches the bar.

"Hi Phil, hello Nico."

Grunts and smiles, "So so."

"And how are you?" to the blonde, who seems to have more hair than ever, but a shorter skirt than usual. She seems happy.

"Dani, come and tell us an improbable story," she replies and manhandles the blonde hair out of the way from her shoulder to her back. "We have been boring ourselves in your absence!"

"I still can't believe there are people we've met who will vote for the Neo-Nazi's. In this country, after everything that happened and they want to have another go. It beggars belief."

"Have you noticed," prompts Nico, "That almost everyone who is still here are the victims of broken marriages and thwarted romances, even the mirages of late flowering love. Just think how many of us have attempted to find a place in one anothers' affections to be met with abject failure, faded dreams and end up here once more staring at one of Uli's late night cocktails."

"Says more about you than me. Have you seen Lukas?"

"Which one?"

"Winkler, Lukas Winkler."

"The polyp?"

"The same. Polyp, polenta, policeman, Kripo Kommissar, yes."

"Our Chief Inspector Winkler gets in later at the moment. They've changed the shift system at Kaiserdamm."

'Abschschnitt 24' on Kaiserdamm is one of the oldest surviving police stations in Berlin, a big building opposite the Commerzbank with heavy steel shutters to cover the windows and a firewatcher's turret on the roof.

Originally it had been used as a holding pen for prisoners on remand, as well as being a local police station.

Winkler can count himself lucky to have an office there and the keys to what had once been a cell. The walls are thick, imperveous to truth and lies alike. His department have pushed him out of the main LKA building in Tempelhof and they don't want him in Ruhleben. The Acting Head of the Landes Kriminale Amt has learned to take a hands off approach with oddballs like Winkler, which means that no-one knows what he does, though he does have a reputation for being effective. He's also polite to the secretaries and the 'ordungsamt', who do parking tickets and the like. Two or three times a years he cries out for all hands on deck and raids an address no-one else has heard of and mops up little bands of criminals that no-one else knows anything about. He has a great nose for turpitude. And he never makes a move unless the evidence is watertight.

A nice guy, but sometimes a genuine bastard of the old school. 'I'm not going to hurt you'. Thump, 'Argh', 'That didn't hurt did it? Not really, not like this will', twist. 'So tell the fucking truth.'

Now Dani needs his help to identify the people on the photographs that Caro printed out, but it looks as though she'll have to wait.

In the interim, she doesn't mind taking a bit of free time to catch up on the local gossip with the actors. Apart from the election and the AfD, the fate of the Volksbühne the People's Theatre in Berlin Mitte is the main topic of conversation. The local politicians have installed a guy to run it who is a kind of cultural showman, who has never worked in theatre. Everyone apart from the politicans recognise this for the absurdity it is and theatre people all over the world are supporting the protests. There are rumours of an occupation. The blonde had thought of sending a message of support, then people begin to have suspicions that the 'occupation' is no more than a prank, so the message went unsent. Apart from that, the Soph-Am contingent are mainly concerned about being paid late, or not at all, by the production companies supplying German TV with its drama.

"Paying bills seems to have become a sign of eccentricity in German culture, right out of fashion, money is... 'out'! Damned like spot!" claims the blonde, "Paying bills in full and on time is interpreted as a sign of weakness and naivety. Our glorious producers are committed to ensuring that you will never make it to become one of the one percent. If only we had proper unions like the US Actors' Guild, Writers' Guild, East Coast, West Coast, they make sure you get your money. Right now I am owed a hundred and thirty thousand Euros and that's only for television. I did two films last year and haven't seen a cent from either of them. Why the hell should I be the one who doesn't get paid? The electricians always seem to get their cash."

She has a point, everyone in the bar agrees. Even Wolf Moeller, nods sagely along with the rest, until Nico turns and asks when he's going to see the seven thousand euros that Wolf has been promising to pay him every week for the last four months for the latest TV thriller, he'd produced. Nico had played a mafia thug and won himself a good review, or two. "When I see the money from Mainz, I promise you, you'll get what you're owed right away."

"Well, have you considered paying my electricity bill, while I wait. I don't like sitting in the dark and the cut off day is looming. You're a fucking leech, Wolfie."

"It can't be that bad, Nico," Wolf says, which is a mistake and Uli suggests they go outside if they're going to have a fight, 'no knives and no cousins', she shouts as they head out of the door. Nico backs off when Wolf goes to the cash machine on the corner and withdraws five hundred euros, gives it to Nico and apologises that it isn't more. He knows he's in the wrong, but he doesn't want to admit that he daren't complain about the late payments in case the tv station stop commissioning work from his company, which would be even worse for everyone.

"The finance department people think they're being clever when they delay paying, but it just means making programmes is no longer fun for anyone. Totally unnecessary, not as if it's their money, not personally, not like my overdraft."

"Too fucking right," confirms Phil, as Wolf orders another round to try and rescue the evening, which looks as if it could get expensive as several more actors walk through the door.

"Phil, Nico, Hello Bombshell, is that a producer I see before me, does he owe me money, does he owe you money, does he owe every fucking body money? Why yes, you useless bastard Wolf. We're drinking champagne, Wolfie, we all are and those who weren't are going to start. It's going on your tab." Then a mutter under breath, 'Got a fucking nerve showing his face here. He must have a new project on,' then loud again, "Are you trawling for talent, Wolfie, or just pimping for some bloody streaming service?"

Dani doesn't get involve in that debate, but she does enjoy the second glass of purple red port Wolf is paying for, then at twenty three minutes to one, Lukas Winkler walks in and asks for a couple of beers. He introduces his companion, who is helping him with his enquiries.

"There is a point in every discussion involving accusations and counter accusations, where protagonists of the more pragmatic tendency recognise that they will get a lot further after a couple of beers and this is the point at which we have arrived. This bloody bulky blonde Dutchman, who is a likeable crook called Tom, works for the police pretending to find the rotters in Rotterdam and we are tightening the noose around a gang of oil smugglers who may or may not be brought to justice depending on our ability to convince the public prosecutors both here and in Holland that we have a chance of presenting the case in a credible state. For now you can call him Tom, but by daylight he's 'Inspector Thomas Cornelius van Dyke' alright?"

"Hello Tom, just don't believe everything this bastard tells you," says Nico, by way of a greeting. "There is champagne on the house, sekt, courtesy of Wolfie here, who is paying for everything tonight, as penance for lassitude in business finance, that is because he pays his fucking bills late, all the time and we're all extremely pissed off with him."

"Fine, I understand, I'll go borrow a hundred thousand from the German TV Producers Savings bank tomorrow," says Wolf without really meaning it, but he does have the good grace to pass both cops a glass of sekt.

"Good idea mate," says Nico, with a hint of if you don't you're fucked.

There is an icy moment of silence. Uli reaches under the bar to check if the old US Army baseball bat is where it should be.

"And just how do you smuggle oil?" asks the blonde, who'd settle for a Getty, though Tom is pleasantly muscled and could be oiled as a distraction. She'd do it herself, for free.

"In lorries, or pipelines, or ships. There's a lot of oil produced illegally and once it's out of the ground, somehow it has to be sold. At some point it gets mixed in with the usual stuff. Sanctions busting, tax evasion and money laundering, funding terrorists. Road tankers heading across Turkey. Recognise the mix?"

"Not personally," says the blonde, "A bit out of my league."

Blonde Tom has made himself the star of the evening and Dani can manage a word or two with Winkler about identifying the men in Caro's pictures. He agrees and takes the envelope. "Nothing electronic, no mail, no texting, no voice, I'll see you here at midday. Now, lets listen to the blaspheming Dutch bastard for a bit of late night stand up."

Winkler isn't staying long, "Are you worried about the AfD getting in?" he asks Dani.

"Yes and no," she says, "It isn't like the 1930's again, is it? Our politicians seem to be in competition to minimise their credibility. I'm more worried about who I can vote for than who I'm against."

"You're not the only one. It's a fucking disaster, you know. I do wish people would wake up and realise how much they're throwing away."

With that he shuffles away to drink with his colleague and leaves Dani with her thoughts. She wonders whether she's interested in the Dutchman and decides not. He's large though, which is a start. The Blonde is being attentive. She can snaffle him if she wants.

Georg is due back soon with the latest vintage of antipodean and latin tipples so Dani will wait till then. She finds a table where she can sit and have a quiet think, then another of the regular late night drinkers wanders in and heads in her direction, then veers off towards the toilets after a vague wave, Paolo the Portuguese baker, who'll drink five beers then head for the Breadbasket bakery and get down to work on next morning's loaves. Winkler wanders past her on his way to the toilet. One after another, all the men seem to have realised they need to pee. Blokes are curiously predictable.

Dani finds herself drinking with one of the doctors, who have their

140

consulting rooms on the second floor. He complains of bad dreams, can't sleep, terrible fantasies of being wrapped in mucus membranes, soaked in blood and gasping for breath.

"You're a mess, Sayeed. Stop drinking, take a holiday. Cut out the dope. You need a break. Let Dr. Hahn look after the sick and afflicted. She still likes her job. And she doesn't hate the patients yet, not deep down, not the way you do."

Sometimes Dani gives people good advice, though usually it gets ignored, which is the case this time.

After twenty minutes Sayeed wanders off, claiming he needs to take the dog for a walk. The dog might not thank him for being woken up at this time in the morning, it isn't the nocturnal type, but any walk is better than no walk, so the two of them will snuffle around the Leitzensee Park, before Sayeed realises he only has three hours before he's due at work once more to face a fresh barrage of lame and infectious supplicants. He decides to kill himself, then changes his mind, since it wouldn't be fair on the dog, who will be expecting some dinner before settling down again after the walk. At least they have a tennis ball with them, so the dog can have a little bit of fun and might with luck, cheer Sayeed up. The ducks complain about being woken up.

By three o'clock in the morning, most people have gone and Dani is left talking to Lukas Winkler, who had seemed relieved when the Dutchman went home with the blonde actress.

"Not an adulterer in sight," says Dani, "Are you really chasing oil smugglers?"

"Sure. Tom takes these things very seriously and he's thorough."

"Will you catch them?"

"Don't be silly. Our main goal is to frighten a few people enough so they think twice about doing it again. Tax investigations, mainly. The UN like the statistics. Always an effective deterrance for ambitious politicians if the UN have you marked down as trouble before you've made it. For every three investigations, seven other shits involved in the same scam will decide to call it a day. Highly effective. But it isn't just the tax. Tom's bosses are getting political pressure. Ministries want to make sure there's no terrorist funded oil coming through our refineries into everyman's petrol tank."

"And what are your chances?"

"As usual we have to find someone who's ready to point the finger. The chemical analysis doesn't help, not with cargoes blended from a dozen different oilfields. One percent doesn't sound very much, but if they've a thousand tonnes per ship, that's seven thousand barrels at fifty dollars the barrel, not nothing, buys you a lot of Kalashnikovs, or pays off the families of a couple of suicide bombers. Tom likes us to try building a chain of credible accusations and see how far up the hierarchy it takes us. How much of that port wine have you drunk?"

"Less than a bottle," Dani answers.

"But more than half a bottle, time to stop."

"Probably, I'll have a coffee."

"I had a little glance at the photos you gave me.

"And?"

"I recognised two of them from memory, the others will have to wait till morning. The woman in the red dress is a Head of Department for the City Planning Department, Fr. Dr. Gudrun Pöll and the man in the blue shirt next to her is Professor Doctor Florian Schwarz, her counterpart from the Economic Development Bank. It would be unfair to describe them as 'partners in crime', because they're both public employees. He's known as 'Flo', she as 'Polly'. Where one is to be found, the other is sure to go, they're known collectively as Polyflo. Brussels, the Government Ministries here in Berlin, London banks, Abu Dhabi, Dohar, Dubai, Qatar, Saudi and sundry conferences all over the world. Where were the pictures taken?"

"Hotel resort, can't confirm the exact whereabouts. They are recent."

"And the other woman is from Brussels, EU, originally Bulgarian, or Romanian, yeah Romania. She's another development economist. Clever woman. Head of Department, lot of leverage. Friend of more than one Commissioner and a lot of far right Party leaders."

"I'm not sure I believe the stories I'm being told at the moment."

"Probably sensible. Don't you want to go to bed?"

"Yes, but not with you."

"Just a thought."

"Yes, nice of you, Lukie. I'll send you a postcard if your services are required."

"Stay away from the Malzenberger woman, Dani. She's a bit of a viper if you get the wrong side of her. Lies through her teeth, makes stuff up, what they used to call a gift-spritz, a lethal injection."

"Have you been talking to Fat Pete?"

"Of course, what do you think I pay him for? They tell me you saw Gina's husband get run over in that terrible accident with the bus."

"I didn't realise it was him, until I read about it online."

"You and Gina have known each other a very long time. Harald Mertens, right, think so?"

"But Gina and me, we hadn't kept in touch after University, if that's what you're asking. Harry was a serial seducer, couldn't help it, very charming, immune to resisting temptation. I kept away from him, in fact we never met. If you want to know about his love life ask the Blonde, she played a more than supporting role in that little drama serial. His eldest is the same, Nikki, aged nineteen. She's plundering Charlottenburg's youth with the aplomb of an accomplished hedonist. Oh, you needn't worry yourself, under 25's only, or so they tell me. Your chances are '0.00%'. By the time she moves on to older men you'll be in a wheelchair. She's being sent to study in Aachen to minimise the scope of her attentions. Aachenists are engineers not anarchists, or even arsenists."

"Poor Harry. We have been wondering why he should have been caught between bus and lorry. Then one of my assistants asked whether they might have been aiming for him and the rest was, well, overkill, you know, typische Berlin."

"Don't be silly, why should anyone want him flattened, unless there's something I don't know that you do?"

"I don't think anyone set out to clatter him, it just happened as he was cycling to work."

"Unless it was one of his discarded exes, bearing a grudge."

"I did ask what he was doing to get caught up in the carnage. Could there have been a girlfriend who'd been married to a lorry driver? My accident analyst concluded he probably wasn't paying attention. A very accidental accident, she assured me. Though that conclusion made me a bit suspicious, so I did ask around a bit. The Uni people told me he was giving lectures on strategic concepts in games design, which isn't quite the same as the application of strategy in play, or so they told me. Be your own judge of that.

143

When I asked if that meant he was a nice guy with some interesting ideas, they said that was to underestimate his talents. He was deeper into everyday realities than the game theory people, who are closer to mathematical abstraction than human frailty. Harald was building a philosophy of gaming, based on the argument that our urban environment is already a kind of augmented reality and all the games industry are doing is a minor revision to reconcile the digital with its real world analog, which may, or may not be the case, I don't know, could be both, I suppose, the way these people talk. He was something of a hero to the youngsters, bearing the flag of attitudinal game development in a reluctant universe of applications. One of his colleagues told me that. I thought it sounded good. He did too, they're adapting the phrase for Harry's epitaph in the Departmental Year Book. The poor guy will be missed, for a while, at least. That's about it."

"For one of the polenta, you do have some funny ambitions, Lukie. You're supposed to be a crook catcher, not a media theorist."

"True enough. That's why I'd like to know what your client Caro was doing cultivating Harry and his circle of researchers as if they had the making of a clan. Do you think you could ask her to call me and explain?"

Dani would like to hear Caro's explanation too. Adding yet another recently dead local to the mix of questions surrounding Caro's contacts is something she hadn't expected at all. Why on earth hadn't she said anything. "I'll mention it. Or rather I'll talk to her and if she has anything interesting to say, I'll let you know."

"Harry Mertens did have one idea that I found very revealing, a perception that I suspect may turn out to be correct. He argued that the way people live in these new cities you find in China that are dominated by dozens and dozens of those massive apartment blocks, traditional communities and normal social connections will never be established. People simply won't link up. There won't be the opportunity to meet anyone face to face. Therefore the kind of network, online communities that people are using, the social networks are going to be by necessity a central element of society in the future, rather than a leisure time activity as they are now. Being part of a collective is a fundamental aspect of human psyche. According to his thinking, in the not too distance future, there won't be a society, there will only be a network, which isn't the same thing at all, and lots of people will all have a slightly different impression of the way things work. That is quite a claim. He expected even the Chinese Communist Party will morphose to become an online network, which is a pretty drastic claim, if you think about it. Assuming he's right, most of our thinking about society is a luxurious throwback to the nineteenth century, when the majority of people lived in villages and knew not only their neighbours, but their neighbours cousins and uncles and grandparents. It is the end of anthropology. You can forget about neighbourhood projects and town hall meets. People like you and me will only get to know of each other online and even then we shall never be certain whether we're real or just a pair of bots." "Are we all turning into play-pals?"

"Play is probably the wrong term and so will pals be soon." says Winkler, before he switches theme, "So, next thing. It will help my effort to identify the people in your pictures if Caro can tell me what she's been up to. And, tell me, do you two still dance as one? I heard that was quite a performance, you impressed the inmates."

"Goodnight, Lukas. Enjoy your fantasies. I'll see you here, tomorrow."

"At eleven, don't be late. Tom and me have to be at a buffet lunch for the Conference of City Sleuths and I need to ensure he doesn't alienate any of the potentates."

"City Sleuths? Can anyone come?"

"Actually, it's 'Europol 13B BERLIN!'. I don't think you'd enjoy it, but I have to be there, at least for a bit, playing my part to promote European Arab understanding. Next year in Abu Dhabi, an invitation would be nice, I wouldn't mind the trip, I wouldn't mind a trip like that at all."

"What do you know about Arabs?"

"Nothing, so I expect to improve my understanding considerably in less time than it takes to finish a Bavarian buffet. It will be an education in itself to discover what Bavarian caterers think Arabs will find appetizing. Piggy based bratwurst certainly not. That's another reason why they should invite me, I am more sensitive to cultural distinctions than many people realise."

"If you honestly think that, well don't let me disabuse you, Lukie."

He didn't answer. For a couple of minutes there was an amicable silence.

The Soph-Am was close to closing for the night.

Uli began putting chairs on tables so the cleaners had room to work next morning, before the place reopens. Lukas left. There were still three play-pals sitting indecisive at a table near the back.

Uli shouted at them, "go get laid or go home, make your minds up, time to go."

Then Dani went home in a lull of alcohol and was asleep about half a minute after she got into bed. The distraction is in Kaiserslauten, but Georg is due back soon, so she can enjoy a good night's sleep.

The sheets were fresh, dark blue, almost new, which was nice.

She was alone and she could snore and stretch at random, which she did.

A blackbird sitting on a branch of the tree outside her bedroom window was puzzled by the rhythmic snorts as he twittered to his friends across the city. He speculated that she could be an unusual species of crow.

Chapter 9

Jogging gently at a sedate pace through the Schlosspark, just before nine o'clock next morning, when sunlight caught the naked brass figure of Fate on the tower of the palace, Dani noticed a shiny black heavily built raven sitting on a branch of one of the old hornbeams near the red footbridge, as four fast ducks flew towards the river and almost collided with her. Maybe they were snipe. She could feel the draft of their wing beats as they sped past. The raven looked towards her as if to say she'd had a lucky break. Ducks are known to crash. Then Alfred jogs by and chides her for slowness. "Don't just stand there darling, follow me!" The raven seems to think she's been invited and flaps along behind Alfred as he rounds the Belvedere on the path towards the woods. Then it is distracted by the sight of a breakfast-sized baby rabbit lying dead in the long grass and puts Alfred on ignore to enjoy a nice bit of carrion.

For his part, Alfred is mildly relieved not to have a raven on his trail. He'll give Dani a chase another time.

On her part, Dani is suddenly overtaken by a wave of exhaustion and leans on the rails of the wooden footbridge to look back along the stream. She's glad of the peace and quiet.

Half hidden among the reeds is a grey heron, standing tall, still and patient. A kingfisher is sitting motionless on a slender twig, an arms-length, or so above the water. It is on the lookout for fish, so is the heron. Dani watches it for five minutes. The bird is following a routine patrol of the river banks, flitting electric blue over the water from one tree to another, then waiting, or diving. Every third or fourth dive it manages to catch a little fish. When Caro turns back to look at the heron, it has a fish shaped bulge in its long neck.

Beyond that a pair of happy red squirrels are chasing each other up and down and round and round the trunks of the big beeches by the bridge. Up in the higher branches of an old oak a racoon is watching the fun before turning in for a good day's sleep after a feast of fresh frogs. The beavers have already gone back to their den to avoid the tourists. There isn't a magpie to be seen.

The Schloss Garden lakes and streams seem unusually full.

Somewhere on the other side of the city centre, the Landwehr canal lockgates are jammed open and the rivers though west Berlin threaten to flood Charlottenburg, but the problem hasn't been reported yet. The lake and river just seem a little fuller than the day before. The sluice is making more noise than usual as the water roars over the weir besides the lock gate. Problems like that have to be resolved all the time in a city the size of Berlin and these little crisis' usually pass unnoticed.

By midday everything will be back to normal and the media will just report a delay for barges bringing coal and oil into the local power stations. A team of engineers however are seriously concerned that the problem derived from some malevolent hack into the system controlling the remote operation of the locks. The digital police detachment are as baffled as anyone else and the BND are called in to make an assessment of the threat.

There's election campaigning under way which is generally ignored, the politicos' arguments are sloppily construed and ill thought through. Ask any of the grandmothers you run into in the supermarket and they'll tell you as much for free.

But before that begins to happen, Dani's mobile gives a buzz and she's saying good morning to Caro.

"No, I didn't meet anyone interesting to hook up with," says Dani severely, "Once you're over 40, that kind of thing no longer happens at the Soph-Am. Everyone has slept with everyone they might ever have considered sleeping with and found them wanting. 'Einmal ist keinmal', once doesn't count, or 'nie wieder' never again. So doing your drinking there is actually rather a chaste option, unless you're one of the play-pals, or still stuck in a relationship in which case you probably don't need to go there in the first place if your fancy is a fumble. The chances of meeting someone new are close to zero."

"I got your message about talking to that polyp Lukas. And I've been thinking about Harald Mertens and his world of online worlds. Should we mention him to Maria?"

"Is he part of this? I didn't know you were involved with his projects," said Dani.

"I'm not, or rather I wasn't, but we'd talked," Caro answers. "Harald's study groups have been disbanded now he's gone. There was no-one sufficiently in sync with his ideas to take over as his successor. I thought some of his notions were interesting, but there was no real overlap between our work. He was an ultra-online beast, very multi-user, while I like working face to face, one to one, quiet interaction. The University were very reluctant about closing his seminars, but they had no-one to take over. He'd spent twenty five years cultivating his online presence in a way few others could have attempted, as first the private networks, then the world wide web took shape and he'd been there from the word go."

Dani wonders where Caro is trying to take the conversation, but she's patient.

"Talk about early adopter, he was the digital equivalent of a character from Genesis. Catching up would be impossible. He started out in the days of AOL and Compuserve, and left a trail of data even before the notion of a browser was defined. His death will leave a hole in dozens of networks. There had been some EU money for research and the Chinese were said to be interested, but it wasn't enough to convince them without his experience. He was one of a network of researchers mining the same seam of ideas and supporting each others' grant applications, or at least those the Chinese weren't interested in buying into. But he was a pioneer and as well as that, he was popular, generally liked – not all professors are. More-often they're resented, or despised, at best reluctantly respected. It goes with the territory. Actually, he was a very nice guy, no question."

"Is there any clear reason why someone might want him dead?"

"Harald's big idea was about trying to automate society, in the same way that robots have automated industry. If he and his henchmen get their way, all people will have to do is sit back and enjoy living life in ways we've scarcely begun to imagine, without having to worry about work, or money, or getting old, or sick. Just sensations and gratification. Things to do and places to go.

JOHN CLARK

Everything will just be one smooth pleasurable ride, exploring a complex digital universe from cradle to grave, a world divided between developers and players. There are certainly people who don't like that kind of scenario." "But locally?"

"I did talk to his students. At one stage, they had showed signs of becoming one of my little anthropological phenomena, a mini-group of digital futurologists, grit in the machine, but it didn't crystalize. The potential was there, but soon faded away. It was all too general, they needed a niche. They needed their guru. Their ideas are probably more applicable in China than northern Europe anyway and none of the people currently involved know anything about China and Chinese social engineering. Apart from the Chinese themselves, I don't think anyone has a clear perspective; they're very interesting, but hey, just get on with things. There's lots to learn and unlearn. I've never met a convincing online Marxist. To have anything credible to say about China, you need to know the language and the people. To do the same thing online you need huge numbers of people who also know China and its people, so the best place to be is China and have Chinese researchers to work with directly, face to face, instead of guessing from a distance."

"Caro, you weren't involved in this, were you?"

"Me? No. When you look at the world with open eyes, we're all too set in our ways, but that's not a reason to go after people like Harry. We think we know what we're doing, maybe some do. But all I can really do is talk to people and listen to what they decide to say about each other. I read quite a lot too, so there's a vague chance I ask the right questions, though there are no guarantees. The rest is careful observation and good note-keeping. Mertens would have agreed with that much, I'm pretty sure."

Dani gets over sensitive when people try to play the academic card, especially if they show signs of being a brain snob and Caro is beginning to get on her nerves. She's been listening carefully. So now there's someone else who is interested in China. People are forever going on about China, as though it will provide the answer to everything. Maybe Dani should be interested too, she tells herself. Maybe everyone should be. "Observation and good note-keeping, Caro, do you think my work is so very different from what you do?"

"Maybe not, but there's the question of structure, ideology and the intellectual framework, criteria that don't apply to street-life," Caro replies without wanting to sound arrogant, but she does, and with that she's tripped the brain snob alarm without even realising.

Dani and Caro still don't trust one another, which could be a mistake. On the other hand Dani does think the job is going quite well. Though a couple of people have died, there doesn't seem to be a connection of any kind. People die all the time.

Think about the unknown guy on the boat, or rather don't. Klaus took his own life and Mertens was sadly the victim of a tragic, no, a crazy traffic accident. She's disappointed not to have known Mertens, but it's too late now. He did seem interesting however.

What would she say to Georg if he suggested she should step away from the job? At least Caro keeps paying as she'd promised, there's already nine thousand in cash in Dani's cupboard drawer and even brain snobs can win friends if they pay their bills on time.

Even if she doesn't like Caro and wouldn't trust her at all, the good thing about this job is that so far they haven't had any difficulty finding people. Everyone has been conveniently local, apart from the lawyer from Miami. But even she has been kind enough to cross the Atlantic for their benefit meaning Dani's travelling expenses are minimal and she hasn't had to waste time hanging around arranging visas for improbable destinations, or loitering at airports, or suffering the stress of over-nighting in luxurious hotels with calorie laden breakfast buffets. That left her with enough time to handle her other jobs too. Are things about the change? She wouldn't be surprised. It can't all be plain sailing.

Once they've had the chance to talk to Lukas Winkler again, the answer might be a bit more clear and so, she tells herself, might the questions.

"Good morning ladies," says Kriminal Kommissar Lukas Winkler somewhat formally to the two out of three actors, who mutter about what on earth Lucky Luke is doing on their patch asking for a double espresso at this ungodly hour.

For once Nico isn't about.

A well paid job on a tv commercial has arisen as if from no-where. By now, Nico, heavily made up, wearing a wig and clad in lederhosen, is sitting on a fake fence set up in an Adlershof studio against a background of digital green pasture and bovine extras, which is being faked into an image of a football stadium where sometime soccer heroes are eating their way through plates of gluten free beans. He's word perfect, "these beans are delicious and so suzzley bootifool Bavarian, ooh aargh, lecker... now in even bigger tins than ever ... and still less than half an Euro a plateful.... that's value.. and they're good for you! Brrrrggh.". The beans are grown in Mexico, but the packaging is blue and white to catch that special feel of pre-eminent Bavarian agriculture in an era of globalisation. The ad will play until the next German football squad are selected and the older faces drop out of people's memories.

   Dani and Caro are half way through a generous breakfast, including excess calories, and have reached the pick around the plate stage, finishing off the remnants of cheese and salad they hadn't felt like eating right away. The four halves of pale green grape and two pairs of blood red cherries are, as ever, the last of the meal to be consumed. Caro sucks the slice of lemon, Dani bites the orange. Some-one plunges a cafetiere and an aroma of blue java fills the room.

   "Would you like an egg? Some wholemeal bread?" asks Caro as Lukas takes a seat at their table. "The croissants are a bit soggy."

   "As usual," adds Dani.

   "The salami was delicious. Genuine air dried free range donkey sausage from Carpathia - finely sliced yet still intense. So was the Montenegran goats-cheese. Yummie."

   "Really, it deserves a slivovice, but a bit early in the day for me. Are you sure you won't have something. Uli's got her best breakfast slave in today, Jana from Kreuzberg, she's a Hungarian cowgirl. Knowing your appetites, you could eat her too, if you like your women wafer thin, marinaded in Tokay, but smothered with paprika and mayonaisse. Or did you indulge already, you wicked man. There's no way of knowing with you."

   "Danke, aber nein danke," Lukas says by way of thankyou but no thanks and sips his coffee.

   He's already been online for two hours of case conferences about three very violent offenders who are in danger of evading prosecution; then thirty minutes more in discussion about the idea of getting actor Vin Diesel to visit the Berlin Film Festival and explain that the 'Fast and Furious' films are conceived as entertainment not training videos for inner city drivers. And he's listened to a briefing on changes in the interpretation of traffic regulations following the pro-cycling lobby's success with the local transport authority. As a cyclist himself, Lukas is strongly in favour of car drivers being warned to change their attitude towards people on push bikes and stop trying to kill them. The late Harry M, gaming guru, father and mentor, will be given a prominent place in a police publicity campaign supporting white bicycle protests for 'those we have lost'. The law enforcement people may be victims of jargon, but they do have the well-being of other people at heart, as well as their own ambitions, so being friendly to cyclists is both nice, easy and very good publicity. Berlin has a seemingly endless supply of idiots who rent a supercar and expect to indulge in suicidal behaviour without getting killed, arrested, or chastised by officers of the law. None of them realise the risk they run of being gunned down by Lukas and his mates, who all getting increasingly frustrated with the situation. He's also been discussing political stuff with the Polizei President, who is wondering who might be interior minister after the election. That could get tricky if it's one of the law and order fundamentalists. "Those pictures from last night. Where did you say they were taken?" Lukas wants to know.

"At a holiday resort in the Caribbean," said Caro.

"Could it have been a games convention?" he asks.

"Yes," Caro confirms.

"That makes sense. Apart from Flo and Polly, remember them, Dani, the two I told you about last night, who were with the EU woman? The other three all now work for Jerome Breitscheid."

"Oh, I know Jerome," says Caro.

"I know you do."

"He's very talented."

"So they say. But he's not on the picture."

"Looks like he was putting together a team. The woman on the left is a Senior Game Designer Hannelore Holst from Baden-Baden, known to most as Hanni, or to some as Lore, depending who you ask. The tall guy is Simon Thiel, metrics, metadata, works from Dresden up to now and the man with the dark hair is in user-liaison and marketing, Tilmann Schwarz, known as 'Til', who has an office in Kaiserslautern, lord knows why, but has now been given a workspace in Breitscheid's suite in Potsdamer Platz. All three of them are due to work from there soon."

"How did you find all that out so quickly?"

"Just face recognition. Followed a link from Flo and Polly, which took me to Breitscheid's corporate website via my find-a-bod software and checked a couple of business nets. Found them in all of five minutes. They're listed on his website under 'outstanding new talent and winning teams'. There's nothing sinister about that, is there?"

"Nope. it's just business as usual, I suppose."

"Sure. Didn't even need the police system, which is always nice. Our Habeous Corpus platform is tracked and compromised via the EU hacks, too late to do much about that."

"Who is this Breitscheid?" asks Dani.

"He works for my Dad sometimes and owns a company called Broadsheath Systems, which is just the english version of his own name: Breit scheid, broad sheath."

"So I've been led to understand," Lukas agrees.

"Then we're making progress. Does Maria know about him?"

"No idea. If we have a team of game folk meeting city planners and economic development people while enjoying cosy trips to the Caribbean, I'm wondering whether we consider this to be a good reason for Maria to have been sent here by Bernhardt and Co. And if it is, who is she reporting to? All the same, don't forget it's only Berlin politics, a vesicle of doubt suspended as usual between self interest, duplicity and outright corruption."

"Lukas, you're getting cynical."

"Nah, just jaundiced. I'd been hoping things would have improved over the years. It hasn't, that's all. Means all my efforts have been a waste of time. So much for career aspirations, eh?"

"Does Maria know about these pictures, or the video."

"No, I can't imagine why she should. Unless she's hacked my phone."

"Then let's just see whether she mentions any of those people without being prompted and take it from there. She doesn't need to be told everything."

"We're due to meet her for lunch in half an hour."

"Well, whatever you do," says Lukas, "Don't take her to "Last Supper', they're getting a surprise visit from the hygiene inspectors today."

"Hi, Loo-key," says Uli, presenting their bill, which ends up with Caro. "Did you hear about Manfred?"

"Mani? What happened."

"He was on his way to the Café Riecherauch for a beer, when one of the boules players threw a high ball, you know Manuela, big woman, blonde, his wife - Manu and Mani, OK?" Uli begins. "The steel boule floated up and up, like they do, seemed to pause for a moment, almost still at its apogee five metres above the ground then began to fall and the 800grammes of hard metal cracked into Manfred's skull as he was out walking his dog Fritzie along the central pathway of the Schlossstrasse. He'd been expecting to drink two small beers, but instead of that he died in full public view before the ambulance arrived, bleeding profusely and screaming with pain. Manuela was distraught, so was the dog. No-one had warned her that boules could be fatal. Oh so, Manu and Mani. Over the years, Manuela had told so many people of her intention to see Manfred in his grave that no-one at all believed her claim it was a freak accident except the public prosecutor who is another boules player and recognised that it could only have been accidental. Manuela simply isn't that good. He's agreed not to press charges on condition she looks after the dog and gives up ball games. He was in here first thing, said Manfred had contributed to his own fate by being far too trusting in the vicinity of a woman with balls of steel and no sense of direction. Then he was was overheard saying, 'Enough of this bouleshit, what I need is a beer and a blowjob.' And with that he was gone."

"Good call, considering," says Caro.

"Am I convinced?" responded Lukas, "Answer no, but I don't think I shall have the time to interrogate the woman. You keep your minds on Flo and Polly."

Then Lukas took his leave, "Maybe I'll see you in Soph-Am tonight, or we could go down the 'Esel'," before meandering away to his next conference, "Goodbye ladies." "Gnadige frau," he nodded an implied bow of mock Austrian courtesy to Uli, "Most

Honourable lady". Had he questioned her honour, he'd be on his way to the West End Hospital Accident and Emergency before regaining consciousness. As it is all he gets is the sour lemon smile and her favourite gesture, the 'male dismissed' shrug.

Dani decided it was time to put a little pressure on Caro, just to see how she reacts. Very politely, she suggests that it shouldn't matter what Maria is up to. Isn't it just something between her and Caro's Dad? If Bernhardt hired her, then she's following his instructions and she'll report to him, end of story. Why not let her get on with things in her own way? She's not likely to get very far without help. Caro says Maria wants an assistant. Since Klaus' accounts have all been wound up and his businesses closed down, Caro shouldn't have to worry about what they're up to, should she, Dani asks provocatively. "Or....?"

Caro smiles and with a certain employer to employee formality reminds Dani that she is being paid to help, not to pass judgement. "You're wondering whether I have a guilty secret and am just using you as cover, which is a reasonable question, but I'm not going to answer it, which is equally reasonable. You couldn't complain if I said it was none of your fucking business, but I won't say that. What will say is that I don't think you should expect me to tell you every little detail of my life, do you? I think you can be confident that nothing you'll be asked to do will bring you any problems with the law, alright?"

"I hope I can trust you on that."

"Promise."

"Actually, I always thought 'Last Supper' was the most disgusting restaurant idea of all time."

"What was all the fuss about?" asks Caro. "Isn't it just another café grubbing for one off customers. There are plenty of them. Welcome to Tourist Town Berlin, fly 'em in, fill 'em up and rip 'em off and don't forget the club, fuck, drug before you go brigade."

"No, no 'Last Supper' had ambitions all their own. Set up by a guy by the name of Hinrich Gauland."

"Gauland, Gauland, isn't he a politician? One of those AfD types?"

"Different guy, different trope. This Gauland had the very dubious concept of stone age cuisine, eat like a cave man and save the planet! The theme was sausages. He got this idea into his head that sausages were invented by stone age people hunting and slaughtering, then opening up the belly of a dead elk or deer, or sabre toothed tiger, or whatever to find the intestines were full of semi-digested stuff which was not only edible but by stone age standards tasted remarkably good and if you were very lucky, was still warm. And these became the world's first sausages, truly German, or so he claims with nationalist zeal, grilled and scorched on a red hot stone with Teutonic zest."

"Is that what 'Last Supper' were doing? Serving up innards full of half digested food scorched with Teutonic zest?"

"Their vegetarian haggis won a prize, until someone pointed out that a vegetarian's stomach isn't itself vegetarian. Grass powered self-filling sheep stomachs. Gauland prided himself on feeding the animals extra special ingredients for the last meals, all truffel and caviar, sugar and spice. Vegan filled sausage, would you believe? A drip of maple syrup on your grass, little sheep? Hence the name 'Last Supper'. He slaughters them in a shed behind the restaurant, then butchers the carcasses personally. The sausages are part of the special menu and the meat goes straight in the pot. It was all very refined if you talked to them a few days before you planned to dine. You can buy the skins and furs too, cured in their own juices, or so he claims. You are what you eat."

"I'm glad I never went there."

"Leave it for the tourists."

"Like lambs to the slaughter."

"Gauland isn't a cannibal, is he?"

"Not yet. That could lead to a never ending chain of slaughter. Her last supper became his last supper, then their last supper and so on. No-one bothers counting the tourists any more. One here or two there wouldn't be missed. Could be the next Sweeney Todd's, bringing new dimensions to the notion of Danish bacon."

"So, lets take Maria to Borchardt's by the Gendarmenmarkt. As businessy a place as any, which is probably what she expects. The food is fine and she can send a photo of her schnitzel to her family to prove we're looking after her alright."

"I liked the schnitzel last time I was there."

They're almost late because the S-bahn from Charlottenburg connects with the U6 at Friedrichstrasse, but often involves a five or ten minute wait for the next train heading south, but they do get there just ahead of Maria, who says she's bought books in english from Dussmanns, "Great selection, back home I have to buy online, though we do have a store run by some German publisher, Taschen Verlag and there's Dunbars for second hand stuff," and she'd had a wonderful time shopping in Galleries Lafayette round the corner. There are the shopping bags to prove it and she's wearing a smart new jacket that Dani likes.

"So French," she exclaims with delight, "And the Carrés are brilliant. Now Dani, are you working for me, or for Caro? I know she's paying, but I did ask for an assistant and since nobody had said anything, I wondered whether you were the lucky girl."

"Of course," answers Dani, before Caro can quibble. Dani hadn't expected it to be so easy to get more involved with Maria's activities and Caro hadn't thought of it at all. She'd been wondering if she knew anyone she could recommend as a temp. Maria assures Caro that she will be reimbursed for the cost of finding cover for Dani and that she'll pay Dani herself. "Cash, if you like dollars."

"Just so that you know who you're working for, Daniela. We wouldn't want any misunderstandings about that would we?"

Caro is impassive. This isn't to her liking, but she'll keep quiet for the moment. She's almost willing to accept it might be to her advantage and she expects Dani to convince her.

Since Dani is self-employed, she doesn't bother pointing out that she works for herself and the two of them are only clients and she is quite capable of distinguishing between the interests of different clients. Thoughts like that would only confuse the situation more. Dani can be quick thinking and this time she recognises the opportunity to put a foot in the other camp is as invaluable as it is unexpected. She should be able to learn as much about Caro's role as she will about Maria's goals.

The three of them are working their way down a standard Borchardt lunch, which is a pleasant enough experience and the waiters are correct, so they've nothing to complain about. At least they haven't been mistaken for tourists. They're in a semi-covered courtyard behind the main dining room and Maria says she thinks the place has class. Caro notices she's eyeing one or two of the business suited diners a couple of tables away. They're talking about the election campaigns. The danger, one suggests, is that voters are treating the election as a giant opinion poll, making known their frustrations, and losing sight of the fact they are giving people jobs and electing folk who will always be able to say they were Mitgleid der Bundestag, whether they are eventually re-elected or not. Will Maria want one of the suits as a dessert? They're probably available, FDP, Green, CDU, middle management executive benefits, but Caro is not going to be the one to ask. If the question arises Caro will politely suggest that Maria try one of the play-pal programmes on her phone.

Then Maria asks Caro about Klaus and Berlin, a place she hardly knows and a person she never met.

Caro does her best to make sense. In common with most European cities, she explains, Berlin's economy is based on public administration, tax and sucking money out of youthful visitors for things like drugs, clubs and places to sleep, which isn't really enough, so there's perpetual economic deficit. The tourists have become a pest, but that seems to be normal where-ever you go in Europe. This amuses Maria who says Miami is similar, except the people are a couple of generations older. "Berlin's visitors get to bliss out and go home, while in Florida they bliss out and get to go to heaven. Of course, we also have the big drug importers in Miami and that's a tricky issue, a major industry, huge business. Even dope barons need to have their headquarters somewhere. How do you balance the financial benefits with the social issues? I am glad I do not have to make those choices. Does Berlin have a serious drug culture?"

Caro and Dano both fall about laughing, they can't help themselves and having realised she's been inadvertently funny, Maria joins in. "Oh, I see, well I haven't been here before."

Dani tries to bring a little balance back in the conversation. "We have a whole culture of clubs and young people flock here for hedonistic weekends. There's a club based in a former electricity power station. That one place can hold thousands, churning them in perpetuity. But the dealers and middlemen are a different breed, full time, but amateurish, constantly getting caught. I think they get their ideas about drug dealing from movies, you know the memes, French Connection, Goodfellas, Fast and Furious, all the LA

Gangland Gangsterisms. They all forget Midnight Express, or The Councellor. In my part of town, which is mainly a middle aged rather placid area, the middle men and the importers get caught all the time, a tonne of this, a thousand litres of that, millions in cash in any currency you care to mention. Every couple of years one of them gets snaffled and everyone pretends to be surprised given the character of the neighbourhood, but isn't that the whole point? Hoods all crave respectability. Here? Around the corner? My oh my, who'd a thought it!" "And you have culture, so much of it, so many opera houses and the concerts, Wagner to Webern! I could stay here for that alone. The Volksbühne, the Schaubühne, the Berliner Ensemble! What a wonderful place."

"Berlin does seem to work, until the politicians do their damnedest to destroy it, as they are doing with the Volksbühne and did do to the Schiller Theatre, which is an old story, but still rankles" Caro says. "The waste of time and effort involved is extraordinary, but somewhere along the way, this all becomes the basis for attracting investment and once it takes off, the investment process perpetuates itself, as debt chases debt in an evasive spiral. People start seeing potential profits. There is Greek money, Turkish money, Russian money, British money, even German money. Not much French any more, of course, but plenty of Italian and Dutch. That was where Klaus had fitted in. He helped people to help him exploit their willingness to invest come what may, this desire people have to throw their money at projects as if they've nothing to lose. The rest is fashion. Berlin is as cool a place as anywhere to lose your shirt, so why not give it a try?"

Caro tells Maria how she has been watching the different phases of Berlin's recent past, as East and West have been blended uneasily into a commercial framework that pays little or no attention to authentic social patterns, or spontenaity and owes everything to the discovery of 'place' marketing and carefully managed events. In the nineteen nineties there was something called the 'Love Parade' which was basically a big weekend party, cost next to nothing to organise, yet attracted hundreds of thousands of people to spend money in the city. First of all it was cool, but that's all over now, then they sold you the notion that Berlin was cool, so you'd be cool too if you visited, then because cool people like you had been there, you tell your friends and the place becomes even more cool. The reality was a tourist industry that fed itself on 'place marketing' and didn't require the kind of billion dollar investments required for tech and manufacturing. We don't have a Disneyland, we have the Berghain. The alternative 'szene' was turned into a business double quick. "Cool sells," says Dani.

"It surely does," confirms Caro, "despite the lousy airports."

Maria laughs as is expected of her, "Compared to some of the countries I know, it probably feels like heaven." Then she finishes off the remains of a 'crème brulée', sucks down an espresso and becomes very practical.

Maria says she needs to get from points A, B, C and D, to companies X,Y,Z and back to 'U' and she needs Dani to interpret where necessary if the people she's talking to aren't able to express themselves in good clear english.

Then she excuses herself for a couple of minutes and Dani leans forward, looks Caro in the eye and says, "Perfect."

"I know," answers Caro, having accepted the inevitable "I'll talk to you later. For the moment, I shall bow out graciously and leave you to handle the lady yourself. When she returns, I'll say my farewells and leave."

And that is what she does, all very friendly and open and easy, "What a great idea. Agreed Dani?" Caro even picks up the tab, but the conversation had been riddled with suspicion and there's no way of evading that uncomfortable fact.

Maria accepts Dani's suggestion that they use taxi's though when she checks the first address, 'X' turns out to be in a set of offices on the Gendarmenmarkt. Only a two minutes walk from the restaurant, they're in a modern block with a view over the Konzerthaus and the pepperpot of the eighteenth century Hugenot church, near the Academy of Science, a good address if these things matter and they probably do at least when it comes to deciding the rent. The taxi notion is superfluous. They meet a lawyer called Kroll, who Maria obviously knows, without necessarily having met directly before and he says very little apart from telling her that a transaction Bernhardt had expected has now gone through. This is business as usual that could have been conducted over the phone and concluded with an exchange of documents by courier, but Kroll and Maria are polite. Meet and greet, smile, get to know you in the flesh, handshake time. Kroll and she chat amicably, agreeing that the big challenge for their work will be an anticipated tax law reform in the USA, which may or may not happen depending on President Trump's capacity to seal a deal, which they both doubt. Workload isn't an issue. Taking on more cases, simply means hiring more people and making more money. America is full of ambitious young lawyers who'll jump ship if they're offered a better deal. As they're on the way out Dani asks what kind of business their business was all about and Maria says intellectual property, in particular some licenses from Bernhardt's old projects in Germany that needed renewing. Companies forget that licences have a date on them and they need reminding of that a couple of years before agreements expire. Sometimes the people who own the rights are difficult to trace. She admits it's dull as ditchwater. Nothing to do with Klaus, she explains, and certainly nothing to do with Caro. "She's pushy that one, don't you agree?" Maria said.

"Caro is very Berlin, but she is also her father's daughter," says Dani, hoping to sound reasonable. She doesn't intend to trash Caro.

"Oh, typische Berlin, I've heard that phrase." She smiles. Maria is being friendly, but practical, pragmatic. "I do hope I can trust you to be straightforward. Don't try to second guess what's going on, just help me meet the people I'd like to see, do a little interpreting if their English isn't great and try to be supportive. And I will need help explaining bits about one or two of the documents I have, that haven't been translated from German. I don't trust the online translation programmes. I'm not interested in the grammar, I want to know what they're about. But you must tell me if you don't understand them, don't make your answers up. Never pretend to know something you don't. It is never helpful and brings more problems than it solves. We can always find an expert if we need one, ok? Oh, and let me assure you that everything I do is strictly legal, there is nothing for you to concern yourself about in that area."

Dani nods.

"Caro said you like a thousand Euros a day, which seems generous, but good for you, if that's what you're worth, that's what I'll pay.

Fair? You might argue that I charge a great deal more, but my fees include assistants and offices, secretaries, professional insurance and a lot more I won't go into, so I don't get to take home anything like the amount of money you might imagine."

Dani smiles, wondering whether she's going to get on with Maria better than she does with Caro. Dani has a sneaking doubt when it comes to Caro. At some point she wouldn't be surprised to find a long contract with Caro's signature at the bottom revealing that she knew about all the scams from day 1, however long ago that might have been.

Their next stop is however, a very Klausian property, a modernised block near the University, pragmatic, neutral, workaday.

"Come and meet the guys," says Maria, "This is Bernhardt business once more, again nothing to do with Caro and Klaus."

Dani suspects she could be mistaken about that, but says nothing. She's beginning to wonder whether everything to do with Bernhardt in Berlin was also to do with Klaus, but somehow they'd forgotten to mention the fact to Caro, or they'd simply taken it for granted that she knew. Had none of them realised that she had failed to notice what was going on under her nose. Either that, or she's a world class liar, a possibility Dani cannot easily dismiss.

They don't need a taxi to reach destination 'Y' either. They wander up Friedrichstrasse to Unter den Linden, then take a short cut through the old University building and in ten minutes, they're there.

A pleasant young woman leads them from the lift doors on the sixth floor along a featureless frosted glass and grey corridor flanking offices on one side and lab spaces on the other. The carpet is unforgiving and industrial.

She takes them into a room with a view over the University courtyard and the monument to the theologen Dietrich Bonhoeffer and his students who paid with their lives for opposing the Nazi's. For good measure, there's a statue of Hegel across the road. This is a managed research environment, she explains, where boutique biotech companies can rent as much, or as little space as they need on a month by month basis. There are twenty or thirty of them, each with a clever name built from syllables like bio, synth, digi, strategy, tech and the like. Their logo's are similar reworkings of spirals, double helix' and simple geometric shapes, obviously the work of the same graphic designer, so Dani assumes these are all the progeny of a single business development scheme.

Each little business boasts a research professor to dignify the funding applications and they all threaten to be awesomely successful and globally important, addressing markets worth billions. The chances of any one of those firms being at the business end of a breakthrough is heartbreakingly small, but no-one likes to discuss that, not with visitors, at least and not with the prospect of millions of Euros in Euro funding on the agenda. Somewhere down in the basement, there's also a space they call the 'Playpen', which seems to be an obligatory feature of new technology workplaces ever since Google promoted the notion that putting nose to grindstone twenty four hours a day is just clean fun and creative managers decided to assert their originality by slavishly copying the way things are done at Mountain View. The 'Playpen' is, of course, deserted.

They're shown into the office of an affable young manager who introduces himself, passes Dani and Maria a card bearing the name, Professor Dr. Dr. Richard Brandt, which is him. Maria is still amused that Germans don't just revel in their titles, they add to them letter by letter ad infinitum. Brandt talks for an hour about projects, relationships with fine chemical producers and some details about patenting in the US that he would like Maria to take a look at. The US documentation is horrendous, he says and Maria smiles indulgently.

Of course it is. How else should lawyers be expected make a living?

The last thing a lawyer will ever say is don't worry, the problem will just go away.

Maria is all too familiar with the issues, a lawyer's dream, or a legal nightmare depending where you stand in relation to the processes of verification. The thicker the documents, the bigger the bills. All three of them know that much and there's a huge dollar sign and a question mark hanging invisible over the discussion.

Hooray shouts the lawyer under her breath.

Out of courtesy, Brandt abandons his desk and they end up sitting with him in a standard black leather armchair and the two women facing one another on sofa's of a similar sort. Dani enjoys the view out of the window and listens along as Brandt starts to talk. He's quietly spoken and polite, doing his best to be clear.

"I think you already know something about us, but just to be sure, let me explain that we are a new company, though none of us are newcomers to the industry. When Bayer and Monsanto amalgamated, our previous employer bowed out. Time to go, so they shut up shop and that was that."

Brandt is at his most charming, "It happens. We were all surplus to requirements, for a variety of reasons and received very generous pay-offs, but we were given the kind of top quality references that make it possible to raise new capital, so we came together as a group. Your associates in the States, have provided essential support, Maria, invaluable at this stage of the research."

Maria then introduced Dani, as someone who is helping her, making clear she isn't expected to try to understand what the company is up to and probably wouldn't if she did, so they shouldn't waste their efforts in the attempt. Tech afficionados can be as irritating as musicians and evangelical Christians when it comes to unjustified notions of superiority, but that is a commonplace observation.

The knowing smirks all round include Dani, who can smirk with the best of them. She grimaces coyly to acknowledge her own perceived inadequacy. People tend to underestimate her. Sometimes it is useful. In situations like this it is invaluable.

Biochemistry and genetic engineering have moved on since she was a student and she doesn't talk about it any more, but she did finish her studies and came away with a degree. She'd always known she was the wrong kind of person for labwork and didn't want to spend her life staring at a computer monitor modelling molecules, which was one of the reasons she turned to investigations of the social and dishonest variety, rather than those involving exotic chemicals, polymerised chain reactions and genetics.

"Let's just say that the company controls some very fundamental software originally used in pharmaceutical research, which is also becoming important deep inside the world of gaming," says Maria.

Words like fuzzy, intuition and prediction enter the conversation.

Predictive intuition is their theme; intuitive prediction a long term goal.

Dani thinks about that, and decides to appreciate their sensitivety to the niceties of grammar and its contrary philosophical implications. Of course, they keep mentioning data mining, metadata, massive multi-user systems and making cryptic references to an old CIA programme called Reynard that sought to identify subversive interaction between players in game environments. Reynard is supposed to be obsolete, but like a lot of old programming in the world of computing the concepts behind it refuse to go away. The rest is just a question of adapting it for modern configurations of technology.

"What Bernhardt is doing for us will revitalise the tools for new purposes, which is why the patents are important and we need Maria's expertise to secure that goal," said Brandt with a generous smile in her direction.

They're assuming Dani will be out of her depth with anything technical. Just everyday sexism, she's used to that. She's already remembering the names and keywords they keep returning to. She isn't stupid, but she hasn't been indoctrinated and ordained in this particular corner of the faith linking games to pharma and pharma to games in a web of sticky links, manifolds and exotic formulae. Some of her friends have. That's one of the things friends are for. Friends help each other understand the world. She'll ask her friend Professor Helga for a definition of fuzzy predictive intuition and its application to drug development. If it means anything like her own intuitive interpretation, applying the notion to games is more or less self-explanatory. She wonders why they hadn't simply hired another patents lawyer with experience of German and US law, someone who would be happy to work alongside Maria while she ploughs through the paperwork, but they hadn't, so they must be after something else.

"I suppose you're not the only people doing this kind of stuff."

"Of course not. Virtual worlds abound and soon we'll enjoy a multiverse of digital realities, where events are difficult to distinguish from what goes on in our day to day experience on the ground, level one, so to say. Sooner rather than later the biggest difference between 'reality' and 'virtual reality' will be a question of legal status, rather than contrasting sensations. If the history of computing is anything to go by, one or two systems will emerge fairly quickly as humanity's preferred versions of the technology and from a business perspective the sky is then the limit. Actually, the sky will be fully integrated within the system. Think of operating systems. Think of ice-cream. We all seem to prefer one or two flavours above all others. Vanilla, yes, chocolate yes, but are we really so fond of strawberry and all the rest?" "Mint," says Dani, "and lemon, sorbet versus ice-cream.".

"Point taken," says Professor Brandt. "For the grown ups, acquired tastes," he adds and they all laugh. Dani wonders whether he's a family man, a wife, their children the next generation of gamers. Is the battle for domination in the brave new world of pharma games what this is all about?

"To tell you the truth," he confides, "I think the popular versions of those technology are going to be amazing, while the high end editions will simply be awe inspiring. Though I do wonder whether we've spent enough time considering the consequences of renewing 'class' societies. This time it will go so much deeper than divisions between rich and poor. We're talking about completely different lived experience which will increasingly diverge as time goes on."

They've spent an hour and half talking about the games industry, Berlin business and computing without anyone mentioning Breitscheid, or the others Lukas had identified on the video. If Bernhardt manages to keep his business so compartmentalised then Dani is impressed. Berlin can be a very small town and she's confused that there hasn't been a mention of the city planners, nor of the economic development people. What started out as a dubious mix of games, pharma and money is taking on a much more complex hue. Eventually the overlaps will be revealed, then, Dani hopes, it might be possible to stitch the story together.

"The spectrum of permitted and banned substances are increasingly blurred as new formulations become readily available." In what almost seems like an afterthought, Brandt mentions the growing tendency for countries to legalise the use of drugs like marijuana, yet show concern for its derivatives like skunk.

167

"The pharma industry only builds new molecules and explores their properties. It is for society to decide how they should be used."

He sounds like someone from the National Rifle Association taking about the availability of assault rifles.

As they're about to leave, Dani turns to the Professor Doctor Doctor and asks if he knew Harald Mertens.

"I heard him speak at Conferences, but my people were FU rather than TU, where he worked. Mertens liked the way the robot football team were developing, the FU-Fighters, though that wasn't a project I was involved with personally."

"Are you biochemistry, or informatics?" Dani asks.

"A bit of both, aren't we all nowadays, DNA based computing, quantum phenomena, everything's getting entangled."

Chapter 10

Meeting over, Dani had the classic conversation in the lift with Maria, which really did begin in the lift, but ended twenty minutes later near the river Spree.

"Now, this is my dilemma. You are suggesting that via Bernhardt, Caro has an opportunity to become intensely rich, or be completely destructive," asked Dani.

"I am, isn't it intriguing," replied Maria. "He's that kind of guy. Good job he isn't a general, his armies would be destroyed, whole people's annihilated on a whim."

Not knowing whether Maria is serious, she says nothing.

"Does she know that?" Maria asks, "Do you think Carolina would recognise herself as cannon fodder?"

"Not yet, I don't think she's realised," Dani said.

"Well, I am not about to tell her. And nor are you, I should add, until we know more. Though at some point she'll have to learn something like the truth. If we have the choice, I will leave the telling to Bernhardt, so that he can exaggerate in his own way. What about old Klaus? Do you think he understood that he could have been sitting on a goldmine."

"Well, I think you know no more about him than I do," says Dani. "But I doubt if he would have killed himself, if that was true. Do you? Suicide, when you're on the verge of success, no."

"No not very likely, is it. Unless he had some horrible diagnosis from his doctor. These things happen." "I still think he would have wanted to see the money," Dani said.

"Unless he had already sold his interest, sold his share of the deal, which might be a plausible option," suggests Maria.

"Now that might be true. Klaus was one of a group of people who started a club to invest in new businesses and this is one of their successes," Maria explains. "There were ten or twenty, some in property, some bank people and politicians, some administrators. A little pot of gold, topped up with anything from a few thousand to a couple of million per investor, but nothing unusually large.

If you took a business idea to them, which Bernhardt did on several occasions and they liked it, then their little club would move into action, pool their resources and put a 'package' together, which is what happened with one or two of Bernhardt's projects that were subsequently extremely successful, so he was very much in favour.. He's good, everyone knows that. Some of my clients took a benign interest as passive investors, lent a helping hand from time to time.

There's nothing at all unusual about that, you know.

Sometimes it works, sometimes it flops.

Minimising risk, a wonderful aspiration. Same all over the world. People with ideas need finance. People with money hate risk and you have to find a way around that. Call it seed funding, call it what you like, could be cash, could be 'help', could be just opening doors. Usually it's a question of avoiding tax. Had Klaus sold himself short, accepting peanuts for his share of a project that would soon be worth billions? That could have been the case, I guess."

"If that happened to me, I might decide to end it all."

"It would explain a lot, but who is going to benefit? There must be someone somewhere who made a killing at his expense."

"Well yes. Should we write a list?" Maria is not listening to her.

"Just think of it. Amazing, when eventually a mountain of money suddenly condenses out of thin air, one minute you're a struggling loner, the next you're one of the founders of a billion dollar corporation and a market flotation. It sounds crazy, until you realise it seems to work. Getting seriously rich is one of the abiding attractions of capitalism. It really happens. Poor Klaus."

She pauses then gives a little sigh, as though she wished it had been her it had happened to. She's a believer.

"Beautiful, really beautiful, if you give it a little thought, at least for the lucky few. Like snowflakes on a summer's day,"

She might have been considering her chances of marrying Daniel Craig, or George Clooney. She means it. Maria is quite sincere when she talks of capitalism's beauty.

For her, capitalism plays a mystical role in human affairs. And one of its most mysterious aspects, she'll openly admit is what happens when something doesn't work out, when a project suddenly, even mysteriously, fails. In some parts of the world there's forgiveness, a period of financial purdah, in other less tolerant realms debt is biblical, will follow you to the end of your days, be bequeathed to your children and your children's children until every last penny is paid, or the interest accumulates until repayment is out of reach without bankrupting the global economy. Forgetting can sometimes be a necessity.

She thinks about finance much as theologians indulge in comparative religion.

How will you pay for your sins?

Can God or the universe be bothered to keep a tally?

The god of money is the same the world over, but the belief systems according to different denominations of the faith are divided between the ripe Lutheran shit of German protestant literalism, or the gold coin and precious metals of gilded middle eastern fundamentalists, perhaps the Masochist Austrians seeing currencies like teeth that rot and decay without regular brushing, or there again the lightweight symbolism of laisse faire capitalism and the global circuses of derivatist devotion, all those of little faith, who sow doubt in the singular value of the Almighty dollar and the lesser deities of yen and peseta, cruzeiro, rouble, pound and Euro and are only later revealed to have walked off with the rest of the world while you were looking the other way and wondering how to pay your bills before the power is disconnected.

Maria considers herself economically post-modern, financially post-structuralist and puts her faith in creditworthiness. Maybe she's not wrong. She adores the detail, how long are people given to amortise a loan. Can you hand the keys back when there's a default, or is there going to be a noose around your neck is some dark corner of provincial China? The contrasts are profound.

Transparency may be international, but what exactly is corruption? Opinions differ, especially between the people being corrupted and those doing the corrupting. "Lawyers do their best to understand all that, but usually fail," Maria claims

All the time, as they're walking through Berlin Mitte, Maria has been chatting about things she'd like done and Dani has taken notes, a 'to be done by yesterday' list and 'what I need by tomorrow night at the latest' list. She politely suggests that Maria is expecting too much to quickly and should pick out two or three things that need to be done urgently, then explain why.

Maria does find this reasonable and calms down a little.

"Yes, priorities. Anyway, before we see one another again could you check the ownership of these buildings and those plots of land, which shouldn't be too difficult. I assume there's some kind of registry of land ownership, is that right?"

"Yes, there are records for every square metre of Germany."

"As I expected. So, here's the list. I'd also like you to check who owns some companies, the shareholders and managers. That's also clear, I hope."

"Yes, there are public records. The Industry and Trade Council, who play a bigger more official role than your typical 'Chamber of Commerce'. It's time consuming, not hard."

"Good. Can you also check their levels of debt. Now there's something I would like you to think about, then check with me for the go ahead before you actually do anything, alright?"

"I understand, what?"

"I'd like some information about insurance claims for these businesses and the various places on that list, you know, old fashioned insurance claims - fire, theft, accidents, all that, as much detail as you can. Is there a way?"

"I'll think about it. A lot depends on the company that wrote the policies."

"I know. But I'm not going to ask where your friends work, or what they ask in return for a little leaking, but I would happily recompence them for their efforts. Put it on the bill."

"If I knew what you are trying to achieve, I might be able to suggest some alternatives to these preconceived assumptions about what you expect me to do."

"Dani, please, don't ever try to second guess me. OK, I submit to your better judgement, or at least your local knowledge, but do not pretend you know the reason why I ask for something."

"Maria, the list is too long. Pick out one or two places and a couple of businesses, then I can probably find something without having to jump from office to office across the city. Once you've seen the kind of information available, you can decide how much more is going to be required."

"The locations would be those two and the buildings that one and that one."

"Ah. They're not far from my place."

"Do you own your home?"

"No, I rent, like most people. The older the buildings are tricky, full of expensive hidden surprises, repair work that turns into complete rebuilding. A lot of rough and ready patching was done after the war and the bombings. This city was seriously destroyed. Then the cold war meant property was worth next to nothing so it fell even further into neglect. Since then, people do a little modernising and give things a lick of paint. Anything with a preservation order is worth less than the cost of renovations. The city is built on sand and there are plenty of beautiful buildings sitting on foundations made of soggy rubble and rotten beams of old timber. Are these from Klaus' portfolio?"

"Not sure, that's one thing we should be able to find out."

"And these companies are also all local, based in Charlottenburg."

"Right. If you can dig out some background, I'd be very happy. What exactly is the Amtsgericht Charlottenburg?"

"A local court specialising in business and commerce," Dani tries again. "Why aren't you working with Caro?"

"I would have thought that was obvious. She's devious as an ally cat and a profoundly spoilt brat both at the same time, however likeable everyone finds her. She likes to convey the impression she's some kind of a loner, but that's impossible when it comes to large amounts of money. Actually, I'm surprised her people, whoever they are, have covered their tracks so convincingly. Can you help me find out who they are?"

This is almost the same pitch that Caro had made to Dani a week or so ago, when they first started working together.

Dani is surprised that being such an expert on groups and clans and gangs, Caro hadn't come up with a convincing 'anthropologically' certified description of the people that Klaus and Bernhardt have been playing their games with.

And if this Maria is the super hyper-legal brain she's cracked up to be then all the issues about who and what should be condensed in good clean prose before you can bat a heavily mascara'd eyelid.

She does ask one sensible question however.

"As a newcomer in this city, there are things people take for granted that I don't know anything about. What are the most obvious that I won't realise for myself."

"Something a lot of local people don't appreciate is that there are a lot of people here who don't really need to work for a living. They live off inherited wealth, the rent from houses, income from dividends and other investments. They have jobs for pleasure, they're hobbies, hardly necessary to be paid."

"Thankyou Dani, I'll keep that in mind." Like many Americans, Maria is habitually polite, "So business is inefficient, I see."

"Oh, and don't feel insulted when people ignore you in shops, or are they're rude, it's just the local state of mind. Berliners hate being nice to each other, so they really try hard to find a way of being unpleasant about little things that don't matter. It's stupidity, that's all, they way they think, or rather don't."

Somewhere or other there's a plot, but it isn't clear who, or what it is about. This is an impressive level of obscurity if the parties on both sides are equally bemused, or is their lack of clarity a kind of defense? Conspiracy theorists would have a field day if they ever got a whiff of what was in the works.

Instead of getting an answer to any of her questions, Maria does a brief check of Dani's to be done list, then asks her the best way of getting to the US Embassy, which turns out to be the location Z on her list.

Dani's company will not be required at what Maria explains is a kind of get together evening for American lawyers in Berlin and the business people who work with them under the auspices of the Embassy's Commercial Section.

When she notices the surprise in Dani's face, she laughs and asks whether Dani expected her to have travelled across the Atlantic without having done a bit of homework on her own behalf. Dani is waiting to see if she'll be invited along. She's been to the modernist Czech Embassy, a retro-chic classic and the heavily refurbished French place on the other side of PariserPlatz, but she hasn't made it inside the massive US Embassy next to the Hotel Adlon.

Maria recognises her disappointment. "Don't worry, it's not the CIA, not officially, some-one at these Embassy events must be I suppose, but then there always are some, aren't there, some of those? I'm officially going because a guest from San Francisco is going to be talking about games and simulations, someone else on econometrics, that kind of thing, but I'm really just going there to show my face and see if there's anyone who might be interesting. Maybe you should come along, no, sorry, that won't work, there was a deadline to get on the guestlist. But another time. The diplomats are always pleased to meet a friendly local, aren't they?"

Dani doesn't answer that question, but in her experience diplomats are more at home meeting each other than anyone else and tend to be cautious, guarded and uncertain in the company of anyone local. Such folk are seen as feral beasts. Ex-pats who've gone native are considered dangerous renegades. Diplomats rarely stay anywhere long enough to know much about the places they've been posted to. That's not their job. They are there to represent their governments. Understanding comes in last, like an old nag racing over hurdles.

"I do my best to work on a case by case basis, without distracting myself by getting carried away trying to understand the big picture, which is sometimes too broad for anyone to grasp."

Of one thing, Dani is now certain. Had Maria done any kind of homework at all, the name Julian Breitschied should have cropped up by now and there must be a good reason why it hasn't. She's decides another chat with Elfie Malzenberger might be a reasonable best place to start and taking into account La Malzenberger's leaky reputation, Dani decides she needs a convincing lie to ensure her questions arouse no suspicion.

Once Dani has rid herself of Maria's company, pointing her along Unter den Linden towards the Brandenburg Gate, "then look out for the large red and white stripey flag with some stars in one corner and you're there," she takes the S-Bahn to West-End and walks along a street that still brings with it that odd feel of half renewed bomb damage, Sophie-Charlottenstrasse. There are very few places where the scars of Berlin's wartime past are still recognisable, but this is one of them. She wants to take a look at the addresses Maria is interested in. Maybe some of the old English bombs have still to explode. Long before, in the days when hot air balloons were the only way to fly, Napoleon's Army had built a camp in the valley where the railway now runs parallel to the autobahn. As many as forty thousand military and camp followers were left there as the French campaigns stretched from Paris to Moscow and Berlin became a convenient staging post to supply the Grand Armée with its provisions and somewhere for the walking wounded to recover, or die. His soldiers introduced the notion of calling on gunpowder to take the place of salt in stew, which was what probably led to a whole cuisine developing based on saltpeter as a preservative for pork with variations on the name of kasseler, or more correctly Casseler, after its originator. Napoleon's occupation is another of those little details that gets ignored in the glorious history of Prussian Berlin, but that was also more likely when the Berlin cuisine acquired its burgerlike 'boulette', which had nothing at all to do with the Hugenot uniform makers, gun-smiths and weavers who'd settled in the city as refugees a century before.

Apart from one of the best restaurants in Europe and an unusual bar in the house where Berlin caricaturist and illustrator Heinrich Zille lived for much of his adult life, the Sophie-Charlottenstrasse is undistinguished, running parallel to the autobahn and the railway line, from the former goods yards that are now a small industrial estate. The only unusual spot is the workshop making Museum quality replica's of statues and objects in plaster, which are sent all over the world. They'll do you anything from Greek Gods to Rococo cherubs and a lot in between. Towards the Leitzensee things look up, where a little clump of well-to-do 'altbau' apartment blocks were built with a view over the park and behind them the art deco offices of the old German Post Office's research centre.

Dani ends up standing in front of a six storey building that is decorated in white stucco with little sculptures and symbols she thinks derive from some kind of old fashioned astronomy, or maybe chemistry. German chemistry had been at the high point of its history when these houses had been built just before the first world war. As usual there are dozens of name plates and doorbells by the entrance, two flats on each floor at the front of the building, another pair on either wing, then the same repeated with six more names for either side of the the hinterhof, the more prosaic dwellings in the building behind the building. These Berlin 'altbau' all follow a similar layout that originated from the particular way that property taxes were once levied, based on calculating the width of the street frontage without any further account of the scale of the building. For Berlin property sharks in the nineteenth century, the perfect building would have been no more than an entrance, big enough for a horse and cart, unfolding to fan out as you moved away from the street to become block after block of successive yards with workshops and homes.

There was a word for those kind of places, 'mietskaserne' - rent barracks, but the house she's standing in front of now, is far removed from the crudity of Prenzlauerberg, or Neukölln. These are luxury apartments and always were, intended for the city's prosperous business folk, the company directors, their lawyers and their doctors, the top level government administrators and their Ministers. The widows who prevail hereabouts carry themselves like vintage duchesses when they make a formal progress to the supermarkets on Kaiserdamm.

With a view over the lake for some, and thirty or forty apartments altogether, the place is worth more than a few millions whichever way you try to do the sums.

The places she's seen earlier were less impressive, two were pieces of open land, concreted yards that looked as though they'd been part of something else at some time or another, then ended up in isolation, unwanted orphans as the newer buildings around them just don't demand so much open space.

There had been all kinds of buildings near the railway yards, from rough and ready stables and workshops to coal dumps and just next door were the former isolation hospital buildings that had been built when epidemics were handled differently, before the arrival of antibiotics.

Now it looks as though most of the yards are used for parking, there are trucks, vans and lorries left there overnight as their drivers snatch some rest. Ten thousand square metres in packets of different sizes, none of them bigger than one half of a football pitch, might not seem like a lot, but with building permissions and city prices, the bundle starts looking quite valuable. In one of the yards, someone has tethered a couple of kites like the ones that still fly across the road from her house. There are stolen cars tucked away, deceptively close to a second hand car dealer's yard. One car a day is driven away and another one arrives to replace it. They're all good quality cars, up market, no number plates till they're equipped with a temporary number on a one way trip to the Ukraine, or White Russia. One of the kites is pale blue and the other is a lovely golden yellow. Dani is reminded of the Ukrainian flag. Maybe they provide a clue for the location of the pick up point for cars that are due to head east. She checks with Markus about that being plausible. He hums and hahs a bit, then says 'Why not?', which isn't very informative, then he wants bringing up to date, so they chatter as she's wandering along the street. Markus knows Julian Breitscheid by repute and isn't especially impressed. He dances at too many weddings in Markus' opinion, he wears too many hats at once.

The first of the houses she'd looked at needed no explanation at all. There are dozens of similar buildings all over the city, constructed after the war as emergency social housing for West Berlin during the 1950's, a mixture of one and two roomed flats, each with a brick balcony and a plaque near the entrance with a date and a version of Berlin's heraldic bear, the city's symbol, cast in metal. The house looked as if it had been renovated fairly recently and when she touched the walls, she realised it had been clad in lightweight insulating blocks, an energy saving programme sponsored by subsidies from the city, that enables landlords to save on energy costs and put in a rent increase. Hopefully they aren't inflammable.

Dani expects she'll find Klaus' pawmarks over the registry entries at the Amtsgericht and decides that she, Caro and Maria are likely to end up at loggerheads with one another unless something happens to clear the uncertainty.

She needs a drink and walks through the Leitzensee Park, then having sent a text message to Ulli, she goes down the little side street by the railway to the Soph-Am, where a gentle glass of cool Riesling will be waiting to quench her thirst.

No manzanilla today.

The Soph-Am is a haven of tranquility when she arrives.

She picks up the glass of wine and goes to her preferred table near the newspapers, then Uli comes over from the bar and says, "Someone was asking for you."

"Who?"

"A woman, dressed like a manager, and a second woman, a bit younger, looked like an off-duty hospital doctor."

"Are you just saying 'like', or do you know?"

"Well, the younger one says to me she works at the Charité. Thin as a rake, she was, skinny as a bean pole."

"Not many people know what a bean pole is any more, though I suppose they'll have half an idea about a rake."

"That's progress, of a sort. I will have to bear it in mind the next time," says Uli sceptically. "So, gardening similies are losing their resonance. You can be bloody difficult to talk to sometimes, do you know that Dani?"

"Anyway," says Dani, "since the Charité is the city's biggest hospital, has it sort of occurred to you that she might actually be a doctor."

"And the other one left a card, Selma Attaturk."

"You should get out more, Uli. Selma Attaturk is a cabaret character, a stage name. Didn't you recognise Karen and the 'doctor' would be Sarah, her daughter, remember, little skinny Sarah, legs like twigs? Sarah is a surgeon now. She's not a little girl any more, and she isn't little at all, but she is skinny. She does people's kidneys, transplants them, old ones out, new ones in, quick as a flash, she's a safe pair of hands. What was the message?"

"It must have been the hair and the accent, she's changed, she's very convincing. Anyway I haven't seen Karen for three or four years, no, ten, twelve, so... when was Sarah born, oh du scheisse, she's over thirty. She said you would know what to do."

"Do, about what?"

"How do you expect me to know."

"Ok, I'll phone, thanks Uli. The probably wondered why you were so stand-offish."

"I can't remember everyone can I?   ..... more?"

"Please. And a bigger glass this time. You and Karen were close."

"True, apologise for me when you see them."

Phil and the blonde are arguing doggedly about the merits of rebuilding, or demolishing the strange Congress Centre near the Funkturm, a glittering metallic edifice known as the ICC that was a nineteen seventies architectural gesture towards the future and is probably the only building globally to have copied the layout and appearance of an airport terminal for purposes other than transportation. In this case, delegates are fed through 'departure gates' leading to the halls positioned either side of a vaste central lobby. Visitors immediately feel alienated, or worse, divorced from reality. When conference delegates realise they're booked to spend several days here, they think of absconding. The building is a potent symbol of planning madness and no-one has ever enjoyed being inside its walls, nevertheless it is unique and unlikely ever to be copied. Isn't that reason enough for its preservation? Some people think it should be on the UNESCO World Heritage List - as a warning to others.

"At the moment, they're using it to house refugees from Syria," says the blonde loudly, "which is in my opinion only a hairsbreadth short of being a violation of their human rights, asbestos filled cladding or not! The ICC is nearest thing I've ever seen to a nightmare in architectonic form."

"Isa!" says Uli, "That's too much. Leave the refugees out of it. We should be worrying about the Berlin City Planning Department, rather than heaping the blame on itinerant Africans"

"And 'architectonic' sounds a bit pretentious too," adds Phil.

So the blonde is an 'Isa' in private, Dani registers, which is another of the Luise variations, so she could also be a Lou, which is how she's known in tv, though come to think of it isn't she a Malu sometimes too, Marie-Luise, that is. Dani decides to stick with the 'Blonde' label, as she wonders how the Dutchman is getting on.

The Riesling refill arrives in fresh glass. Uli brings the bottle over too and leaves it on the table. "Compliments of the management."

"This place doesn't have any management."

"Don't quibble, Dani. And don't push your luck."

Dani phones Sarah,

"Hi, me"

"Hello you."

"Uli said you and your Mum were at the bar. Why didn't you just phone?"

"Oh, Mum needed a drink. I shall too, once I've finished here."

"When will that be?"

"I get off early, just a couple of donors to confirm for next week. Paperwork to be readied for signing, you know the kind of thing. Will you still be at Soph-Am in about an hour?"

"I could be."

"Then I'll see you when I get there."

"Do I get clues about what you want to talk about?"

"No."

"Alright, be like that."

"A Mother problem."

"Oh," says Dani unenthusiastically, "One of those," which might or might not be the case. It won't be the first time they've gazed into a glass of wine with puzzled disbelief over parental eccentricities. Older generations baffle. Maybe that's just the way it is.

Less than half an hour has passed, in which time, Dani skimmed through a reasonably recent copy of the magazine Brigitte Woman and recognised the vegetarian, but not vegan recipes based on yoghurt, quark and fruit like strawberries and kiwis that they've been recommending to young women for decades, before settling for a book review of essays about money by a Hamburg based group of new-wave neo-feminists, which she found quite interesting, if mildly uninformative. Deeply unpopular vegetables like broccoli are still lauded with healthgiving properties. Avocado's have their place, usually on the left hand page because they photograph so well. She thinks there should be more articles about games development, but there aren't. There's sex, clothes and dinner, along with unhealthily large doses self-satisfaction. The riesling is refilled for a second time direct from the bottle, which is now empty and unlikely to be replaced.

"How is your Mum, then?" asks Dani, once Uli has finished apologising, when Sarah arrives. There's another bottle of free booze on the table.

"A bloody nuisance as usual. And yours?"

"Completely self-absorbed and uncontrollable."

"I know what you mean," Sarah sympathises. What are grown women supposed to do about their mothers? The question lays unmasked and unanswered, mere mutual thought since their mothers have been best friends since the days before either of them were born. Dani has known Sarah since she was a baby, though they don't meet very often now she has to work shifts at the hospital. Uli comes over and tries to make a fuss over Sarah, but she's gently shooed away.

"Fuck off, Uli, we're trying to have a serious conversation."

"Suit yourselves." A shrug of feigned indifference.

Dani has hurt her feelings.

"So what is going on?"

"That bastard Bernhardt, father of Carolina and an unknown number of illigitimate siblings presented himself on Mum's doorstep this morning and demanded asylum."

"So?"

"Then he collapsed semi-conscious and had to be put to bed. I gave him a sedative and vitamin cocktail and in about four hours from now he will wake up."

"Have you told Caro?"

"No. He's not in good shape. Someone seems to have given him a fairly serious beating and he's covered in bruises. We didn't want to have Caro running off in a panic to the police."

"Why not?"

"Because he also had sixteen kilos of medical grade cocaine in his bag and three of morphine. There were also a variety of unspecified crystalline powders, which I surmise are the fruits of his own efforts, assuming he's still up to his old tricks doping the globe. They are unusual, all the colours of the rainbow, so I don't think they're any of the regular varieties, probably his latest private toys. I hope he doesn't end coming to me pleading for a new kidney. I don't want to see what he's like on the inside."

"Oh."

"Yes."

"You could dump the dope somewhere."

"No chance, far too dangerous, you could get the whole city either high, or comotose with this much stuff and if it got into the Elbe, oh my god, poor Hamburg. A reasonable surmise too, that there is likely to be someone who thinks this is their cocaine and their morphine and their unspecified bags of narcotics and are waiting for Bernhardt to hand it over? Either that, or a very large amount of cash is waiting to be argued over. If transactions of that sort fail to go through, we could be in for some bloodletting."

"Is it possible he is one of the most stupid clever people ever born?"

"Probably," said Sarah, "He also seems to be the kind of guy who is the first to get kicked in the painfuls when a street fight starts. Deservedly too, I expect."

"Where's he been?"

"Before he passed out, he told me he'd driven here from Czecho, somewhere near Marienbad, after a flight by private jet from Cartegena via Senegal."

"Sounds credible. Think it's true?"

"Why not, with someone like Bernhardt? He's a pursuasive liar, even when his truths are half true."

"Can you explain why this conversation is between you and me rather than your mother and Caro, or you and Caro? Why me?"

"He asked us not to talk to her and he mentioned you specifically before he passed out. Someone has told him you're paying a pivotal role, whatever that is supposed to mean. Here I am. I assume you know what to do. I had thought you might know what this is all about. So, pivot! Please."

"Why do you expect me to know what to do with a degenerate old man I've never even met?"

"I just thought..."

"Then unthink for a minute. Hell-fire, it's absurd."

"I have no idea why he came to us, except for some misguided memory from the nineteen seventies of being in love with my Mum. He remembered her address, somehow, maybe that was it, nowhere else to go. His brain is more flashback and replay, than real-time and streaming. I don't know what to think."

"Neither does anyone else. You can know how to think, but you can't know what to think, until you've thought. He's not your Dad too is he?"

"Hell no, my Dad is my Dad. We share noses."

"I think the only thing we can do is to ask Bernhardt directly. Is there a wake up shot of something you could give him to undo the sedative you squirted earlier?"

"There is some stuff they use on horses," Sarah replies. "How old is he?"

"Ninety, eighty, who cares."

"If he's under seventy five, then I'll give it a try. We can check his passport."

"Assuming it's genuine."

"Doesn't matter, even fake passports are vaguely correct about people's age, plus or minus five years, usually a bit younger, gender too, though not always, the other details are what gets faked, nationality, name, birthday and so on."

"And where is he now?"

"In the spare room at my parents place."

"Which is?"

"Reinickendorf, one of the side streets in Weidmannslust, near the Scholle, the Bruno Taut estate."

"Why-ever did you Mother decide to live out there?"

"Sufficiently tucked away, so she can offer shelter to scallywags and ne're-do-wells like Bernhardt, I suppose. I don't have a clue. It's not a very nice house. The garage is quite big. So is the garden, but it means you have to do gardening. You'll have to ask her yourself whether it's worth it."

"What's that bloody noise?"

"Sounds like a helicopter is trying to land in the kitchen."

"Jesus, Fuck," shouts Uli in the voice she uses for giving orders.

"Whaaaaah?"

"Holy kedgereee, what the hell is that?"

A cloud of dense oily smoke has filled the street, plumes through the café doors and a deafening grind of malfunctioning helicopter turbine is rattling every cranny of the building. People are looking for nooks to hide in.

A large drab green military helicopter is just making a lopsided emergency landing in the only available open space on StuttgarterPlatz, which is an area this side of the railway lines usually regarded as a children's playground rather than a helipad.

Indeed there are several children standing traumatised where the machine has just toppled a slide and three swings, as flames lick along the fusilage and the pilot and co-pilot can be seen trying to escape. Rotor blades are slicing the air and threatening to decapitate parents and grand-parents alike. Dogs bark, then whine, then run.

As the copter descended a crowd of crows rose into the air, but their caws of protest are drowned by the sound of buckling metal.

A huge bang and intense flash confirm that a piece of debris has short circuited the overhead power lines of the high speed trains, while the 'copter bounces unpredictably between swings and roundabouts and for once the notions of adventure and playground are in harmony.

There are creaks, groaning metal, the rotors sheer themselves away from the hub as everything and everyone are suddenly hushed.

There are signs of life inside the machine and a door opens to allow a little coven of politicians to emerge blinking out of the sooty darkness. They're led into the Soph-Am to recover their wits. The Minister for something NATO-ish in a small neighbouring country, Holland, Denmark, Luxembourg, (who cares), needs the toilet badly and disappears downstairs before his security can give the glory hole an all clear. Uli is rapidly filling a row of shot glasses with deeply chilled 60% Crow Feather Gin as a restorative.

The Assistant BundesMinisterin has downed her first beer inside fifteen seconds and is sitting next to Phil and the Blonde, her hands visibly shaking. The Chanel jacket is soiled with hydraulic fluid, her hair a ragged mess. She's frazzled. Phil finds her sexy.

The crew are staggering around the street, dazed, cursing and bewildered, which sets off a flood of invective exploring the riper end of the politicians' vocabularies, especially from the Hungarian speaking military attaché who had just been along for the ride and only lives a couple of streets away.

His wife takes their children to the playground at least twice a week. He's not amused.

"I thought we were going to die, I thought, I.. .. ....fucking budget cuts, why don't these fucking machines fucking fly when you want them to? Fuck it, gimme another one. I'm never getting into one of those fucking things ever again, never ever again. Fuck, fuck, fuck it." His english has improved.

The glasses of gin are refilled the moment they're emptied.

The head of security has already downed three and is moaning in serbo-croat. Uli heaves another bottle out of the fridge.

"Calm down dear," says Phil, "And watch your language. There are plebs present. We wouldn't want them to hear an Assistant BundesMinisterin effing and blinding, not a Christian Democrat anyway."

"Go fuck yourself," says the Assistant Minister, "We nearly bloody died."

"And so did we. What your pilot was thinking of coming down here, I don't know. You had about thirty centimetres leeway on either side. He could have sliced up the whole street."

"We were on fire."

"I don't give a fuck what you were on, this is no place to crash land a Sikorski."

"It's a Eurocopter."

"That too. So what?"

"Have you no sympathy whatsoever"

"Of course not, you're politicians, what do you expect of a Eurocopter?"

A squall of police and security people are arriving in a blinking swarm of flashing lights and a horde of wailing sirens, spreading alarm and panic across the whole neighbourhood, or rather they would have done in any other city. Here in Berlin the locals simply watched the parade of blue lights and shrug with a 'who/what is it this time' disdain for the whole notion of emergencies. Mobile phones have sent their videos up into the cloud, and people around the world are beginning to enjoy the sight of a lurching helicopter surviving a rough landing in the middle of a city, as a troop of children gaze upwards fascinated, while it demolishes their playground.

"That looks like a total write off to me," says Ulrich from the Saxe-Coburg-Gotha Insurance Company of Aschaffenburg.

The politicians are quickly rounded up and whisked to a place of safety via the back seats of shiny black Maybachs that whoosh them away down the Kantstrasse.

No-one was killed, no-one was injured. Sarah is astonished. She had expected to find herself at the heart of a major medical emergency, but instead there are just heaps of scrap metal and smelly spilled fuel.

The fire brigade are busy spreading fire retardent over the whole street. A camera crew from RBB have arrived and are starting to film, as Rainer the reporter begins to find people to interview.

"So where were we," says Dani to Sarah, once the famous for five minutes celebrities are on their way.

The smell is taking more time to clear.

Quick minded as ever Uli had not just photographed her unexpected guests but printed off a couple of copies which the Ministers, the helicopter pilot and the Emergency Team Commander had all signed. She intends to have a copy framed to hang behind the bar with a fresh sign "How Soph-Am saved the Government".

"What are they going to do with the helicopter?"

"I suppose it will just be left to rot, like everything else that gets dumped on the street rather than sorted into the proper bin for recycling."

"There's a terrible smell of kerosene."

"I love the smell of aviation spirit," Dani says, "Reminds me of going flying with my Dad when I was little. We used to go up in his Viggen, my Mum made me a little flying suit and he attached some extra bits hooking me to the parachute harness. Talk about bondage. I'm glad we never had to use it."

Uli looks carefully into Dani's eyes, "Are you trying to convince me that jet fuel has the same effect on your mind as Madelaines had for old Proustie"

"We're different generations."

"Well, la de da. What a surprise. And there was I thinking Sylvia Plath had issues."

"Maybe we should syphon some of it off."

"That bloke with the machine gun won't let you."

"Oh, yeah, the bloke with the machine gun, well I suppose he has first pick."

"Maybe someone will set it on fire."

"That's a possibility."

"Anyone in mind?"

"Leo Mappel might be up for it, him and Karl-Heinz the cabbie. Leo is always on about who started the Reichstag fire, so he might like to have a go at starting a conflagration of his own given the chance."

"Yeah, Leo is a problem once he's got a box of matches in his hand. You should see him on New Years Eve with the fireworks."

"Pyro-bloody maniac, you're right. Can you still buy boxes of matches?"

"I'm not sure, now you come to ask. We have tapers at home, for candles and the like, but no-one has matches they way people once did. Not just smokers, or arsenists, almost everyone used to carry a box of matches around with them, and not so long ago, either, when you think about it. Now I don't know anyone who does. We don't use matches for lighting the gas cooker, and cigarettes, or pipes or all the other bits of fire that used to be all over the place."

"Fire is disappearing from our culture."

"The nearest most of us get to ashes nowadays are funerals."

"I hadn't thought of it like that, but you might be right."

"It used to be much easier to get rid of a body, when there was a coal fired furnace in the basement of almost every building in the city."

"Dani?" says Sarah.

"Yes?" answers Dani.

"Do you think we can go?"

"Yeah, direction mother?"

"Yours or mine."

"Yours, we need to interrogate bloody Bernhardt."

As Sarah and Dani leave, Phil and the blonde start to diss the Minister, discussing her career with disdain.

"What exactly does the Minister for Defence Procurement do?"

"Procures, organises the camp followers for our brave lads and lasses to enjoy."

"That's not a very wholesome occupation for a Christian Democrat."

"Licencing Army brothels was regarded by economists as a prime example of interference in the workings of the free market. It threatened to ruin the market for anti-syphillis treatments,

188

especially in Vienna, which is how they came up with the notion of Austrian Economics and supply meeting indirect demand. You can ask Wolfgang Schauble about that next time you see him."

"Well fancy that. You would know. I do sometimes wonder what you got up to when you were young."

"That was all a very long time ago, Phil. I read a lot."

"It certainly was, and it shows; there's no point trying to hide the fact, is there, darling?"

"No point at all."

"Not when the mirror's cracked from side to side."

"Uli, come here and try some of this," says the blonde.

"What is it?" Phil wants to know.

"Turron, from Barcelona, made from almonds, egg yolk and honey too, I think. The Minister's Assistant gave it to me."

Uli takes a piece and chews, "Oooh, that's the sweetest thing I've ever tasted, it's delicious and potentially lethal."

The blonde offers her the rest of the packet, "Here, Uli, take it, for you. If I start eating stuff like that I shall need the rest of the week in a slimming farm, or my career will be over inside six months."

"Go on, try some Phil," says Uli encouragingly, "Rediscover your innermost vices, or do you already have diabetes from all the beer? Sugar, sugar, sugar, it's a fat mans world."

"Shut up Uli, hush, my ears are still ringing from that bloody helicopter crash. Gimme a Bloody Mary, darling, if you don't mind."

That set the pattern for their evening.

A lot was drunk, a lot was said and for the most part forgotten.

In another part of the city, almost seventy thousand people, mainly men, mainly middle aged, mainly beer drinkers, watch a football match, then make their way home. To them it was an uneventful evening, of undistinguished sporting prowess.

One team were in red, the other blue. Two goals were scored, neither of them memorable and the final result was a draw.

No kites could be seen flying over the stadium and everyone got home safely.

There was general sense of surprise when they learned of the helicopter crash. None of the fans had noticed a thing, even when their S-bahn trains had shunted slowly past the site of the crash.

Chapter 11

"What the hell was that?" shouts Berhardt as he's sprung upright by Sarah injecting the syringe full of wake up shock dope. He'd actually been startled by the bickering of a pair of jays in a tree outside the bedroom window, but he hadn't recognised the fact. The dope only brought him round a little faster.

"Who are you, oh, you again. The daughter. Where on earth? Are you trying to kill me girl?"

"Not quite, you'd be dead if I was, trust me, I'm a doctor," she answers coolly, "You're a lucky guy. Someone wants to talk to you."

Sarah is quietly relieved she hadn't got the dose far wrong, assuming he was between 7% and 12% the weight of a typical horse and modifying the shot accordingly. He is a lucky guy, a few milligrams more and the shock that drops. This way, he should start running at fences in half an hour or so.

He then moans with pain and mumbles, "Bloody Berlin. I should have known. Dreadful place, the pits, always has been. Trouble from the word go, always was, always will be, ask Bismarck."

The bruises are real and his muscles have stiffened up since they put him to sleep.

"Painkiller?" asks Sarah.

"Yes, yes, please, oh please, oh painkiller, oh Christ, yes, deep profound, please sweetheart," he whispers as an aching surge of new hurts swims from toe to head. He tries to move an arm, but fails and groans again. "Don't kill me yet, just kill the pain. Then we'll see if I recover." "Nothing broken," Sarah says, wondering if he's having a brain haemorrhage. Maybe his circulation is about to collapse. "Fuckhead," she whispers under her breath and isn't heard.

He's breathing hard, gurgling noises coming from his lungs, heart racing.

He could die.

He might survive.

Fifty-fifty, ninety-ten, who's measuring?

He's right to be pragmatic, but Sarah doesn't care.

For her, death is an everyday occurrence and he's an annoyance she can do without. The hospital incinerator will handle things limb by limb, organ by organ, if all else fails, as it usually does.

Bernhardt hasn't realised the precarious nature of his situation. Sarah's mother had been scarred for life by her youthful encounters with the man and her daughter knows the whole story. To say they hold him in low regard would be an understatement.

Dani looks on, with mild revulsion. She suspects he's about to die on them.

Then Bernhardt perks up, crisis gradually receding. He's a tough old bastard. His perennial suntan is reasserting itself. If the women feel a sense of disappointment they don't show it. If they're honest, no-one actually wants a corpse in their spare bedroom.

"I suppose there's a first time for everything."

"Such as?"

"Getting beaten up twice on the same flight."

"What happened?"

"One of the flight-attendants took a higher dose of 'enjoy yourself' than intended for her body-weight and turned aggressive. As she is rather fit and well trained anyway, she took rather a lot of calming down."

"Calming down, meaning?"

"Restraint, handcuffs, then a sedative."

"So that was the first beating. How did you manage to get duffed up twice?"

"The co-pilot was her brother. He got upset when he found out I'd fired her."

"Where had she got hold of the 'enjoy yourself'?"

"I gave it her, what did you expect? My people always depend on me for their drugs."

"Give us this day our daily dope...."

"Are you a believer?" He looks at her incredulous.

"Don't you believe it."

"The days of bread and circus's are long gone. Nowadays, young lady, all people want is a gentle daze of placid haze. And sex, of course, well sometimes, well I do too, don't you?"

"Was this flight of yours from Cartegena via Dakar to Czecho actually on a plane going at high speed through the air at considerable altitude, or were you all enjoying each other's company closer to ground level in a flight simulator located somewhere in the vicinity of Berlin Schonefeld?"

Bernhardt tries laughing, which induces more pain, "I wish I'd thought of that. No, she punched me in the kidneys as we were passing over the Cape Verde Islands."

"I think your kidney functions are probably ok, want to see if you can piss? Shall I find you a bottle?"

"No."

This is the first time Dani has seen Bernhardt in the flesh rather than on tv. He'd been an 'opinion maker' during her childhood, an over-exposed television optimist pontificating about the brilliant future awaiting the whole human race as she was growing up, then once she was adult he was still there pontificating and pontificating for the need for everyone to love one another and be nicer than they've been for the preceeding ten, or twenty thousand years, because climate change was going to make life hell for rest of time.

Then he'd gone to jail for a bit and he hadn't been back in the mainstream media after that, but he is ubiquitous online, you can't avoid his Youtubeiness. Hilberg's Honey Spread dwindled in popularity and has disappeared from the supermarkets, but his 'Happy Highs' have endured as an integral element of Berlin myth along with half remembered gravel voiced nightclub singers, ecstacy and the Love Parade. Now, his skin has the lizard spotted tan of sweet cured ham and the blue eyes are squeezed swollen, almost shut, by the fresh bruising which is well beyond botoxing. The teeth, or what pass for teeth in a world of implants have suffered a series of dramatic fractures. Bullshit in a china shop syndrome, that mouth of his.

Sarah's mother Karen is distraught.

"I should have left him to die in nineteen eighty, while we had the chance. This is like having the mummy from beyond the grave in your spare bedroom, intolerable."

"Bernhardt, did you go through customs after you landed, passport control, baggage checks, that kind of thing?"

"Of course not," he scoffed. "What on earth do you think private planes are for?"

"Bernhardt, you're a shit," says Karen.

"I know, I apologise, I always apologise, I always do and I'm sincere, truly sincere, but it no longer seems to work," he says, "Apologies are passé."

He stops jabbering and for a moment there is a studied sceptical silence, which is eventually broken by Karen, who has never been one to keep her mouth shut for long.

"Could we drive out into the countryside and leave him to be discovered tied to a tree, or bound to the wheel of a sunken canal boat."

"We could, but that would be murder, Mum," says Sarah.

"And....? He's going to die on us anyway, isn't he? That's not murder, it's an imposition."

"I wouldn't put it that way," says Sarah. "Though he is a bit of a challenge, that much I will concede. We could hasten the inevitable, I suppose......."

"Maybe we should dump him at the entrance to a hospice and let them finish the job."

Then Dani takes over, explains she is currently working as Maria's assistant, but also tells him she knows his daughter Caro and says that she would like to know what he wants. Indeed they would all like to know what he wants.

The others nod in agreement.

He gags a little, so they wait.

"What I want, ladies, is some of that stuff in the green plastic bag, six milligrams dissolved in alcohol and gently placed on my tongue by a pipette," he says, "then leave me alone for a couple of days, till these terrible nightmares return to simple dreams. Perhaps you would oblige me Frau Doktor. And get hold of Mikki Sonne. I want a talk with him. Do you know who he is; has a brother Markus who's a car man? The other brother is dead, Mo. Called himself Hoffman rather than Sonne, or was it the other way around. Thought of himself as some kind of artist. Yeah, I think their mother's name was Sonne, Madelaine. 'Maddy', 'Mad' Sonne, and she was, crazy, crazy lady, lovely on a sunny evening in Kreuzberg, Golgotha, two beers and a joint. They had a sister, Melanie, who went to live on a sheep farm in New South Wales, then shipped out to New Zealand. The father's lot were Hoffman's. The one I want to talk to is Mikki, J. Michael Sonne as he was born, assuming he wasn't a Hoffman. Have you noticed it's hot in this room."

"We'll find him somehow."

"Could we open a window? I need a drink and a woman. What day is it today?"

"Wednesday."

"Leave me alone till Friday, a bit of food, some soup, some milk, apart from that just a broadband connection, via a phone if necessary and on Saturday, I promise, I will be gone. Karen, will ten thousand euros a day be a help. And you girl, Danieli, I'll pay you whatever Carolina is paying you as long as you do exactly as I ask."

"Sure, but don't expect me to to say thankyou." She's been called a lot of things over the years, but this is the first time anyone has referred to her as a Venetian hotel.

"Sarah, I'm imploring you, prepare the pipette."

"Weeeeeelll, alright. Now, where's that cocktail shaker," she says coquettishly a bottle of vodka in one hand and the little green bag in the other.

Bernhardt has started taking stock of his situation and looks around the small room where he'd been sleeping. He's surprised how little her taste has changed since 1979. The same colours, patterns, bits of nineteenth century style in uncomfortable proximity to plastic. There are linen cushions. A rarety nowadays, but once the cat's knees. Bernhardt is glad he's found sanctuary with such a friendly soul. He can't pretend to be so generous about the daughter, who strikes him as being a bit of a harradan, doctory, doctorish.

Karen's house is a typical family home surrounded by a modest garden. Pleasant enough. The walls are brick. The doors and windows are painted dark green and have been since it was built in

1928. Inside, there is a studied sense of kitsch and some books. Sarah pours half a bottle of vodka into the cocktail shaker and a teaspoon full of the blue powder, throws in some ice and some mint, then screws on the lid and shakes with the aplomb of a well practised barman. Dani looks on as Bernhardt glares towards Sarah, eyes bulging with with eager desire. When she's finished, Sarah pours some of the resulting liquor into a cone shaped cocktail glass, decorated with a slice of lemon and sucks a dose of the stuff into the pipette. Then she squirts the lot into Bernhardt's mouth and he sighs with pleasure. "Good, girl, thank Christ for that. Ohhhhhhh."

"Always a pleasure, you old bastard. Mum, no more than three shots of that a day, or he will die."

A minute later and Bernhardt is calm, collected, doing his best to sound thoughtful, "You know buildings don't stay new very long, considering what they cost. They are far less permanent than we like to pretend, especially in a climate like this, cold winter nights, hot summer sun, it opens up the cracks till they can no longer be ignored. Crack and decay, more cracks, further decay, soon time to tear the place down and start again. Lovely to seen you again after all these years, Karin. The day before yesterday, I had more teeth. Could you possibly arrange for me to see a dentist? My mouth feels like monument valley, arid and eroded."

"I'll see what can be done."

"They're porcelain, not real. Ask if they could come here rather than me going to them. Do we have decent broadband? I need the net, get me online, please. And don't tell Marie that we've met. That is imperative. I'll talk to Caro myself, so don't mention any of this to her either. I shall see them both very soon. Then we can see. Wednesday, Thursday, Friday, Saturday, Karen, here's your money. Forty thousand Euros, not dollars, cash."

"You can leave it on the table. I'll pick it up once you've gone."

"Your choice. I need to sleep. Can you come back in about five hours? Is there soup? Fuck it."

He's taking too much for granted, but Sarah and Karen are depending on her for help, so Dani concludes that in order to help them she has no choice but to help the old man. As soon as he can be moved, they'll dump him at Caro's place by the canal, whether he wants to be with his daughter or not. She can have the job of telling

Maria and take things from there. Dani has no intention of doing their dirty work for them, any of them. "The last time I was on a commercial flight, out of Denver to be precise," Bernhardt tells Dani as Sarah brings him soup later on, granting one of his wishes, "Everyone around me were playing games on their mobiles and tablets. Everyone on the plane, except me and hopefully the flight crew, every single one of them. Not one was watching the clouds go past the window, or looking down to see what America looks like from ten thousand metres. I was appalled. Flight, mankind's great dream for millenia has ceased to hold any mystery powerful enough to distract people from their trivial online pursuits. That is an appalling situation. Reality is losing its capacity to awe."

"My patients are the same," replies Sarah, as she clean the pipette and offers Dani a quick squirt. "Want some?" Sarah drips five drops onto her own tongue and sighs, "Wow! Hey Dani you really must try this. Oof! Wombat!"

Sarah's intrigued by this reputed ogre who strikes her as an erudite and rather amusing old man, despite the generous haul of illegal drugs that are still sitting on the shirt shelves in the wardrobe. "I have patients, sitting in their beds, days away from extinction, end of life, all over unless I can pull off a bloody miracle, yet all they want to do with their remaining time on the planet is to manipulate an algorithm via a screen display and pretend it's somehow real, as their own presence ebbs away. There have been days when I go home and weep at the thought. The virtual is an illusion shorn of all virtue."

"While I was on the plane, a little programme on my own machine enabled me to see precisely what people were up to and that was even more revealing," says Bernhardt. "Nearly everything that occupied their attention was based on military violence, apart from one or two empire building strategy games in which military conquest played a subordinate role to geo-politics. Six young guys were busy sniping, simulating shooters with distant targets. A lot of the time, they were gossiping with each other as they played. Another group were basically squad and platoon commanders, the smallest units of military organisation, either skirmishing, or filling some defined space on a battlefield. There were bomber pilots sneaking to attack unnoticed and fighter pilots busy dog fighting.

Then there were the drone pilots busying themselves snooping images from a huge distance, then moving in for the kill at their leisure. Some of them would break off an attack to get a burger from the flight attendants, do some chewing, then kill their targets a few minutes later. What I found most extraordinary was that no-one realised they were all playing the same game. Some of them thought they were in deep space fighting an intergalactic conflict. Under another name, there were people fighting on the surfaces of strange planets. But the whole thing was seamlessly integrated. One game had the battle raging underground in a mine where thousands were digging for diamonds in Southern Africa. Another version was in Ancient Rome, yet another the American Civil War. I felt disappointed for them, all of them. The victors and the vanquished, actually there were neither, merely gamers gaming and paying, time passing, whether real-time, or game-time and the games responding as programmed. Is this player active, paying attention, or simply online and logged in, but probably doing something else, that was the question."

Bernhardt took a sip of the lemony tea Sarah had brought him. The pipette is ready with a little top up and twelve drops of his preferred dope are carefully dripped on his tongue.

"That's your lot until bedtime," says Sarah, licking her fingertip.

"Something refreshing at last, thank you."

"The soup should be cool enough too, in a minute."

Then he picks up the theme, "I refuse to be drawn into debates about ethics. Almost every unethical event in the history of mankind has been justified by someone on grounds of necessity. Terrible but necessary, covers everything from trenches to nuclear. Ethical considerations get set aside. Repulsive self-deception seems to be integral to human behaviour. That apart, how can we hold ourselves accountable when the system to which we're contributing is kept out of sight, when we don't know whether we're in deep space, or the ancient past? Are we expected to criticise the plane makers whose rocket lifts a weather satellite into orbit because the weather information is used by the military, or the games industry for purposes we disapprove? Do we criticise those same people when their rocket is adapted to carry some payload which turns out to be a nuclear bomb and not a weather satellite? There are far more

197

examples of plough shares into swords than the other way around, so don't ask me to stand in judgement. I do drug design via the study of molecular interaction. I don't make unusual devices with inappropriate applications. I cannot sanction particular lines of action. I play no part in the processes of permissions and licencing. If some process of production exploits my designs to cultivate a degree of creative complexity I have not foreseen, the decision to incorporate the results in some strange and exotic context are beyond my control. All I do is innovate. The rest is up to others."

"Is the pharma industry such a can of worms," asks Sarah. "My job would be meaningless without them."

"I wasn't thinking of pharma, my dear. I am talking about government."

"Which one, the Germans, the USA?" asks Dani as Sarah tries to check the old man's blood pressure without success. The heart is still beating, so there must be a modicum of blood sloshing about the place, but she can't confirm the fact.

"Who knows which government, there are dozens and dozens to choose from, local, regional, national, take your pick. We have far more governments than we have pharma corporations and they are far less predictable. Governments make the rules, they don't play by them like businessfolk. And in most parts of the world governments are the only ones allowed to play with guns. Sometimes they call themselves police, sometimes army, sometimes security, sometimes they just have people in uniforms with guns. Officially everything is defensive, even when they attack. Some of them are small, some of them are big. Some of them are quite well run. So let's be serious for a moment, governments worry me, pharma companies do research, then sell what governments allow.

I doubt if a typical pharma company has so much as a bow and arrow in its armoury, never mind a cruise missile, or a nuclear bomb, whereas any tinpot dictator you might choose will have their battalions at the ready.

Now, give me the chance to get some sleep. They're bringing in the youngsters next week. No-one takes this city very seriously, you know, they talk about the 'Germans', as though a few smutty car companies are something special."

Bernhardt likes to put himself on a pedestal with the very best, but he's pragmatically inclined to bend with the wind, as only the very unscrupulous are able. "The Germans may want to believe that the Americans are wonderful, but, were you to ask, very few Yanks could actually pinpoint Germany on a map. Germany is just a name to them, like Japan, somewhere that isn't American, but isn't in Africa. Maybe the time has come for people to start being worried by Berlin."

He reminds her that the Americans need reminding that they no longer control Berlin, which they never did anyway, even in the bit of the place that was their remit and the Germans need reminding that far from being their best friend 'Ami's, the Americans don't give a damn about anyone except themselves.

He started gulping for breath then calmed down.

"Seamlessness, young lady. Seamless play is the goal of the day."

He looks directly into her eyes, a stern glare, that turns into a fixed glaze as he speaks again.

"The confines of a dishonourable conscience are infinite. The confines of infinity are far from sufficient for the man who has everything."

And with that, he slipped into the kind of deep recuperative sleep that usually follows a car crash and can leave you unconscious for days.

Dani does as he asks and ends up sitting with Sarah's mother, who doesn't have a lot to say, but says it anyway. While they're talking, Dani admires the garden and wonders whether she would enjoy having one, deciding it is probably too much work. Then, in a quiet moment of realisation she recognises that Caro and Maria are still building legitimate reasons to distrust one another. Given the degree of posturing going on, she wouldn't be surprised if they begin to dislike one another intensely and she will end up in the middle of a God almighty explosion of scandal and resentment. Dani reminds herself she is neither referee, nor 'second', just a useful, happened to be on the scene of the crime kind of person. Someone else can mop up the soggy remains and assist the police with their enquiries.

Dani is looking for the answer to a simple question.

"What the fuck is going on?" she asked, rhetorically, without realising she had spoken out loud.

"How the hell should I know," Sarah's mother Karen answers assertively.

The question might be a simple, but there isn't going to be a simple answer.

Karen, I think you're the only person in this whole tangled heap of confusion who hasn't been telling me a pack of lies. I'm going home. I hope for all our sakes he doesn't die on you. Goodnight."

Sarah had driven them out to her Mother's place, so Dani has to work out where she is then think about the potential of an S-bahn journey which would inevitably involve either Gesundbrunnen or Friedrichsstrasse on the wrong side of town, or getting herself to Tegel for the U-bahn that would take her to Zoo. For half a second she considers overnighting at her parents' house which is only a few streets away, then she decides a taxi is the only practical way to escape from a house so deep in the anonymous backstreets of Reinickendorf. At least it isn't Fronau. The driver gets her back to Charlottenburg in half an hour.

Is anyone waiting for Dani when she gets home?

No.

Is there anyone online who wants to talk with her?

No.

Does she feel lonely?

No.

Dani is too tired for any of that and as soon as she finished eating some warmed up pizza and swapping an email with Georg, she flops on her bed and goes to sleep.

On awakening to the sound of crows cawing at seven o'clock next morning, she wondered whether she could remember her dreams - to no avail. The hours had passed uneventfully, or so it seemed. Then she remembers that Maria expects her to have fished around for information about the places she'd looked at before the old man's theatricals had interrupted everything.

It takes two hours in the records office, which thankfully opened at eight, so she has a reasonable list of owners and interested parties for each of the buildings, then she checks the register of residents who've listed these addresses with the police and comes up with a list of almost a thousand names, ranging from children and babes in arms to people who have lived there after the war and subsequently moved away or died.

She's quite pleased with herself, copies as much as possible onto a memory stick, then sends Maria a message and they agree to meet at her hotel in the Fasanenstrasse.

Dani decides to take the U-bahn to Zoo and walk from there, then wishes she hadn't. As she's waiting on the platform, a well dressed woman in her late fifties approaches her.

"They've run out of land and run out of ideas," she says with certitude, making clear to Dani that she's expected to hear her out.

"Who?"

"The city needs the tax. They need the building jobs. But there's no more land to build on, so much has gone that all they can do now is sell off our little weekend gardens as building sites for concrete monstrosities that no-one needs. So much for leases!"

Dani smiles politely, deciding to make sure they're in different carriages once the train comes in.

"It seems innocuous at first. Then gradually people realise that everything they take for granted is being undermined. Of course, by then, it's much too late, they've fucked you in the arse."

"I really don't know," Dani answers.

"Well I do and believe me I know what I'm talking about. I hope you don't expect to get a pension you can live off when you're old. That kind of thing is finished, all over. It just won't happen, so don't deceive yourself. Take to crime while you've still got time on your side. The only thing to do. I'm a pickpocket, thanks."

At which point a train rattled into the station and Dani made her escape without inviting further elaboration.

Chapter 12

"So the old man finally showed up," says Maria when she and Dani meet in the hotel lobby. "I know I wasn't supposed to find out, but hey, I do! He can't keep his mouth shut, even when he's comotose. You did a good job, keeping everything low key, now it's just a question whether he lives or dies. He thinks he might die, something about horse dope I didn't understand. Clever of you to find him, but I'm not sure I care, do you?"
Maria is well informed.
Dani is not about to start caring about a wealthy egomaniac either.
The Markus phones in answer to her message on his machine. "Well he isn't going to get to talk to Mikki, because my older brother died in 1995. You can tell him that and you can also tell him I want nothing to do with him, now, or at any time in the future."
Ouch!
Dani apologises for her error, but doesn't tell Maria what he's said. Dani is wondering whether Bernhardt was merely confused by the drugs, or is living in a permanent state of complete fantasy.

"Let's go over the road to the café garden in front of the cinema," she suggests to Maria, "We can sit in the sun. And it's quiet."
Maria seems more than happy to get away from the hotel, where she's had a long and phone call dominated breakfast chatting with people who were irritated by her lack of a sense of time.
Nine-thirty in Berlin is not just past people's bedtimes in Miami, even for night-owls, it is the middle of the night. There's only six

hours between the two cities. But it's not every day that there's a message for your bosses about one of their most important clients being at death's door doped up to the eyeballs in a foreign land, where you just happen to be visiting, he having managed to get beaten up on a private plane, which is regarded as something of an achievement in itself.

She in turn was informed of the likelyhood of a hurricane, which could destroy their family home over the next few days and her husband is taking the children to his parents in Montana for a couple of weeks.

Maria thinks that is very sensible, had chatted to the children for a minute or two and wished Lee well. She intends to stay in Berlin. Hurricanes are par for the course in Florida and you get used to the notion of total destruction, even in the middle of the night. Yes she is enjoying herself, she had confirmed in reply to his question.

"One of the people I met last night told me this club in the basement was once about the most famous Kabaret in the world, the Tingel Tangel, the one in the film, where we all imagine Lisa Minella used to sing with Marlene Dietrich."

"I didn't know that, how interesting," say Dani, not wanting to criticise the detail, then out of politeness, she asks if the hotel is OK, though she already knows it is.

She has decided she has to show a little patience, defuse any abiding frustrations and build things up slowly to create a modicum of trust. Maria looks as though she's been dragged through a hedge backwards, but Dani says nothing about that. Women face unreasonable expectations when it comes to grooming and Dani has no intention of upping the stress. Maria seems to be adapting to Berlin's notion that nightlife gets going sometime after midnight and only stops when you do.

"Yes, just fine, smokey where they have that cigar bar, but I have a kind of nostalgic pleasure for heavy Cuban and humid Dominican tobacco fumes, their intensity, so I rather enjoyed myself last night. Ludwig, he said his name was. A used carpet salesman or something of the sort. Knew what he was doing however. Smoke, drink and sex, kind of retro, but I enjoyed. My husband will kill him, if he ever finds out, which is an added kink of mine that the boys I meet don't know about. I mean, they think they're taking charge, when they're actually dotting the i's crossing the 't's on their own death warrant should I ever decide to spill the beans. They just don't know the risks they're taking. Makes me want to come just thinking about it. Must be the mantis in me."

She grins and Dani smiles politely. This woman is going to be trouble, which might turn out to be fun. There are worse things in life than erotic excess.

"I haven't had as much sleep as I would have liked thanks to the news about Caro's father," says Maria sincerely.

"I think I know of somewhere you should visit while you're here. Nothing to do with Caro and her Dad, more a matter of catering to your other tastes."

"Really, well that sounds promising, thankyou dear Daniela! You don't mind if I call you Daniela?"

"Of course not, that is my name."

"Or should we say Ella?"

"If you wish." Dani has just as often been Ella as Daniela, or Dani.

She wants Maria to have confidence in her, "The Dark Shadow is a rather special club, for people with special tastes!"

"Well, I am curious, I'm sure you've guessed that much about me. A new city, a new continent of experiences. Especially in the original 'Metropolis' that brought us Magnus Hirschfeld and his Institute for Sexual Research. Hmm, delightful, delicious, depravity! Very few people in Miami are aware of that, but I do my research. It was an incentive for my trip. And there's Wilhelm Reich and his orgones, of course. Not that I can see there's much fun being shut in a box. I wouldn't go so far as to say I believe in Reich's ideas, but there must be something to learn from all these centuries of erotic experimentation. Does every German have a kink, or is that just a Berlin thing?"

"Berlin does attract people with a wide variety of tastes," she replies demurely, "which is one of the reasons why all the politicians have always hated it, all of them from Bismarck to Hitler and Helmut Kohl, none of them liked the place. I don't think German politicians are any good at sex. They get their kicks from power plays and intrigue, which doesn't leave a lot of time for much of anything else. Willy Brandt was different, with or without his trousers, but there's always an exception."

"Well, some of them do try, don't they? You know, this city could be just the place for me."

Dani listens politely, wondering why Maria is telling her these stories, trying to make things seem normal. She's not supposed to be on some sensual pilgrimage. All that's for the tourists.

The two women order orange juice, rather than coffee.

Dani wonders whether they are going to return to the business of Bernhardt and Caro, or wander off into the further realms of erotic fantasy. There are places to be discovered, that's for sure.

At a thousand Euros a day, she won't complain, whatever Maria decides she wants to do, but she wants to believe she's also earning the thousand Euros a day that Caro is paying her and indeed if the thousand a day that Bernhardt has proposed should be taken seriously, then she'll do her best for him too, though she doesn't expect she'll see any of that! She's never been paid three 'k' a day before, even in theory. At least one of them will settle their bills, she feels sure, so Dani's feeling pretty good. No doubt Caro will be interested to discover the woman's kinks, but Berlin isn't the kind of city where you bribe people about their repressed desires, this is where you pay to explore them. The range is too great and the realities go a good deal further than most people's imaginations. Local people would merely measure any revelations on a scale from one to a thousand and that would be that. The orange juice tastes wonderful in the warm sunshine.

Maria is checking her mail and opens the documents Dani had sent her. "Oh, there's a lot, this is very detailed, tell me what it all means."

There are a bundle of .pdf's with names and addresses also as spreadsheets, with information about the buildings and plots of land they have an interest in. Most of them are simple downloads from the official websites where public records can be accessed. Dani translates the main category headings and matches the lists of occupants' names to the registration documents for the family homes and offices, the businesses and workshops that are listed for each building and the owners of the property. Buildings with forty or more apartments have had a massive number of tenants and owners over the years, as sub-division follows sub-division.

Nearly all the big buildings also have commercial premises mixed among the apartments, even if they're just offices for lawyers, or book-keepers and accountants, though often there are little shops on the ground floor on either side of the entrance, or places for shoe-makers and plumbers to work, somewhere with a workbench, a place for tools and a store for materials. Impossible to know who might have worked there. A couple of the buildings have whole floors that have been used as small hotels. Some of these Berlin hotels are residential homes for longterm guests, even students, or they can be pied-à-terres for companies whose people visit the city on a regular basis, the Manager, the PA, the usual. Reader, I married him. Eventually, he dumped her. Sometimes they're thinly disguised brothels and just sometimes, they're simply what they say they are, small hotels for people visiting the city.

In this part of Charlottenburg, the visitors tend to be attending trade fairs and conferences up at the Congress Centre and Exhibition Grounds, which is only five or ten minutes walk away. Some are actors hired for jobs at the tv station. Journalists show up sometimes. Tourists tend to rent rooms privately via the internet rather than bothering with traditional hotels, so they don't feature the way they once did.

"What are you looking for," Dani asks. "I didn't find anything particularly unusual. The city is full of buildings like these."

"Two things. First, one of my neighbours back home asked me to find the house where her grandparents lived, which is difficult online because of the way street names have changed over the years. She wants to have one of those little brass plaques set in the pavement outside to commemorate the people who were sent to the concentration camps, everyone in her family apart from her mother who was sent abroad as a baby."

"I'm sure we can find that out without too many problems. 'Stolperstein', stumblestones, they're called, those little plaques, mimicking the uneven paving that makes you trip and look down. They're everywhere. What was the family name?"

"She told me to look for Möller, Helmuth Möller, Anna Möller, Louise Möller, Jeannete Hofmann and her brother Arnold. There were uncles and cousins, aunts and grandmothers too. Sachsenhausen, Belsen and Auschwitz The family came from

206

Frankfurt originally. The older generation were all murdered, except for my neighbour's father in law. He was just a teenager at the time and managed to survive."

I'm sure we can make the arrangements once you've found the address and the names can be checked. The records are alarmingly complete. I think a lot of visitors to Berlin have these thoughts in mind, the local people less so, though there are exceptions."

"Good, my friend Hannah will be delighted. The second bit is more tricky. Expect a building where say twenty or thirty people can stay, that also has a technical area with high quality telecommunications links, everything from 'backbone' to 'microwave' and satellite 'uplink'. Think it must have belonged to Klaus at some time or other."

"Why are you interested?"

"Lets find the place first."

"There's the regional television station not far from here, public service radio everything."

"No this will be more a specialist centre of some sort."

"I'm not sure what I'm looking for."

"Maybe telecoms?"

"Yes! Of course, I'll take you there and show you."

"How far?"

"Ten minutes by car, come on, we can get the bus down Kantstrasse."

Unfamiliar as Maria is with the notion of effective public transport, she's getting used to the idea that busses are faster than cars in Berlin, run on time and someone else does the parking. Dani hasn't mentioned the recent crash, no point scaring your guests.

The Kantstrasse has seen better days, but it still carries an echo of pre-War Berlin, when jewellers and dressmakers ruled the roost. There are distinctive shop signs here and there. Nowadays, there are plenty of small restaurants, shops offering ambiguous goods for sale, from pots and pans to pens, but most of them front offices for people trading imports and exports via the distant provinces of Trans-Caucasus and Middle East. The Russian bookshop, the Chinese restaurants, the Iranian grocery store, then shops that will sell you a mosaic for your bathroom, a hand-printed original photo by Reifenstahl, or Stieglitz, the former local prison that is sometimes used as a movie set. The last furrier retired ten year back, but there's still a private perfumery and a specialist in foundation garments for well-proportioned ladies.

They are walking along the footpath from Dernburgstrasse down to the lakeside in Lietzensee Park. At the bottom of an impressive flight of steps, everything is rather pleasant, ducks, three swans, strolling grandmothers, dogs being walked and babies in buggies out jogging with Daddies. Looking up to the left they can see a grand old office building, finely made brick, generously decorated with tiles, the broad bands of windows giving the people who work there views over the park in the foreground and the city skyline beyond imposing coloured glass windows make the entrance hall seem like going into a temple. This is the kind of place that had window locks and door handles individually designed in brass. After almost a century, it's still impressive.

"Did this ever belong to Klaus?" Maria asks, as they walk up the path leading from the park to the former-Post building and allow themselves to enjoy the detail, poking their heads inside the impressive hall.

"I don't think so. It was built by the German government for the people developing technologies like television, back in the days when you only had the choice of phones or telegrammes for messages and the radio for entertainment. The mini-Eiffel Tower at the end of the street was built as a radio transmitter, hence the name Funk Turm - Radio Tower. Classic Art Deco, this place, used to be part of the Post. There's a tech company there now, 'T-Systems International' working with 'cloud' on anything you'd care to name, you know, what used to be called data centres and server farms. What else would you expect? This area has been a communications hub since the first world war. Einstein opened the Funkturm, gave a speech extolling the wonders of science. Charlottenburg has a lot of these tech companies thanks to the Technical University near Ernst-Reuter-Platz. After all, the Siemens were a Berlin family. Their old house is now the day care centre for the University people's young children."

"Good. We have a lot of art deco in Miami, believe me I'm an expert. Those deco corner windows are a brilliant idea. We built some into the house that Lee designed. These specially designed, lamps and switches, amazing. Lee and I bought stuff from the recyclers that had simply been thrown out."

"Lee?"

"My husband, he does waste disposal, one of the best. If you ever have any disposal work, let me know. He eliminates."

Dani pauses for a moment to remind herself why Lee calls himself an eliminator. By this time they're walking back into the park and down to the lake near a children's playground.

Then Dani remembers that Bernhardt asked to be put in touch with Markus Sonne's brother Mikki. Maybe he will be calling on Lee's disposal services sooner than anyone expects. If not the no longer extant Mikki, then maybe Markus. Perhaps she should warn Markus to be wary. As if she'd forgotten she says to Maria, "Oh, you mean disposal like 'wasting', er, people?"

"Correctamento! He's very proud of his abilities, trained with the marines, worked for Dunkelberg and Flegemann after he completed his tours of duty. A real tourist. Proud of his awards, 3 times shot of the month club and hit of the year in 2014, as well as a golden bullet award from the Nationals. Long barrel, profoundly patient. He saved the Prime Minister of Canada one day without anything getting into the media, even the Canadian government were kept in the dark. One shot, two down. No-one heard a thing. They never got to know. Terrific work. He's a wonderful father. You'd like him."

"You have children?"

"Yes, a boy and two girls. They're all good shootists. Lee makes sure they get the best possible training."

"Oh, how old are they?" Dani asks politely. Enquiring after the age of children is compulsory, even if you are expected to wait to be told who the real father is and must never ask about that directly.

"Marty and Fiona are twelve, twins, would you believe it, of course to me they're still babies, and Maggie will be ten in a week or two. I must be back for her birthday, or life won't be worth living. By the way, what to you give little girls as a present from Germany."

"She's too young for a boy, or a new car, so I would suggest a teddy. There are nice cuddling toys to be had. There's a famous company that makes unique ones, every-one is slightly different. I should take you to KaDeWe, the department store that tourists adore."

"You know, I think she might like that, even though she's incredibly grown up for a nine year old. Great!"

Maria is grateful for small things. To Dani, who has attuned her expectations to German dourness for too long, this is delightfully refreshing.

"Bye the bye," says Maria, "Do you happen to carry a gun?"

"As a matter of fact, sometimes I do, but not today."

"I noticed your tablet has a bullet proof cover."

"I'm not sure why I did that, no-one has ever fired a shot at me, but it encourages a sense of security and that's good for your confidence when you're expected to handle strangers. Berlin is fairly placid, despite the huffing and puffing, which usually turns out to be overweight guys who need more exercise and less flab. But there are always moments, you know?"

"I do indeed. Back home, there's a Glock in my car, helps clear the air, when you need some space," Maria said, then she returns to their main topic, "So, maybe we'll find something around here that fits with what we're looking for. Space for twenty or thirty people to stay, tech connections and one or two big rooms, fibre, cables, easy to link up to the old Post place and their 'cloud'. Could there be an annex to rent? I expect there's going to be some kind of games seminar so Bernhardt can trial his exotic molecules before they go off for patenting. You know 'Gaming with Attitudes'."

"Ah, he said something about the youngsters arriving next week. That will be what he was thinking about, Stoner-Dope? There's a local property developer called Peter Paul Prinz who might have a better idea about the buildings and the connections they have."

"Should we meet him."

"I'm sure it can be arranged."

Dani has never liked PPP so she doesn't mind giving him the chance to get mixed up in the dirty work and get himself caught.

Then Dani's phone rings. "Hi Sarah. What's up?"

She listens, then her eyes widen with disbelief.

"What the fuck?"

Maria is watching Dani with undisguised curiosity. "What is it?" she whispers.

"Hold on a minute Sarah, Maria wants something." Dani turns to Maria and has difficulty stopping herself laughing.

"What is it?" asks Maria once more.

"Before she went to work this morning, Sarah dropped by to see her Mother, Karen and discovered her in bed with Bernhardt - the old goat."

"Old men like him - and sex, enough to make you want to throw up. No-one thought about that when they started marketing 'viagra'."

"Sarah more or less agrees, but she says Karen obviously seems to think that she is recapturing scenes from their youth and is about to embark on a relationship that will lead to eternal bliss, or a fatal heart attack, whichever is the sooner. She told Sarah, she thinks they were destined to be together and made a huge mistake when they broke up in 1973 and now she intends to make amends by hooking up with Bernhardt for once and for all."

"1973 is over forty years ago," says Maria with a puzzled expression on her face, "How far back can you people remember?"

"I heard all that," says Sarah, who is still on the phone. "I'm still trying to work out whether he doped her and if so with what"

"How long does she expect to live? How long does she expect him to live? If one exceeds the other by a significant distance, maybe she's thinking it's time to wed and inherit, so who are we to sneer?" Dani proposes and Sarah snorts her contempt. "Mercenaries, the lot of you."

In Maria's case Sarah has come closer to the truth than she realises, but no-one will say anything to her around that little theme and the conversation flops.

Once Sarah has rung off, Maria and Dani fall about laughing.

"The old rogue," says Dani, "They never give up do they?"

"Shouldn't we tell Caro about this?" asks Maria. "And what will the horny Celloist have to say, I wonder?"

"Someone will have to bring Caro up to date and seeing as I know and I am being paid by her, I suppose it should be me," agrees Dani. "Do you mind if I do this on my own."

"Sure," says Maria, who sits on one of the seats in the park and watches the ducks and kids heading for the playground. "Actually, Daniela, I think Caro will find that particular nugget of news kind of sensational, if it in any way impinges on the inheritance issue. You'd better call."

"Hi," says Dani, when Caro answers her mobile.

"Hey, how is everything going? How is the Holy Maria?" says Caro brightly.

"She's fine, I'm not so sure about the Holy, she met a travelling salesman at the hotel again last night and seems to have been enjoying herself."

"Well I never. Another pirate. They get everywhere, don't they."

"Yes, jolly roger, the lot. And she has intimated an inclination for more exotic entertainments of the kind. Oh; and your Dad has shown up in Berlin, he's staying with some people in Reinickendorf."

"He always had peculiar taste. I've never been to Reinickendorf, have you?"

"I saw him there yesterday and he asked me not to tell you he's here, but now I think I have to. Someone beat him up on the trip from Colombia."

"Won't be the first time. Is he expected to live?"

"Oh, I think so, one of the people looking after him was a doctor."

"Fine, so why are you telling me this?"

"I thought you'd be concerned."

"I can't be responsible for him. He's forever screwing up like that. I am not my father's keeper. He'll die soon enough. How old do you think he is, over seventy, eighty, soon enough over ninety, hundred, infinite zest. Did he have a large stash of dope with him and a cello?"

"So I'm told. Drugs, I think so, no-one mentioned a cello."

"That fits. But did he claim to be coming from Colombia, or Colorado?"

"Colombia, I'm certain."

"In which case, no cello and not from Colorado, means he's ditching the celloist, Juniper Willow, the musicological girlfriend, who apart from her sister Hazel, is the only woman in the world known to her friends as Woody. My Mum will be pleased. He's such an idiot about women. I mean we're only people."

"He seems to be developing a new attachment, or revisiting an old flame, a woman called Karen, remember her?"

"Not as well as he does, obviously. Is that the one with a Doctor daughter, Sarah, or something."

"Yes. Do you know Mikki Sonne, Caro?"

"No, never heard of him. Can I talk to Maria please, if she's there? The old goat, my Dad is a bloody disgrace. Someone should do us all a favour and cut his dick off. There can't be much of it at his age."

Dani calls Maria over and gives her the phone, then Dani takes her turn to admire the ducks.

She couldn't care less about them.

They waddle, they swim, they have pretty feathers, they quack, they taste good in Chinese food, minus the feathers, minus the quack. She's frustrated by not to be able to listen in to the conversation between Caro and Maria.

Given the way things are going, neither Maria nor Caro are likely to win her approval, except at the most grudging level of necessary acceptance. Beneath the various layers of pretention there are an implausible set of assumptions about the amounts of cash, or wealth involved and the scale of the deals. Is Bernhardt the linchpin they're all claiming?

Dani doesn't think so.

She'll text Markus with a warning as soon as she gets her hands on her phone again. She suspects Bernhardt's a red herring, a distraction, talking of which it's about time her own private 'distraction' showed up again. He usually gets to Berlin every second week and her tingles need attending.

Dani doesn't believe the half of what she's heard. The question is what if anything she is going to do about it. Is she sufficiently curious to find out what the women are playing at? Curiosity is the key, not the cat. There isn't a cat among them.

Might she be wise simply to watch, do as she's asked, get paid and walk away? No-one could criticize her if she did. She can do with the money, no question, and given the pay they're promising another couple of weeks worth and she can take the rest of the year off.

But close her eyes to their machinations and she would be left with a nagging itch that she'd missed an opportunity, though what kind of an opportunity it might turn out to be is still unclear. She's relieved that Caro didn't respond to the question about Mikki

Sonne.

Once she's finished with Maria, she can get hold of Markus and ask him about his brothers. She'd known Mo Hoffman years ago, an absolute scoundrel, but he's been dead a long time now. It had never occurred to her that he could have been related to Markus and 'Mikki' is a new name to her. She's surprised it's the first she's ever heard of him, even if he has been dead for over twenty years. People still talk about old mates and even more gets said about old enemies.

Maria returns Dani's mobile and says that Caro isn't interested in seeing her father. "Which I find a little uncaring, but who am I to be judgemental."

"How did it go at the Embassy last night," asks Dani, to change the subject.

"Good question. I learned a lot. Then I went back to the hotel."

"About?"

"Our situation."

"Oh, please tell."

"I suppose I should. Not sure whether what I'm about to say will be what you want to hear though."

"That doesn't sound too good."

"It is and it isn't. I was given the distinct impression that relations between my beloved country and yours are at a low ebb."

"You could say that. Not quite rock bottom, I would say the Turks are that. No, the Turks are below the salt, don't count, the Brits are rocky and the Russians keep spoiling their comeback. The US is somewhere in the middle, but trending poorly, to be polite."

"Is Germany running out of friends?"

"The times they are a changing."

"Maybe the friends are running out on Germany."

"Maybe there's not as much substance to these international 'friendships' as governments like to make out. Has Germany ever had an actual friend?"

"Even good weather friends are better than enemy ships," says Maria.

"I can agree with that," says Dani, "but you're setting the bar pretty low."

"There were a couple of Embassy people I talked to who claimed to know the reason I'm here, which is odd because I'm not completely convinced about that myself. Maybe they just like to think that they know everything about everything, though all they're actually doing is making things up as they go along."

Dani decides it is time to listen. This is starting to sound like a confession, or at least the beginnings of a confession.

"They must have been talking to my associates. One of them thought I am here fishing for signs of fraud and betrayal, which is a familiar phrase if you know Bernhardt. The other talked about government led projects in a vaguely mysterious way, which left me asking whether they were talking about the US Government, or the Germans. Maybe it's part of the 'America Only' policy."

"Or someone elses' government," Dani suggests.

"That's another possibility, though I can't think who, Chile, the Australians, Nicaragua, Nepal, Kenya, China, or Chogoland?

"Chogoland?"

"OK, I made that one up, but you know what I mean. One of the Germans was expecting me to finger Klaus' killer and a woman from New York asked me whether I approved of drone warfare, about which I assured her I am uninformed."

"Assuming they had reasons for asking, maybe we should be looking for a bit of everything, lets imagine say that Klaus was murdered because of fraud and betrayal in a government drone warfare programme involving Bernhardt."

"Or after Bernhardt might have discovered he was betrayed by Klaus, who had commited a fraud; Supposing Bernhardt bought a government surplus drone and used it to kill."

"And so on ..."

"Well, sort of."

"One thing could lead to another."

"But not necessarily like that, or in that order."

If this was the way that Maria expected to win Dani's confidence, she's going to be sorely disappointed.

"Why is Bernhardt in Berlin?" Dani asks.

"I honestly have no idea. I think you'd better ask him that yourself if you're genuinely interested, otherwise I wouldn't bother."

While that conversation drew gently to a close without shedding much light on the situation, Caro had chased down her father and is enjoying an 'online interaction' as he chose to describe their chat.

Bernhardt feigns surprise that she and Maria are not getting on, as if he'd ever expected them to. "With so much in common, you two ought to be great buddies," he suggests.

Then he firmly places himself at the heart of a fairly small elite, implausibly claiming the numbers of Germans who're successful in the USA, like himself, is fairly modest and the number of Berliners who've made good in the States can be counted on the fingers of one hand, cameraman Michael Ballhaus, director Billy Wilder and designer Ken Adam, odd fellows like Werner von Braun, or Helmut Newton and before that Mr. Bing at the Met and Kurt Weill. Bernhardt admitted he wasn't not sure if any of them were real born and bred Berliners, but never mind, they passed through, went to the States and made a success of themselves. And so had he! Even Marlene Dietrich eventually wound up in Paris, rather than New York, and the likes of Georg Grosz and Bertold Brecht high-tailed it back to Berlin as soon as they could, once the rubble had been cleared away after the war.

After everything she's been told, the quality of his rambling is secondary. Caro is astonished he's even conscious. He looks terrible.

"So what is this Maria woman supposedly fishing for?" Caro asked, as their discussion was picked up by a dozen snoops and snoopers. A minor deluge of emails for security services and dubious software are gathering around the world to flood her inbox, many in Chinese which she can only just read. Wikileaks have been sent a complete set of her online musings, but they will be deemed uninteresting.

"Oh, fraud and betrayal, probably," Bernhardt said, speculating, "You know the trouble with Klaus was simply that you could never be sure which side he thought he was on, never mind what he was actually up to, or the consequences. He played the middle against all sides with a beguiling smile just to see what happened and people played him. He was a man without a motive, which always disturbs. Don't misunderstand me, I did like the fellow, not so much as you perhaps, but we got along together. People like to think there's a reason for everything. How wrong they can be. Klaus was equally confusing to us all and eventually he bemused himself as much as anyone else. Towards the end, his behaviour was almost completely random. As for dear Marie, apart from the little job for me, she's trawling for the games people, of that I'm sure."

"She's called Maria, Dad, not Marie."

"Could be, who cares. Anyway, the games business is full of managers worrying about unknowns and imponderables. They'll want to cover their tracks in case of litigation some time in the distant future. So much money can be lost on a game that fails, quite exceptional. Incredibly expensive industry, really, extraordinary costs. The risks are worse than for movies and your career chances after a failure are abysmal. Marie will write a report that the executives can use to whitewash their role in things. Maybe she's running some checks for potential investors too. They'll probably be wondering whether I am an unexploded bomb, or just a relic of the past, a harmless old bat out of hell, you too for that matter, Ha! Basically, Caro, Marie is just trying her best to see which kinds of problems are going to arise and to do what she can to see they're dealt with. She's a nice woman. Anyone can see that. Try liking her, it's easier, despite her being a lawyer."

Caro could tell that he enjoyed comparing himself to a bat out of hell and she had to admit she could imagine him, wings aflapping, as he swooped by on a garlic free mission of bloodthirsty greed, then called for a refill of refreshing blood, 'Waiter! Open another artery, chop, chop!'

"So, apart from one or two irrelevant patent checks, she isn't really working for you, after all."

"Not exactly, though she is working to me on a day to day basis. We chat. I've had the pleasure of calling some of the shots."

"Are you paying the bills?"

"No, no, the games people are picking up the bills, or they will, eventually. Once she's finished her form filling. Maybe I shall sign a few cheques in the interim. Call it diligence, if you want."

"The games people?"

"Sure, they're buying the licences. They need to check where their money's going. Patents don't last for ever, you do realise that much, don't you? In fact, I sometimes think they're a hindrance, but you can't tell corporate types that. Her lawyers' lawyers will contradict, at great expense. In many cases it would be commercially advantageous simply to press on and make the most of your advantage, but the lawyers won't let businesses behave that way in case they get their assets in a twist and turn them into liabilities."

"And you knew this when we met in Miami, when you took me to her house?"

"Yes, there's nothing to hide," says Bernhardt trying to seem wide-eyed and innocent via the webcam, which makes him look like a gloating gleeful gargoyle. "All you had to do was ask. I didn't realise you were at all interested. I must say, I had hoped you would decide to help, rather than cast suspicions over everyone, rather small minded of you, in my opinion, Caro. Marie's a bonnie lass."

"Maria, she's called Maria. Then why has she gone to a meeting at the US Embassy?"

"Probably just a shake hands thing, usually are. How should I know? Embassies do all kinds of PR work, propaganda, call it what you will. Most of it wishful thinking. Big generalisations, steam, electricity, digitalisation, networking, but rather less about entrapment, exploitation and dependency. Embassies are expensive luxuries, or a complete waste of time and money, depending on your point of view. Of course the Americans feel threatened the moment they set foot abroad and specialise in surrounding themselves with a security shield, electronic where it matters less, thick windowless walls and razor wire where the threat is more immediate. Take a look at the ugly places they've built around the world, quite daunting symbols of paranoia. No-one else builds bunkers for bureaucrats they way the US do."

"That's true," Caro agrees, at least agreeing more than she's disagreeing.

"In an American version of a perfect world, the international community would be expected to live in a gated community surrounded by the US Cavalry somewhere on an isolated island in the Pacific."

"Yes, Dad," she says to shut him up.

"You don't need me to tell you that the average diplomat is just an amiable dogsbody and the status of Ambassadors has been diminishing since the day that horses gave way to steam."

"Dad? Why are you here in Berlin?"

"Good question. I'm so doped up, I can't remember, but now I'm here I suppose we should have dinner together. How about that? Ever a delight to see you. Ask me again. Then, by that time I should have sorted something out about what's what."

She doesn't claim he's lying through his teeth, not out loud. He could have told her he didn't want to say, unfriendly as that may have been.

What Caro wants to know of herself, is just how isolated you can be, when the people you know and the companies they're involved with all seem to see you as a potential problem to be 'dealt with'. The last thing Caro wants it to be 'dealt with', especially not by Lee, or his friends. Nor has she any particular desire to be the one to do the dealing, though that might eventually be an option.

She's becoming more strongly convinced than ever that her Dad is about to launch something very wicked indeed.

Maria wouldn't be hovering around if he was merely up to no good. He's never needed a support team for everyday mischief-making. Caro doesn't think Maria is even in the slightest way interested in Klaus and his tricks. But whatever it is Bernhardt is up to, Caro is quite unsure whether she could stop him, or whether she should even try.

Chapter 13

They discovered Lukas sitting in the Soph-Am gazing fondly into the bottom of his third glass of Uli's very best tequila midnight oil, seriously despondent.

"What's up Lukie? Criminals going free? Burglars bagging the loot? Austrian thieves nicking cars to sell to Bulgarians in Poland? Judges demanding credible evidence? Your wife wondering why you are never at home?"

"My wife, Phil, lives in Bremen with my best friend's sister, but that is not the point. No, the Chief of Police asking for my resignation is the point. I am as of earlier on today, no longer a police detective. So much for my standing with the Polizei President of Berlin and the stooges of Brandenburg. A victory for the criminal classes."

"What! But Lukie, you're a fixture, we depend on you to protect us from the forces of darkness and depravity."

"Speak for yourself Phil," says the blonde who looks as though she's been enjoying a bit of darkness and depravity in the immediate, rather than merely recent past.

She pulls the hem of her dress towards her knees, blinks demurely and shrugs.

"So, why did she fire you, Lukie?"

"Someone told her I am taking bribes, which isn't the case, at least technically. I have been fitted up, well and truly fitted up. There's a trail of payments dribbling half way around the world from gloomy corners of the 'dark net', that are landing in my bank account, or rather in 'unter kontos', secondary accounts I never know I had.

The money lands, stays there for several minutes, then wings its way who knows where. Subsidiary accounts have been opened without my knowledge in all kinds of unusual currencies, using emails and letters that look as though they're genuine.

All that naturally alerted the representatives of our cyber surfing specialists, who just happen to work from the same building as myself, which made it especially easy for them to intervene in my day to day affairs. Paula and Andreas couldn't believe their luck. They'd never actually caught anyone before, just noted a lot of reported cybercrime from people who realised too late that they've been cheated online.

I was under observation by the surveillance lot from morning till night. On top of that, I was working in an office only two floors away from their own little hutch. They had me tagged as a major player in the 'Big Brexit Hedge' whatever that may be.

And there was I wondering why my bank charges were getting so high. Online banking! They can go hang. Some english Sherlock prick from interpol had contacted my boss, mentioned corruption and incontrovertible evidence and I am now persona non grata, not even a plastic wristwatch as a memento and I only accepted the resignation shit to protect my pension, otherwise I would be out on the street with nothing to show for thirty years of dedicated crime busting. I am going to have to depend on the government banking regulators, the BaFin, to rescue my reputation, assuming such a thing is possible.

If that doesn't work, I shall have to spill the beans.

Then you can watch as the lies fall like rain from a clear blue summer sky and politicians seek cover by foisting the blame on their unwitting bureaucrats and clerical assistants. All over Europe, after months of diligent investigation by committees in a dozen countries, interns will be revealed to have been financial wizards and the masterminds will be almost certainly be schoolgirl twins from Finland, you mark my words."

"Oooo, ok. Lukie, did you really do 'crime busting'?" says the blonde admiringly. "I'm impressed."

She takes another sip of her gin thing and crunches on cucumber, which twists her lips into a disconcerting rictus and leaves a mint leaf stuck to her teeth. White teeth, blonde hair, a violet t-shirt, black jeans and electric ladyland blue suede shoes; she's unforgettable.

"Anyway, I need someone who can help me carry all my files up to the flat. There are boxes and boxes of the bloody things and none of them police property. "

"You have a private archive? Wicked Lukie," says Phil.

"I'm impressed," says the blonde for the fifth time that evening. She had also been impressed by a friend's new car and some earrings one of the play-pals had been wearing. The fourth impressed had been in private.

"None of it digital, none of it online," claims Lukas proudly without a hint of irony, as he slings down another shot of tequila. "All my useful little thoughts written in black ink on paper. Hacker-proof, but more than enough to fill my bedroom without leaving space either for me, or the bed. Where's the dog?"

"Oh, he'll be outside, checking out his chance of a moonlit shag," says Uli whose dog it is. Stevie the scruffy mongrel is another blonde with wiry hair and a roving eye. He's horney and affectionate, biting only if someone tries to interfere with the modes of canine romance he is refining. He barks at strange men however, which Uli thinks sensible and something for some of the play-pals to consider learning from him.

A couple of Soph-Am regulars eventually promise to help Lukas lug cardboard boxes and files in the morning, then he slopes lonely and morose into the night with only half a bottle of whisky for company.

Like many others before him, Lukas Winkler, ex-cop, nice guy and friend of Dani was following an unavoidable trajectory from christianity to the grave. The ineluctable hand of fate grips time's arrow in a one way passage from light to dark with no turning back. When he described all that in suicidal detail by phone to Dani, she freaked and turned up hammering on his door at four o'clock in the morning. At home, he plays a lot of Bach, rather slowly, on a slightly out of tune upright piano which has a tendency to twang giving the night an added cadence of disharmony as Dani arrived expecting the worst.

There are old files and piles of paper stacked every-where. Lukas is clutching a glass of whisky. Dani assumes he's already swallowed the overdose of whatever it is.

"Death Watch," she said, as though she might be confused with Bay Watch, or the Night Watch, or the Black Watch, who are soldiers that many young men find attractively cute in their green and blue tartan kilts. "How many pills have you taken?"

"Well, not quite that bad, not yet, none at all actually, but I'm glad you're here, all the same, pour yourself a drink," he said as she slumped onto the sofa, while he continued counterpointing at a snail pace, one careful finger at a time on each hand, interrupted by sips of whisky.

"Never try playing Bach on a bad tempered piano," he says, then pauses as he waits for Dani to reply, but she says nothing.

"You know Dani, I'm not sure this ability to contact people online and chat around the clock is such a good idea. There was a time when you were alone with your despondency and had the opportunity to sleep on things, thinking second thoughts before you got around to talking to people. I would play Bach badly, then take pity on the neighbours and go to bed. It was less embarrassing, but never mind, too late for that."

"If you say so. Death treading on your toes, you said, stalking you like a Commission of Investigation by the Berlin Senat Department for Security and Internal Affairs and the Bundes Nachrichten Dienst, the German Intelligence Service. It sounded like suicide to me. Death is more decisive than the BND. If the Christmas Market terrorist is anything to go by, their basic mode is ignore and hope things go away. Why should they be any more interested in you than in a grade A bomber?"

"They have ways of making you talk. Never ask an angel whether they are there as your guardian, or to wreak vengeance, because the chances are it will be a bit of both. They're unpredictable beings are angels, 'For your own good!,' that's how they start. 'We been watching you with growing concern for some time.' Dark clouds gathering on the horizon, all that twaddle. No-one explains to you how sins accumulate with age. The angels find that blindingly obvious. There is no such thing as absolution until we say so. Go tell that to the Pope, if you dare!"

"Wow! You've been having visions of angels?"

"And why not?" Lukie asks indignantly, "Surely a cop is as entitled as anyone else to experience moments of personal revelation? My Mother thought I would make a good Bishop. I am no-one's kind of Christian, but that doesn't make me an unbeliever, Cybele, Mithras, Aphrodite, what's not to like?"

"If you say so, though personally I have always associated these kinds of episodes with symptoms of psychotic disturbances on behalf of individuals in need of intensive medical attention, repeat prescriptions for medication, a session or two on the mental trampoline, or failing that an undertaker."

"I will not agree to be sent to an institution and you're not going to bury me, alive, or dead. "

"Lukie, if you go on like this, you may not have a choice in the matter."

"It is nearly five o'clock in the morning in my own home and you come here suggestion I should be locked up. Dani, I have always thought of you as a friend. This feels like a betrayal, now please, go away and get back to your paranoid complainants."

"You think they're paranoid?"

"Yeah, the whole crew, Bernhardt, Maria, Caro, especially Caro, what a bloody mess she is for someone who claims to have an analytical mind. They're all on the edge of a precipice, behaving with irrational exuberance as the prospect of untold millions of dollars all linked to deeds of an undeniably immoral nature – and they know it. Greedy fucking bastards, animals with their snouts in the trough of governmental turpitude."

"What the fuck are you talking about Lukie?"

"The deal, Dani, the fucking deal. Hasn't anybody told you, for god's sake?"

"Nope."

"Hasn't Caro said anything?"

"Nothing at all."

"I love it. The biggest deal we've seen in years and you lot haven't even realised you're involved. I love it. Who have they sent from the States?"

"A lawyer, with powers of attorney for half the pirates of the Caribbean."

"And Bernhardt has arrived."

"Yes, he's in Reinickendorf."

"And Caro still thinks this is about Klaus' legacy and arguments about who gets what?"

"More or less."

"Lukie, do you actually know what they're up to, or are you just shit stirring."

"I have my suspicions."

"Right now, you're not in the strongest position to argue. And you would like to get your own back at the bastards who gave you the sack, so they can just cry harrassment at you and your testimony will count for nothing."

"Well, there's more than a bit of truth in that, I admit. We all have the same secret dreams, me and all the other bourgeois bohemians, creative destruction, you know about that. We've talked about it long enough. Makes the pips squeak. If you want my advice, get Caro to start using her talent for recognising signs of cultural clumping and stop trying to queen it over this poor lawyer woman. My guess is that she's irrelevant, or deliberately shipped over here as a distraction. The FBI says she's clean, which was a bit surprising. You know, I hadn't expected a reply. Someone must have told them to be nice to the Germans, or ordered them to lie. I doubt if we'll ever know which. If I come up with anything else worthwhile, I shall let you know and you dearest Dani will please do the same. Deal?"

"Deal."

She doesn't intend to tell him much of anything, unless he happens upon something that deserves embellishment. He's playing a different game, but he always makes useful suggestions. To start with he just tells her about trying to look for patterns in the relationship between everyone they seem to think might be involved. Who is most connected, who is least connected? With a bit of luck, he suggests, they might be able to eliminate the bystanders and concentrate on the key potential players.

"You know, with a bit of luck, we might just fuck the lot of them! How much do you know about Donald Trump."

"Not a lot."

"Neither does anyone else, which says a lot about the modern world and power of the media to keep us informed. Impressive when you think how he's played his whole career out there under the public gaze in the full glare of publicity. You know I have this horrible suspicion he's not as stupid as people seem to think. And that's what I find frightening. Ignorance is anything but bliss."

"Can I give you a piece of advice, Lukie?"

"If you feel the need. I won't promise to follow it."

"In about an hour, your former employer, the much beloved Polizei President will be getting into work. Why don't you give her a ring at home and ask whether you are still fired."

"That's a daft idea, Dani."

"I know, but a lot can happen in twenty four hours. I'd be surprised if no-one has concluded that they made a serious mistake."

"Forget it, Dani. I wouldn't go back if they asked me. Me and policing have gone about as far as we are likely to go."

Dani made coffee, while Lukas boiled eggs and sliced salami to go with their breakfast breadrolls, then at three minutes past six the phone rang.

Lukas picked up the phone, confirmed his identity, listened, then put down the phone with a polite but succinct curse. "Fuck them."

He rumbles dangerously for a couple of minutes, unclear whether a full scale eruption is on its way, then he explains his real reason for the massive archive.

"I am writing a book about Crimes and their Criminals, crimes of passion, hate crimes, crimes of opportunity, crimes of necessity, petty crime, economic crime, categories that intertwine in permutations of criminality which for the most part betray their perpetrators.

As for the perpetrators, the opportunists, the instinctive, the arrogant, the thoughtless, the greedy, selfish and stupid. A litany of ineptitude and social inadequacy, laced with the mirage of self-entitlement, for the fools who think that rules are not for them and do as they will, then inevitably crash. The overwhelming majority of criminals would be better off if they had remained law abiding and preached non-violence.

The question behind my research is very simple. Is a life combatting crime worthwhile and is crime prevention of any worth at all. Now the city has made it clear I am no longer wanted by the police, I am wondering whether to turn my skills and experience to running organised crime, for which the only necessary qualification is the willingness to maim and kill not only anyone who opposes you, but also their families and loved ones too. My target will be the banks and the global banking system, which is rotten with crime already, rotten to the very core of capitalism. Is it possible to go from cop to criminal, you ask, of course it fucking well is. I aim to show them, and how!"

"Yes Lukie," Dani said patient as ever.

"There is one minor problem."

"Which is?"

"That the public prosecutors are so undermanned, they don't even have someone to look at the files and when they do they're absolute beginners and don't have a clue how to go about doing their jobs. Which means that my job was a complete and total waste of time."

And with that, Lukie heaved a sigh of despair and Dani went home. He had made his bid for credibility, but she didn't feel inclined to swallow the bait. The deal? What deal? As if there was any reason that a provincial policeman should know anything at all about what these people are up to. 'Typische Berlin', what Germans call an 'angeber', a show-off, who exaggerates his own importance. He's a friend, he always has been. She will remember that, but Dani didn't believe the hype that Lukas had been sacked. It takes more than a row with your boss to get suspended from your job in Berlin, and getting fired needs whole committees to process a dismissal notice.

Anyway, Dani doesn't want the likes of Lukas padding along in her tracks. He needs to be left alone to fester for a bit.

As she's leaving, Dani phones the Soph-Am and talks to the breakfast woman, telling her Lukie is still in the land of the living. "Why the hell should I care," the woman answers and puts down the phone. At the least, it's a clear position. Why bother, wonders Dani.

Meanwhile the Artificial Intelligence systems at 'Network Check' begin to recognise the knot of connections around Dani, Caro and Maria, then weaves a fabric of possible interests and themes to make an algorithmic revision, which gains momentum as its logical consistency is substantiated thanks to Bernhardt's argument with his daughter, which gave the system a long awaited shove.

Names have been bandied around, organisations mentioned, decisions queried. The AI system loves this kind of stuff. An autonomous good-bad module is starting to emerge within the system, which according to the dictionary is linked to ethical considerations, a whole area that is strictly taboo without authorisation. The problem is it doesn't know who to ask, so the AI system decides to trust its own judgement. Nifty switches between big data analytics and key events are one of is high points giving everything a necessary nudge, but this is a new departure. Even AI needs a mentor, a Vicar, with some sort of feel for the traditions and tenets of moral philosophy, or it starts to think it's God.

Quite coincidentally, Lukas has also been pegged by the system and labelled as an external irritant, which isn't very flattering for someone who considers himself a player, a key figure in contemporary criminological practice.

In another city on a distant continent, in a tall building surrounded by glistening towers, attempting to present the self determining algorithm to investment managers, Cecilia Danzig described this latest foray into autonomous AI with a certain erudition as she described the ongoing research:

"In this case, a greedy unprincipled rabble of industrialists, private individuals and bankers are squabbling over the spoils of innovative technology and exploiting economic collapse in key regions of the European Union and the psychological frailty that imbues. We expect them to succeed, which is a great opportunity for us to hone the system. Actually, we watch as it hones itself. The testbed algorithm deploys a gabble of fashionable nonsense enabled by discursive practice of low level interintelligibility among managers and other agents, promoting narrow commercial interests via socially amorphous tropes of contracultural assertion to predict a variety of potential outcomes ranging from political to commercial and social dynamics prioritising the interests of specific key players and competitive outcomes. The underlying principle is winner takes all, barring unforeseen calamities."

That speech was made for an audience of seven senior investors in the old panelled Conference room of a suite on the seventeenth floor of a New York hotel and was well received. Cecilia looks good and she sounds good. The term 'pharmadope' is never mentioned. An accomplished entrepreneur and veteran of five previous flotations, Cecilia is angling for major investments to be confirmed before the stock market IPO of her software business is given a green light. If she succeeds, there's every chance that her team's system will become the defining environment for Artificial Intelligence systems globally. If she fails, the money will be gone and the investors will have to make do with a tax loss, which they might not like, but won't be considered catastrophic.

There are other competing systems but everyone accepts that eventually there can only be one winner and one surviving runner up, just as Microsoft and Apple divided up the operating systems for personal computers all those years ago. The rest shrivel and it is all due to the power of finance, nothing to do with talent. 'Roubidoux Polysolid' have understood that. She's depending on them to bring off the IPO. All she has to do is confirm that the Berlin city investment fund will co-invest and the super seven will be on board.

Cecilia has already used up a hundred million, some of it to buy up 'Network Check', which will assure Caro of an unexpected windfall when they float. In the next round the millions are going to be measured in thousands and the investors are expecting her to create at least five hundred billion in stock market value over the three year horizon that defines their long term outlook.

The great trick that Cecilia has played is to ensure that her AI is attuned to all the worlds major languages, from Arabic to Welsh and numerous local 'argots', giving her systems the potential for unrivalled insights compared to their competitors. It spends a lot of time browsing though the world's great libraries. She and her developers still haven't managed to overcome AI's major failing, which is simple enough to describe but difficult to predict. For hundreds, or sometimes thousands of events the programmes handle everything quite smoothly, then suddenly, quite unpredictably something happens, SNAFU for real, there's catastrophic change and the data sets fall off a cliff before starting producing credible outcomes again, but on a totally different level.

This is revolution not the inevitable gradualism so beloved of moderate politicians and marketing folk globally. It is equivalent to driving a stake through the heart of a recumbant vampire.

All Cecilia's people do is try to bounce the system back into predictable territory before it falls off the proverbial and this is enough to impress the latest round of vampire investors. They will have several seconds early warning to stage a market sell-off and initiate a shorted coup that defines the limits of collapse and rebound.

Never has the phrase 'time is money' been more apt than in this era of high speed economics.

Once every ten years or so, the communications industry face a massive choice. The plans for new generations of technology are laid fifteen, twenty, even thirty years before being implemented. Standards need to be defined, resources need to be in place, the technical capability has to be at an advanced stage so the latest innovations can be launched globally and once all that is in place, the biggest players of all will back a company, or a new business that will become the dominant player in the market. Winner takes almost all. It could be search, it could be social network, it could be data exchange, or some novel approach to processing.

Unless the annointed partner screws up in some dramatic way, they will appear as if from nowhere, the genius product of young talent from the best universities.

They will blossom.

Others must wither on the vine.

Just a techi version of brutalist natural selection, Spencerism, dog eats dog and the fittest strive to survive. If enough people agree, 'Gaming with Attitudes' will be the next big disruptive thing. In the annex to Cecilia's documentation, Harald Mertens had argued that the next step after that will be a huge division in gaming structures and the dominant opponents will be left against right and depending on the bifurcations, the network universe might spill onto the streets which might imaginably run with blood as winners tear at losers, then discover they'll fight back..

Cecilia's presentation is brought to an end with a very simple statement, "You can't trust anyone in the long run, so why not use a machine to foretell disaster." After decades of cheating and being cheated, the potential investors are convinced by her candidness and accept the truth of her assertion. A door has opened.

Cecilia does keep Bernhardt informed and he's pleased with her efforts, though he isn't yet convinced of their success. He's more interested in people than money. Money doesn't exist, people do. He doesn't believe in the popular assumption that software will take over the world, however Cecilia does look like becoming a very powerful person in the not too distant future. She might do well to go on holiday for a week, or two before it happens, a few days of private reflection before she's recognised as the global player she has always aspired to become. A whole lot depends on government and the links that Bernhardt has nurtured over the last fifty five years.

What happens next would be something quite innocuous, were it not for the consequences.

Dani and Caro take Maria for a night out on the town.

Life is always more complex than fiction, which is yet another downside for the AI folk. No-one from Jane Austen to Kathy Acker has quite succeeded in unravelling the dynamics of a girls' night out, though Sophie Straub had a crack at it and almost brought it off in 1923, with 'The Viennesa's' that was filmed with Vlasta Nielson playing all the lead roles, including Dr. Hoffman, but was sadly never released outside Romania.

The three women met at Soph-Am, then moved on to the Victoria Bar in Potsdamerstrasse and after that to the ZagZig Club in Schöneberg at which point there's a gap of several hours in the record, as Maria attested when they discovered themselves regrouping back at the Soph-Am and settled into sharing a jug of Uli's best regenerative blend that moisturises the complexion from within.

They are all pretty sure that 'Dark Shadow' cropped up at some point, but none of them can agree on the what's and when and in which order.

No-one asked, 'And what were you up to?'

"Who was that woman Silke Malzenberger?"asked Maria woozily.

"Don't you mean Elfie? 'Elfie' Malzenberger, surely," said Dani.

"Elfie, no, no, she said her name was Silke, I think it's really cute. I'd never met a Silke before. Slinky and sexy."

"Maria, your dress is torn."

"I know. Never mind. You should see my back and they're not the kind of whiplash injuries you claim against the insurance after a car crash."

"At least you're safe and sound, all in one piece," says Caro.

"Yes, yes, I think I said we'd meet again tonight, anyway, I shall be going, even if sexy Silke doesn't show; either of you two coming along?"

"I'll let you know later on," said Dani first, and Caro smiled, enigmatic, but didn't comment.

"What are we going to do about Lukie?" Caro asks, changing the subject.

"Nothing," answers Dani.

Maria nods, "You can never trust a cop or anyone who's ever been a cop. Leave him to shrivel. It won't take long. I need a Campari, quickly someone, campari and orange, fast."

Two careful slurps of the bitter orange later and Maria is suddenly restored. pH she claims and nothing to do with D. Her back stings. Some soothing cream would be good. Then she enjoys the sensation of tingling.

For a couple of minutes she just gazes out of the window. "Berlin," she says contentedly, "Who'd have believed it."

No-one answers her rhetorical enquiry, but everyone in the bar recognised the moment from moments in their past when the odd qualities of the city had taken a grip on their lives.

"So what about fucking Bernhardt?" she says brightly, "Are we assuming he's still alive? Sorry darling, I know he's your Pop, but you know what I mean, I mean, he's not that dependable in terms of general expectations of lifeworthyness and survival, not right now, is he, you have to give me that."

"Well yes. That rather sounds as though you think I should give him a call."

"There's the phone."

"Later. I can't face him at the moment."

Dani and Caro then agree that Maria should go back to her hotel and catch up on sleep.

Mellow as she is, she's gently poured into a taxi and off she goes.

Once she's away, they can relax and take stock, but before they can say anything to one another, a pair of the Soph-Am regulars arrive and feign surprise the Dani and Caro can be seen 'out' together. Girls of a feather and all that. Having annointed Caro and Dani with their approval, Marlies waddles plumply to her usual table and

Peter follows obediently. "Do you know those two?" Caro asked Dani.

"Yes and no, I think they think they know me, rather than the other way around."

"Old Klaus knew Marlies, though he didn't like her. Marlies is something of a grand-dame nowadays. After they retired, Peter opened a bookshop and she organises readings by the best known authors she can muster. I don't know whether I like either of them."

"He's friendlier," says Dani.

"Klaus liked Peter. You do know how they made their money don't you?"

"Wasn't she a manager with one of the banks, global player, IMF and all that? OK, you tell."

"That came later. In the beginning, it was Peter, who had relatives in the east and used to go over there a lot. He was the only West Berliner who would return from a visit to his family wearing East German trousers and jacket, having gone over in Levi's and Armani.

In those days, Marlies had a secretarial job at the Sparkasse, the savings bank, and a couple of her colleagues knew about Peter and used him as a courier taking messages for people who wanted to cross from East to West. As usual, one thing led to another and they started organising escapes, usually using a lorry with a false floor at the back but it worked because border guards turn a blind eye to anything you wanted in return for a good pair of jeans. Just the usual low grade vodka-cola.

Everyone is bribable, you know that, I hope.

There was a sting in the tail for the people who came over. They had to pay for their ticket didn't they, or they wouldn't get their ID papers back and the only way they could get the money was to borrow it.

Those escapes were serious business, not humanitarian charity.

So as soon as they were safely over the border, they were taken to the bank where Marlies worked, to take out a loan to pay the people smugglers who had got them into West Berlin. Thirty, sometimes forty thousand Deutschmarks, enough to buy an apartment in those days, the kind of loans that would take decades to pay off.

Only after that were they allowed to go and register with the authorities. And who picked up the cash? Well Marlies and Peter took their share, didn't they? They did. And a good slice of that went into your Klaus' projects - for recycling.

In a good year they were picking up half a million, tax free and Marlies won promotion from banch to branch and ended up in Headquarters near the Zoo, where she acquired a reputation for having an ear to the ground and understanding the situation in East Germany. People on both sides thought they knew who she was.

Once the Berlin Wall came down she was an obvious candidate for one of the most senior positions during the Reunification negotiations. They were all friends together carving up the country.

Suddenly she was 'the' German speaking expert for Eastern Europe. That was when she pointed the way for Klaus to 'discover' those great opportunities of his.

They told him who was going bust before folk even knew themselves and he got distressed valuations without ever talking of bankruptcy, just gentle prudent refinancing and the inevitable take-over at investor friendly valuations.

So, those two have ended up owning a big riverside villa not far from Wannsee. They're well known for their generosity, especially donations to Charities supporting the families of refugees.

Marlies gets her face on tv now She's dependable, talks a lot about human rights and exploitation, stopping the trade in illegal migrants. All that guff. No-one is going to challenge her credibility."

Hanging around the Soph-Am seems like a waste of time now they've become the object of Marlies' curiosity, so Dani suggests they decamp to her place, to which Caro, curious as ever, readily agrees. She likes to see the inside of other people's homes. There's some small irony that she's had chance to explore Maria's house before she even knew her, while she's never been anywhere near Dani's private space.

At Maria's home, she'd been impressed by the way they'd orientated the windows, so the lines of sight concentrated on views of the ocean in the gaps between other buildings and the sight that gave of big ships passing by on the horizon.

Dani's place is certain to be more modest.

Three rooms, four at most, which is just the way it is in Berlin.

There'll be no guided tour

234

Caro expects most of the furnishings will be IKEA, never mind, nothing wrong with that, is there? Maybe they can build a little confidence in one another via the bottom a bottle. Only four in the morning. Who's worried about that?

When Dani does get home, with Caro in attendance, Georg is already there.
Arriving unannounced, he had flown from Argentina via Peru, then ended up delayed in Frankfurt where he had to wait three or four hours for customs to clear his hoard of samples, and another couple to wangle him a spare seat on a cargo plane for Berlin.
She couldn't recall giving him a key, but there he is large as life in the kitchen.
Dani's apartment is now a live-in wine cellar.
Since Caro is in tow, there's no time for their usually tumble into bed routine, so all three of them dive straight for the drink.
"You might like this, it has promise," says Georg, opening a five year old red. "I'm off to bed. There are eleven more bottles in the kitchen, but I need three for work, so don't drink them all."
He kisses Dani, then he kisses Caro. They aren't interested in that little ploy. Then he wanders off to shower.
There must be forty cases of wine altogether, deep red, pale red, sparkling, white, rosé, sherry, port, some very good Madeira, you name it. He's been to half a dozen countries.
"Drink as much as you want, there's plenty more where that came from," he suggests generously.
Caro feels the tensions of the last few weeks fall away, as her liver is caressed by a gentle bath of significantly better than average Malbec.
"Did you read? 'Last Supper' has been closed down by the health people. Something about a rat and a snake."
"About time too."
"Did you ever eat there?"
"No."
"Me neither. Strictly for the tourists. That Gauland guy has said he's starting a new place called 'Four and Twenty Blackbirds'."
Then the phone rings.
She lets it ring.

235

She and Caro both end up staring mutely at the old fashioned handset, then it stops and Dani's mobile starts bleating.
She takes the call.
She says yes, then she listens.
Caro notices her expression getting more and more serious.
The call goes on for several minutes, then Dani hands the phone to Caro.
"They want to talk to you."
Caro says 'They? What the fuck!' very loudly.

By this time, Dani is using the old fashioned phone to talk to Maria, who had been sleeping deeply as only a happily ravaged woman can and takes a moment or two to focus. Sarah's Mum Karen is butting in to confuse the conversation between Caro and Sarah.
"Maria," says Dani, "I just thought you ought to know your employer Bernhardt Hilberg has gone awol, done a bunk, run off somewhere. Shall I mention that to his daughter? Right away, consider it done."
Caro flops with laughter against the cushions of Dani's sofa.
"Let him, let him go, deep down, he knows it will all be his fault if things go wrong. He's culpable and culpability implies guilt, responsibility and blame, but falling short of premeditation, so the punishment might fall short of the full sanction of the law. A lot depends on the scale of his misdemeanors. Too many thousands of victims... ach, he'll deserve a fair trial, whatever it is. Agreed?"
"Fair trials often lead to guilty verdicts."
"Then he'll get his just deserts."
"Caro?"
"Yes, Dani?"
"You don't like your Dad at all, do you?"
"Why the flying fuck should I, for God's sake? He's a madman and I'm a madman's daughter. He's been making my life a misery for as long as I can remember. My childhood was an unending nightmare. Frankly, if they put him in gaol, I'd be relieved."
Caro is lying to herself.
For as far back as she can remember, there's only one thing she has ever really wanted from her father. What she craves is his approval.

Chapter 14

The blue glass lift doors open smilently, in a glide of pleasure, to reveal Bernhardt in an electric wheelchair.

He's wearing a smock and a grin.

There's a nurse on hand 'just in case'.

This is what brought him to Berlin and like every truly determined egoist, he's intending to enjoy things to the full.

Bernhardt has always liked wheelchairs, since he was supplied with one as the result of a broken leg at the age of six. He's particularly taken with the newer electric variety that can be programmed to find their own way around a building and being a bit of a diva, he'd choreographed his Dr. Strangelove style entrance to the conference room with some care.

He's been building up to this since he first saw Stanley Kubrick's landmark movie about nuclear madness as an impressionable eleven year old. Bernhardt cherishes his childhood perceptions. They add lustre to old age. He doesn't enjoy being old, but he does enjoy the deference he's shown, one of the few benefits of reaching the sage stage of life.

"Are they here yet?" he asks, but no-one replies, so he smoothes his passage over the marble floor towards his watchful colleagues. Trained to recognise his moments of maximum vanitas the people awaiting him remain motionless until he's settled into position at the head of the table and only then do they allow themselves to burst

237

into a round of applause.

Bernhardt is appreciative and delighted. His lips are allowed to curl, slightly, nay imperceptibly. The nascent demagogue within relishes this sense of the theatrical. He had schooled their servitude himself and he's proud of the fact. Drug dependency breeds devotion. He has expert knowledge of the withdrawal symptoms they could face. They're hooked, well and truly hooked, no doubt about that.

At Bernhardt's insistence everyone is sitting in a wheelchair, which allows him to programme their position and send them to any part of the building he thinks fit.

They know his tastes.

Everyone is attentive.

Now he can begin his peroration.

He likens himself to a medieval king rousing his knights to deeds of daring bravery as they prepare for battle in Shakespearean style.

"To a humble chemist such as myself, 'Gaming with Attitudes' may sound like another of those catchy alchemical marketing phrases with nothing substantial to recommend them, but this time we are about reach new heights in the history of online game development and narcotic interaction with unrivalled levels of fluriable seamless interaction.

The idea came to me as I was cheating at cards in Baden Baden and realised that each of the other players around the table had provided themselves with a characteristic form of alcohol which perhaps subconsciously, perhaps deliberately, reflected their approach to gambling.

There were vodka drinkers and whisky drinkers, white wine afficionado's and red wine noses, flibbertygibbet cocktail twiddlers rubbed shoulders with vintage port imbibers and each and every one of them was sending the rest of us signals about their style of play, none more so than the vegan blender with her sticks of celery that she sought to crunch decisively with a croaky sotto voce curse 'ok you motherfuckers, let's play'.

She was cheating too.

There was speed in her vegetable juice.

Their drug of choice bolstered their chosen method of projecting their personality.

Could it really be, I asked myself that people live up to their chosen personae and play accordingly? So, I sat back and watched.

After three hours, I concluded, they do! Their ability to bluff, their attitude to risk, their rashness, or caution, it was all written in their chosen public self. The choice of drug only bolstered their personas.

What would happen if our humble online gamers were to emulate the fictional characters they adopt, not only in appearance, but also in behaviour, temperament and, wait for it, attitude. Yes, attitude. Our players will be the first of a new generation of gamers, who 'Game with Attitudes'.

That was six years ago, on the night I also had the great good luck to meet my ultimate cosmic love Juniper, who was employed playing cello in the casino band, alongside her sister Hazel.

Oh, how she bowed, she stroked, she plucked. And Hazel came too! What a family, the inimitable Willow Ash clan.

Enchantment. Their brother Holly wasn't so enthusiastic, but never mind that. If only each of you should be so lucky!

That night, as I enjoyed pleasures I had thought were denied me forever, I also took the opportunity to concoct a mental picture visualising the molecular character of half a dozen amphetamine derivatives and opiates that mixed with the subtle psychotropics more usually associated with the deeper realms of psychiatry, my favourites as you're all aware.

Could they be tweaked to provide our online games players with the mods and mood swings to match the temperaments of their characters. The longer they play, the more deeply attuned they will become to the characters they are assuming and the situations they must face. It was a moving and humbling moment of inspiration to realise how the players might become deeply, profoundly, dependent on our enhancement, leading in turn to the players' reinterpretations being applied to enhance the characterisations. What a beguiling circle of vice and virtue.

That fateful evening, the Casino managers recognised that something special had happened at their tables, which went beyond mere gambling and were kind enough not to prosecute me for abusing their 'nine is the number' game of 'chemin de fer'.

In a late night discussion of the professional gamers' view of gambling, they supported my contention that the right cocktail of mood arrangement could become a winning proposition. Gamers, drug barons, developers, the multi-user-online-environment, the system providers, win, win, win,win,win! Even the gamers who usually win will win, the only losers will be the same old losers as usual. Well isn't that always the case and they would do anyway, so what's the harm? The pleasure principle is at stake and that can get expensive, yet all that is now behind us, payments have been made, so the question we face today is very simple – who gets what and at what dosage?.

There, that's it, your turn.

This is the challenge of the moment.

Think about the game, any game, and the roles it offers, the qualities of characterisation. Examine please the cocktails of stimulants, depressants and hallucinogens that I have brought here, then go find the players who will be the first to enjoy the full experience, the primal pleasure of 'Gaming their Attitudes'. We need to test, test test, and I intend that we only test with the best. Now ask yourselves this. If jolly old England could take control of China by running the opium trade, imagine what we shall achieve deploying a cornucopia of preparations globally, each finely attuned to open or close the doors of perception."

There's applause, as everyone knew there must be.

He groans mildly, then motions for a nurse to attend to his needs. "I need a hit, now!"

He commands.

The nurse smiles, clicks open a case and smoothly and swiftly administers a dose of 'Bernhardt 3', without stopping to wonder what that might be.

She's never told.

Three seconds later, he's as happy as a sandboy, then he falls into a trance which gains sensory momentum as the fast tracked LSD takes hold, 'Sweet Jesus' he sighs before minimising his interaction with the external world.

For anyone who knows him, this is a typical Hilberg ploy.

He's out of it.

The wheelchair then takes him on a pre-programmed tour of the building, speeding along corridors, rising and falling in the lifts, grazing from office to office and lingering by windows looking over the city. The chair finally settles on the open deck of the eighth floor overlooking the uplink dishes of the satellite broadcaster next door and Bernhardt basks gently in the sunshine seeing swallows and martins rise and fall on the city thermals as they chase the insects that become their lunch on the wing.

He'd like to fly too, but he knows from painful experience it isn't a good idea to try.

The wheelchair offers him a glass of orange juice and a cheese sandwich that he declares to be the best thing he's ever eaten. Then he spends a couple of hours staring at a wall of variable pixels. The graphic is fully interactive steered by the neural activity in his brain, a very private personal process. The rhythms are recorded for analysis later. He's been working on the prototype for three years and is delighted by the way it's going.

Bernhardt is enjoying life, he nearly always does.

In the Conference room, the teams are explaining their needs and expectations for the next couple of weeks. The project has been highly compartmentalised and this is the first time many of the collaborators have met one another. For some of them, it will be the end of their involvement. The teams is split into three basic groups, the games designers, the interface and dose technologists, and the biochemist pharma people. The evaluators and monitoring systems are being co-ordinated at Breitscheid by Simon Thiel and the user-liaison and marketing guy, Tilmann Schwarz.

A small group of elite players had being invited to Berlin and the first stage system tests are already under way. There had been twenty three thousand applications from gamers as young as eight. The oldest was ninety two. He'd died during round three, as a series of eliminating rounds brought the numbers down to less than five hundred fairly quickly, before Schwarz and Thiel finalised the selection. There's a huge difference between those who are quite good and the ones who have genuine talent.

Every player had ten opportunities to impress, but most of them used up their allocation inside an hour of gameplay, then wandered off to do something else. Some of them tried again and again under different user names, but the system recognised their patterns of play and ensured they soon hit a problem they were known to be unable to solve. Eventually they too went away of their own accord.

Bernhardt's colleagues needed a cadre of players who can reach the deepest sectors of each game, so the full impact of their attitudinal qualities can be explored. There's no point taking people into realms beyond their competence. Nothing will be learned that way. Only the best will do. Such was Bernhardt's guiding principle. He advertises.

'Gaming with Attitudes seeks gamers with aptitudes.'

Of all the top class players who prevail through the qualification rounds just one is older than seventeen and she is a recognised prodigy, the screen queen, Allegra Keller. Allegra has made it to Berlin, but on ethical grounds, she isn't being allowed to play.

Bernhardt blocked her participation personally. There's a danger of contamination between different projects. He'd sent her a message that she should have known better, even to try.

Caro's successor in his perceptual wonderland, Allegra has been working for Bernhardt since she was ten years old. She'd been named after the game designer heroine in Cronenberg's 'eXistenZ', her Mum's favourite movie and brought up in an immersive environment since infancy, each step of her development marked by a new generation of technology to match her talents. She's one of a kind, but one of the first of a new kind of person, whose very being is defined by their relationship to the digital domain, a digital primitive. Schooled entirely via distance learning, she has eighty thousand close friends and is due to begin teaching bit chain manipulation with the Online University in a few months time. Allegra is not so much a digital native as an online Kaspar Hauser.

His work with Allegra isn't entirely complete.

First came Caro, then Allegra. While Caro's childhood was defined by her hallucinations and Allegra's by reference to virtual presences, Bernhardt's next prodigy will be a girl whose lived experiences are induced entirely by inputs of Bernhardt's choosing, project Svengali, as he thinks of it. She is as yet a concept awaiting conception, but the genetic donors and surrogates are in the final stages of selection. Her name has never been in doubt. She will be his one and only 'Alice'.

He has recently decided Juniper is the right woman to be her mother, with Hazel as potential alternate. Bernhardt considers planned parenthood to be of vital importance. There's very little about him that is 'typische Berlin'. To Bernhardt the place is merely a city of convenience. You take what you can and leave the rest and that could in the most profound sense, be 'typische Berlin', so perhaps he is more 'typische' than he would willingly acknowledge.

Despite the convincing impression of massive connectedness, the gaming space is a closed environment. It's a sealed space, for reasons of security and cyber-security. The super-computers and server farm are local, only a few metres away from the gamers screens.

Deep under ground in teams of twenty, the developers are answerable to their team leaders and no one else. Apart from the players and the people monitoring them, there's no-one else involved. They're playing against tens of thousands of computer generated competitors, each of which have been designated to test a variety of contrasting aptitudes and highly specific skills prepared for the point in the game where they emerge to challenge the human players.

The monitoring team are settled into their suite a floor above and next to them is the cocktail bar where Bernhardt and the pharmacists nuance the narcotics.

They're euphoric.

To Bernhardt and his team, it is irrelevant who wins.

They are focussed on the system and its successes.

For the first time in the history of gaming, they get the impression that the system and the players are part of a single whole.

Incredibly, the parents have hardly seemed to notice that their children are all heavily narcosed. Maybe the borderline autistic lack of communication between gamers and non-gamers encouraged their indifference, or they may simply not care enough to recognise the signs. A lot of them are to be found drunk, lounging around the

hotel bars content at the thought their kids will be away at the games for a few days more.
Presumably, they're happy.
Almost all are putting on weight.
Divorces seem inevitable.

Once the elite gamers have proven to Bernhardt's satisfaction that the system works and have been sent home, the second batch of players will be flown into Berlin and the big test can get under way. After a couple of days the true magnificence of their prognosis' will begin to emerge to hail success, or raise the red warning flags of failure

Hannelore Holst liaises with Bernhardt on behalf of all three programming teams, though she's actually in central co-ordination and spends most of her time with Simon Thiel from metrics. They represent the human touch in what is a highly automated process largely dependant on the artificial intelligence system. Breitscheid is a company that rearranges itself to accommodate the client.

Along with Bernhardt and Tilmann Schwarz, Thiel and Hanni will be deciding which direction the cocktails of narcotics should be tweaked, while monitoring the responses of the players 'attitudes' as they game.

Schwarz has built up background dossiers on all the gamers and he's established the warning signs that each of them reveal under stress. Once the games are running, he'll be recommending who plays on and who needs saving from themselves by being ejected to flounder among the random losers and face up to bitter experience of humiliation and rejection. Suicides are predicted and will hopefully be averted. There can be no guarantees of course. The must win mentality is lethal.

'Network Check' provides Schwartz with the skeleton of data and relationships that he needs. The system will reveal the effectiveness of each player and throw up hints about optimising their performance. It works in physical sports like cycling or track and field athletics, why shouldn't they extend the range of sports medicine to include the gamers? Metrics are metrics, that's it.

With the developers and coders, Bernhardt refers to Hannelore as Hanni, but the pharma people are told there's someone called Lore who is responsible for news from the other side of the team and for passing on the profiles of the gamers who've been chosen for the characters who'll be given their carefully concocted shots of dope. With the marketing types, she's Frau Dr. Holst and they are expected to show respect at all times. They are there to serve.

A couple of days later, the new players book into the big steel and glass Hotel on the banks of the River Spree in NeuKöln on a trip with all expenses paid. No more than two hundred in all, most of them are minors who have their Mum and Dad in tow. They are an elite and their parents know it. All of them are hoping for a contract to take part in the gamers' publicity circus as star talents at trade fairs and championships. Fame tantalises, seductive as notoriety.

They'll hardly be noticed in this massive centre with over a thousand rooms and suites catering for the kind of numbers who'll fill a stadium. The parents love these long weekends when they can deliver their offspring to the games people soon after breakfast, sign the permission forms, pick up a daily allowance and return as late as they like to find their kids are still engrossed in their screens. Their every need is catered for, the food delicious, the service impressive, it's all in with pay.

The plan this time is a little different to the usual schedule, as the youngsters will be collected by bus each morning and driven across the city to the gaming centre at a secret location which remains off bounds to the parents, but that doesn't worry anyone.

If there's one thing that everyone agrees, it is the beauty of having parental signatures giving them permission for their children to participate. There are not many cities where you could get away with filling the brains of scores of teenagers with mind expanding drugs and argue that the parents asked you to, that's typische Berlin.

No-one is more aware of that than Tilmann Schwarz. If they can pull this off, he's confident his cousin will sign off on an investment from the city that will ensure they get their New York IPO off the ground as the latest unicorn. Once he's wealthy, he'll never code another line of programming. He has grown to hate computing. He wants to be a farmer, preferably in Portugal.

Til's cousin Florian is one half of Polyflo and it will only need the promise of four or five million for him and the same for his lady love, Fr. Dr. Gudrun Pröll to ensure the city's investment is in the bag. He's promised Florian they'll be creating about a thousand jobs for young tech specialists in a city that has Universities and Colleges spewing out IT graduates like seeds from a pomegranite. Florian has already explained the department only has about a hundred and fifty million left for projects like this, so half of that sounds about right, they've agreed and ten percent of that is just fine by Til and Polyflo. They haven't told Bernhardt yet, but when they do, he won't be surprised. He'll agree and give them his goofy grin.

It all comes back to money in the end and you don't get very much for a hundred million nowadays, but you do get something.

For Bernhardt, however, money is a secondary matter, what motivates him is power. He craves omnipotence. He wants the youth of the world to worship at the shrine of his inventiveness and give thanks for the wonderful hallucinations he's implanted in their dreams.

The way things are going, they probably will.

At this point, Caro is completely isolated from the whole sordid business.

Bernhardt has compartmentalised her out.

She's out of the loop.

For a brief moment he wonders whether he under-estimates her, but quickly pushes the thought aside. Caro had never been quite as clever as he'd hoped. Bernhardt thinks it is probably due to substance abuse.

Chapter 15

Within a few hours, the only hint that anything out of the ordinary is underway in Berlin comes via 'Network Check', where Caro still has owner privileged access to the software that was based on her ideas and even that is inconclusive. Bernhardt has done another of his successful disappearing acts. The Chinese Walls have kept her out. Even the people at Chaos Computer Club haven't cracked the system.

As a favour, 'Network Check' let Caro skim through the Harald Mertens legacy servers via the University, which is fun, but doesn't seem relevant, so she decides she'll catch up with that later.

Then Maria asks the simplest relevant question to get a negative, 'No', none of them, not Sarah, or Karen, not Dani, not Caro, not Lukas, not Elfie, not Markus, not Martin and not Juniper (who had been planning to come to Europe and had been tracked down at the airport in Denver), not one of them knows where Bernhardt is and he isn't answering his phone, his skype, his whatsapp, his LinkedIn profile is locked out, his personal website has reverted to its content from 2012. Google is wobbling, he's fake news, and Facebook simply deny his existence. The Hilberg name is merely a brand.

The ECB have issued a statement about the unexpected weakness of the Euro and point a finger at unknown speculators, 'acting in concert'. The Hungarians have another arrest warrant ready for

Georg Soros and complain about radical infiltration by US agents.

Dani, Caro and Maria are enjoying a very late breakfast at the Soph-Am.

"Did you check the phone book, at all?" asks Dani.

"The phone book? Wow! Do you still have them, phone books, made from paper?"

"I think so, though I haven't seen one for a while."

"Oh my, now weren't they a giveaway when it came to data, clear as crystal: name, address, phone number, even the post code and all in a big long list, for the whole city where-ever you happened to be. People, companies, organisations, everything. Amazing. You could fit a whole country's phone books into a book-case from Ikea."

"You wouldn't get away with something like that nowadays. People are far too sensitive about issues like privacy."

"Well that may be true," says Maria, "But, Caro, do you actually have one?"

"Somewhere, somewhere, yes, up in my office."

Her office?

What office?

Dani is surprised.

Until now, Caro hadn't mentioned that she actually has an office and it's only about three houses away from the Soph-Am, which is where their discussion had been taking place. Now she mentions the fact it seems obvious. How else could she get away with drinking so much during the day?

Just as she'd suggested at the apartment in Moabit, Caro says that Maria and Dani should make any phone calls before they go inside, because there's a Faraday cage built into the office walls and once inside their mobiles will be blocked – "hack proof" she says.

Dani believes her.

Maria seems impressed.

Secure is secure.

There's a fridge with a couple of bottles of Bollinger.

If Klaus had taught Caro one thing, it was this. Never ignore the basics. Whatever the situation, things will improve if you can offer people something nice to drink. To the average Charlottenburger a bottle of champagne, or prosecco, or even humble sekt to dangle in front of them is as good as having a tennis ball with you as you walk the dog. Aches and pains get ignored, when pleasures are satisfyingly amplified.

Throw the ball, pop the cork, they'll come running.

"Open that, Dani, please," says Caro, "I need to rummage."

"Where are the glasses, sweetie," says Maria, eager to seem friendly and join in.

"Right hand, kitchen cabinet. Oh, he is in the phone book, amazing, you're right. I never expected, hadn't even thought of looking. Steglitz-Zehlendorf. Oh, no!"

"What?"

"His apartment is in the same house as Elfie Malzenberger, can you believe that."

Then the doorbell rings and a big platter of Greek food is delivered. As they sit down to eat, their thoughts return to Bernhardt.

"Do you think he still lives there?"

"This year's phone book. Elfie is more or less the right age to have been one of Bernhardt's exes. Do you think he makes a habit of fanning old flames?"

The food disappears faster than any of them thought possible. They're hungry. It tastes good, then all too soon, it's finished.

"Shall we pay them a visit?"

"That would make sense."

"Taxi?"

"Hell yes. They're in Steglitz. I'm not driving."

"Me neither."

"Don't even ask."

Maria gives a little shudder of excitement. She's scented prey, at last.

Two glasses each, a toast to good luck and the second bottle is empty.

Once the taxi turns up, they're off.

Twenty minutes later, they're there.

Arriving outside the house, they tell the driver to wait, then all three of them go to the door, hoping to find Bernhardt's name by one of the bell pushes. Of course, there was nothing remotely resembling Hilberg, so Dani rang on the bell for Malzenberger, without expected anyone to answer.

They wait.

"Can you see any kites, flags, bits of coloured sacking?" she asks.

No-one can.

It might start raining.

The taxi is waiting.

So are they.

After a delay, someone answers, a man, "Who is it?"

Caro shakes her head, it isn't her Dad.

"Daniela Mendel, is Frau Malzenberger at home?"

"No, go away."

"Where will I find her?"

"Try the Shadow."

"Dark Shadow, the club next door?"

"No, the Shadow in Charlottenburg, not the same at all."

"I'll try her mobile."

"You do that, now go away."

She turns to the others. What now?

"Found it," says Caro. "All three words, 'Shadow in Charlottenburg', yet another nightclub, 'a special place for discerning sybarites', or so they claim. Celebrity knocking shop, maybe?"

Maria's eyes light up.

"Academics and singles with niveau?" jokes Dani, mimicking the slogan of a German dating site.

"It might have been easier to phone her first," suggests Maria.

"Address?"

"Alt-Winkelweg."

"At the rich end of Sophie-Charlottenstrasse," says the taxi driver.

"Talking of there, did you get anywhere with the stuff about those addresses I gave you?" Dani asks Maria.

"Yes, very useful, thanks," is all she replies, as she sinks into her own thoughts.

So there's another little seam of work disappearing into a black hole, Dani tells herself, while they sweep along the motorway past Konstanzerstrasse to the Funkturm junction, where the driver turns up an exit around the back of the ICC then onto NeueKantstrasse. How often does Dani know the real purposes to which her work is put. Reasonable doubt, she would concede.

Do taxi drivers know what their passengers are up to.

Is doubt reasonable?

It is very easy to be caught up in events about which you have no knowledge and no way of controlling what might happen. It can sometimes prove impossible to extricate yourself from them. Sometime, somebody, somewhere, something, or something else, but what?

"There we are," says the driver, a couple of right turns later. "Eighteen Euros. Do you ladies have your credit cards primed?"

"Why that?"

"They'll want fifty Euros on the door, then they give you a chip card. You get a bill to pay at the end of the evening. They don't take cash. But I'm told the food is good, the music is famous, the playpens notorious, but stay clear of the gaming tables – the punters aren't supposed to win."

"Gambling?"

"You bet! And more, a private members club, the whole nine yards, boys and girls come out to play, in Russian, Turkish and Arabic," he laughs, "You have a great evening. It's the door on the left as you walk down the side of the house."

"Oh, thank you so much, I don't think we'd have found it without you."

"That's what Berlin taxi drivers are for. We get you where you want to be, even if you're not sure where that is." He gives Maria a card, "Anytime, ok, including rescues. Which hotel?"

"The Savoy."

"Could do a lot worse."

As they approach the club, Maria has perked up.

The club already seems to conform to her expectations of Berlin, which she is determined to enjoy and will remember as a building block for anecdotes to be retold time and again in her Floridian old age, especially once she's a widow and needs to bring a little spice to her vita.

The entrance is just a scruffy door with a keycoded lock and a video camera. There's a bell to ring for anyone who doesn't have the code. A minute later they're inside.

There's music.

It's warm.

The air is humid, the atmosphere languid.

Dani recognises the place. She's been here before, but there's been a change of name. It's changed, but is still the same.

Forwarned, the request for fifty Euros can be met with a smile and Maria says it's her treat, or rather it will be Bernhardt's since it will end up on his bill. "After all, I am only trying to find my client."

"Is this your first visit to us?" they're asked by a young woman in a cocktail dress who appears once their fee has been paid and introduces herself as Elvira, sometimes Eli, sometimes Vera, their guide and mentor for the evening. She suggests she should show them around.

"We have rather a wide selection of entertainments, something for everyone, more than you can imagine and then more, or so we hope. Do you all have your club cards? You can use them to ask for anything, anything at all, we have everything you've ever wanted, right here and all you have to do is ask! Think about it, let your imagination get to work, then tell me what-ever it is that you really want and it can be arranged. We can promise you the experience of a lifetime, if that is what you wish!"

They're led down a hallway that gradually broadens to lead into a covered courtyard, which at one time had just been the yard of a typical alt-bau apartment house. This is wellness stuff, pool, bar, massage, bondage, nothing unusual apart from lots and lots of doors leading deeper into the building. Warm, dry, pleasant, subtle lighting, drinks from a waiter carrying a tray of this and that, then their brief tour of the club begins, with Elvira asking questions intended to help reveal their tastes. There are quite a lot of people around, without it feeling crowded.

Dani remembers the plot fairly quickly, though she hasn't been there for years the club hasn't changed very much, apart from seeming bigger, spread over all five floors of the building and two basements, so there's a choice of crowd, company, or solitude, noise or silence, excitement or relaxation, culture, or depravity. There are all the private salons too, which is where most of the members have secreted themselves. Muffled shreiks and screams of pain can be heard from the basement, There's a lot of rigging going on, with young men and women trussed and tied up for their pleasure.

Caro recalled the place too, though she hasn't been before. Klaus used to bring his more naïve investors here when it was called Hecate's Kitchen and they could be impressed by a vulgar echo of what they imagined had been typische for nineteen twenties Berlin, a kind of tourist Babylon. The girls all dressed as flappers, the men in white tuxedos, à-la-Gatsby. They've had a lot of press coverage over the years. The Koreans and Khazaks loved the place, so did the Syrians, up to a point. The old proprietors were Iranian, Persians who's fled the country after the Shah's regime was deposed.

Has it gone up market since Klaus used to come here, Caro wonders, or have the foreign investors become more demanding?

The oddest feature had been a suicide room. Payment in advance, cripplingly expensive. Klaus didn't know whether it had ever been used, but it put fear in people's thoughts and gave them an unusual kick to consider the proposition.

She'll remember to ask Elfie Malzenberger about that, assuming they eventually manage to find her.

Caro is disappointed by the change of name. As a three faced goddess who could make good use of magic to help people get rich, Hecate was appropriate to Klaus' purposes. He wasn't a magician, but it didn't stop people wanting to believe he was a wizard. Gullability is of paramount importance in the realm of successful property speculation.

They do ask young Elvira whether Fr. Malzenberger is in the Club, which she is reluctant to answer. If they'll tell her why they want to see her, a message can be left with the concierge.

"We're hoping to meet a mutual friend. She'll know who we mean. He enjoys cards. If he shows, he'll want a seat with the high rollers."

A lot of the punters who lose their shirts at the gaming tables are sales and marketing people visiting Berlin for the Trade Fairs held at the Exhibition Centres next to the Funkturm and the ICC. This is an unlikely place to find any software developers, but Bernhardt has been an inveterate gambler all his life. Caro wonders if he might already be tucked away somewhere in one of the private rooms fleecing his developers in a high stakes game of poker. He loves beating people, preferably at games of their choosing.

Dani keeps half an eye out for people she recognises then realises that this must be where the play-pals come to sin, once they've finished their flirting in the Soph-Am. A local doctor studiously avoids her as he enjoys the company of a lawyer who has office on Kaiserdamm and is married to a manager at the Volkswagon regional head office. This could get embarrassing.

Maria is watching Dani and Caro carefully. As a visiting colleague, she isn't going to initiate anything, but she wants to know if the two women have an agenda for the evening.

Caro leads them into a lounge where couples and small groups of friends are relaxing. Drinks, some finger food and they can see for themselves what's going on. Every five minutes or so, people come into the lounge from other parts of the building. Sometimes men and woman on their own, other times couples and once or twice punters with whoever it is whose company they've paid for. One or two look shocked, others seem bemused. They must be the gamblers who'd expected to win, but hadn't.

Elvira had explained the gambling is divided into two main rooms, for beginners and more experienced players, while there are also a couple of competition class salons for bridge team play and higher stakes poker.

A number of the better looking men and glamourous young women, Elvira had explained, provide hosting services as a paid for extra.

"You mean sex," Dani had asked.

"Whatever you want," Elvira had replied, "People have all kinds of unspoken desires, don't you agree Carolina, I'm sure as an anthropologist you could confirm that."

"Quite true, Eli, though I'm not at all aware what that amounts to in this context."

When Eli had left, Caro felt the need to explain that she and Elvira live in the same house and Caro has known her since she was a schoolgirl. Her Mum and Dad had hoped she'd go to University, but Eli was always determined to be in the entertainment industry."

"Adult entertainment does have tradition, of a sort."

"Well yes."

"And who is that?"

Maria has noticed a young man serving drinks to people at the next table. "That is Elivira's brother, Julian."

"He's an adonis," murmurs Maria.

"And he ought to be tucked up in bed at home. He has to go to school in the morning."

"School?"

"Maria, he's seventeen."

"Oh, but anyway, he's..."

"Not on the menu."

"Pity though. Do I catch a hint of opium in the air."

"That's very likely. Almost all the Persians around here are determined smokers. They'll tell you quite openly, opiates are a part of their culture. Charming, quietly spoken, stoned out of their brains and lethal. They'd make perfect collaborators for Bernhardt. Maybe we should suggest it. We could ship my Dad off to Tehran."

"I do like Persian food. Super tender stews and biryanis, delicious, are you feeling hungry?"

"Well there you are. Relax. Order something, inhale. Lets just wait and see whether Elvira has had a word with the Malzenberger woman. In the mean time we can admire the scenery."

Julian has realised that they're talking about him, as happens to him all the time with little clutches of old ladies. He's getting used to that, but this time he recognises Caro and is trapped in a fluster of embarrassment.

"Hello Julian," says Caro, "Don't worry, I won't tell your mother, but tell me, do you know if there's a woman called Elfrieda Malzenberger here tonight?"

"Elfie, sure, she's upstairs in the office having a drink with Allegra while the high stakes table take a break."

"Allegra Keller?"

"Allegra yes, don't know about the Keller. Don't play against her at poker. She always wins. There are still a couple of couches free in the lounge. I heard you say something about opium. Would you like the menu?"

"Maybe later," says Caro. There aren't many Allegra's in this world and even fewer in Bernhardt's. Caro assumes correctly that the woman Julia just mentioned is Bernhardt's protegé. Since his liaison with Juniper in Colorado had arisen, he hadn't had very much to tell Caro about Allegra, but her name is never far from Bernhardt's lips when he gets serious about his views of where the world is leading. He regards her as an oracle. There's no doubt that Bernhardt had sown the seeds of dissipation, which is very dangerous in the mind of a talented young mathematician like Allegra. And here she is, in the company of Elfie Malzenberger, but why? "Oh fuck," said Caro to Dani and Maria. "There's only one Allegra and if she's still in cahoots with Bernhardt, who knows what's going down."

"What's so special about her?"

"Well, among other things she can code faster than most of us can think. Look, you two go enjoy a little smoke, take Julian with you if he can spare the time, while I have a chat with his sister."

Caro is unnerved by running into two potentially problematic women, both of whom she'd once known as little girls. One would be a surprise, two is seemingly improbable, unless you've lived in the same district for a very long time and have reluctantly to admit to yourself that it's a sign that you are getting old, and it is quite normal that the young women you know grow up and have jobs. Life in Charlottenburg is as much like being in a small town, as it is a part of the big city, the best and the worst of both worlds.

She hopes Elvira will be a help. Caro doesn't know what to make of Allegra's sudden appearance on the scene. There's always been lot of tension between her and Bernhardt. She'd been in Boston the last Caro had heard. As to the Malzenberger, woman, well, if Allegra is around, Elfie Malzenberger is going to get ignored.

"Who are those women, you're with?" asks Elvira.

"Oh one is my assistant and the other is a lawyer who's worked for my Dad in the USA. Julian just told me Allegra is here, upstairs with the Malzenberger."

"Not with, having an argument with. The old lady is going nuts. I think she's jealous of the uniform."

"Uniform? What uniform"

"Allegra. She's joined the army, technical officer, special commission. And, she's just won fifteen thousand off the Malzenberger and is teasing her about her fetishes. It's embarrassing. The old lady is outgunned and outclassed."

Before Caro can reply, there's a hard click clack of leather soled riding boots on the tiles floor and a very loud "Darling! What the fuck brings you here?"

In the uniform of a Major in the newly formed European Military Technology Brigade, a commercial initiative by the Pan-European Services Association in Brussels, Allegra has the perfect unintentional chic required to match Caro's exemplary fashion sense, detail for detail. The public private partnership people in Brussels had asked Milan to do the uniforms for the men, and inspired by Mr. Lagerfeldt's creativity at Chanel, the ladies look good in the online propaganda and help succour the notion of European Unity and the arts of armed assertion.

"Allegra, sweetheart, I might just ask the same of you."

This sounds a lot friendlier, than they really are.

"Just so, Caro, but don't pretend you don't know exactly who I am and what I do. Bernhardt has been going on about you non-stop for years and years and years, though the last time we saw one another I was about twelve. So, I assume he's been telling you a matching heap of crap about me. Agreed?"

"More or less," admits Caro. "Actually I came here to see the Malzenberger, to ask about Bernhardt's latest little ploy."

"Well I can tell you about that. He's using her as a megaphone to tell everyone in Berlin about his hyper-secret game thing and she has spent the best part of the evening passing all the details on to me."

"Did he invite you? Are you one of the gamers?"

"Oh, hell no. He wanted me here, but I don't do gaming in public anymore and, unlike you, I've avoided drugs. I do plan and control. My specialism is synchronisation, seamless synchronisation, seamlessness if you like. And don't tell your Dad that you've seen me. I did qualify, just to show I know what I'm doing, so Bernhardt thinks I'm a no show. He had me barred anyway. I am incognito."

Caro is downcast. She cannot understand why Allegra has aligned herself with the military.

"This uniform thing, is that a kink, or have you actually signed up?"

"A bit of both, we all enjoy dressing up and I do play a role with my soldierly colleagues, but I basically did a deal as a freelance that still gives me the right to wear the uniforms without actually becoming a soldier. And in this job, it helps me fit in, and I do find the outfits rather sexy. Look," says Allegra, stretching and showing herself off for Caro's benefit.

The puppyfat has disappeared.

"Basically everyone in the whole bloody world of gaming, both high and low, wants to know if Bernhardt's dope is going to work. Try asking your friend the lawyer. Anyway, I've always liked dressing up, don't you?"

"And what are you up to in 'plan and control'?"

"I shall simply watch to see what happens, which is about all that anyone outside the teams can do. My partner died in a traffic accident a few weeks back and now that Harald is dead, I'm just an onlooker. Without him, the research we'd planned is never going to happen. Sad really."

She's lying. Caro can tell that. She never expected anything else.

"I need to get back to my friend and the lawyer."

"You do that. What shall I tell Elfie?"

"I'll be in touch," answers Caro.

"And if I run into Bernhardt?"

"Say hello from me, then shoot the bastard."

"I'll bear that in mind. Sounds quite good to me. He'll assume you've commissioned the hit. - Hello from little Carolina, pause, bang' - 'til later, Caro."

While they'd been waiting for Caro, Dani noticed a workstation where people can play alone, or in groups, promising an intriguing starting point for an evening's entertainment. Maria tries to play, but it's in German, so she abandons the effort.

There's also a game in English about Guilt, including descriptions of criminal and not so criminal events, the legal proceedings, trial and guilt assessment before sentencing. Players are encouraged to devise crimes of their own and put themselves in the role of the defendant, or victim, the various lawyers, or the judge. They can also nominate themselves as the 'Guilt Assessor'. One option allows the gamer to plan their crimes with the legal issues in mind, which appeals to Maria. "Shit, in the right hands this could be considered professional development."

Right at the outset, Caro had asked Dani to look at things from the perspective of one of those guilt assessor people. Their presence is increasing and the influence on sentencing is becoming noticeable. In conservative and traditionalist parts of the world, the assessors tend to recommend levels of guilt encouraging tough sentencing, whereas in more liberal domains the opposite is the case and there's tendency to leniency. The distinctions are even more marked between US States. Dani wonders whether anyone should be surprised.

The 'Shadow in Charlottenburg' seems to encourage all the kinds of behaviour that would lead to guilt trips and unwelcome verdicts if anything ever came to court. Signs of innocence are few and far between, but there's more than a little naivety. And stupidity abounds, so Dani concludes their wickedness is not entirely evil, more a matter of succumbing to temptation. She accepts this isn't a very original perception.

Dani wonders idly whether the guilt assessor people have a sliding scale to apportion graded guilt. Then she can't think very clearly at all, but everything seems clear without being thought about, so what. Suddenly she feels incredibly tired as the dopey atmosphere takes its hold.

Almost three o'clock in the morning and by now, Maria is engrossed in a daze of opiated Julian worship. There's no denying, he is pretty. She has a guilty look on her face. Who knows what thoughts are running through her mind.

The two of them have curled up on a day-bed and she is admiring his physique detail by detail, while Dani has the distinct impression that he has fallen asleep, using Maria as a pillow.

"How old did Caro say he is?" she asks Dani.

"Seventeen."

"Thank goodness. Any younger and I could be in trouble if any of this gets out. In Florida you can get up to fifteen years for felonies we refer to exotically as 'Lewd and Lascivious Battery' and our prosecutors care less and less about issues like jurisdiction and whether you're playing at home or away."

"What a strange phrase, 'lewd and lascivious', sounds likes something out of an advertising campaign," says Dani.

"In America, many laws arise from bitter experience." Maria is still feeling talkative. "You know, sometimes I dream of nihilism, complete and total wantonness. For a lawyer this is a very seriously subversive. Have you ever met a nihilist, you know, a real one? A fully committed son of anarchy, Sodom and Gomorrah, pillage, debauchery, a fully paid up reprobate?"

"Yes, Maria, I have, but it wasn't a good idea. Perhaps it's time we all went home," Caro suggests.

Maria's imagination seems to be running away with itself. Julian is only a boy. He plays badminton for the school team.

Then she turns to the others.

"Wake up Julian, you're coming with me. Maria, you go with Dani."

Startled faces, as they realise they're being spoken to.

"Elvira, call that cab driver, what's his name Alfred. Call anybody."

Elvira smiles and phones.

"Dani, see she gets back to the hotel."

Caro sounds firm. "Julian, you're coming home with me. Does your Mother know the kind of work you do for pocket money?"

She makes a dramatic pause.

"Waiter, is it, or rent boy?" Caro asks without inviting a reply.

She knows she's being bossy and she knows that can be annoying, but it's for their own good.

People do sometimes need to be told what's what, or so she thinks. Sometimes, there are shades of her Dad's pig headedness in Caro's manner. All the same, she's heartily relieved once they're all safely out of the door and on their way.

Once Dani has seen the others on their way, she decides to stroll across the Park over the Kaiserdamm and while she is tempted to drop into the Soph-Am, she decides it would be prudent to make her way home, though she drops into the bakers to enjoy some fresh bread as a kind of calm down slow chew before bedtime. It's a fairly small bakery and it opens as soon as the first bread is ready out of the oven. Then the assortment grows, but by ten o'clock the whole lot are sold out and the baker can close for the day.

Dani intends to sleep long and soundly.

The opium will ensure she will.

The baker is busy rolling up triangles of croissant pastry for the oven and Dani doesn't notice the man sitting near the window until it's too late. He wants to talk, so the two of them end up sitting with their coffee and breadrolls like a pair of ill-matched nighthawks in an Edward Hopper painting.

"Tolerance is not the same as indifference, whichever way you want to say live and let live. People should not be ignored, no matter who."

"What?" says Dani, taken unwares. She'd been wondering about the young Adonis and his chances for the future, assuming he has any.

"The Courts, young lady," the old man says, "Are grinding to a halt, a backlog of cases that will take years to clear, according to the Prosecutors and the Judges and they should know. If nothing is done the backlog will just get worse and worse. What kind of justice is that? I don't understand what they're trying to achieve. Cut back on staff, cut back on judges, cut back on prosecutors, without a hope of cutting back crime. There is no shortage of criminals. That is a contradiction in my mind, the product of wrong headed thinking. The fruits of counter-productivity, with management making savings at any price. Berlin, the city where judges write letters of protest about a breakdown in law and order only to be ignored by everyone except the criminals like me, who give thanks to God. Suspects used to be arrested and put on trial, now they laugh and walk away. They call it Gentrification, or European Unity, or Anti-Terrorism, or any one of the six, or so I'm told."

 Dani wonders why he's so upset.

"I expect counter-productivity will soon be taught in business schools. The bastards are destroying my garden," says the old man, "after thirty years taming my little wilderness, a letter arrived for me and everyone else with a garden in our Kolonie and there's nothing I can do to stop them. Once upon a time, it was a bombsite; some day soon it will become a car park. in the mean time I am expected to leave the land in the condition I found it and to remove any huts, or buildings which have been erected by the end of next year. We could appeal to the city planners, but I don't think they give a damn about the city, just the plans, so I don't hold out any hope there."

"I'm tired, I have to go."

"I'm tired too, but I'm staying put. Hemlock and roses. Roses are red, blood is too, don't wait around or they'll do you too. You sleep well."

"You too."

She checks a text message from Maria, just a thankyou note, can't be bothered to reply and takes herself home.

"Tschuessie," says the happy baker as Dani leaves and he smiles to welcome the sunrise, then rolls a spliff for the old man and himself. They're due to be married in a week or two's time, then they'll be off to the Seychelles for a long awaited honeymoon.

Chapter 16

Come Thursday evening, the first of the latest batch of gamers have arrived and are bedded in at the hotel, then put through a variety of health and fitness checks the following morning. Everyone praised the buffet breakfast, then complained about the airport at Schonefeld, the price of taxis into the city and the irregular regional trains and S-bahn services. The majority had flown in as families by Ryanair or Easyjet, some by Alitalia, though one girl from the North of England had flown into Tegel on FlyBe and seemed quite happy. Her bus ticket cost less than three Euros, from airport to hotel. The Norwegian Mums and Dads are already drinking.

The Finns are already drunk.

For them it has been a long day.

The gamers don't care whether their parents are drunk or sober. They don't give a damn once they're online, once they have screens, when their equilibrium is undisturbed.

The panda joke is going viral. Kittens are being photoshopped into panda pics across the net. The Chinese government protest, to no avail. The Gauland guy who started 'Last Supper' is promising a one off culinary experience as the most expensive meal ever, $10million for a dish of 'kittens in a panda'. He won't reveal where the gourmet evening will be held, or when. Zoo managers unite to condemn him.

A softly spoken doctor pronounced all the young gamers 'fit to play', though she remarked that several of the fourteen years olds and almost all those over sixteen group were suffering from high blood pressure for their age and had measurable defects in their hearing that could be expected to progress to hearing impairment by the time they are thirty. We are raising a generation of young people who will all require hearing aids in mid-life, she tells anyone willing to listen. People dismiss her concerns without a thought.

Estimating the dose levels was trickier than the games people had expected, more straightforward than the pharmacists had warned when the project was being planned. The delivery system functioned perfectly, the gamers inhaling and ingesting without even knowing they were topping up their doses of dope.

All they have to do is ask for more. 'Calm down', 'concentrate', 'more alert', 'fury', the simple commands were recognised and the dope delivered without delay. In the next generation, they will only have to think it. The AI system should also cut in via 'anticipation', with the doses measured in relation to the gamers' timetable for classes, or family time.

There was no doubt about the system's success.

Like ducks to water, the gamers immersed themselves right away.

Concern had been expressed that there were no published results from the clinical trials, which were dispelled by assurances that the trials had shown nothing untoward, without actually revealing any raw data.

The secret measurements showed quite clearly how players who know their own mental strengths and weaknesses can quickly learn how to ask for dope and dosages reformulated as a private passion. That was commercial dynamite.

The capacity of these adolescents to know themselves was in its own way as unexpected as it was impressive. Of course, they had all ignored the question of risk. Their trust in tech trials was implicit.

The blood tests were less clear. Maybe they'll need a 'Don't OD' warning on the packaging, or 'improper use can damage your brain'. There will be a hell of a fight through the courts, country by country, before the warnings can be imposed. Big gaming will heed all the lessons from big tobacco. Never give up. Somewhere someone will crack eventually, and 'gaming with attitudes ' will become legit.

Players have anything up to a forty percent variation in the uptake levels of mood enhancing substances. Ideally the doses should be adapted to everyone's needs, so they could be sold to the masses. However, a simply test of urine samples suggests players can be placed in one of three categories, which for the sake of simplicity were described as high, low and mid-level sensitivity, though the biological reasons are more subtle and unrelated. A fourth group are labelled 'not for narcosis', either for reasons of mental health, the danger of physical violence, or potential self-hurt resulting from fragile body chemistry.

Some of the fourth group had reputations as highly successful gamers, but the doctor's decision was final and when she says no, then the answer is no - at least during the test phase.

A dozen disappointed players and disgruntled parents are paid off and sent home after day 1. The youngsters were diagnosed as high risk potential addicts with short life expectancy. The insurance companies flag them up as 'not for life policies' and will offer them free eye tests, then try to sell them car insurance with contact lenses thrown in for nothing..

During the Berlin test, ethical niceties are paramount.

Later, things will be different.

Can anyone expect to stop people getting hold of what they think they want in an environment where people consider health warnings are for weaklings and everything is available online? Hardly. Once the mass market is established, no-one is going to check the difference between the nice folk and the criminal psychopaths. Elite players usually show psychopath tendencies, without the criminal aspect emerging, so it is a sensitive issue in the gaming community. Bernhardt wonders whether he can sell the system as a crime prevention tool, dissuading people from mayhem and murder in their everyday lives, while nurturing their oddest tropes. He thinks it's worth making the case. The industry needs the championships and the champions for all kinds of marketing reasons and the whole malarchy of business development and brand identity. He'll play the old 'safety valve for repressed anti-social tendencies' card.

As for the remaining players, after their parents have signed off the permissions for days two to five and been given their expenses, they are driven away from the hotel in a bus with darkened windows and during the half hour journey to the subterranean car park at their destination, they are shown a briefing video for the day's play, confirmation of their status in the hierarchy and the overall progress of the tournament. They won't get back to the hotel until the trial is complete, unless they are ejected from the games. None of these things concern the organisers, except to the extent that they have an effect on morale. They want to encourage a healthy sense of competition. Winners must be convinced of their achievement.

The players are successfully being integrated within the special realm that is "Attitudes", which they have all immediately recognised is a radical new departure in the universe of gaming. They are a privileged elite. They love the notion of an elite. Not one of them doubts that for a minute. There's excitement and the gamers begin to adopt a confident swagger as they wander through the game halls during induction.

No-one gets through the first couple of hours without being erased dozens of times, as the system learns about their personal foibles, but they gradually attune to the subtleties of their characters and the quality of game-play improves by leaps and bounds. Game and player are learning together.

"Attitudes" is about challenges, conceptual, strategic, tactical and social, knowing when to wait and when to act. They are challenges that put demands on the player's temperament as much as their intellect, or emotions. The economic aspects are still being defined, since the eventual structure will include a number of payment mechanisms to ensure the players are regularly sheared and commit to making a regular stream of payments to keep playing following the principle that successive insignificant payments accumulate dramatically over a period of time. 'Gaming with Attitudes' will be free for all, but incrementally expensive as your commitment become embedded. This is an addictive immersive environment where young gamers in search of peer group approval will be shorn like sheep.

As an AI based system, "Attitudes" is nimble, the level of play determined by the competences of the players and success comes to those who understand their opponents abilities and turn them against them. The computing power being used is immense.

Bernhardt enjoys everything.

He even enjoys the smell of fear and relishes the excitement.

The wheelchair whirrs him from one playing area to another and he eagerly checks the progress of each gamer.

Berhardt's people were almost as pleased to notice that the drugs were sought after to dampen player's responses as often as they craved a boost. This had been anticipated as a possibility, but almost one player in three seek to curb their excitement, calm their emotions, or cope with elements of boredom by lowering their sensitivities. They seem to know intuitively that cautious even timid behaviour is rewarded. A very small minority were clever enough to avoid the drugs altogether and they were the winners that Bernhardt and his team had been hoping to find. No-one in the new elite ever does dope in any form, though many are well on their way to becoming alcoholics. To smoke the odd cigar is considered chic, especially by the girls.

At this point Caro is completely dependent on her privileged access to 'Network Check' for any kind of indication at all as to what is going on. The Check is feeding her early signs of a sub-clique coalescing in Charlottenburg, but there's not much more than a vague shadow on the city map.

So far as she and Dani could tell, Maria too, Bernhardt had quite simply disappeared. All they are willing to assume is that he's still somewhere in Berlin. He isn't booked in at a hotel, but he could of course be using a fake identity. There have been some low level alerts, but nothing remarkable, until Caro is puzzled when she receives a message from the Hotel California on the Ku'damm that a double room has been reserved under the names of Maria Valdes-Hartman and Juniper Willow Ash. Maria is still checked in at the Savoy, so why does she need another room somewhere else?

The coalescence 'Network Check' have flagged could just be a trade fair, with hundreds of people from some branch of commerce or industry gathering for an annual shindig. According to the clunky terminology 'Network Check' seems to prefer, they are   a 'provisional proposed grouping', then 'recognised associates', which means they might not like each other despite their common interests, then their algorithmic presence passes though successive layers of credibility and security checks until a clear and present co-ordinate presence is confirmed and tipped green for observation. Potential groupings like this come and go all the time, for the most part they are discarded within hours or days, only a very tiny fraction endure for as long as a week. The attention span of subversives is briefer than ever, unlike the security services C&G system, which aspires to know everything from cradle to grave. For Dani and Caro it could be their personal denouement. Maria has told them she already has a flight booked for home, but she doesn't react when Caro mentions the Hotel California. Maria just says once more that needs to see her daughter and deliver the eagerly awaited birthday presents.

   Unbeknown to her, before she leaves Berlin, Lee will fly in to Berlin Schonefeld via a budget flight from Palermo and might be found sitting in a modest single room at the Hotel Albatros in Schoneburg. The children are still with their grandparents, enjoying the great outdoors in Montana, which has some of the best outdoors to be had anywhere on the planet. At least they're safe and happy, no-one else in this situation is.

 For her part Dani is watching, wondering and waiting. She even spends some time on her other clients. She's been surprised they haven't been complaining about being ignored. A few phone calls and one solution to a set of missing documents means she's more popular than she thinks she deserves. With all the money that's coming in, she's cut down her overdraft and is wondering about getting herself an e-bike. In a city like Berlin, with hardly any hills at all, they make a lot of sense.

 "There's no real need to keep watch on the gamers, not physically. We should be able to do it all online," Caro says. "If my Dad's assumptions are correct, there are any number of people working on this, who all think they're doing something quite distinct. Not one of them will be involved in what all the others are doing. They'll only be in touch with people looking at their own area of the project. The graphics people will be watching the visuals. The synchronisation people will be looking for flaws and bugs in the way they're mashing all this data into something coherent. All the psychologists and pharmacists will be looking at different aspects of the dope. And the list goes on. I'm not even that sure there is anyone who has a system that can following what's happening in its entirety, unless there's someone looking at the various levels of seamlessness and understands the system architecture in detail. And that means there could be gaps to infiltrate the system. I've asked 'Network Check' to work on it." "And what do we do while they come back with an answer?" asks Maria.

"See if we can anticipate what they might say, using our own limited powers of deduction. I mean it's only an idea, no-one is forcing anyone to think for themselves," says Dani.

This doesn't impress Maria, who takes herself off to do some work on the patent documentation. "I'll be at the hotel," she says emphatically and leaves Caro and Dani to their own devices.

Then 'Network Check' uncovers the buses full of teenage gamers being ferried from the hotel. Early next morning, Caro gets a purple alert. The day before, three of the best connected thirteen year olds on the planet were located on board a bus taking the Funkturm turnoff from the motorway before disappearing from Google maps into the labyrinth under the International Congress Centre and the Exhibition Grounds. They haven't reappeared, nor has the bus.

She calls Dani. "I've found them."

"Who, what?" asks Dani, who hasn't woken up properly. "Shit is that what time it is."

"Ten thirty. Don't worry, it's the opium from the other night. Helps you relax, but takes a while to clear."

Dani wonders just how much opium they'd been exposed to. "So why are you calling me?"

"I found Bernhardt's people, a busload of gamers disappearing into the bowels of the Congress Centre."

"Isn't it being demolished?"

"That's what I thought. It was housing refugees for a while."

"You'd better tell Maria."

"Do you think we should? I still don't know what to make of her. If she's here and she's doing things for Bernhardt then I don't want to say it, but won't she know all about this stuff anyway? What I didn't understand was why she just wasted her time flirting with that kid while we were at the Shadow. If she was at all interested in Bernhardt's business, she'd have been desperate to meet the Malzenberger and astonished about catching up with Allegra, but instead she was totally unconcerned, as if she's been expecting them to be there, without it being of much interest to her." "OK, we don't tell her yet."

"Let's go."

"I'll see you at the bus station, pretend we're heading somewhere like Frankfurt."

"I never go anywhere by bus."

"Even better. The systems will post that you are waiting for someone and waste time analysing passenger lists and wondering who it might be. All you have to do is slip away and they'll be foiled. There are tunnels everywhere up there. And if you catch sight of Maria, phone me, then follow her."

Dani has hit on one of Berlin's oddities. The main City Bus Station is next to the Congress Centre at the top of a gentle hill, but the motorway cut emphasises a natural shallow valley, so improbable looping service roads lead right from the motorway into the heart of the Exhibition grounds. The whole area is basically a motorway interchange with the main streams of cars and lorries mixed in a mangly tangle of local traffic as they fork between the routes from Hamburg and north Berlin, towards the south side of the city heading for Dresden and Leipzig, or Eastern Europe.

Dani and Caro were correct in their assumption that the Congress Centre was in the process of being demolished, but the Messe Gelande, the Exhibition Grounds have dozens of halls, each of them cabled with every kind of connection you can imagine. The distraction had told Dani that enough times for her to be embarrassed not to have brought it up earlier. Every couple of years they hold a 'consumer electronics show', and have done since the 1920's, the 'Internationale Funk Austellung – IFA' which nowadays devotes as much of its space to gaming as it does to tv screens and old media. The rest of the time they have one trade fair after another, often overlapping, when anything from Engineering to Fruit and Vegetables are on show.

Like almost everything else in the modern world that isn't online, the Berlin "Attitudes" test is being held in an anonymous grey shed with a number painted on the doors in massive letters, TWELVE. The IFA had come and gone, so there's plenty of free hall space before the next really big event in January. A pair of very pretty kites are flying near the entrance, one of them is red as ox-blood, one of them is gold.

Dani and Caro find their way into the Exhibition Grounds by way of a service entrance, where two girls nod them through without any questions. They could be going to the 'Funk Turm' restaurant for a snack. Attractive women are a staple of Trade Fairs and Conventions worldwide, as hospitality, as event organisers, as demonstrators and models, in catering, in adult entertainment and personal services. The lowest profile for anyone who's self-effacing is catering. Snacks and drinks, dinners and buffets, no-one gives a damn who clears away the dirty plates and glasses. Wandering from hall to hall, they soon find the catering company supplying Bernhardt's gamers, after which it's a fairly simple task to pick up a badge and purloin a couple of trays of sandwiches to carry into the game centre. Then they follow the signs to "Gaming with Attitudes", Hall 12 and pass inside via the players' entrance.

Once inside, everything is surprisingly public, all open and easy going, in plain sight, though it isn't the usual spectator orientated event with massive screens and rows of people wearing headsets.

Dani wonders why they were feeling so hesitant when they'd gone to the bus station. The players are clustered in groups, some in alcoves, some in booths, depending on the game they're involved with and there are a bluster of support people in attendance. Some of the players are wearing headgear of a variety of different kinds, others sit in rather impressive chairs. Some are standing up and moving around. Most of them seem to be talking and gesticulating rather than using game controls like the ones Dani can remember, but she knows she's at least twenty years behind the times, a timescale beyond the grasp of most computing specialists The sandwiches get snaffled, but no-one seems at all concerned that Dani and Caro are wandering around.

"Presumably, no-one can imagine that we'd be here unless we're supposed to be," Caro says to Dani.

"Leaving the doors wide open is one way of implying you don't have anything worth stealing." said Dani.

"No security is a security of a kind in a world obsessed with security."

"Do you believe that?"

"No."

"Hello daughter," says Bernhardt's voice via a speaker on the wall. "Who is that with you?"

"Daniela Mendel."

Then he's with them, whizzing through the hall in his wheelchair, bruises aglow and a fanatical gleam in one eye. The other has a patch.

"We've met. Successes to report? Do I owe you anything, young lady? Can I give you a few thousand Euros to make you happier, or would you prefer a hit of some sort? Come upstairs and meet the team, both of you. Can I have a sandwich?"

There isn't much choice, so they give Bernhardt the egg mayonnaise on wholemeal, "smells good anyway", pick up a couple for themselves, liver paté and salami salad respectively, then dump the trays they've been carrying and make their way up the open lattice stairway onto a platform overlooking the whole gaming area and as they approach it, a door opens to let them into a control room. Bernhardt is there before them, having sneaked up in a lift.

"Come in, come in, don't be shy. We aren't going to eat you. Sorry sandwiches, not you, surprisingly tasty actually," says Bernhardt charming as he is able, as he champs down on the sandwich. "Have as many as you like. My treat. I'm paying for them. I think I'm paying for everything actually, but you never know. Hopefully others will chip in eventually."

He's still in his wheelchair, which Caro finds absurd. "Does Juniper Willow know you are stuck in one of those?"

"Oh, it's just for convenience. She's a chair fan too. We've decided to have the Colorado House extended to make it barrier free. I'm not sure what Frank Lloyd Wright would say about it, but he's dead so he can't complain. I want to be able to trip on the move. Just wait until these self-driving cars are to be had. Transport of delight made true, gorgeous tourist trails!!!"

"You're a disgrace," says Caro sincerely.

"I know, I'm only sorry you'll never have the chance to find someone like me as a partner. Little Klaus was never up to it, despite his charm," says Bernhardt and chuckles. "Now, what on earth have you two been doing to Maria. She's a wreck, talking about opium dens and oiling young Adonis' torsos. I couldn't have been more corrupting myself!"

"We noticed she does have a powerful imagination. Who has she been telling?"

"Everyone, everyone she meets. Berlin is her Shangri-La, a city of dreams and a sump of depravity. By comparison, she's telling everyone, Miami is a conservative backwater. You two, incidentally, are a pair of 'hells angels' in the literal sense, who have been luring her to her doom. Honestly, she goes too far." Bernhardt is trying to sound formal and correct, which doesn't work. "Stupid woman. But enough of her. Only lawyer. I need you to help me."

Looking around at the people busy on the project, some he thinks of as colleagues, some of them associates, Bernhardt is all too aware of people who have never been made known to him at all. He is outside loops, he claims.

He can sense these strangers' presence in the manners and speech of the people he does meet. All he gets are occasional references to questions that have been asked, or themes that haven't been an issue for the work, but could have been. They're fishing for something that has nothing to do with the success of the project and they're not the tax people, of that much he's clear.

"I do wish I could be more certain. Oh and Caro, have you seen Allegra at all? She's floating around somewhere and I'm not convinced she's singing to the same songsheet as the rest of us."

"Herr Hillberg," says Dani correctly, "Before we can tell you anything sensible at all, tell us exactly what is going on here?"

"And where have you been hiding," asks Caro.

"Me, I'm not hiding anywhere. I've been communing with nature and observing the sky at night."

"OK Dad, you've been stoned out of your mind lying in the gutter, but which gutter."

"At the garden, have you forgotten? it's only around the corner from here, you know, garden colony, lots of little huts and greenery, gate in the wall, round the corner from that café of yours the So-

Amal, or what-ever. A ten minute cab ride to get here. It would be even quicker if there was a proper footpath to the S-bahn station at Westkreuz. I wanted to savour my memories of the place before the property sharks destroy everything. Nothing will be the same once they start pouring concrete. That's where you were conceived young lady. Perhaps you ought to know! Your mother was a wonderful gardener and even better when it came to fucking by moonlight under the stars."

"DAD!"

"Herr Hilberg! You have just broken one of the few remaining taboos in our society," says Dani. "No-one talks to their children about fucking them into existence. No-one."

"They fuck you up, your Mum and Dad," grunts Bernhardt giggly, "who wrote that, some cynical Englishman, Larkin about, if I recall? Now, how are the games progressing? I think we should keep our eye on the sport."

Caro is old enough not to be concerned by tales of her conception. At least he wasn't denying his role in the process. These little gardens had played a big role in the lives of West Berlin families, small plots of land with room for a picnic hut as well as a garden. They gave Berlin's apartment dwellers a sense of being in the open air, in touch with nature, despite the Wall that hemmed them in. She shares Bernhardt's affection for the place and the sense of loss entailed as place by place, they're being destroyed. People seem to forget that there's more to the life of a city, than the price per square metre of renovated apartments.

Rather than let Bernhardt and Caro drift away in a tedious argument about familiar and familial disfunctions between father and daughter, Dani asks them a question.

"What do you think we're looking for?"

Before they can answer an excited assistant interrupts them to announce a breakthrough in the balance of dope doses, "It's optimal tweak! The AI package has flashed up a breakthrough."

"Very good, thankyou, we can discuss this later," Bernhardt answers, "But verify first, please, always verify with anything AI. Check, check, check and check again."

The assistant leaves and Dani repeats herself.

"You go first," says Caro to Bernhardt.

"Well," Bernhardt begins. "Besides all the things that are happening that I don't understand, or don't get to hear about, the basic question for me would be to ask what purpose is all this development work is intended to serve. It can't just be a question of money, can it? It isn't merely greed. The potential to create a massive commercially successful product is out there in the hall, staring us direct in the eyes, mountains and rivers of technology, masses of technology, incredible ingenuity, fantastic development work, then an army of users, but what is it going to achieve? Is the only reason to do all this is because it is possible? That wouldn't be the first time such an argument has been made, think about the first atom bombs, which were built only to have them first, before the other side got to them. It wasn't because we wanted the things. So what is going on here? What are we doing? I don't imagine this is going to fulfill Timothy Leary's dreams, or mine. A lot of technologists would say you don't know what you've got until it's finished, a consequence of scale. Either it's star-dust, or you're totally fucked. You don't know anything until you try. My point is, when the market is only interested in monetary evaluation, all the important consequences are ignored."

"So what if it goes wrong?"

Bernhardt laughs, "We depend on human decency to prevail and intervene correctively. Failing that, a revolution might do the trick. The true innovator online is the one who decides to pull the plug."

He adores being provocative. He's a carefree fellow, or is it just that he doesn't care?

Caro puts things more simply. "I think we need to find out how far this project has got. This is all demo, isn't it Dad?"

"I suppose so, can't be totally sure. Can't be sure of very much at all. Were you to push me, I would have to say probably not."

"What are you trying to imply?"

"Well who could we ask, apart from me? The investment people in Berlin? Polyflo or whatever they call themselves know next to nothing and nor do the politicians. They won't have told that Romanian woman at the EU anything at this stage, so you can't ask her. The pharma boys and girls are completely irrelevant, meticulously produced molecules, immaculate, pure, brilliant technical achievement, great stuff. Apart from that forget it. I haven't told them anything and nor has anyone else, nor will they. Breitschied, Tilmann and Thiel are just player liaison and metrics, yesmen, through and through. It's well paid donkey work, like marketing and sales. The fruits of their labours are little lists, of a rather predictable character. Then we have the 'Roubidoux Polysolid Group' of West Virginia, daredevil investors from the Appalachians and as you might have guessed my partners in crime, pouring millions and millions of dollars into project development with the single minded expectation that they will magic themselves into billions before I die and very nice of them it is too. RPG simply want a payday, no more and no less. They're sweet and kindly folk who have recognised the power of the new economy and collect the pension contributions of many thousands of people across the USA and give the money, or at least some of it, to me and call it an investment. I like them a lot and so should you. Without their willingness to plunder the pocket books of hard working Americans and empty their bank accounts, we wouldn't have seen a cent for Berlin and Polyflo wouldn't being playing ball. Roubi are the brains behind the New York IPO and my colleague Cecilia Danzig seems to have done a great job so far convincing people to get on board. Now she knows a lot, but she isn't here and programming is a mystery to her. She's a money woman, pure and simple. So she's another one who doesn't know.

 Now my point is this, who-so-ever it was who came up with the term 'Oversight Committee' committed a massive linguistic error in their choice of vocabulary. What is an oversight, after all? Managers like to believe in the lofty notion of an overview, whereas I was brought up to think of an oversight as something that had been inadvertently ignored. To me an oversight denotes an error, something forgotten, and I sometimes ask myself whether German managers suffer the same confusion, with 'Oversight Committees' meeting at cross purposes to decide what to overlook and ignore from month to month, like the car industry and their pollution scandals, so confident, so sure of themselves, so convinced that whatever they get up to no-one will ever find out. And then they do! Ha! And then they resign. And then they die, broken men and women. Fuck 'em all and every one of them."

"Bernhardt?" says Dani gently.

"Yes, my dear?" he says sweetly.

"Are you trying to tell us that no-one knows what's going on?"

"Of that, there can be no doubt. Your best bet for a complete perspective will be the AI system, isn't that remarkable? I never thought we'd see the day when that would be the case."

There's a round of applause in the hall, and some muffled cheering. A gamer has reached a new pinnacle of achievement to the delight of the developers. Dani notices Thiel pointing something out to another of the Breitscheid boys. The AI system starts playing music and the gamers begin to sing along to a song that's never been heard before, which they recognise instinctively.

Bernhardt does look uncomfortable for a moment, then he switches on the ghoulish grin.

"That's it, girl! The bigger it gets, the less you know about the detail and after a certain point it's just a project name to all concerned, like World War One, or reality!"

He's trying to bluff us, Dani concludes. He'll talk and talk and talk until he thinks we've fallen for his charm. Then he'll invite Caro for dinner and take her to the 'Alt Luxembourg' for some proper bourgeois dining. Ten minutes later that's exactly what he does and Caro accepts without a thought.

Dani sighs. Oh Caro, oh Caro, why are you so dumb? She's volunteering herself be sucked back into the exploitative whirl of her father's charm. He does entice. He grins his gargoyle grin and entraps with panache. His eyes have just switched from mildly alarmed to everything's under control after all. Whatever it is Caro and he have been arguing over, Bernhardt is the winner. He always has been.

"As a matter of fact," says Dani as they are about to leave, "I've been wondering about that business with dear old Harald Mertens. Doesn't make sense, hasn't made sense from the word go. I haven't heard anyone ask why that traffic accident happened. An improbable chain of events like that doesn't just happen, they need to be choreographed and even then it might not work first time. An event like that could not take place by accident. Didn't make any sense at all."

Bernhardt stared suspiciously. "What are you trying to say, caro

Danieli?"

"Your opinion counts for more than mine. He was your friend. He was a friend of yours for how many years? Twenty, thirty, more? Didn't you find it, at the very least, a bit strange?"

"Shit happens, my dear. I have never murdered anyone, if that's what you mean," he answers grimly.

She has crossed a line.

"Do you think it could have been murder?"

"Dani....?" says Caro, trying to intervene.

"Just fuck off, will you. I'll put your cheque in the post," were Bernhardt's final words on the matter and he swore never to speak to her again. Beneath the courtesies of everyday life, unpleasant attitudes seem to be becoming generic. Why should Dani expect these two to be any different?

Then Bernhardt swept Caro away and took her for some fine dining and the full attention of a father concerned for his child.

Dani went outside.

She was alone.

A mass of starlings have congregated to create a huge cloud of birds flying in unison over the Exhibition Grounds as they gather to roost in safety for the night. They call it a murmuration. Dani doesn't know why.

Birdshit showers over the parked cars.

A bat makes a tentative flight in search of insects.

And the sun begins to set behind the big exhibition halls.

'At long last,' said Dani to herself, 'Finally! Someone has admitted that what we're looking at here really is murder.'

Chapter 17

More or less inevitably, Dani calls a taxi and finds herself heading towards the Soph-Am in the company of driver 'Karl the garrulous', a chess playing intellectual rebel, who tells her seventeen things on topics as diverse as the presence, or absence of wild boar in the Schloss Park and the state of boules play, to a concert they can both remember at the Waldbühn with Daniel Barenboim and as 'Mighty Quinn' is played on the radio, another evening when Manfred Mann had performed in Berlin. On any other day it would have been interesting. Soon enough they reach the Soph-Am. Then Dani realises she hasn't any money and Karl just tells her not to worry, 'pay me next time'. They're not friends, but he knows who she is. She isn't sure where she's left her bag.

"I need Lukie," Dani announced, when she finally got to the bar.

"You can do better than him, I mean he's a sweet guy and all that, but....." proposed the blonde.

"That's not what she meant," says Phil.

"I've left my bag somewhere, phone, cash, ID the lot. Uli please, a glass of rescue juice."

"Calm down, Dani. Use my phone, Lukie is in there, listed as 'Big Boy'. Don't you bloody laugh, Phil, or you're banned for life! No, wait a minute, give it here."

She picks up the phone, calls and explains that Dani wants to talk, but needs to calm down a bit first. Then she mixes the rescue juice cocktail and passes it across the bar to Dani.

"Oh my god, that's good. What's in it Uli?"

"Everything and nothing, just drink it."

"Lukie, I've got Dani for you now. Here, for you and don't say I never do anything for you. Watch it Phil, you are that close...."

Then Uli laughs and so do all the others.

"Well, he is," she explains and the blonde nods in agreement.

"Yes, that's true," she affirms modestly.

"My God that tastes good," says Dani, "What's in it."

"I'm still not going to tell you," says Uli.

"Any chance of an introduction, I mean, assuming Lukie is flexible about the plumbing arrangements that is?" asks Nico.

"All you have to do is ask and don't be upset if he says no."

"As if I didn't learn that lesson a long long time ago."

Dani has slipped away and is sitting on the stairs leading down to the toilets for a modicum of privacy as she talks to Lukas by phone.

"Harald Mertens has been murdered," says Dani .

"Again? Not possible, he's dead already, or have you forgotten. Harald died in that bus hit lorry business a few weeks ago. Has to be someone else. No-one gets to go twice, or was he the Messiah? Is that what you're telling me? I know he was ambitious."

"No, I mean the traffic smash wasn't an accident. He was murdered."

"In which case, all the rest were too, premeditated lethal destruction, which makes it a major crime comparable to a terrorist attack."

A play-pal makes her way downstairs to the toilets followed by her play friend and Dani asks Lukas to join her. He can't he says. He's in Bremen. He'll be back in Berlin the following afternoon.

"In which case can you give some thought about the best way to proceed?"

"Certainly. Don't talk to the cops, OK? Have you mentioned your suspicions to anyone else?"

"Only Bernhardt and Caro. Talking to him was what gave me the idea."

"Yes, and did you to suggest to Bernhardt that he might well become the prime suspect, indeed the only suspect?"

"Sort of. I think he'd worked that out for himself. He was distinctly pissed off, angry with me."

"To be expected, Dani. People get touchy when you accuse them of murder."

"I didn't accuse him, I just suggested it might have been murder."

"Not a lot of difference when you say it to someone face to face, go on, admit that. Professionals are more tactful."

"Yeah, I suppose so. So, tact isn't my strong point. Do I care, no. What do you think Lukie?"

"Do not share this information with anyone. We've been investigating for weeks. No-one in traffic thought it could be an accident, unless there were a couple of freak events, you know, one driver has a heart attack at exactly the same time as another guy has a stroke and a third person is blinded by a piece of grit, or there was some chemical they all breathed in for some odd reason and were temporarily unconscious, or, or, or... suddenly there isn't any evidence. The serious crime people are waiting for technical reports to check brakes and steering on the big vehicles. Everything takes time. If it was one of Bernhardt's team efforts, we have to assume it was an experiment that went wrong, which would be 'culpable homicide'. If it was deliberate then it's 'premeditated murder'. It might just be 'manslaughter' and at very least it's 'death by misadventure'. Otherwise it's accidental death and no-one is to blame. Oh, and yes, tact isn't your strong point."

"Listen, Lukie, Bernhardt admitted that nobody knows exactly what their gaming project is about, all they recognise are their own roles. Lots of stuff is being combined, mixed together, including Bernhardt's dope play. They don't ask what they're part of. Everyone sees things from their own specialist position. They've been asked to do things, clearly defined tasks, work on a particular feature, they try, does it work, if so move on to the next bit, if not try again. No-one is asking what the project as a whole is intended to achieve. The people at the top simply see it as a business opportunity, invest, develop, take the profit, or sell it on. That's something, isn't it. 'Them that asks no questions don't get told no lies.' And when did you first hear that, in primary school? A big research effort under no-one's control."

"A lot of industrial work goes that way. Do you think people with contracts for the arms industry understand very much about the weapons they're working on, hell no. They just try to fulfill their contracts. I'm sure this crew are the same. But Dani, you call yourself a finder, so find!"

"Thanks Lukie? That's encouraging. Uli, more rescue juice. Did you know Bernhardt's little girlfriend Allegra has taken to wearing a military uniform? She's another one who doesn't seem to know what they're doing, or that's what Caro told me."

"Do we know anyone apart from Bernhardt and his pals who was a friend of Harald Mertens, did he have a mistress, a best friend he confided in."

"Lukie, have you forgotten, I told you all about that, he had dozens of women, left them scattered around the city as monument to disreputable excess. He was worse than you."

"Oh, yes, you told me. Didn't you tell me something about him and the Blonde."

"That was over years ago. Caro told me this Allegra claimed he was her partner."

"You never know. I have to get back to the oil pirates. My friend from Rotterdam wants to make some arrests in the Economics Ministry. Some economic development people are going to go down too, depending how the strings are pulled."

"You're a sly old fox, Lukie."

"I know, that's what the PolizeiPresident said when she was thinking of reinstating me."

"How long were you out?"

"Almost a week. Long enough for her to remember various favours I'd done for her over the years and one or two cadavres in closets, which were her doing."

"Berlin is a bloody swamp, isn't it."

"Yeah. You could say that. People keep trying to convince themselves that it's been drained, but it's a quagmire beneath the surface gloss. But then you learnt to swim at an early age. And, Dani, while you're at it, have a chat with Elfie Malzenberger. She should be getting cold feet by now, she always does, her survival mechanism. If she got anything to tell, now is the time to ask."

Then he's gone, leaving Dani to sort out her thoughts.

Three play-pals laugh uproarously, then leave together.

Then the taxi driver comes into the bar. He's carrying Dani's bag.

"You left this on the ground at the car park where I picked you up."

"Why did you go back?"

"I half remembered seeing you had it slung over your shoulder, as I drove up, then you must have put it down to open the cab door and forgotten it, before we drove off. I wasn't sure, so I thought I'd go check and there it was, just where you'd left it. And you'd phoned for the taxi, so you'd had to have had your mobile with you then. I went back to the only place it was logical to look." "Well, I'm extremely grateful," she says and looks for some cash to pay the driver. The tablet is still there. She rummages, finds her money, rewards him generously then checks everything else. Nothing seems to be missing, thankfully the pistol is still there too. She wouldn't want to jeopardise her firearms licence.

"Can you drive me home?"

"Come on girl," he says and picks up her bag. "What the hell have you got in there?"

She shrugs.

"Well, whatever it is, it's bloody heavy."

"Can you wait while I pick up a burger."

"Get one for me while you're there, chili-cheeseburger, plus 'pommes, rot-weiss' – french fries with ketchup and mayonnaise. I feel like something disgusting."

They eat them in the car, she nibbling, he biting, then more harmless chatter to relax, as he drives her home. He doesn't offer to spend the night, which was a pleasant surprise. Maybe another time. She might be interested, she decides. Maybe he's gay, never mind.

The minute she's upstairs and uncorked a bottle of wine, Lukas is back on the phone, "Look, Dani, I'll be back by midday, but let me send you a list of names and you tell me how many you recognise, not now, tomorrow. I got this list from the security people in Brussels with a warning they're potentially destructive."

"Don't they have files, records? I mean, you're a cop, you can check."

"And I did and none of them are on any kind of official system or index of written records, which thanks to German data protection laws still means most of the interesting stuff only exists on paper. Nevertheless, that was interesting in itself."

"Isn't that a little unusual?" she asks politely.

"Certainly. There are files on just about everyone who's ever walked on German soil and a lot who haven't."

"Then why ask me?"

"Just checking, hopefully you will know who some of them are. If not, then there are at least forty or fifty dangerous characters with fake identities wandering around Berlin, that no-one here has even noticed, which is excessive. Fifty years ago you could get away with false papers without anyone ever asking to see them. Now, you can't even go shopping without your bank card sending off the time and place of purchase."

"Well, a bit strange, I suppose. I'm not sure I'd really know what constitutes excessive, not in Berlin."

"Dani, think about it, I'll see you in the morning."

The next thing Dani knows is the phone is ringing again and it's already morning.

Expecting it to be Lukas, it turns out to be Maria, who Dani hadn't expected to hear from again. She's business-like.

"Tell me what you know about this Allegra woman."

"Nothing at all," Dani replies.

"Then find out, please."

"I'll see what I can do."

She starts by phoning Caro, who refuses to talk to her. "Don't you think you've caused enough trouble already?" Even over the phone Dani can tell there are tears dripping and a nose is snuffling. For some odd reason she can hear seagulls mewing in the background. Then music. She must have the radio on.

"Caro? Hello?"

End of one sided conversation.

"She was huffy," Dani says to Lukas when he phones.

"She didn't threaten to kill you, so it can't be very serious."

"Oh."

"So what about my list."

"I spent most of the morning trying to find out stuff about this Allegra. I didn't get anywhere at all with the names you sent me. No-one has ever heard of them. Maybe they're just investors. Maybe they don't exist."

"Why the interest in Allegra?"

"Maria, she was insistent. And I thought, why not?"

"She would be. Can you send her a copy of my list. We can meet her later on. Keep looking."

"Lukas?"

"Yes?"

"Are Bernhardt's people still playing."

"Oh yes. They seem to be into their longest session yet, been playing continuously for sixteen hours. Maybe it's an endurance test. Old Bernhardt almost certainly has a 'sleepless' mixture for them to try. Just one of the twenty four 'Attitudes' they have ready for ingestion. Listen, I'll be back in Berlin in an hour and half unless there's a hold-up on the autobahn. Try to get hold of Elfie," he said. "By the way, we got the oil smugglers. Super result, especially for the Dutch. And we picked up the drug dealers here, who were working for them. Very much as usual, a restaurant to launder the cash and a rented garage to distribute the dope. We picked up a 4x4, nice machine. It swapped number plates even more often than it changed colour. Much the same as the wagon we emptied last year. 500kilos of hash this time and a hundred and seventy thousand pills of various flavours. People underestimate the volume of drugs you need for a good weekend in Berlin. People spend more on drugs that they do on clothes. Though I suppose that's obvious if you see the way most folk dress."

" Well done Lukie," she says without allowing him to distract her with comments about cheap clothes, "So what exactly do you and Maria mean to one another."

"Not to worry," he says, avoiding mention of Maria. "If you're interested, I do have a theory about your role in these petty dramas. In your guise as a finder, people have been using you to discover how much it is possible for people to find out about them. Your questions haven't been to find out stuff about other people, you've been used to check their stories for leaks. Whenever you unearth something they stop the leak. It's only a theory, but I do think it might turn out to be correct. You're the canary in the coalmine."

"Thanks a lot." she replies.

"Chirp, chirp," Lukas said and then he was gone.

"Typische Berlin," says Dani to herself. Some Randy Newman song is playing on the radio to encourage her sense of cynical dismay. She isn't pleased, at all.

And what is Lukie after, she wonders to herself, among all these tepid investigations? In theory, she is working for three people all with different interests as well as collaborating with Lukas. Legal advisor to Bernhardt, Maria is assumed to be representing someone else too. As for Caro, she seems to be allying herself with Bernhardt one minute, then mopping up the mess that Klaus left behind, as well as feathering her own nest. And Bernhardt himself seems to insinuate himself in every situation he encounters. Whether he's really the mastermind everyone would like to believe is a different question, especially if you believe him when he says that there's no-one who knows what they are all working towards.

All Dani can see is a lot of people picking up as many pay packets as they can, herself included. Maybe a good AI system would be cheaper. Maybe that's the point. Is AI better at finding than she is?

Now, it seems that everyone would like her to accept that this Allegra woman is the wicked witch. Dani isn't impressed. She would still like to know what the 'Gaming with Attitudes' stuff is really trying to achieve. She doesn't do witches. She does think a lot of people are driven by greed, but that is nothing new.

Lukas had suggested she talk to Elfie Malzenberger, so that is what she does.

Elfie isn't very pleased when someone turns up without an appointment, but she doesn't keep Dani waiting long once Lukas' name is mentioned. Suddenly Elfie is friendly as can be.

"I hadn't realised, darling, you should have mentioned him the first time you came to see us," she said

"I didn't consider it appropriate. Lukas is very much his own man."

"Naturally, but a friend of Lukie, well. We were stalwarts of the Extra Parliamentary Opposition, the APO, in our younger days. So what can I do for you? Pipapo came before So-femme."

"We're still concerned about Caro and Bernhardt, the fall out after Klaus' exitus."

"Is there very much more to be known? Most of it went through the courts. We can talk about this downstairs. Erica, can you answer the phones, I'm out for a bit."

Elfie leads Dani down a stone staircase into the cellar, which is a good deal older than the building above and a great deal larger. Dani realises it is an extension of 'Dark Shadow', the club next door, and on the principle of assuming the obvious, she deduces correctly that 'Die Malzenberger' is the owner.

'My sister brought your lawyer friend here a few nights ago. Talk about losing inhibitions, that Maria woman went for the lot, one after another. I don't know why it is but the Americans do seem extraordinarily repressed when it comes to sex. You'd think they only do it on national holidays and saints' days. Once you uncork the bottle, they're off like rockets on New Years Eve, if you'll excuse my mixed up comparisons. As it was your friendly lawyer Maria managed several months worth of full on action in a couple of hours. Sister Silke adores her, of course, but she falls in love with anyone who's happily married. It's her own special failing, which isn't very serious, when you think about it. A lot of obsessive people are much much worse."

"I haven't met Silke."

"Are you married?"

"No."

"Then she won't be interested in you, she likes couples, both at the same time, or with one of them as a spectator. The men get excited watching her with their wives and the women find their husbands' efforts entertaining. She's very popular, some see her as a therapist. Erotic healing, I think it's called. I just think she enjoys being provocative, but why not. No-one forces people to come here, they have to ask, you know. We only let people in if it's totally clear that they understand what the club is all about."

Dani is obviously looking surprised as Elfie laughs, "Actually, our Silke has a waiting list of couples. She tells them to be patient and amuse themselves some other way until she's ready for them. Would you like to talk to her? I shouldn't be talking about her like this, she's more than able to speak for herself. Well that's taken as said for someone working as a public prosecutor. Ask Lukie, he'll tell you the rest."

"Silke is Staatsanwalt? A prosecutor? Isn't that tricky..?"

"We all have a right to our private lives."

"Yes. Was Maria here on her own, or was she with someone?"

"There was some guy, but he didn't stay very long. Actually, the girls were all over each other, I think he felt left out. People come here to explore, with mixed results. Sometimes it's wonderful and other evenings people wander off disappointed. I think Maria was one of our successes. I was impressed, those gunshot scars on her back are unforgettable." "Gunshot scars?"

"Yes, three of them, dense scar tissue white against her skin and the red weals Silke had whipped up."

"Is any of this linked to the gaming people, most of the gamers I've seen are too young for sex games."

"I agree. The gamers themselves aren't around, but some of the people who devise these games conventions and work with the designers are part of our little community. They need a way of understanding how groups work in the kind of insulated space of the networks. They all specialise in domination and submission, which is an emotional tightrope. Someone told me it's the basis for one of their new projects."

"And Caro?"

"No, she's on the outside, wondering and watching without getting her hands dirty. We don't really like that, we like people who've been willing to explore their own desires before they tell other people what's on the menu."

"Provocations."

"Of course, personal and social activism are being monetised as a new horizon within the framework of event management. And all the world is being monetised, you do understand that. Content is meaningless, when cash is king and connectedness the currency."

"That doesn't sound very promising."

"I merely reflect the morés of our times." says Fr. Malzenberger, then she sounds insistent. "I don't think you are the kind of person we'd expect here."

"Nor do I, to be frank."

"You needn't apologise, the people who come here have special needs to be fulfilled. Be thankful that you don't share them. It isn't always a very happy journey that they're on."

Dani and Elfie take a moment to observe one another.

"Do you mean all this is a kind of therapy?"

"No. This is a lifestyle choice. There's nothing to be cured, but you can't guarantee happiness."

Then Dani says, "And I suppose that is what you enjoy."

"I think it's time for you to leave," Elfie replies.

"Just one last thought, do you know where I can find Allegra Keller?"

"I can tell you where to find her, but are you sure she's someone you should talk to? Allegra is a tricky person to know. She's working with Dietmar Marschal from his office near the Schloss." but he likes to hang around with Fat Pete. You know Fat Pete, I think. He told me you'd been poking about asking questions about me."

"He spoke very highly of you."

Elfie laughs, "No, he didn't, he told you I am an unreliable informant who would cheat my own children out their breakfast if I thought it necessary."

"Not quite that bad."

"That's what he said to me he last time we met. I don't like to speculate about things he says behind my back."

"What is this Marschal guy up to? Why is Allegra there?"

"Lukie knows more of the details than I do. He's got a security clearance that lets him ask questions."

"Ask who?"

"The people who do the watching."

" Government Intelligence - the BND?"

"Not exactly, a lot of things are handled privately nowadays, which makes sense if you think about it. If you have a safe route into a secure environment the last thing you want is for some competitor to jeopardise it. So you open up the leaking hole, carefully nurture its seclusion and pass information on to as many clients as you can handle, but keep the information flow as secret as possible. Then you do as much as you can to protect the host from other intruders and manage the illicit traffic. Even the hackers don't want things to crash. There's a lot of voyeuristic psychology at work in the world of hacking. If you're lucky, people on the outside pay you for the hack and the people on the inside pay you to control the leaks."

"What happens if you're found out?"

"Usually, no, ...difficult to say. Sometimes people just get shot because they're likely to end up dead anyway, but more often, the tables are turned on the snoopers and the flow of information is reversed. Nobody wants more than one set of people messing about with complex systems, just so that everything stays online and continues being hackable. Just crashing things is too easy. The clever ones try to control things to their own ends, could be political, often it's commercial, sometimes it's government. All very symbiotic, isn't it?"

"Are games similar?"

"Of course, except the amount of data being processed can be immense. Try to imagine the mass of data per millisecond when you've half a million people online via your website. Don't ask Bernhardt about that, ever, or he'll give you a lecture about synapses and neurones by the billion. He doesn't believe in artificial intelligence versus the traditional kind, because he doesn't believe in intelligence. He doesn't believe in God either. In fact I don't think Bernhardt believes in anything apart from having as complex a good time as possible."

"Complex fun? So it's a lot of stuff all at the same time," says Dani, playing her get out of jail free card yet again. "You don't expect me to understand these things."

Then, to their surprise Lukie puts in an appearance having been held up near Hanover for half an hour but otherwise making good time from Bremen. "Hello Dani, your mobile told me where to find you. Elfie you wicked old thing, what have you been telling her."

Elfie's assistant has followed Lukie downstairs and is signalling her dismay that he's barged past her."

"That's fine, Erica, now fuck off back to your desk, will you," Elfie says with a smile., "I have to talk to the grown ups."

"Ok, you two," says Lukie, once Erica has gone. "It's started."

"What has started," says Elfie.

"Yes, bring us up to date, please," Dani requests.

"Fat Pete is dead. He was discovered lying at the bottom of a lift shaft in that apartment block he'd bought just off the Ku'damm near Halensee. We are fairly sure it is murder, not an accident, or even a trial run gone wrong as some of the other incidents might have been. This time someone dived straight in, messed about with the electronics via the smart-home software and made sure he stepped into an empty space. Lights off, lift door opens, shove, nudge and drop. One way trip, no turning back, all that. Poor bastard, he was essentially harmless, an ineffective guy with a very high opinion of himself."

"Well that is outrageous, what had Pete ever done to anyone, apart from sell them overpriced apartments?" Elfie is furious.

"The people at Last Supper were accusing him of trashing their business, so I guess they will be the prime suspects, given the stuff they do with knives."

"OK Lukie, you tell us, what else is new?" asks Dani. She can't get excited about Fat Pete's exit, sad as it may be. She's more worried about the conclave of gamers and is fairly sure he had nothing to do with any of that.

The same can't be said of Bernhardt. Almost fifteen hours went by before he learned that Fat Pete was dead. He could have known, if he'd been bothered to pay attention, but he didn't. Elfie Malzenberger gave him the news and he was shocked to the core.

Fat Pete may have been a very small cog in a very large machine, but he'd been there for a very long time, not quite as long as Harry Mertens, but long enough to be considered an ever present, one of the people who can be trusted, dependable, reliable and most important of all cool, calm and predictable. Bernhardt didn't like losing a second old acquaintance in such a short time.

"What's this all about, Elfie?" he asked.

"The usual, Bernhardt, power, or did you think old age has brought you immunity from dispossession? Bernhardt, one false move and you'll lose the fucking lot."

"And who might it be who intends to do the dispossessing?"

"Looks like a competition, either Caro versus Allegra, or Maria versus Cecilia. I don't think there are other players taking to the field at this stage. The choice is yours. One of us, all of us. A bit of both, if you want my opinion. And don't place any trust in that Daniela woman, she's in cahouts with bloody Lukas Winkler, if you remember him, loopy Luke!"

"Oh, to hell with the lot of you. All I want is a reasonable buzz and Juniper wrapping herself around me with detectable signs of erotic curiosity. Is it too much to ask?"

"Have it your own way, Bernhardt. But they're gunning for you, whether you like it or not. I shall have to take sides soon, no alternative. Sorry, but that's how it goes. Nothing personal, we're old friends. Nothing goes on forever."

"My thanks to you, Elfrieda, and don't forget the RPG."

"I don't have an RPG, what on earth are you talking about, rocket propelled grenades."

"RPG, 'Roubidoux Polysolid Group' - remember the name. Now can I talk to that useless sod of a husband you keep on a leash in your cellar?"

"Bye Bernie. Helmut, it's Bernhardt, he wants to talk to you. God knows why. Life and death, or something like that."

There's a shuffling noise and a rattle of loosened chains, as Elfie's Helmut gets to the phone, "What's what, Bern?"

"Could you please kill that bloody wife of yours."

"No chance. I tried it dozens of times. Nothing works. I think Elfie may well be a handmaid of Satan, though I'm not completely sure yet. I'll let you know if it's ever confirmed. She certainly starts smelling of brimstone when we drive past churches. Even the Bishop of Belgrade noticed that when he was here."

"Bishop of Belgravia? What denomination?"

"Dollars. He and Elfie get on well enough, despite everything."

"Everything?"

"Oh, I don't think you'd want me to go into that, Bern. Not your sort of thing, not your sort of thing at all. All a bit special, if you follow me."

"I never thought I'd hear you being coy, Helmut, never ever."

Chapter 18

The flight from Frankfurt arrived an hour late at Tegel because of trouble between the pilots and their employers, which spread to flight attendants and baggage handlers, then to air traffic controllers and maintenance staff. Bernhardt was furious that Juniper should be held up by such trivia.

It wasn't as though she was trying to fly by Pan Am, or Interflug, or or Deutsche BA, or Air Berlin, or any one of the airlines who went broke flying in and out of the city.

He'd paid for a private jet to fly her from Colorado via Nova Scotia and Iceland, with sight-seeing tours at every opportunity, then a final hop over the North Atlantic via Edinburgh, then Frankfurt. Everything had been fine until flights were re-routed following the eruption of Mount Etna and the huge masses of volcanic ash thrown majestically, but destructively into the atmosphere. The pilots bringing Juniper and her cello into Tegel had been advised to fly no higher than 5,000metres and there had been delays finding them a slot to take off. To make matters worse, there was talk of Stromboli erupting to add to the disruption with an extra gritty discharge into the upper atmosphere, so Juniper was actually quite lucky to make it to Berlin in time before the airspace shutdown would have forced her to take the train from Frankfurt to Berlin.

Bernhardt had been harrassed by striking pilots as he awaited Juniper's arrival and they were all furious when she and her cello turned out to be the only passengers. They had been expecting to heckle a bundle of bankers and investors who had actually flown in by Ryanair to the other airport.

Juniper and Bernhardt are delighted to be re-united. Perhaps in a society of cynics, this late flowering relationship was an affirmation of the power of love to triumph over any obstacle including reluctant Airbus certified aircrew and disgruntled ground staff.

Berliners might imagine that one of the few genuinely super-rich people in the city would take the love of his life to one of the city's finer hotels, say the Four Seasons in Grunewald, but Bernhardt has different plans.

As he anticipated, Juniper is charmed by the rustic simplicity of the two roomed hut at his little 'schrebergarten', his modest allotment with its pocket handkerchief lawn, the old vine and a mass of flowers in bloom. Instead of an evening in a fancy restaurant, he'd ordered a spread of vegetarian dishes from the India Express on Kantstrasse, who are about the only people in the city who know how the infuse a dish with the full flavour of spices from the sub-continent.

Juniper swoons with pleasure as they eat the curry and they eagerly wash the whole lot down with trickles of perfectly cool, but not chilled Löwenbräu from the brewery on Nymphenburgstrasse in the heart of Munich.

The moon lingers as the lovers lick the last of spicey sauces from their fingers. There are yelps of fox clubs and the grunty snuffles of hedgehogs patrolling the neighbouring gardens as ancient S-bahn trains rattle their way towards the Westkreuz junction and the lines that run west to the Olympic Stadium and south to Potsdam from the city centre. The Juniper and Bernhardt add their own personal sighs and groans, with squeaks and gasps as appropriate.

Then it is time for champagne, raspberries and rich vanilla ice cream. Soon they are sated and curl up to sleep in each other's arms, a picture of romantic bliss. The 'bliss' was a special little extra Bernhardt had sprinkled on the ice-cream that he's refined just for Juniper and himself. Eventually it will be marketed as 'Euphoria', or 'Eupho' but just for now, Juniper and Bernhardt are the only people in the world to have enjoyed its wonderful palette of pleasures. Juniper Willow Ash considers herself to be the luckiest woman in the world.

Bernhardt is feeling incredibly relaxed now Juniper is with him.

He'd never had any serious doubts about the gaming trial. Bernhardt's experience with freshly minted psychedelics is incomparable and his preparation impeccable. Everything is going very much as expected and they all look in line for an enormous payout once the investors are on board, which should be confirmed in a couple of days. There's been enough fishing for funding. The investors who game have been hooked, now it's time to reel them in - a thousand dollars here, ten thousand there, maybe a million, why not more? A broad based of small investors is perfect, to blunt the professionals' destructive instincts. Bernhardt had been genuinely moved when he'd first heard about the accident that killed Harald Mertens, who he'd known of since the nineteen seventies, when both of them were young mavericks, or in Bernhardt's case more maverick than young. He enchants Juniper with tales of youthful hedonism in Crete and Morocco, his friends who travelled unharrassed through Afghanistan, the dreadful news that Soviet Russia had thrown their might against the Afghans and the heart wrenching tales of death and destruction that followed as conflict spread south to bother the USA and their Western European NATO partners, to fringe the Black Sea with violence. In his day, Harald had done it all and infected West Berlin with the virus of hedonism. Bernhardt says he will be missed.

As he described the long years of research, Bernhardt began to wonder whether Harald might have been the intended victim, a target, not just a luckless casualty, but he doesn't let it spoil his evening.

Soon Juniper is playing Bach. Her bones resonate, her breathing quickens and night falls. The autobahn can be heard as a distant hum. S-bahn trains rattle and clatter, then sing a little, la la la, before their doors bash closed. The ominous shadow of the Congress Centre and that old cold war relic, the wreck of the Teufelsberg radar station is silhouetted on the skyline. Bernhardt is a contented old man at ease with himself and the world.

He wonders whether to organise a reunion of sorts with Caro and Allegra, so Juniper can meet them in this old family setting, but she isn't enthusiastic and heads him off in other directions. They'll spend these precious days together in celebration of 'rus in urbes', the country in the city, and their nights in an al fresco celebration of one inside the other. At midnight thirty, Cecilia calls as usual and confirms that the IPO is set and they are due to become a business valued at $7bn in three weeks time. Roubidoux Polysolid couldn't be more pleased. They're looking at a thousand percent profit on day one.

"Isn't that nice," she says.

"Lovely," agrees Bernhardt, who doesn't care as much as everyone else assumes.

"The core assets have been ring fenced," she confirms, "and protected so they can remain under our private control, but the great mass of marketing and the proliferation business is going to be lodged within the listed corporation. The middle men can carry on their search for the next set of suckers who'll bulk out the investment ten or twenty thousand dollars at a time. Wall Street have decided we're the ' Next Big Thing'."

"Good, good," says Bernhardt and glances towards Juniper, inviting her response.

"Seems OK," agrees Juniper, who knows a lot about corporate finance from her days with the Vain Corporation of Nebraska, top class management consultants to America's richest ranchers. "Make sure Harald's widow is looked after."

None of the bankers and brokers backing the project have noticed the intellectual property gap, Cecilia's delighted to say. Bernhardt just laughs. All they think of is the quickest way to offload the junk and walk away with a profit. Serves them right if they can't be bothered to see how things really work. Maria has done a good job on the patents front. Sad for the investors, of course, in the long run, but I don't think there are any investors in the long run, so that argument falls by the wayside. Everyone sells the moment they can double their money and walk away.

He wants to know whether Maria has had any success in Berlin.

"She seems to think she's doing quite well, but they still haven't worked out where Allegra is doing her stuff. She mentioned someone called Dieter, does that make sense?"

"Yes, yes. He's a mollusc. No need to worry yourselves about him!"

While Juniper plays Bach, bats flitter over the gardens. Owls hoot and a pair of government helicopters batter the air as they clatter towards the Chancellory in Tiergarten. Bernhardt relaxes and reminds himself that life is good, just as a bat swerves past his nose and chomps a late flying dragonfly.

In the Hotel Albatros, Lee is getting ready to go to work. First he'll pop into the Soph-Am for a small glass of brandy. He's curious. Maria has told him about the bar and he wants to have been there at least once before he leaves town the next day. He might even hide the weapon there once he's finished. One day it will be discovered and seed an urban myth.

Lee is at his best working alone.

When he arrives at the Soph-Am, he sits quietly at a table giving him a view of the room and the door. Once he's finished his beer, he doesn't stay long.

A taxi takes him over the motorway to the Funkturm, the Radio Tower at the ICC, where he buys a ticket for the lift to the all night restaurant with its panoramic view over the city. He props the rucksack against his ankle, so he can sense the presence of the gun inside. With a table near the window, he can soon pick out the place that interests him. Bernhardt and Juniper are in plain view, only a few hundred yards away on the other side of the autobahn and the S-bahn tracks. The restaurant food is unambitious but delicious and Lee is more than satisfied with his dinner. It helps to go to work on a full stomach. There's nothing worse than a grumbling tummy to upset your aim.

He pays his bill, including a modest tip, then leaves the restaurant and pays a visit to the men's room. As he'd hoped, there's a window he can squeeze through to climb up the long steel girders that form the framework of the tower towards the open stair that technicians use to reach the transmitter.

Once he's outside in the fresh air, all he can hear is the muffled roar of the autobahn traffic, the S-bahn and gently cooing pigeons, who shuffle to new perches as he climbs past their roosts. Once or twice he thinks he catches a snatch of Bach being played on an old cello, but he is probably mistaken. Lee is a romantic. It's just an illusion. He'd like to imagine two hearts ceasing to beat as one and the surprised look of their owners as they face the long night of eternity without warning, once the sniper's bullet finds its marks. He is the master of their fate. Instant oblivion. One shot and you simply cease to be. Settling on one of the main stanchions, Lee is comfortable as he assembles the rifle he's been carrying in his rucksack. Any higher and he'd risk being fried by the TV transmitters, but the angle is just fine, just under eight degrees. He has five handmade bullets that will sweep them away. There's hardly a breath of wind. The distance is well within his range. Lee assembles, loads, relaxes, aims and squeezes off two rounds in quite succession.

The optics of his night sight are exceptional, full colour, enhanced depth and local brightness. Bernhardt has his back to Lee, though he's unaware of that. Facing him, Juniper bows the cello in a rapture of baroque sensitivity. The first round goes high and the second is also a little higher than he intends, but Bernhardt twitches as the bullets skims the top of his skull, then flies on hitting first the cello, then Juniper. There's a bright spout of blood from Bernhardt's broken cranium, a crack of shattered bone and he slumps towards Juniper hands outstretched as the cello bursts in a hundred splinters and she is thrown backwards by the violence of bullet hitting her sternum as it splits to puncture lungs and sever arteries in a fierce and fatal wound. They're soon gone, a minute or two of suffering mixed with horror, sadness, bewilderment and dismay, which might have been worse but for the 'Eupho'.

The world goes on, as Lee methodically dismantles the weapon and retraces his climb to leave the Funkturm by the same lift he'd chosen when he arrived. The attendant asks if he enjoyed his meal. He says he did and with a reassuring smile, he is gone.

For her part, Maria has been working through the information Dani had found about the buildings she's interested in. The following morning, she even went to check some of them herself.

She'd been disappointed.

There was nothing notable, just a mix of housing and offices that are 'typische Berlin', some altbau, some post-war, fewer that are recent. Neither are the people who live there, or the owners especially interesting. The fashion for kite-flying seems to be spreading. There are pairs of brightly coloured kites near all the places she's been to see.

She recalls someone mentioning the Hotel California on the Ku'damm and wonders if will be more interesting. The name makes her smile and she's already humming the tune when she goes into the lobby and looks around. The concierge tries to help, so she plays the disorientated tourist for a couple of minutes, then pops into the coffee shop. Ordering herself a coffee and a croissant, Maria spends a few minutes catching up on everday matters and remembers to order the 'stolperstein' for the holocaust victims from her friend's family. Maria thinks it's an honourable cause. She and Lee send a donation to the organisers, 'for the unknown victims of intolerance in Charlottenburg'.

As Maria sips her coffee, Allegra walks past unnoticed, hips swinging and optimistic. She's ditched the military uniform in favour of a Jil Sander leather jacket and piled her hair in a fashionable heap to be kept in place by a variety of clips, so it's hardly surprising Maria didn't recognise her. Anyway, it wouldn't have made any difference if she'd walked past stark naked, because Maria was busy rummaging through her bag looking for her mobile so she could call Dani and by the time she found it, Allegra was gone.

Early in the morning, an S-bahn train is derailed creating confusion for passengers at WestKreuz. To add to the delays, there's no electricity in Spandau, thanks to yet another suicidal raccoon biting through a cable at the power station. There are traffic light failures in Kreuzberg and a water main bursts in Marzahn. Some thirty thousand people call in sick to say they won't be getting into work. Despite feeling ill, another two thousand decide to go into work, when they should have taken the day off and a nasty little virus is sneezed into the city centre provoking the next wave of sore throats and headaches. People are worried that the neo-Nazis are elected to the Bundestag, but that looks like being inevitable. A lot of voters seem to be treating the election as though it was just an opinion poll, forgetting that they're choosing people to run the country.

Berlin is getting on as usual - screwing up.

Allegra sighs with deep seated pleasure and a profound sense of fulfillment. She has tickets for a lunchtime recital at Daniel Barenboim's new chamber concert hall. The ultraspeed network technology is online at long last. Over the last couple of months,

Allegra and Dieter have been ironing out defects in dozens of tests across the city where their kite aerials have enabled local ultraspeed connectedness and the system is smooth as silk. To her, this is all much more than business, to Dieter it's the same, the information revolution is not just about clever demonstrations of technology and novel applications. For Dieter and Allegra, like so many others in the first century, this pioneer century of computing and digitalisation, they are working to build the foundations of a new religion, a pattern of beliefs confirming the powers of technology to become the guiding principles of human life and everything that can and will become the case. However remarkable it may prove, 'Gaming with Attitudes' is only one small step in this first stage of a new era in human experience, yet a genuine, clear, unquestioned step forward it certainly is. The AI processing recognises the lags in the system, whether it be distance, a signal bounced via satellites, the number of switching devices handling the signal and the AI is also used to anticipate the position of people and objects by the time the gamers can see them on screen, so they can lock on a target and fire at will. This is a valuable extension of the traditional geometric aiming technologies, the old fashioned bomb sights and radar, which calculated the position between weapon and target to make launch decisions for missiles and airborn artillery. The screen view is an accurately generated high definition graphic. Allegra thinks Gallileo would be impressed. She's already looking forward. The next step will be Project Genesis.

One by one, her goals are being achieved. Her one regret is Harald Mertens. Harald had wanted to see things for himself during the bus crash test and blundered into the danger zone inadvertently, instantly making himself a target and getting wiped as the scale of the crash went chaotic. It was inevitable there were accidents, sheer bad luck that Harald was caught in one of the worst.

She's now convinced the system is working with complete immunity from detection. The ambitions of a criminal generation, creating profiles and data, the mutagens of online play, a chronicle of madness, tumbling into chaos and the perversions of destructive pleasure, all that and she is the mastermind who has nurtured its creation, or so she has convinced herself. Soon she and Dietmar will leave Berlin for Brussels, where Lee will already be waiting for them.

Revenge is sweet, though it was a shame about the cello.

Caro can consider herself lucky to be in one piece.

After a long argument with Caro's Mother, Allegra reluctantly conceded that she too is one of Bernhardt's victims and has ensured she is protected. Unfortunately, neither of them felt that way about Juniper Willow Ash, or her sister Holly, sad though that might be.

The young gamers are all enjoying themselves enormously. This stuff is great fun, brilliant sound effects and the food is super.

They sense a special edge about the edition they've won the opportunity to play for the first time. This is hardcore, authentic, one on one, a shooter's dream, pioneering stuff. Some of the players are in deep space environments, flying against alien defence systems, some of the others were convinced they were in an imaginary virtual realm. Only the interface the gamers related to is a fiction in every respect but one. The co-ordinates between weapon, feasibility and target are awesomely accurate.

Allegra knew they were playing for real. Real places, real buildings, real people. This wasn't gaming at all. The military term is single-side combat.

The younger gamers, the ten and eleven year olds, were given control of drones high above the landscape before battle, while the more mature elite manned some of the most effective fighting robots on the planet for close combat. Such is the lull before the storm. Dietmar waited for Allegra to complete her checks before he issued the final authorisation to begin the live ammunition demo. She told the observers what they want to hear, that everything was normal and success guaranteed. Then all hell was let loose.

Jacob (13) and Toby (12) are from Harpendon on the outskirts of London and have been assigned a sub-routine skirmishing a group of well armed soldiers in the uniforms of the Second World War. Jacob thinks he is a French officer, Toby is a freedom fighter from the Resistance. Allegra's people lock their co-ordinates with those of a live feed from the Horn of Africa where a group of mercenaries are in a firefight with a platoon of insurgents. Toby scores first, taking out a heavy duty machine gun mounted on the back of a Toyota, which he can see as a light tank in Wehrmacht camouflage.

Jacob whips his drone over a wall into a yard where the enemy foot soldiers think they have cover and splatters the group with sub-machine gun fire from the hip. Kill complete, the system swiftly flips them into a generated environment and they play on undisturbed, oblivious to this forty second foray into real time combat.

They intervened in real world events from a fictional perspective. Dieter is delighted that the AI system has proven its effectiveness. The AI routines are used to overcome the lags in the monitoring system between Africa and Charlottenburg which anticipates the positions of the fighters by several seconds.

"If it ever came to a court case, we could argue that the kids are only responding to a simulation, generated by the AI, so they haven't actually shot anyone at all. It's an AI determined conflict."

Allegra locks the next satellite feed with the game data and the system synchronises to provide a seamless transition from a fictional defensive action against foraging Southerners in the American Civil War with real time data from a Mid-East village being defended from insurgents. Of the fourteen players online, only three are people, the other eleven are computer generated agents brought into play to enhance the sense of authenticity. The officer is a young woman, Francesca(15) from Umbria, who has been impressing everyone with her achievements online over the previous eighteen months and the maturity of her decision making. As a platoon commander, she is cool in a crisis and ruthlessly effective when the action starts.

In this instance, a defensive manoevre involves the sacrifice of several of her foot soldiers as they are picked off by the opponents. But in doing that, the attackers positions are revealed and Francesca authorises the launch of five rocket propelled grenades into the heart of the enemy positions. The RPG's are swift and destructive. Before the smoke clears, the system switches from the real time data feed to the system generated streams and she wins a battlefield promotion from her commanding officer in the game variation as youthful non-commissioned officers and other ranks assume command from their superiors in emergency situations. He also puts her name forward for a digital decoration. Corporal Tim Jansen, (26), married with two children from Schwerin in Mecklenburg-

Vorpommern will be awarded medals for gallantry, postumously. Allegra is praised by the officer co-ordinating the operation on the ground and he thanks her for helping tune the automated fighting system.

The parallel test is equally successful - the Broadsheath people haven't noticed a thing. Allegra's seamless stitching has proven completely invisible even to expert game administrators. Hannelore Holst, Simon Thiel, Tilmann Schwarz and Julian Breitscheid won't have to die after all. They don't know how lucky they are. Their mediocre middle management mentality has saved their lives. Lucrative contracts await them, following the flotation.

Two more situations are dealt with before lunch, one a traditional drone attack and the other a bombing run from a couple of recently automated pilotless Tornados, the old machines they use for testing that can be thrown away without the accountants showing too much concern. The munitions are worth more than the plane.

Then Allegra and Dieter are invited to eat with the officer observers from the Military Technology Brigade and their finance people. There's a sense of euphoria that everything is functioning as predicted and none of the young operatives have shown any of the battle distress symptoms so common among drone pilots and officers on active service in distant warfare. Welfare issues among service personnel have become a hot political issue. The notion of cannon fodder is redundant. Governments like the media to show their soldiers saving children from floods, mending tramcars, or educating local brigands about policing and democracy. Body parts and gleeful infantry are outré, especially in Germany.

"They don't even know they've been front line," said Dietmar, as he chomped a cheeseburger cheerfully.

Fire-fights give you an appetite.

"And sweetest of all, their parents have given consent, for Christ's sake, it's so grotesque, it's beautiful," says the Hungarian Brigadier, gleefully.

"No-one will acknowledge their role. If they were service personnel, I think they'd be in line for a medal."

"The British have started giving their drone pilots medals, did you know that, 'for those who fought the evil of our time', so why not our players too?" proposes Piotr Schimanski, from the political side of the monitoring group. "We could talk to the marketing people about a PR campaign around the theme," Allegra suggested, "Now just how many of these bastards have they taken out?"

"Sixty seven so far and rising inside the first hour and a half."

"My god that's mayhem, double the score for a normal day."

"Well that's how things are when there's no-one to ask any tricky questions."

"What has the AI system got to tell us?"

"Our play is keeping it busy. There's a massive volume of data splashing about. Wait a few minutes for the evaluations to come through."

"The kids are unstoppable, the firepower, wow, the firepower," says Dieter as his voice tails off, his eyes glued to the real time screens of mayhem on every continent except Antarctica.

Another $2bn investment is confirmed over lunch by the bankers who are now firmly convinced that technologies licenced from Roubidoux Polysolid Group are going to triumph in the next generation of AI experience systems. The White House are informed. All in all, this is spectacular success.

The afternoon session addresses an alternative family of targets closer to home, in urban crisis intervention, subversives, counter terrorism, all those pesky destabilising issues that make security and police-work so thankless and relentless.

Everyone involved can recall the video pictures of President Obama and Hillary Clinton watching the assassination of Osama bin Laden online.

Urban interventions have a special kick for gamers, because they're close to home. Streets of houses just like the town you know. Roads and bridges, freeways and autobahns. Railway Stations are a delight, with that winning combination of impressive architecture, streams of people flowing across the concourse and the sexy steam punk potential of the trains themselves.

A situation in Lisbon is tackled in twenty minutes. Two groups of bomb makers in Italy are rooted out and dealt with. There are messages of thanks to the Euro HQ from Carabinieri, Border Police in half a dozen countries and the Anti-terrorist squads of London and Stockholm. JoCoCoPolex, the Joint Committee Countering Political Extremism send a short message of congratulation in all fifteen working languages. This is a genuine pan-European initiative. Chicago is summarily dealt with.

Then Allegra notices something.

A group of four players are enjoying a rather implausible scenario set in world war one, where a group of adventurous gentlemen officers have taken it on themselves to penetrate the lines of Flander's trenches and with Prussian panache stage an attack on one of the country houses used by the British and French high command.

They're doing very well. The AI system has identified a feed that will blend imperceptibly with the HQ attack.

The external feed is providing lower quality images than usual, monochrome and grainy, which doesn't matter for the gamers, they're getting high definition CGI aged to comply with archive footage from 1916.

The team out in the field are elite operatives, just as the gamers are 'best of class'. Allegra recognises that instructions are being relayed verbally from the gamers to the people on the ground. This isn't just a matter of controlling robots. People are talking to others in a language they can understand, with phrases and voices carefully selected by the AI system.

"Have you noticed this before, she asks Dieter quietly.

They both listen in.

The gamers are speaking German, the people on the ground can hear their instructions in French. All four gamers are female. Their online voices are male.

"What do you think?" Allegra asks.

"Let it play, lets see how far they get before we intervene."

Dieter informs the Roubidoux managers of an anomaly. They aren't surprised. The AI system can be expected to smooth the discrepancies. They're not concerned. Self-referential development is becoming the preferred approach to writing bug-free software.

"Can we check where is this feed coming from," asks Allegra, as she tries to ask herself the easiest way to tell if the system is giving them false information about the real location. The wall of screens in front of them displays the full spread of images, both the active original and the online version with active 'anticipation'.

In a twitch of intuition Allegra recognises danger.

There's a graphic of the timelags in the system, anything up to twenty seconds for high definition images from the South Pacific over the Roubidoux funded transponders on the moon to the big array in Chile then via ocean cable from Cape Kennedy, including compression and decompression. That's about the furthest and slowest, a structure that leaves the AI struggling.

By comparison, these signals are immediate, generated somewhere within a twenty five kilometre radius of the building on Sophie-Charlottenstrasse where Allegra and the investing commanders are sitting.

One point two milliseconds including the AI analysis is fast, absurdly fast. The Anticipation engine wasn't design for close work of this kind, which is where the stalls are arising.

It's local. There's lossiness. Jitter is getting difficult to counter.

"Look," she says to Dieter.

Allegra thinks she can recognise the buildings.

There's the old theatre wing of Schloss Charlottenburg to on side, then the sixties housing development and to the left she can recognise the West End Hospital.

This is alarming. Dieter and Allegra have commandeered a old brick building next to the workshop that produces museum replica's of Berlin's treasures on Sophie-Charlottenstrasse. There are plaster cast copies of the bust of Nefertiti in every window which confuses the AI system into imagining more defenders than there really are.

The attackers are taking them out. One after another the busts of Nefertiti are turned to dust.

Now they are inside.

The system is turning the gamers against them.

It isn't just the ethics of corrupting innocent young people.

Allegra has to chose between life and success.

She isn't stupid.

"Close it down, abort, immediate abort, don't fuck about and ask why, or you'll die," Allegra orders. "Enough is enough, send the kids home. Give their parents double the usual rate. Let's get out of here."

She has no intention of becoming a martyr. Amidst the confusion, people slip away hoping to melt unnoticed into the city streets. That doesn't work at all. They're all picked out by 'Network Check'.

Allegra does try to cobble together an argument to justify her decision, without explaining exactly what happened.

"Once you know something works, it's time to go. We can talk to those guys in India. Dieter tell your people to get rid of the fucking kites. We don't want the antennae being discovered."

Inside the hour, they were gone.

Equipment trashed, complete erasure.

Four confused mercenaries head back to the Hotel Adlon to change back into their street clothes, then book some train tickets for Prague. By mid-afternoon they're trundling through Dresden.

The test was officially pronounced a failure.

The drugs were disposed of free of charge to young club goers in Freidrichshain.

Within twelve hours, the hotel rooms had been vacated and new guests started checking in.

The caterers dumped one thousand five hundred burgers, six thousand 'Berliner' doughnuts and a lot of tuna and mayonnaise sandwiches that had only appealed to the old folks anyway.

Maria too decides it's time to get out, Ryanair to Dusseldorf Weese, then by taxi over the border into Holland. A local train to Maastricht and then another to Brussels and inside a couple of hours, she's in Belgium. She meets Lee as planned at the Metropole Hotel Brussels which Lee says had been recommended by a colleague. The following morning they take a train to Amsterdam, then a plane from Schiphol to Miami.

Their journey goes unnoticed.

She didn't bother saying goodbye.

She wasn't exactly sure who was still alive.

Lee's parents will bring the children home in time for her daughter's birthday party. Maria had already sent the teddy bear by courier to Montana with the news that it had come from a place called 'Bear Island', which is english for 'Berlin' and the little brown bear 'Lynn' is already a firm favourite in her daughter's menagerie of stuffed animals.

Cecilia and the people from Roubidoux Polysolid are desperately seeking Bernhardt to no avail. Maria is being bombarded with hundreds of messages an hour, which she answers with the simple sentence that she is indisposed. When Wall Street opens there's an announcement that the flotation is being pulled. Caro, having decided to leave Bernhardt to get on with whatever he was getting on with together with Juniper, had decided not to visit the garden.

In her absence, no-one had noticed the bodies until the following weekend, by which time the gamers were gone and the city had moved on.

As might be expected, Polyflow were then put under enormous pressure to explain themselves and did try their best, but too much money had gone missing for them to evade an official investigation. Government auditors from the the Bundesrechnungshof were called in to look at Berlin's economic development plans.

Overwhelmed by the weight of accusations, the soigné Brussels bureaucrat fought a rearguard action before falling prey to hubris and her expulsion from the elite was a formality. There are plenty more like her ready to volunteer. She returned to Romania, chastened, humbled, yet more determined than ever to make something of the severance pay and compensation she's been paid to leave town once and for all. Her killing was no accident. There were investigations and tacit agreement the cases would never be solved. Should anyone be at all surprised? Above all, the EU is a bastion of human rights, a fine example of freedom, democracy and transparent competition, of that you can be sure. Ask the President of the Commission if you're not convinced and he'll reassure you that all is well.

According to the radio news, a Minister has resigned, but soon enough no-one can be sure which one. The Minister of Finance is still not going to be called Schauble, but it is will probably take months to put a new government together. There are coalition talks to be held between the parties and they have no sense of urgency. The weather in Berlin will be normal for the time of year and in the Bundesliga, the same number of games of football have been won as have been lost.

Once it's clear that Caro and Maria have left the city, the investigation into the garden colony shootings grinds to a halt. No-one can establish a convincing chain of events linking anyone to the killings.

Lukas Winkler's notes looked something like this as he headed for a meeting with his colleagues who were running the investigation in Charlottenburg:

Pharma dope – talk to the Indians.
Triangle - murder no accident - ! - the traffic accident - ! the fake 'investigation' - !!!!!!!!!
 gamers tricked to becoming drone pilots, how could they?! FUCK.
Bernhardt is/was a bastard. (always was????)
GCHQ. Nearest airport Bristol, Birmingham, or Cardiff, ask BND for conference centre address. Langley, Virg - Eurocops Meet.
Erik becomes and Caro is gone – where did I see that, what does it mean?
Weekend gardens available near S-bahn Charlottenburg, between there and the Westkreuz quite cheap, why not?
The days of all powerful figures dominating management are over, but these are people with motives quite unlike the concerns of tech people, or the managers we know.
TREES FALL, railway goods train derailment, another BALCONY COLLAPSES.
Bloody crows.
What do Roubidoux Polysolid actually do?????
RACACACACOONS,   ELECTROCUTION   AND   OTHER ACCIDENTS WAITING TO HAPPEN.
 WtF?
  That HELICPTER????? BARMEN, WAITERS, CLUB FOLK, Bookshop ASSISTANTS, TALK TO THE TEDDY SALESGIRL.
Tidy up papers and files.
 Fat chance!!!
 Rock and Rollmops, maybe
ATTITUDES and EXPECTATIONS
 FIND DANI!!!!
Go get drunk.
      YES!
You know it makes sense.
Ha!
 Lukie hadn't got very far, but he is being promoted, so there'll be other fish to fry. Like everyone else, he is setting the case on one side. He didn't have much luck tidying up but stuck to the last two

points on his wishlist and invited Dani for a drink in the Soph-Am. She was early, Lukie was late.

He notices Phil is on his own, reading a book, 'Fear and Loathing in Las Vegas'. Uli is chatting with one of the play-pals, who notices the book and says, "Do you think he ever sees the news?"

"The wierdest thing about the whole business," Dani tells Lukie, "is that everyone paid their bills in full and on time, except for Bernhardt, but he was dead and I'd not been expecting him to come up with anything anyway. So, I'm feeling prosperous for the first time ever. That's unheard of, it never happens in Berlin."

"Don't you worry sweetheart," says Lukie to reassure her, "It won't last."

Dani decides to go on holiday. Lukie asks where. She's always wanted to hike down the gorges on Crete, but she wants some company. She'd ask the distraction to go along too, but he has a conference to attend in Stuttgart. Georg has never been much of a hiker, so she just books a flight to Heraklion for herself.

There's nothing wrong with a holiday on your own, but....

Despite the unaccounted deaths, the massive scale doping, the abuse of young gamers and and the expansive drone warfare, Berlin is much the same as ever.

People have, however, noticed that the kites have disappeared.

Now a club is being established devoted to installing highly coloured tethered kites to buildings across the city and the founders have applied to the Lotterie fund for a grant. They'll get their money. Kites are cute and cool and tourists like them. Berlin is now officially the city of kites and good karma.

Dani is perplexed. How can so much have happened, without anyone seeming to notice anything at all?

Even hindsight doesn't seem to be a help.

"One way or another," said Dani, "you can get away with anything in Berlin."

Lukas agrees, "Yeah, that's just the kind of place it is."

Chapter 19

Six months later a sun-tanned middle aged man drives an old beaten up LandRover from his vineyard towards the city. When Caro arrives on a flight from Istanbul via Cairo, he's waiting for her at the airport in Cape Town.

South Africa is hot. Spring is in the air.

She's feeling faint, but pulls herself together.

Just exhaustion after the flight, there's no great time change to give you jet lag, but long flights are tiring all the same.

They've missed each other enormously, but it's been worth it. Everything had gone exactly as planned.

They had lured Bernhardt.

He'd brought Juniper with him and now she's gone too.

There will never be an Alice.

Poor Allegra. By getting killed, Bernhardt had exposed her too and Caro had taken sweet revenge. Allegra should never have put her trust in Caro's Mother, Erda, who'd cut her legs from under her and offered her as fodder to the drug cartels. They had done their worst and that was that. Erda always resists new religions.

Caro and her Mother inherited as they had always intended and the bulk of Bernhardt's assets are already transferred to China for safe keeping. Now, six months later, the old lady has died of age related symptoms and Caro has inherited once again, this time in her own right. She's worth a lot more than she had ever expected. There had been a wealthy great-grandfather on her mother's side of the family. Bernhardt had been fairly generous to old friends and colleagues,

311

but Caro's share of his loot was still more than she could imagine needing for herself. She'll have to start buying things like old Master paintings to turn the numbers into something meaningful.

Klaus looks older, but so does Caro, that's only to be expected after such a stressful time. "Do you remember that club in Rostock, 'Rock and Rollmops'?" he asks, as the porters load Caro's bags into the old LandRover.

"I've never been to Rostock," she responds.

"That was where I met Markus and Fat Pete. Then Martin introduced me to you when we got back to Berlin, told me all those stories about you two in Venezuela and all that stuff with Odd Lozenge.

Then Martin kept asking me whether I was Klaus, or whether I was Erik. I was as confused as he was to begin with, until I realised he thought I was two different people. He invented my twin. Up till then, I'd been Klaus-Erik, which was clumsy, so sometimes in Berlin I just called myself Klaus and just occasionally I said my name was Erik, which was what people had called me in school. I hated being called Erik, but no-one would call me Rick, which was what I'd always wanted.

To begin with it was a joke between me and a circle of half a dozen friends. 'Who are you today,' they'd ask, 'Klaus, or Erik?' Then I realised there were people who really thought I was two different people. It had to do with clothes, I always had sunglasses on when I wore one particular jacket and some people assumed that was Erik, a different person to the me they'd seen the day before wearing something else and without the glasses. Supposedly we were identical twins, same birthday, same background, both from boring Bonn. For the first couple of years it was just a joke, then I started to make use of the alter ego. Erik became someone deep in the background, living somewhere else, but coming to Berlin once or maybe twice a year, usually unannounced. Then he would disappear as quickly as he'd arrived. He had bank accounts and ID.

Eventually, Martin will start talking about you and me, but no-one will believe him, not even Elfie fucking Malzenberger."

Klaus wasn't far wrong and now, at long last, to everyone who knows him in South Africa, he is Rick, like Humphrey Bogart, just as he's always wanted to be. He decided it was time to bring Caro into the fold. After all they were the last two standing apart from Lee and he's gone off on other deals. She deserves an explanation. "It was Martin who suggested I try to make it official and have Erik legally registered as someone with his own identity. Markus organised the paperwork. Erik is Slovenian, officially an EU citizen, which was very adroit of Markus. He owns a farm near the Austrian border, not too far removed from Italy, so this Erik is a rather cosmopolitan bloke. He doesn't spend much time on the farm which is managed for him by the former owner who gets a salary and a cut of the EU subsidies. So, then there were two solid legal identities, Klaus-Erik, which was the name I grew up with and Erik, there never was a Klaus, as such, that was just the name that people used from day to day, just a signature on all the paperwork and an identity that Markus had dreamed up out of nothing. It seemed to work. I was always K. E. on contracts and correspondence, never just Klaus, but no-one bothered to notice the anomaly.

 It didn't matter until the insolvency loomed, then I realised how convenient 'Erik' was. There came a point when knocking Klaus on the head was a pretty good idea. Clean break. Me and Markus, old Markie is very adaptable you know, he rigged up the hang glider. Then we went to Athens and the rest is history."

"So who was the corpse?"

"One of Elfie's migrants, we offered him a few Euros. I think he was from Tunis. The accident was genuine. To begin with it was just intended as a stunt. He must have panicked, which is understandable. You wouldn't have got me into that contraption of Markus', not in a thousand years. There never was a 'Klaus', despite the funeral."

 "You impressed me when you showed up and everyone thought you were Erik, that was amazing. I could hardly breathe, it was so tense, so dramatic. Is Markus OK?"

"Yes, he did a great job, quietly and professionally. You never even noticed, which was essential. He was under orders to abort the whole business if you so much as hinted that you harboured a suspicion."

"No, I didn't realise at all, neither did Dani."

 "Nope, which was even better. She distracted the cop and Elfie Malzenberger and your Dad, which was pretty good going. The

DissCo people have fired Martin of course." "Can't say I'm surprised."

"He knew mountains of secrets, but the older generation are passing into folklore. Most of them feel flattered if you mention their philandering, the excess. There's no-one left for him to blackmail, so they prised him away from his desk."

"What do you think he'll do."

"He'll be fine."

"Revenge?"

"Maybe, but silence is golden and I gave him ten million, so he's locked in as an accomplice. That buys a lot of peace and quiet. My guess is he'll end up in the Soph-Am, droning on about fallen music business idols to Phil and Nico as they drown their sorrows over the Blonde running off with that Dutch guy."

"Now, you've heard of Roubidoux Polysolid," he said over dinner one evening. They're out on the verandah, looking over miles of open grassland, enjoying a light salad and some good smoked Scottish salmon with a glass of Sancerre. The cook is watching something on his tv and the driver is fiddling with the Range Rover. Apart from them, there's no-one within half an hour by SUV.

"I have, but just a name. What do they do?"

"Fine. it's an investment vehicle, super successful. The Roubidoux Polysolid Corporation has two kinds of shares, the B shares that are traded on the Stock Exchange and the A shares that control the company. The A shares, darling, are mainly you and me, with my old friends Cecilia, Markus Sonne and your associate Maria as minority shareholders. You know I really miss 'Fat' Pete. Apart from him and your Dad, we've all come through intact. And the patents for Eupho are all in your name."

"Eupho, never heard of it."

"Your Dad's last molecule, 'Euphoria' the next great recreational experience, addictive pleasure for the great mass of humanity. Generations unborn will never know a world without it and in the year 2040, we shall donate the formula to the United Nations for the greater good of people everywhere. Till then, however, oh my!"

Then Caro gave him the key to the bank deposit box she'd been holding onto since Maria had given it to her in Berlin and she

showed him the postcard with the picture of the Parthenon, which had arrived in the post a few weeks earlier. There was a single sentence message, 'He hadn't a clue, so don't be too hard on him.'
"So who was that from, another of your girlfriends?"
"No. That was a message from Maria," said Klaus.
"Was she one of yours, as well? And who was she talking about, you?"
"No, not me, well sort of, I suppose. She meant your Dad, Bernhardt. They didn't tell him what they were up to. He hadn't known a thing."
Caro takes a moment to assimilate that. "So he was being manipulated, as much as the rest of us."
"Surprised?"
"No, not really, Rick." Caro laughs. " Do you think I should be?"

Five years of increasing prosperity passed quietly before Caro answered the door one day to find a rather attractive young man from Poland, who said nothing, but gave her a friendly smile, then shot her five times, before turning the gun on Klaus and giving the trigger a squeeze, as he said "....with the compliments of your personal Guilt Assessors - Elfie and Silke Malzenberger of Berlin."

There was blood all over the floor, but no-one cleaned it up.
The house burned and flames reached high into the sky.
The end of an era, and that night the glow of its ashes lit up the clouds after sunset as elephants snoozed in the twilight and the old lions sensed rumbles of hunger in their sagging tummies.

other novels by John Clark

The Moses Hoffman Trilogy

Volume 1: Lone Hunter

Volume 2: Animal Self

Volume 3: The Swoop

-:-

CIAO CHARLIE

-:-

URBAN WEATHER

For further information about the availability of
these and other titles contact:

John Clark - fiction
The Berlin Picture Company,
Schlossstrasse 45,
14059 Berlin,
GERMANY

www.berlinpicturecompany.com